BLACKEST OCEAN

J.N. CHANEY
TERRY MAGGERT

VARIANT
PUBLICATIONS

LAS VEGAS, NV • PORTLAND, TN

CONNECT WITH J.N. CHANEY

Don't miss out on these exclusive perks:

- Instant access to free short stories from series like *The Messenger*, *Starcaster*, and more.
- Receive email updates for new releases and other news.
- Get notified when we run special deals on books and audiobooks.

So, what are you waiting for? Enter your email address at the link below to stay in the loop.

https://www.jnchaney.com/backyard-starship-subscribe

CONNECT WITH TERRY MAGGERT

Check out his website
http://terrymaggert.com/

Connect on Facebook
https://www.facebook.com/terrymaggertbooks/

Follow him on Amazon
https://www.amazon.com/Terry-Maggert/e/B00EKN8RHG/

JOIN THE CONVERSATION

Join the conversation and get updates on new and upcoming releases in the awesomely active **Facebook group**, "JN Chaney's Renegade Readers."

This is a hotspot where readers come together and share their lives and interests, discuss the series, and speak directly to J.N. Chaney and his co-authors.

facebook.com/groups/jnchaneyreaders

CONTENTS

1

I STUDIED the alignment sensor intently, watching as the two circles gradually converged.

"Okay, Torina, a little more. And a little more. Little bit more——"

"Van. Please. I can see the alignment, dear."

"Forgive me for being obtuse, but what I'm hearing is that mansplaining is… unwelcome? Perry, are you shocked by this?"

"Stunned, boss. As the kids said in 2015, I can't *even*." Perry waved a wing over his chest, as if wounded. Unlike me, Perry wore no suit, because unlike me, Perry was not made of meat.

"I think they may have started saying that in 2013 or so," Torina mused, her voice taut with effort. I stayed silent, letting the moment of humor fade. We were, despite our chatter, working.

And working in space is *never* simple.

I looked up. I was perched on the *Iowa*'s hull, adjacent to the empty well of a weapons hardpoint on her starboard topside. Above me—although, really only above relative to the *Iowa*—hung the *Fafnir*'s workboat with a missile launcher slung beneath it.

Torina was nudging it the last few meters into place, using deft puffs of thrusters to slowly ease the base of the launcher into the well. It was a delicate operation, depicted on the alignment sensor's display as a pair of circles, one slightly larger than the other. As long as Torina kept the entirety of the smaller circle enclosed in the larger, the mount would mate properly.

And she didn't need me mansplaining to do it. In fact, I really had no reason to be out here at all. Torina, Zeno, and Icky were more than capable. I just felt like coming out for a spacewalk because the grandeur of it all hadn't gotten old, and my life—and job—were an endless source of fascination and wonder to me.

"Close now," Torina muttered.

"Dead on, Torina. You've got the perfect rate of convergence," I told her.

Another meter to go. I pushed myself back, making sure I was well out of the way. A faint glimmer in the distance highlighted Orcus, the dwarf planet near which we'd parked the *Iowa*. The hard spark of distant Sol, a bright point like a far-off welder's torch, gleamed off a bit of ice on the dwarf planet. It, and the scattering of stars, provided the only relief from the otherwise unrelenting blackness all around us.

Sol. I smiled. I'd taken to thinking of Earth's star as Sol, no longer "the sun." That's because there were lots of suns, at least as far as known space was concerned. Tau Ceti was the sun in the Tau Ceti system. If you stood on Torina's homeworld, Helso, then Van Maanen's Star was the sun. It struck me that automatically thinking of Earth's sun as Sol, instead of the sun, meant I'd crossed a subtle but important boundary. I was no longer strictly a citizen of Earth. I had dual citizenship now—Earth and "out there."

Or out here, at least at the moment. The missile launcher slowly crept the last half meter and finally seated in the hardpoint with a thump I felt through my hands where they gripped a stanchion on the *Iowa*'s hull. Icky immediately flipped a recessed lever in an open panel nearby and slid the locking clamps into place.

"Okay, Torina, you can cut 'er loose," Icky said. Zeno had already plugged a data slate into an access port inside the same panel and was now frowning at its display.

"Netty, I'm showing everything green. Do you concur?" she asked.

Netty, the AI that oversaw both the *Fafnir* and the *Iowa*, immediately replied over our shared comm channel. "I'd like to traverse the launcher to make sure the T&E motors are properly engaged. Is everyone clear?"

Icky and Zeno pulled back. "Go ahead."

The launcher began to turn, slowly. At the same time, it elevated and depressed as Netty tested the T&E—traverse and elevating—system. She did one full traversal in about thirty seconds, then reversed it and did another, faster. The launcher smoothly obeyed all of her commands with no lag whatsoever.

Zeno was still studying the data slate. We left the nitty-gritty of our weapons' operations to her since it was her field of expertise.

"Okay, no power surges hinting at any binding in traverse or elevation. I think we're good."

"Excellent. One down, one to go," I said. I glanced behind me and down, relative to the *Iowa*, to where the second missile launcher hung motionless about a hundred meters from the ship. I could see the stern of the *Fafnir*, docked on the Iowa's flank, between my feet. The two weapons we'd removed from the mounts sat in their own spots, waiting to be stashed in the *Iowa's* open hold.

My gaze lingered on them. They were both twin-barreled cannons retrieved from the wreckage of an ancient battle and installed by Icky's father. They were an esoteric design that promised to fire bolts of high-energy plasma enclosed in magnetic bubbles to long ranges at a good chunk of light speed. The guns used physical principles on the very edge of understanding, which is how the plasma bolt was able to generate its own magnetic containment bubble, and should be devastating weapons.

To quote Icky, they *wrecked major ass.*

To me, they were a weapon with that dirtiest of words. *Potential.*

First, we had to make them work. Unfortunately, ancient alien weapons didn't come with owner's manuals, and although we tried mightily, we couldn't get the damned things to do more than squirt clouds of plasma that immediately started dissipating. There was something about their operation we just weren't getting. Rather than have them clog up two perfectly good hardpoints, though, we'd decided to replace them with the missile launchers, and here we were—

"Van, I've got a pair of intermittent contacts that I *think* are inbound," Netty said.

"You *think* they're inbound?"

"That's the intermittent part, boss. They seemed to be on a trajectory that's at least in our general direction, originating from somewhere in the vicinity of Rhea, one of the moons of Saturn. Sorry, I'm getting what I can from their signals."

"Good work. Just... curious, that's all," I muttered.

I frowned. It was peculiar enough to encounter any other ships in the Sol system. It did happen, but they were usually some sort of legitimate research expedition, charting and documenting the system or, more disturbingly, doing some sort of cultural anthropology study of Earth. A not-insignificant number of UFO sightings on Earth were actually alien researchers, particularly grad students doing field work for their dissertations. Apparently cattle mutilations had been the idea of an Eridani anthropologist who'd just wanted to study the reaction to it he got.

Which meant we were kind of like lab rats running around in an Earth-sized maze, a fact that managed to both amuse me and piss me off at the same time.

The only other sort of contact in the Solar System tended to be criminals up to no good, and that's where my interest was piqued. I'd put out the word through the Guild to lay off with the cow mutilations and power failures and stuff, but that didn't stop bad guys from haunting my home star system. Flickering, inconstant contacts heading toward us from Saturn didn't sound like a research team, so I had Netty prep the *Fafnir* for an intercept.

I started toward the airlock. "What's their ETA, Netty?"

"Uh—"

"That intermittent, huh?"

"Yes. If it's supposed to be some sort of stealth, it sucks. But it does make getting hard data a problem."

"Maybe that's the point."

"We'll go with that. Anyway, using the *Fafnir*'s weapons ranges as a standard, they'll be in effective missile range in... about two hours."

I stopped just outside the airlock. "Two hours?"

"That's right."

"Two *hours*."

"Are we having comms trouble?"

"No, it's—Netty, two *hours* from Saturn to here is awfully damned fast, isn't it?"

"And yet, there it is."

A faint chew of anxiety started in my gut. Two unknown contacts with weak, flickering scanner returns and insane velocity, both heading toward us—

Every one of my nerves went to high alert, and Torina felt it too as she opened a comm from the workboat.

"Buckle in?" she asked. Torina's combat awareness was second to none.

I felt the workboat thump into place. "Come on inside, dear. Choppy air ahead."

"I'll put my tray table up while I'm at it."

"Tudor Airlines thanks you for your cooperation. Now, then. Prepare to receive our *guests*."

I SETTLED into the *Fafnir*'s pilot's seat with a comfort that was becoming second nature and let my eyes adjust to the low light of our screens.

"Perry, my favorite mechanical bird, what's the latest?" I said.

Perry turned his amber eyes on me. "I hate that word, you know."

"What word?"

"Mechanical. It makes me sound like I'm all gears and pistons and grease and stuff."

"Okay, so what would you prefer?"

"How about synthetic?" Zeno asked, scanning her panel.

"Makes me sound fake."

"Artificial?" Icky suggested.

"Too vase-full-of-cheap-plastic-flowers."

"Okay, how about—"

I cut in. "How about we concentrate on the business at hand and discuss respectful nomenclature of our valued crew member *after* we resolve these two bogies?"

"See, Zeno? *Nomenclature*. That's why I feel valued," Perry said.

"No need to crow about it," Zeno deadpanned.

Perry's head whirled, then his beak dropped. "Well played, whiskers."

Zeno inclined her head while grinning, or at least as much as she could given her thickness.

Torina slid past me and settled into her own seat, her hand trailing over my shoulder as she did. It was a small gesture, but the meaning was… significant, and I smiled at her with a warmth that told a story. She cocked her head, grinning. "What'd I miss?"

"Perry bitching about being called a bunch of greasy flowers," Icky said. "He's so weird."

Torina stared. "What?"

"I—what? I didn't—" Perry started, but again I cut him off.

"Guys, focus here? Let's try this again. Perry, status please," I asked.

"The two ships haven't responded to any comm challenges. They have no transponders, or aren't using them, so we can't ID them. Their scanner returns are still pretty wonky, so we can tell they're about class 6 and—well, that's about it."

I nodded. My earlier thoughts about alien researchers doing bizarre things on Earth just to provoke a reaction gave me an idea. "Okay, Netty, let's disconnect from the *Iowa*, then set course, uh"—I pointed—"that way."

"You want to head to the Large Magellanic Cloud? It's going to take us about eight hundred thousand years to get there, so you might want to use the lavatory first."

"Any random direction at full power will do, Netty—well, as long as it doesn't crash us into anything, of course. I just want to see what these incoming ships are going to do, come after us, keep on track for the *Iowa*, some of both, or neither of the above. Let's force their hand, so to speak."

The *Fafnir* undocked with a clunk, and Netty eased us away from the *Iowa* with thrusters only. Once we were clear, she lit the fusion drive, and the *Fafnir* shot forward on a heading of *that-a-way*.

"Engine is cooking hot, boss," Netty said.

"Keep it at a medium boil. Onward, if you please. And this is a general order, but keep our weapons at more than a boil. I want us —and our sharp ends—ready."

"Van, the new missile launchers on the *Iowa* have passed all their diagnostics. They have a far longer range than the *Fafnir*'s launchers, they accelerate a lot harder, and those warheads are absolute haymakers," Netty said.

I grinned at her enthusiastic report, then drew my focus back to the targets. Both incoming ships were clearly aimed at the *Iowa*, either because that was their intent or they simply hadn't detected the *Fafnir*. "I'm sensing you'd like to test fire them at some live targets, Netty. How bloodthirsty of you."

"I'd call it pragmatic. This is an excellent opportunity to test the targeting, firing, and tracking capabilities of the missiles."

"By blowing up a couple of unidentified ships."

"The only thing we don't really need to test is the warheads. My suggestion is we fire them unarmed and inform those incoming ships about it. If they're hostile, I can arm them remotely. If they're not, they'll just sail on past and we can recover them at our leisure."

I smiled again. "That is pragmatic. Okay, broadcast three warnings at thirty second intervals, then loose a missile from each launcher." I glanced at Torina. "Maybe that'll provoke them into talking to us."

"Actually, Van, they may not be talking to us because there's no one to *do* any talking, aside from an AI," Perry put in.

I turned to him. "You think these ships are unmanned?"

"Possibly. I've been analyzing the scanner data, and although these ships are roughly the length of a typical class 6, they seem to be a lot less massive. If we assume conventional power plant and drive specs, then they'd have almost no internal space for a crew. One guy in a cockpit, maybe, like a fighter, but that's it."

"Or their crew is really, really small," Icky said.

Perry gave a slow nod. "Yes, that's a possibility, too, that these ships are crewed by tiny aliens."

"Van, no answer from those ships," Netty said.

"Weapons hot, Netty. Do your thing."

Two icons streaked away from the *Iowa*, one from each of the new launchers. The missiles were fast—at least fifty percent better acceleration than the *Fafnir*'s comparatively small ordnance. They immediately pinged their targets and began to track them.

"So far so good. We're looking at about eight minutes to detonation if we arm them," Netty said.

I watched the icons representing our two bogies on the tactical overlay. For the moment, they just maintained a steady, unchanging course. We were closing with them at a phenomenal rate, though mainly because of their enormous velocity. The *Iowa*'s missiles had shot past us and closed even faster.

"So if they don't answer us sometime… in the next seven minutes, I guess, are we actually going to just blow them up?" Torina asked.

I looked out the canopy, a useless reflex because I wasn't likely to see much many millions of kilometers away. I sometimes wondered why the *Fafnir* even had a canopy, since virtually everything we did relied on the ship's suite of sensors anyway.

"Probably not. For all we know, maybe they can't contact us and are coming for help," I replied.

"If that's the case, they'd better start decelerating pretty soon or they're going to overshoot us," Netty said.

I regarded the scans and knew she was right. "Still, I'm not excited about attacking two ships that haven't actually done anything hostile—"

An alert chime cut me off.

"The incoming ships have launched missiles. Four inbound, high rate of acceleration. Detonation in seven minutes," Netty announced.

I sighed. "Or, they could start shooting at us and make this whole conversation kind of moot."

"We did shoot at them first," Zeno pointed out. "Just sayin'."

"We also broadcasted several warnings. In fact, given their approach profile, I'd say we could reasonably assume they were on what could be construed an attack run." I looked at Perry. "Right?"

"It's an argument."

"A good one?"

"Depends how well you make it."

"That's… not helpful."

"I'd argue that it's not unhelpful."

"Perry—"

"Sorry, Van, but there's no firm answer to this. Yes, you could argue that these ships were flying a threatening profile, didn't answer any comm calls, and just came straight at us. The best I can say is that if it comes to some sort of inquiry, it would be a decent defense."

I sighed. "Decent will have to do," I said, then turned back to the overlay and watched as the drama played out in colored icons.

"One minute, Van. Do you want me to arm those missiles?"

I sat back in my seat. The inbound missiles, which the oncoming ships had fired after the *Iowa*'s launch, were still about three and a half minutes out. We had to commit to destroying these incoming ships long before their missiles were going to reach us. And they may have only fired at us in self-defense.

Screw it. As I'd mused back at the *Iowa*, the only people that tended to come to Sol were researchers or criminals. I had trouble believing these were the former, and I wasn't prepared to stake my life and those of my crew on the possibility this was all some big misunderstanding. Play stupid games, win stupid prizes, right?

"Arm the missiles, Netty," I said.

She did. The seconds ticked past. I expected the two bogies to open up with point-defenses, but they remained strangely silent.

"Twenty seconds," Netty said.

The two ships finally opened fire and coughed out streams of mass-driver slugs. They weren't rapid-fire point-defense batteries, though, but bigger, slower-firing weapons more like the *Fafnir*'s. One of our missiles vanished in a flash and a cloud of debris. The other one scored a direct hit, though, blasting the bogie to whirling fragments.

"One down," I said. No one else spoke.

I considered our options. The other ship kept barreling on toward the *Iowa*.

"My ship," I said, then took the controls, flipped the *Fafnir*, and burned hard in reverse. Two of the inbound missiles were locked onto us, while two more streaked toward the *Iowa*. Our battlecruiser could look after herself. I wanted to bleed off some velocity to make it easier for us to reverse course, but it meant losing the incoming ordnance in the flare of our own fusion exhaust. Their icons winked out on the overlay.

I watched the time carefully. "Zeno, let me know how much longer I can burn like this and still give us time to flip again and engage—"

"Thirty seconds," she said. "We're at fifty-six seconds now."

I nodded. "Got it. Appreciate the fine-tuned numbers."

"It's what I do. Forty seconds," Zeno said in a crisp tone, then paused. It was dead silent in the *Fafnir*—until she said one more word. "Thirty."

I flipped the *Fafnir* again and cut the drive. A few seconds later, the missiles reappeared on the overlay. As soon as they did, Torina opened up with the laser batteries, their beams lancing out in silent fury. And a moment after that, Zeno started firing the particle cannon. One by one, the missiles vanished again, blasted to scrap—in no small part owing to the fire control system gifted to us by Master Gerhardt.

"Good shooting, folks," I said, then rotated the *Fafnir* yet again and relit the drive. The surviving bogie shot past us and would probably pull irrevocably away. But it seemed determined to pass close to the *Iowa*, which, unless I was missing something, was a bad idea.

Sure enough, it loosed another salvo of missiles at our battlecruiser.

I thought about Admiral Yamamoto and sleeping giants as the *Iowa* responded with a hurricane of point-defense fire and a laser barrage that seared the bogie's stern to wreckage, killing its drive. With a second burst, the enemy missiles vanished, leaving debris and a dead bogie on a steady course to nowhere.

I relaxed a notch. "Okay, let's catch up to this asshole and see whose breakfast cereal we managed to piss in."

Torina gave me a sidelong glance. "Yuck."

Icky waved all four arms in disgust. "And you say *I* eat weird stuff."

BY THE TIME we matched velocity with the damaged bogie, we'd passed the *Iowa* again and were on our way to the outer margin of the Solar System. Voyager actually plied its stately way into deep space ahead of us and off to port. I really wanted to do a flyby sometime, but I had no idea if it still had the ability to collect images. If it did, then a picture of me gawking out of the *Fafnir*'s canopy arriving back at the Jet Propulsion Lab in California might raise a few eyebrows.

We kept our distance from the bogie and studied it through imagery and scanner data alone. While it was now just a collection of fragments traveling the same general course, there was still enough of it intact that it could detonate in an uncontained fusion or, worse, an antimatter explosion. Even in death, the bogie had a last punch it could throw.

"It doesn't match anything in any registry or records I can access," Netty said.

"So a truly alien alien, then," I replied. I made to go on, but Zeno suddenly made a *huh* sound. We all looked at her.

"Have something you'd like to share with the whole class, Zeno?" I asked.

She frowned. "I'm not sure. I'd really like to take a close look at a piece of that hull before I commit to anything."

"Van, there's a fragment on a divergent course, about a meter across. If we wait twenty minutes or so, it should be far enough away from the bulk of the wreck that we can safely retrieve it," Perry said.

"Sounds good. Netty, let's intercept that fragment so Zeno can commit to something."

The remains of the ship didn't explode, though, and just

continued their long, lonely journey into interstellar space. We matched velocity with the stray fragment, and after a brief space-walk, Zeno and Icky brought it aboard. We shut off the *Fafnir*'s inertial dampers, which also generated her interior gravity, so they could nudge it into the cargo hold.

As Zeno and Icky pulled off their suits, I studied the fragment, which was covered in frost condensed out of the *Fafnir*'s air by the fierce ambient cold of space. I knew better than to touch it with anything even resembling bare flesh until it warmed up. Still, even taking the rime of frost into account, it looked like another chunk of hull plating to me.

"Okay, I'll bite—what the hell is this thing, Zeno?"

She studied it for a moment. "I think I know, but I really want to make sure before saying anything."

"Oh, for—can you give us a hint, at least?"

"If it's what I think it is, it originates outside known space, from a place that's not on the maps."

"Oh, okay, that *totally* doesn't raise about a hundred more questions."

Zeno shrugged. "Sorry, Van, but I'm bound by some pretty old promises here. If you're willing to burn some gas, I can find out for sure."

"If it gets us some answers, then yes. Where to?"

She didn't take her eyes off of the chunk of wreckage.

"Home."

2

ON OUR LAST visit to the P'nosk homeworld to visit Zeno's collective of mothers, we'd established an important fact—

Zeno and I were not dating.

Her mothers, as a group, took the whole *when are we getting grandchildren?* thing to a new, almost epic level. And as one of only two males aboard the *Fafnir*, where Zeno now spent the vast majority of her time, I had been firmly caught in the eye of that particular hurricane, emphasis on *had*.

But as we arrived at the door to the apartment Zeno's mothers shared aboard the lush and park-like P'nosk orbital, I still found myself gritting my teeth a little. I'd assumed that my best protection against the idea of Zeno and I being—well, Zeno and I—was the fact she's P'nosk and I'm human. Even if we were so inclined, creating offspring was… difficult.

But it turned out that wasn't quite true, and I was a living, breathing demonstration of that. My grandmother, Valint, hadn't been human. She'd been a member of a race known as the Hu'warde, a tall, elegant people with slender frames and regal bearing. Their gothic beauty was matched only by their shrewd intellect—and a penchant for strategy that, for them, was religion. It turned out that when a mommy and daddy loved one another very much but also happened to be different species, there were *ways* of making offspring happen.

And those ways involved molecular genetic manipulation, which sounded neither sexy nor romantic but was effective—at least within certain genetic limits. So Zeno and I probably *could* have offspring because our respective DNA had enough commonality. Me and Schegith, not so much.

All of which was to say I braced myself for that hurricane to come thundering back ashore, determined to storm-surge Zeno and me into some sort of relationship that wasn't going to happen.

Zeno must have anticipated it. As soon as the door opened and her mothers appeared, mouths open to start talking, she spoke up and preempted them.

"Honored mothers, so good see you, and I have exciting news—Torina and Van declared for one another back on her homeworld, so they're together now! Isn't it wonderful?"

The mothers' faces fell like the curtain on a failed Broadway show.

As we shuffled into the apartment, I leaned close to Zeno and whispered, "Thank you."

"You'd better play it up. They'll be watching you two more intently than a targeting scanner."

I nodded and stepped back, then took Torina's hand. She

glanced at me, surprised. We'd agreed to keep the overt displays of affection to a minimum. We were crewmates, after all.

"Go with it," I said through what I thought was a loving smile.

She looked down at our clasped hands, then raised her voice. "Oh, Van," she said, a little breathless, then turned to the gaggle of mothers. "He's just so... demonstrative."

I chuckled, and it even sounded forced to *me*. "You are irresistible. Dear."

The mothers looked dubious, but Torina and I just smiled blandly, choosing to wait them out.

It worked.

They turned their attention back to Zeno, grilling her with questions in a rapid-fire interrogation. She finally held up her hands.

"Honored mothers, please, this isn't strictly a social call." She turned to one of her mothers, neither youngest nor oldest but in the middle of the pack.

"Mother Tendothir, we're actually here to tap into your expertise," she went on, pulling out a data slate. "We retrieved a piece of debris following a recent attack. It reminded me of something you once described to me, so I wanted to get your take on it. These are both macro- and micro-images, a materials analysis and chemical composition data we collected on our trip here."

Tendothir, the mother in question, sighed theatrically and accepted the data slate. She spent a moment scanning it while the rest of her mothers resumed the ceaseless barrage of questions about Zeno's *wandering lifestyle*, her potential to *settle down*, whether she'd met anyone *nice*, and so on and so on. But my attention caught on Tendothir.

Zeno had told me that this particular mother had an expansive background in material science, and despite being retired still did consulting work for the P'nosk government. As she scanned the data on the slate, her attitude and even her body language changed. The fussy doting mother gave way to a brusque professional. She stepped into the middle of the conversation swirling around Zeno, her manner abruptly cutting everyone off.

"Zeno, where did you find this debris?"

"The Sol system," she replied, then went on to give a brief description of the attack. When she was done, Tendothir turned to me.

"Van, we need to talk."

"Okay—"

She shook her head. "Not here. There are security implications. Let's go to your ship. That's where the debris is, right?"

I blinked in surprise but just nodded. "It is. And, uh—certainly. By all means."

As we left the apartment, I overhead one of Zeno's other mothers hiss something quickly to Tendothir.

"While you're there, check to see if he and that other woman are sharing a cabin." The mother leveled a stink eye at me, then went on in. "And one bunk. If there are two, we shall require a maternal meeting."

"A meeting," one of the other mothers agreed. "I don't trust him. He's shifty."

TENDOTHIR ASKED for access to the piece of debris, then spent a few moments scanning it with a device she'd brought with her. She frowned at the readings, then stepped back and nodded.

"Well, this isn't good news."

We waited.

"Do you have imagery of the ship it came from?"

I nodded. "Netty, can you put it up in the galley, please?"

A frozen image of one of the mystery ships was waiting on the display over the galley table. It was the clearest image we had, depicting the ship that had managed to pass close to the *Iowa* before it had been disabled by our battlecruiser's shooting. Tendothir stared at it for a moment, then nodded again.

"And that confirms it," she said.

I exchanged glances with Perry and Torina. "Is there something you can, you know, actually share with us about this? Aside from ominous statements to yourself?" I asked her.

She stared back for a moment. "The trouble is that I'm bound by a Seal of Writ."

It was my turn to stare; then I looked at Perry.

"Think non-disclosure agreement," he replied, but turned to Tendothir. "Fun fact—a Seal of Writ is a Peacemaker Guild instrument."

She nodded. "It is."

"Okay, hang on. You mean to say you've got some sort of non-disclosure thing in place with the Guild? The Guild I work for?" I asked.

She nodded again. "Just because you're a Peacemaker, Van, doesn't mean I'm suddenly not bound by it."

I crossed my arms. "Oh, for—this is shades of Gerhardt's slavish bureaucracy. You know something potentially important to us, but you can't tell us what it is? Because we've told you not to reveal it? To *us*?"

"Need-to-know is a thing, Van. Peacemakers keep secrets from one another all the time," Perry noted. "It's somewhat of a hobby among your profession."

I sighed and closed my eyes. "Okay. Who *can* lift this veil of secrecy, so you can tell us what you know?"

Tendothir shrugged. Perry answered. "A Master could," he said.

"Naturally. I've gained a lot of respect for Gerhardt, but he still has a pedantic streak a light-year wide. And if I ask him to unseal this or whatever, and he says no, I can't even go the *it's easier to get forgiveness than permission* route."

Tendothir finally shook her head. "You know what? I don't care. I've been sitting on this for years now. And what are they going to do, throw a decrepit old P'nosk in jail for revealing old information to someone who's not just a Peacemaker, but a Peacemaker with a legitimate need to know it?"

I looked at Perry. "Are you and Netty going to report this?"

"Report what?"

I nodded and turned back to Tendothir.

"Okay. About, oh, fifty standard years ago or so, I was called in to do some material science consulting by the Seven Stars League. They'd retrieved some debris just like this in the wake of a battle apparently fought near a star system about two hundred and fifty light-years outside known space. It was—" She paused and glanced at the display.

"Can you have your AI put up a star map?" she asked.

Netty did, and Tendothir scrolled through it, hmming until she found what she was looking for. "There," she said. "It was found in or near that system right there."

I looked where she was pointing. "HIP 102152. Sounds like a happening place—" I started, but the stellar data caught my eye. "Huh. A yellow-white star almost exactly the same mass as Sol, just a lot older."

Tendothir nodded. "Anyway, it seems that there were a series of wars fought out there between three races who have nothing to do with known space. The wars, or the place they were fought—something, anyway, was called The Clearings. Somehow, despite being outside known space, the Seven Stars League got involved. So did the Peacemakers. I think they called themselves Galactic Knights, though."

I exchanged a look with Perry. His voice came back in my ear bug.

Sorry, Van, means nothing to me. But I don't have access to much of anything about the GKU. It's how they operate.

Tendothir had carried on. "Anyway, one of those races, the"—she frowned, thinking—"Pelo—Pola—no, wait. It was—right, the Puloquir, that's it. They were one of the races involved in the war. They ended up being exiled by the League and the Peacemakers, or Galactic Knights, or whoever they were, anyway. So they're still somewhere out there, somewhere near that star, HIP-whatever."

"We've got no records of any race called the Puloquir," Perry said.

"Probably because of that Seal of Writ. The people I talked to described them as something like—okay, memory, do your thing." Tendothir frowned again. "Nu—yes, nudibranchs. That's what the humans called them."

I looked at Perry again. "Think sea slugs," he said.

"Except they live in liquid methane-ammonia. Anyway, it turned out that they weren't particularly good at warfare—"

"Sea slugs that live in ammonia-methane oceans aren't masters of space combat? Go figure," I said. I was trying to wrap my mind around the concept. I'd run into a lot of aliens but only a few that were *truly* alien, in the sense I couldn't really identify with them at all. Methane-loving sea slugs would definitely fit that category.

Tendothir smiled a thin smile. "Right, go figure. I gather that they were both aggressive and vengeful, on top of which they did have one advantage—their lifespans are measured in centuries. Many centuries."

"So *ancient* sea slugs who hold a grudge. And just when you didn't think they could get any cuddlier," Torina said.

"You have no idea," Tendothir replied. "Their animosity can outlive empires, and it's reflected in, ah, that piece of wreckage you've got back there. It's from a weapon the Seven Stars League labeled a 'sinking fish.' They're basically AI-controlled warships that can lie dormant for years, decades—centuries, even. When their triggering protocols are activated, they come to life and start to attack."

"To what end? Just causing mayhem?" I asked.

Tendothir could only shrug. "No idea. I don't know if the League and Guild people knew, either. Whatever their purpose or strategy, the Puloquir never shared it with anyone. The only thing that did seem to be clear is that the triggering protocols, whatever they were, would always be in effect. A year later, ten years, a thousand—it doesn't make any difference."

"So like a minefield after a war. They kill indiscriminately, forever," Torina said.

"Or at least until they just cease functioning or are destroyed," Zenophir put in.

"That might explain that ship you called a junkyard dog—the one that attacked us at that old battle site near that neutron star. The one where—" Torina said, then cut herself off.

I nodded. She was going to say *the one where Rolis died.* "Maybe, but that one was invulnerable and built to destroy things by ramming them."

"Sinking fish was a category of weapons, not a specific type. And the League people did mention one they encountered that they simply couldn't knock out. Their weapons wouldn't even scratch it. Being into materials, I really wanted to get a look at it. But you're saying you encountered one?" Tendothir asked, her tone suddenly eager.

I nodded. "We did, but it's gone, flown into a neutron star and destroyed." I went on to give her a brief rundown of what had happened at the neutron star called Arx.

"Yeah, that sounds like one of these damned things," she said. "But now you've run into two more, in the human home system."

I nodded, but something still puzzled me. "The ones we destroyed at Sol were fast as hell, but they didn't put up much of a fight. In fact, their shooting was pretty anemic."

"Don't let that fool you. If they didn't shoot at you much, it wasn't because they didn't want to. The things are basically just a powerplant and drive, weapons, and an AI to control it all. For some reason, they just *couldn't* put up much of a fight," Tendothir said.

"They'd probably exhausted most of their ammo, maybe even

took some damage long before they ever even got to Sol," Zeno said.

I scratched my head. "But what were they doing there? Why were they at Sol in the first place?"

No one had the answer. But Tendothir did have a suggestion.

"The League people, in their background briefing, mentioned that the Puloquir had actually been beaten more than once. Or, at least that's my understanding, but the source of the data can be pretty prickly."

"What source is that?"

"Based on what Zeno's told me, you already know them. It's the Schegith."

WE LEFT the P'nosk homeworld with a promise to Zeno's mothers that they would definitely be invited to our wedding—or so Torina said, holding my arm with open delight.

"I haven't been treated to that kind of suspicion since I was a teenager," I said as the *Fafnir* backed away from the P'nosk orbital.

"Same. Did you see the second mother roll her eyes when I touched your forearm? You'd think Zeno was left on her Declaration Day," she replied, giving me a coy smile.

"We call that being left at the altar, but I get your meaning. Human grandmothers have got *nothing* on those ladies. Zeno, is that standard operating procedure? To regard every competing female as a nuclear threat to your familial honor?"

Zeno waved airily. "Not at all. You should see how they treat *males* who have—as the mothers would say—made the wrong choice."

Torina snorted. "Can you imagine? I thought having *one* mother was a challenge, but—"

Netty interrupted. "If you two can stop being the adorable couple for a moment, there's the small matter of where we're going. I'm assuming it's going to be something more than just *that way* again."

I turned to Perry. "Can I assume that The Quiet Room has something like safety deposit boxes?"

"They do, right up to full-sized vaults."

I nodded and turned back to Zeno. "Can you cut our piece of debris back there into two pieces?"

She frowned for a moment. "Probably, with a plasma torch. We're going to want to do it outside, though."

"Perfect." I swung back to the instrument panel. "Netty, take us out to our twist point. Zeno, on the way there, you can help Icky cut that wreckage into two. They don't have to be equal halves—in fact, let's make it so one person can carry the smaller piece. Once we've done that, Netty, we'll twist to Procyon and make a deposit at The Quiet Room."

"You want to hide away a piece of that wreckage? Why?" Torina asked.

"Because we're going to hand the rest of it over to the Guild as evidence, which I suspect is eventually going to disappear."

"Disappear?"

"Let's call it a hunch. In any case, I want to hang onto a piece of it just in case. And if it isn't clear, that means this is totally hush-

hush. Consider it top secret, need-to-know by the present company only, no one else. Everyone get that?"

They all understood. There were questioning looks but no actual questions, which was a testament to just how good my crew was—but regardless, I didn't offer any details. All I knew is that the moment Tendothir referred to the Galactic Knights being involved in this, it got much more complicated. I wanted some insurance against that complexity.

Because although I might be a part of the Galactic Knights, I frankly didn't trust them. Like Perry said, parts of the Guild had no idea what other parts were up to. I had to assume that would be doubly true for a reclusively paranoid outfit like the Galactic Knights.

This felt like an old, important secret. And those are the kind that get buried.

At any cost.

3

WE ARRIVED to good news at The Quiet Room. Dayna was back.

Dayna Jasskin had been our original contact with The Quiet Room, but she had been shunted aside in an insidious and deceptive operation tied to our old enemies, the Fade, that was intended to trap us. The Quiet Room had subsequently cleaned up its ranks, something Dayna made abundantly clear.

"We take things like that very seriously. The Quiet Room really is just its reputation," she said. "Without that, a reputation for absolute integrity, then we're just a bunch of people who handle money. Anyway, you can rest assured that anyone even remotely connected with that... unfortunate unpleasantness has been dealt with."

I smiled across her desk. "Sounds ominous. What'd you do, space them?"

She didn't smile back. "Not all of them."

"Ah. Okay, then. Anyway, I need a safety deposit box big enough for"—I gestured at the case on the floor beside me, a repurposed tool chest—"this."

"I think we can arrange that."

"Not too expensive, though. My people tell me we're getting a little tight on funds again," I said, glancing at Torina and Perry. They'd gotten caught up on our finances on the way here, and our buffer of bonds was getting thin. As she got bigger and more powerful, the *Fafnir* also got more expensive to operate, and it was starting to show.

Dayna sat back. "Well, I may be able to help you with that, too. How would you like a good-paying job?"

"I'm listening."

"There's a planet called Landfall in a star system just outside known space, roughly equidistant from space controlled by the Seven Stars League, the Eridani Federation, and the Tau Ceti Alliance. It's what you would call a super Earth, I think, but what makes it special is some unusually rich mineral deposits exposed on the surface through erosion and weathered down to essentially gravel. You can basically mine them with a shovel."

"Let me guess—all three of them, the League, the Federation, and the Alliance are claiming it."

"Unsurprisingly, yes, they are. None of them have fought a war in a long time, thanks to a series of treaties and agreements and such—but those don't apply to Landfall since it falls outside of the space covered by those."

"So you're actually expecting them to fight over this place?" Torina asked.

"Technically, they already have. No actual shooting—yet—but

there have been some cyber attacks on ships in the system, and someone laid some mines around one of the closest twist points to the planet. And now, someone has placed some satellites in orbit, which may be armed. The Quiet Room would like those satellites to be... removed."

I sighed. "What is it with this veiled speech and innuendo? We want this person *dealt with*. We want that ship *taken out of the picture*. We want these satellites *removed*. Why not just say killed, destroyed, blown to bits, or whatever?"

Dayna shrugged. "Beats me. I guess it's tradition. Anyway, yes— we want those satellites blasted to their constituent atoms. Better?"

"Much, thanks."

"Uh, whose satellites are they? Shouldn't we know that before we"—Perry paused, then spread his wings and made his tone dramatically ominous—"*cause them to no longer be a concern?*"

Dayna shrugged again. "No idea, nor does it matter. They're unauthorized, which makes them navigation hazards."

Torina held up a hand. "Wait. You said this planet is outside known space and covered by no protocols or agreements. How can any satellites, or anything else for that matter, not be *authorized* to be there?"

Dayna smiled. "Ah, I was waiting for someone to ask that. Technically, there is a protocol in place. Three hundred years ago, a mining consortium filed a notice of intent to conduct surveys in that region, over a volume of space that includes Landfall. At the time, The Quiet Room was acting as a neutral agent to regulate affairs outside of the accepted boundaries of known space, so that notice of intent was filed with us. We don't act as that neutral agent anymore, but as it turns out, there was no provision for any end date in any business we conducted while we were."

Torina smiled. "So that notice of intent still applies."

"Why yes, I suppose it does," Dayna returned.

"I can't believe that the League, the Eridani Federation, or anyone else still recognizes your authority based on a defunct, three hundred year old notice of intent," Perry said.

"Oh, they don't, not at all. But whether they recognize it or not, there it is."

I'd been following the conversation but thinking through the implications. They led inexorably to one question.

"Dayna, what's in this for you? For The Quiet Room? Are you saying that you guys have a claim to this planet, Landfall?" I asked.

"No, of course not. The Quiet Room doesn't hold territory. We're a bank."

"So then what—?" I began, but stopped. "Wait. You're expecting a war to break out over this planet, aren't you?"

"Relations between the Seven Stars League and the Eridani Federation are already strained, over the matter of your homeworld, Ms. Milon," Dayna said. "The Federation is supporting the Schegith taking over from the League as the protectorate of Helso, which has infuriated their new Satrap. Or, that's the story, at least, but the League and the Federation have been itching to go to war over several border disputes for some time now."

Perry raised a wing. "So you're expecting a shooting war to start over the ownership of Landfall. Correct me if I'm wrong, but wouldn't the Quiet Room stand to make scads of money by funding such a war?"

There it was, the place my own thoughts had been going. I leaned forward.

"Dayna, a war between major powers like the League and the Federation could kill millions of people. The Quiet Room can't possibly—"

"Have any wish to see millions of people die? No, of course not. If we're going to fund a war, we prefer it have survivors. Dead people don't tend to make their payments."

"Wow. I can feel the altruism all around me. Gives me the warm and fuzzies," I said. "So how does having us destroy some satellites around Landfall help with that?"

"It's one piece in a bigger machine, Van—one that your Guild has agreed to help us build, I might point out. We've assessed that, barring something unforeseen, an eventual war between the League and the Federation is inevitable. We do *not* want that war to occur in known space, or if it does, we want it to have minimal impact. We would prefer that war to happen outside the boundaries of known space, and Landfall gives us a convenient flashpoint to make that happen. So we're going to start by asserting our three hundred year old authority to regulate Landfall based on that dusty old notice of intent, and clear some navigation hazards from the planet's orbit."

"Okay—and? What then?"

"The League, the Federation, and the Alliance will all object, probably quite strenuously. That's all they'll do, because we're The Quiet Room and we control all the money. But we'll listen to their objections, accept them, and then hand the governance of Landfall over to all three of them with our best wishes for a glorious future. That will last about ten minutes, then collapse into strife and conflict —but out there, around Landfall."

"How do you know it won't just spill back over into known space?" Torina asked. "War has a nasty way of refusing to go to plan."

Dayna smiled. "Because we will make it clear that if it does, that if one side starts anything here in known space, we'll exclusively fund the other side."

"But if they keep the fighting out there, then you'll fund everyone and no one has the advantage—except you, The Quiet Room, who profits from the conflict," I said, sitting back.

"And now you see why we need to establish our authority over Landfall right up front, by destroying some satellites. I mean, we have to give the League and company something to object *to*, don't we?" Dayna replied.

"This is... incredibly Machiavellian. And convoluted. It could go wrong in a lot of ways, Dayna," I said.

"Oh, absolutely. We're not dealing with accounting ledgers here, where things either balance or they don't. We're dealing with people, and people can do unexpected and often idiotic things. But if war is inevitable, don't you think we should at least try to minimize its impact on the citizens of known space?"

"Not to mention customers of The Quiet Room," Torina said.

"That's just a happy coincidence. As Van said just a moment ago, our true motives are altruistic."

I snorted. "I never doubted the purity of your intent."

WE DEPOSITED our fragment of debris in a secure vault buried under The Quiet Room's facilities in the Procyon system, then prepared to get underway. I couldn't help turning over the cunning but intricate plan Dayna had outlined.

"I keep thinking I should be morally outraged about it all, but if a war is going to happen anyway, then this seems to be the best way to contain it and minimize the damage," I said, watching the status board as Netty did our preflight checks. "Still, it just seems so—"

"Manipulative?" Torina offered.

"Yeah."

"That's because it is. It's extremely manipulative. And it sure puts its toes right up against a moral line or two, but it doesn't seem to cross them."

"Hey, look at it from The Quiet Room's perspective. They offset the worst impacts of an inevitable war, while making a bunch of money doing it. It's win-win," Perry said.

I shrugged. "I guess."

"Besides, the Guild's backing it," Torina said.

I shrugged again. "Probably for a cut of the profits."

"Sure. But it fits nicely with the Guild's mandate—you know, the *Peace* part of Peacemaker. And if it puts some bonds in the treasury, so much the better."

I nodded. It all made sense. And yet, there was still something about it, like that faint, barely perceptible taste milk gets right before it turns sour. The milk is still perfectly good, but there's something not quite right. It was the echo of something foul, just at the edge of my senses.

"So how did we end up with this job, anyway? The Quiet Room had no idea we were going to show up to stick something into a secure vault," Zeno said.

"Apparently, we were on their short list of Peacemakers to offer the job. We just happened to show up before they contacted any of the others," Torina replied.

Icky spoke up. "So, we blow up these satellites. What happens if whoever owns them just puts up more?"

"According to Dayna, we destroy those as well and keep getting paid to do it—at least until the League and the others get tired of the Guild and The Quiet Room being in the way and agree to a joint stewardship agreement over Landfall," I said.

"The agreement that's gonna fail," Icky said.

"That's right."

"What if the League and Federation and whoever else decide to join forces and just kick us and The Quiet Room out of the system right away?" Icky persisted.

"Worst case scenario, it amounts to the same thing, everyone fighting over Landfall. But The Quiet Room's going to put out the word that if they try that, then they're going to pick one faction and fund them exclusively, which would totally screw over the other two."

"But what if—"

"Icky, we're going to go and blow up some satellites. That's it, that's all. The bigger geopolitical—or should it be astropolitical? Anyway, the bigger picture isn't our concern. Or are you tired of making money?"

"What? No, 'course not. Got my eye on a new hammer."

"Why? Isn't a hammer a hammer? What's wrong with the one you've got?"

"For one, it's not a proper warhammer, just a plain old sledge," she said, then grinned. "Besides, after you swing 'em enough, they wear out."

LANDFALL WAS A *BIG* PLANET. It was twice the size of Earth, although with an internal makeup that resulted in its surface gravity being only about fifty percent greater. Still, that was enough to make a two hundred pound person on Earth weigh three hundred on Landfall.

And that would get old *fast*.

Fortunately, though, we didn't have to descend to the surface. We only needed to fall into orbit, find the satellites, and shoot them down. Not that I was being complacent about it—Dayna did say the satellites might be armed. But as our list of risky jobs went, it wouldn't even make the top ten.

Which I hoped wasn't going to end up being famous last words.

"Van, I've got hard scanner returns on the three satellites. There aren't any other ships in the system," Netty said.

I nodded. "Okay, then. Let's go do what we came here to do. Torina, you may go weapons-hot at your discretion."

The big planet loomed closer. We didn't actually need to fall into a completely stable orbit, just pass close enough to shoot. Our trajectory would bend around it, and we'd pick up some velocity, doing a gravitational slingshot. Landfall had a hefty moon, so the plan was to do a one-eighty around it and come back at the planet for another pass, just to see the aftermath of our attack.

"Okay, the first satellite is rising now, dead ahead," Netty said.

"Got it," Torina replied, triggering the lasers. On the zoomed image displayed over the tactical overlay, the satellite, a chunky cylinder with wing-like solar panels, flared brightly. For a moment, it shone like a small star as it scattered laser energy, then puffed into a cloud of debris.

"One down," Torina said.

"Good shot. Avoid debris, if you please?"

"Nudging accordingly, boss," Netty answered.

I thanked her but kept my attention on the overlay. I wasn't convinced that this wouldn't get more complicated and wanted to be ready. And if it didn't, and it just ended up with Torina pressing the trigger three times and us flying back home, then I'd be pleasantly surprised and nothing more.

Sometimes, simple is good.

The next satellite died, and we waited for the third to rise over the limb of the planet. Beneath us, the terminator demarking day and night swept past and fell behind.

"Third satellite—" Netty started, then cut herself off with a contact warning.

"Six launch signatures from the surface. Two of them are ships, each about class 7 mass. The other four are missiles."

I sighed as the new icons popped onto the overlay. "Of course. Nothing's ever going to be this simple, is it?"

"If it makes you feel better, the third satellite is now in range," Netty said.

"It doesn't, but thanks anyway. Torina, once you've taken care of that, can you turn your attention to—"

The third satellite flashed into wreckage.

"—our new friends, please and thank you?"

"On it," she said.

"Van, both those ships and missiles are climbing out of a pretty deep gravity well. If we light the drive, we'll probably pull away before they can pose any threat to us," Zeno said.

"That's actually happening anyway. It's going to take them a while just to climb into orbit," Torina observed.

I nodded, but watching the icons slowly creep out of Landfall's gravitational depression, I was struck by an idea.

"Netty, if we do light the drive and make the fastest possible slingshot around that moon ahead of us, can we get back here before those assholes are able to break orbit?"

"Before they can break orbit? No. But we would be able to come back at them before they'll be able to get up to any significant velocity."

"Perfect. Please do that. Oh, and if you can, design our return trajectory so if we brake hard enough, we have the option of dropping into orbit around Landfall, if the reception doesn't get much hotter than this. There's something down there, and I want to know what."

———

It took the Apollo astronauts about three days to get to the Moon from Earth. Of course, they only had the energy from their Saturn V launch vehicle, plus a couple of mid-course correction burns from a chemical rocket. We had a vastly more powerful fusion drive that we could burn for hours if we wanted to, so we did roughly the same trip—both ways—in a little over two hours.

It made for an exciting pass around Landfall's moon. It was a little larger than its Earthly counterpart, and we passed over its surface at an altitude of about a hundred klicks. The barren, rocky surface blurred beneath us, giving us the rare sensation of moving like a bat out of hell.

Even Zeno, old spacer that she was, noted it. "Out in the big black, there's no noticeable difference between standing still and traveling a bajillion klicks a second if you've got nothing to compare it to. That, though—"

She gestured out the canopy at the surface of the moon racing by beneath us, seemingly close enough to touch.

I nodded. "Yeah. I kinda think I should be able to feel the wind in my hair—if there was, you know, wind out here."

"Not to mention the fact that if there was, it would rip the hair right out of your head at this velocity," Perry said.

I shot him a glance. "You've got no sense of romance, Perry."

"I could download and install one, if you'd like."

"Romance version 2.0. You charmer, you."

The massive disk of Landfall rose over the rugged gray horizon ahead. Netty had to periodically flip the *Fafnir* into different orientations and apply brief bursts of thrust from the fusion drive to tweak our course the way I wanted it.

"The ships have entered orbit around Landfall. Those four missiles have been tracking blindly after us—oops, and there we go, they've got lock on us again," Netty said.

I turned to Torina, but she was way ahead of me. "On it. Zeno, you want to stand by on the mass driver and particle cannon in case this gets up close and personal?"

"Delighted to, ma'am."

"Okay, everyone, battle stations. You know the drill," I said.

We did. We'd already suited up, so we put our helmets on and decompressed the *Fafnir*. We'd adopted this as standard practice at Icky's recommendation because, as she put it—

"I'm tired of explosive decompression turning little holes into big ones. It just makes extra work when I've gotta fix it all."

She gave me a thumbs-up and moved aft, ready to join Waldo in doing damage control. It was a smoothly oiled machine at this point, and I was pretty damned proud of that.

Torina opened fire. The lasers lanced out, seeking the incoming missiles. They were big ordnance, the sort of thing fired by a capital ship, but also surprisingly slow. I noted that and Zeno replied.

"Those are surface-defense missiles, intended to shoot at things in orbit. They're not really designed to break orbit and chase things into space."

One by one, Torina took out the four missiles before they even reached our point-defense envelope. As for the two ships, both were burning to break orbit, but we had a huge velocity advantage on them. It meant they could maneuver more tightly, but this wasn't a dogfight so that wasn't much of an advantage. This was, as my father had once explained it to me, more of a "boom-and-zoom," fighter pilot lingo for taking advantage of a superior energy state to do an attack run—*boom*—then speed away—*zoom*.

Which was exactly what we did. I *almost* felt sorry for these guys. They did pretty much everything wrong, so much so that it wasn't even a contest, really. Torina waited for them to open fire, which they did, with missiles that had virtually no hope of climbing out of the gravity well to catch us. She then blasted one of the ships to fragments with the lasers. The second one decided discretion was the better part of valor and bugged out, trying to plunge back to the safety of Landfall's surface, but Zeno caught it with a mass-driver shot that sent it plummeting toward the surface, out of control.

"Okay, Netty, can you drop us into orbit?"

"No need to ask, boss. Got us turning right now."

She spun us around and fired the drive to full power. Preceded by a plume of fusion exhaust, the *Fafnir* braked and dropped neatly into orbit. We did a complete loop around the planet, then scanned the surface for any sign of the second ship. We found it, or at least its remains, scattered on the ice covering a nearly circular glacial lake in Landfall's northern polar region.

"Perfect. Netty, take us down. I want to see if we can recover anything from that wreckage to identify these guys. Dayna specifically said there was no one on the surface, but apparently she was wrong."

"Yeah, about that," Perry said. "Van, while we orbited, I kept an eye on the scanner data. We've got about eighty percent coverage of Landfall and there is nothing, and I mean *nothing*, down there, aside from rocks, water, and native flora. It makes Wyoming look like Manhattan."

"Kansas or New York?" I asked.

"Geography jokes. You know, they don't come around often, so when they do—"

"We seize the day. But back to that howling wilderness down there. Any sign of, ah, missile launchers? A base? A Dollar General, maybe?"

"Nothing at all."

"Hmm. Curiouser and curiouser."

Torina lifted an eyebrow. "Curiouser? Is that a word?"

"Thanks to a man named Lewis Carroll, yes, it is."

"I'll take your word for it."

Netty fired the drive long enough to start us dropping from orbit, along a path that would ground us at the crash site.

Technically, we didn't need to do any of this. We'd destroyed the three satellites, which is all we'd been asked to, and were being paid to do. But my gut told me that there was more to this, and I wanted to know what it was.

Curiouser and curiouser indeed.

4

WIND GUSTED AGAINST ME. If I could have felt it as anything but pressure, it would have been cold as hell, but my b-suit was designed to resist the cold of space, so this was nothing.

The bigger problem by far was the gravity. I'd idly mused that I'd weigh close to three hundred pounds here on the surface of Landfall, which had just been an interesting fact when I had no plans to come here. Now, though—

"Does this outfit make me look fat?" Torina asked, stomping up beside me. "Because I feel like I've gained, like, sixty pounds."

"You carry it well, and you've got such a pretty face—" I said, and got a half-hearted slap on the arm.

"I'd hit you harder, but that would take too much work."

We stood on a small, rocky rise overlooking the round kettle lake into which the class 7 had crashed. Apparently formed when a receding glacier hived off a massive hunk of ice, which then melted in the resulting depression, it was about a klick and a half across.

J.N. CHANEY & TERRY MAGGERT

According to Netty, the lake was about two hundred meters deep in its center. Patchy gray-white ice covered most of it, which was a warning sign. Dark, vitreous blue ice—actually more black than blue—was sturdy enough to support any reasonable amount of weight put on it. The ragged ice on the kettle lake had been corroded by the rising temperatures of local spring into stuff that I didn't even want to test.

"What the hell is it with work always bringing us to these frozen hellholes, anyway?" Torina groused. "That planet where we found Group 41 doing their bullshit recruit training was all rock and ice and snow, too. Why don't the bad guys ever go to lush, tropical worlds, where we could do our crime fighting in casual beachwear. You know, with style."

"I thought you were worried about your weight," I deadpanned.

Torina snorted. "I'd punch you, but it's too much effort."

Icky strode up beside us. The Wu'tzur physiology had evolved for higher gravity, so she'd just lost some of the exaggerated strength she enjoyed in our standard one g. It also meant she had to take a daily supplement to offset things like losing bone density, but to her, this was just normal gravity.

"So what's the plan, boss? That ice doesn't look like it's gonna hold up that wreck much longer," she said.

I gave a grunt of agreement. The crew of the class 7 had apparently tried landing with whatever control they had left, and they had nearly succeeded. The ship had slammed into the ground a few hundred meters from the lake. Instead of simply turning into an impact crater and a cloud of debris, though, it had hit at a shallow angle, and the bulk of the wreckage skidded out onto the ice. A starburst of ominous gray cracks radiated out from the hull, and when I put a hand on the ice, I felt the echo of movement. The ice was *alive*, and not in a good way.

"Could we try lifting it with the *Fafnir*?" Torina asked.

Icky shook her head. "We'd still have to get it slung into a cradle of some sort. See, her keel's broken right there, behind the cockpit. We lift her without a cradle, and she'll just fall apart."

"Zeno, any ideas?" I asked. She'd stayed aboard the *Fafnir*, being Icky's opposite when it came to high gravity. Her physiology wasn't suited for it, particularly when it came to her respiration, so she remained in the safe one g of the *Fafnir*'s internal gravity.

"No, sorry. The only thing we can really do remotely is scan what's left of her. We want something more direct, then some brave soul is going to have to walk out there."

I shook my head. "Valor aside, no. We're not risking it."

"Okay, okay, I get the message. As usual, only the bird is up to the job," Perry said. He stood on a rock a few meters away. He could still fly despite the stronger gravity, but only for short periods and distances.

I turned to him, a small movement that still took effort. "So you're going to do what, exactly? Fly out there and——"

"And find an external data port to see what I can find out. That's an off-the-shelf class 7 hull, so there should be a maintenance access panel about two thirds of the way back from the cockpit, along what's currently the top of the wreck."

"Anyone strenuously object?"

"Everything I do here is strenuous, Van. If this is going to let us get the hell out of here, I'm all for it," Torina said.

I turned back to Perry. "Okay, bird, you're on."

"On my way," he said, hurling himself into the air, with limited

47

success. Through a combination of gliding and beating his wings, he sailed across the ice, did a hammerhead stall at the other end, and landed on the flank of the wreck.

"Confirmed, boss, there's a maintenance port right here," he said. "I'm going to hook up and see what I can pull out of this thing before it—"

A loud crack, like a gunshot, snapped apart the cold air.

I took an instinctive step toward the lake. "Perry, get the hell out of there!"

"Van, relax. Ice cracks all the time. I've hooked up and—"

Another whip crack cut him off. A second later, the wreck shifted, then water gushed up and spilled onto the rotting ice.

"Perry!"

His tone was aggrieved. "Really? I'm the bird that broke the camel's back—?"

With a shuddering crash and fountains of water, the wreck broke through the ice and quickly began to sink.

I LUMBERED down the slope in sluggish, awkward steps, headed toward the lake. By the time I reached the shore, I was wheezing like a chainsmoker singing opera.

"Perry—!"

The wreck had vanished under a slurry of water and ice floes by the time I stopped. I couldn't see Perry, either in the water or the air above it, so he must have gone down with it.

Torina stumbled up beside me, Icky with her.

"Perr—" I sucked in a breath. "Perry!"

Nothing.

"Netty, are you getting anything from him?"

"I'm not. But water is a poor medium for transmitting radio-frequency energy, except at very low wavelengths. And that requires a big antenna, which Perry isn't."

I cursed. Of all the places I'd worried about losing Perry, a lake wasn't high on the list.

I turned. "Okay, let's get back to… the *Fafnir*." I gasped in more air. "We'll fly out over… the hole, where the wreck was, and—"

A garbled rattle of noise in my ears truncated my words. I turned back to the lake.

"Perry?"

More noise.

"Netty, is that—"

"It's coming from beneath the surface of the lake, yes. And the signal's getting stronger."

"Perry?"

This time, I thought I heard a recognizable word—or sound, anyway.

I heard one… sound.

Wheeeeee!

"Perry? What the hell are you doing?"

His voice came through distinctly now, although rough and full of static.

"Who'd have thought it'd be easier to fly through water than air?"

"Are you okay?"

"Yeah, fine. Better than up there, in fact. Well, slower, but flying's a lot easier."

I took a last, deep breath. "Can you get out of there?"

"A little reluctant to try and come back up through that hole. All those chunks of ice banging together like hammers and anvils—anyway, I'm on my way to you."

While we waited, I asked Zeno for an update on the bigger picture around us. "Still nothing on the scanners?"

"Nope. Nothing on the surface or in space from horizon to horizon."

"Then where the hell did those missiles and these ships come from? Missiles that big must have had some sort of launcher," Icky said.

They did, which meant we should have just been able to track their launch signature back to their origin. But atmospheric interference meant we only had a rough idea where that was, and that assumed they weren't launched from something covert, like a stealthed base or ship or—

I stared at the ice in front of my feet, thinking of Perry in the water beneath it and how missiles could be launched back on Earth by launchers that couldn't be found.

"A submarine. Or some sort of mobile, concealable launcher," I said.

"If that's the case, then someone put some real effort into establishing a discreet presence on this planet," Torina said.

"Yes, this resource-rich planet, with mineral deposits that, as Dayna put it, you could mine with a shovel. Laterites, they're called. Ore deposits exposed on the surface and weathered down to gravel. There's lots of money to be made here, and three major powers who want to make it."

"Okay, Van, I'm here—kind of. I think my inertial nav is pretty good, but I got tossed around when that damned ship sank, so—anyway, all I see above me is ice."

"I've had enough of this," I growled, then drew the Moonsword and plunged the blade downward in one smooth motion. I was profoundly glad the blade was so preternaturally sharp and basically cut the ice under its own weight, because if I had to work and hack at it, I'd have been left a gasping heap of sweaty exhaustion.

Icky levered the piece of ice I'd cut out and heaved it away, the massive block sliding several meters before grinding to a halt.

"Reminds me of ice fishing," I said.

"Why would anyone fish for ice?" Icky asked.

"They—no, they're not fishing *for* ice, they're—" I sighed. "Never mind. I'll just show you when we're back aboard the *Fafnir*." I turned back to the hole. "Perry?"

"Sorry, Van. I can't see any hole, and my scanners are really degraded by this water. Try thumping on the ice where you're going to cut, and I'll see if I can zero in on the vibrations."

I shook my head. We had technology that could detect things light-minutes away in space, that could target something the apparent size of a dust mote with accurate laser fire and discern small differences in the composition of a ship's hull at a distance. But despite all that, we were reduced to what amounted to a game of Marco Polo, with Icky thumping her foot on the ice near the shore so Perry could follow the sound and we could finally cut him out.

He clambered out of the water, vibrated himself to shed water, then paused.

"Uh oh."

"Uh oh? What's wrong?"

"I'm freezing, that's what's wrong."

I frowned. "How could you be *freezing*? You can't feel the cold."

"No, I mean I'm literally freezing. I've still got some water droplets stuck in tight places, like my actuators, and for some reason my deicing system is offline." He sighed. "In exchange for much of my dignity, can I get someone to carry me back to the *Fafnir*?"

Icky gleefully scooped Perry up—then held him over her head and began to run back to the *Fafnir*, making jet-engine noises as she did.

Torina and I slogged along after her, grinning. "Actually, Perry, I think you've exchanged *all* your dignity for this," I said.

He sniffed, a noise I barely heard over Icky's ridiculous whooshing sounds, and then he turned back to give me a smug wink. "Dignity can be regained, but being chauffeured in this ridiculous gravity is worth a month of jokes at my expense. Onward, Icky, and see if these laggards can keep up."

"What's a laggard?" Icky asked, never breaking stride.

Perry's answer was instant. "A sucker who ain't gettin' a ride."

IT DIDN'T TAKE LONG for Perry to work his actuators free once he'd warmed up. As he did, shaking himself like a preening avian, I pulled off my helmet. I suddenly felt about ninety pounds lighter, because I was, thanks to the *Fafnir*'s inertial dampers.

"Perry, did you get any data from that ship?" I asked him, unsnapping and pulling off my gloves.

"We've got a bigger issue than that to deal with, Van."

I stopped, tensing up at the bland tone. "What?"

"My deicing system. It needs—"

"We'll get it looked at, don't worry. Now, about that ship."

He flexed his wings. "I didn't get much before I was, you know, plunged into that frozen hell. What I can say is the crew was dead, killed by some combination of our weapons fire, explosive decompression, and crashing into the planet."

"I think we could have assumed that. Anything else?"

"Judging from the comm logs I was able to access, they were mercenaries—and before you ask, no, I can't confirm if they were from Group 41 or not."

"Again, not really a surprise. The League, Federation, and Alliance would all likely employ mercenaries to give themselves some plausible deniability about being here in the first place," Zeno offered.

Perry bobbed his head in agreement. "I'm assuming you're not interested in mundane maintenance data about the ship, so I'll cut right to the chase—the other significant bit of information I pulled is some nav data. This ship has twisted to a set of coordinates on the edge of the Wolf 424 system three times in the past eight weeks."

Zeno sniffed. "Effectively neutral territory, so it doesn't narrow it down. It could still be anyone."

"Still, repeated trips to the same place—resupply runs, maybe?" Torina said.

I shrugged. "Could be. So let's find out. Netty, preflight us, if you please. Let's see if we can find out who's paying these guys to be here."

"And then?" Netty asked brightly.

"Simple. We make them pay *again*."

I BLINKED AWAY the residual fuzz of twisting and watched the tactical overlay. It quickly filled with data.

"Busy place for a random spot on the edge of a lonely system," Torina said.

I whistled, watching the scanners reveal their data. There were four ships within just a few light-minutes, including a class 12 freighter registered to what was now known as the Schegith Protectorate, two class 9s—one fast freighter and one armed cutter—and a class 6 workboat with a signature so bland it might have been a civilian craft. Wolf 424 was indeed almost empty, being populated mainly by small scale, transient asteroid-mining operations. The Schegith freighter's flight profile suggested it was just heading out of the system, probably with a load of ore concentrate. The other ships were more inscrutable.

"That class 6 workboat is registered to a small mining consortium based in this system. The two class 9s are registered to different corporate fronts. One based in Procyon, the other on the Gajur homeworld," Netty reported.

My attention zeroed in on the class 9s. They were flying similar, though not identical profiles. Their respective registrations were unremarkable, which meant they could belong to anyone. Corporate shells within shells, like Russian nesting dolls, were turning out to be the norm more than the exception.

In other words, it told us nothing.

"So what do you want to do, Van?" Torina asked

I tapped my chin. "Well, even if some of these are bad guys, all they have to do is ignore us, right? So let's make it so they can't.

Netty, broadcast a demand that all four of these ships heave to and prepare to be boarded for inspection."

"Even the Schegith-registered ship?"

"Yup. All of them. Let's see what happens."

Netty made the broadcast, including our Guild credentials. The Schegith ship immediately cut its drive. So did the class 6 but only after altering course in a way that would make it a pain to catch up.

"Probably small-time smugglers, running booze or chems to some supposedly dry mining operation," Perry said.

I nodded and watched the class 9s. The fast freighter reduced power but didn't cut its drive entirely. The armed cutter, though, immediately turned into us, accelerating and firing a spread of missiles. As soon as it did, the other class 9 slammed its drive back to full power. It would be able to twist away in less than ten minutes.

I swore. It meant the fast freighter was probably going to be able to give us the slip. Not that we could do much about it, though, since we had four inbound missiles.

A new voice came over the comm. "Hey, Peacemaker, what's your weapons load-out?"

I blinked in disbelief. "Uh—a battleship's worth of ordnance and a thousand photon torpedoes."

"What the hell's a photon torpedo?"

I noticed the traffic was coming from the class 6. "Do you really expect me to just announce the details of our weapons to you?"

"Hey, we're trying to make odds here. Right now it's three to two in your favor, but I've got a couple of guys who're leaning toward that class 9."

"You're *betting* on this?"

"Well, yeah. Wouldn't you?"

"I—no, I wouldn't. Now clear this channel, or I'll give you a weapons demonstration, right before I haul your asses in for interfering in an investigation, or harassment, or… or whatever other charges that happen to occur to me."

"Somebody's grumpy," the voice said, but the channel cut off.

"You haven't seen grumpy, shithead," I said, but my attention was already back to the matter at hand. Combat.

We accelerated directly into the attack. Torina took down three of the missiles with the lasers. The point-defenses missed the fourth, and it detonated close enough to do some minor damage. We returned the favor, pounding the class 9 with laser fire until it broke off and desperately accelerated away. Unfortunately, it meant the other class 9 was now certain to escape—

"Van, the Schegith freighter is firing."

I snapped my attention back to the overlay. It was firing —at who?

As it turned out, it seemed to be targeting just an empty bit of space. But then a drive lit, and a ship that had been hanging cold and silent suddenly came to life.

"They must have been sitting in it with life support off, in their suits," Perry said.

"Yeah, that's not suspicious at all." I dismissed the fleeing class 9s and focused exclusively on the new player on the field, a class 8. It was making a break for a twist point, too, but the Schegith missile caught it handily, since it had to accelerate from a relative stop. It finally opened up with point defenses, but too late. The missile detonated close by, and the ship's drive died again.

While we maneuvered to match velocity with the disabled ship, I called up the Schegith and offered my thanks.

"That was a good catch. We hadn't even noticed them," I said.

"This one suspected there may be another ship nearby. This is a common tactic among miscreants. To whom should this one send the bill for the missile?"

I smiled. "Send it to Anvil Dark, attention Master Gerhardt. And thanks again."

We closed in on the damaged class 8, coming to a relative stop a few hundred meters away. I transmitted an open comm message.

"Unknown ship, you can either stand down and be boarded, or you can be pounded to scrap, then cut open like a can of peaches and boarded that way. Your call."

"What are peaches?"

"Seriously? *That's* the part you fixate on?" I rolled my eyes. "Things that can't fight back, that's what peaches are."

A long pause. We waited, our fire control scanners hammering away on the other ship.

"We will surrender," the voice finally replied. "We further declare diplomatic immunity under the auspices of the Seven Stars League and demand to be transferred to their custody immediately."

I looked at Torina, who just shrugged.

Perry flexed his wings.

"Anyone see any rust anywhere?"

5

WE ENDED up taking three prisoners off the disabled ship, two human and one Yonnox. All three were churlish, only giving us their names and refusing to say anything else until they were brought to a Seven Stars League consulate. Their apparent leader, a cipher named Jameison with the bearing of an ex-cop, only broke his stubborn silence to ask a question.

"What are the charges against us?"

"You're implicated in an illegal smuggling operation in which we were fired upon."

"So the charge is—?"

"Threatening a Peacemaker engaged in lawful performance of his duties with violence."

Jameison's face started in the direction of a smile but didn't get very far. "It'll be interesting to see how you make that stick."

We placed them in the *Fafnir*'s brig, marked their disabled ship with a salvage beacon, then started back to Anvil Dark.

On the way, I pulled Perry into my cabin.

"Did you find anything incriminating aboard their ship?" I asked.

"A leisure outfit in a storage locker that was a definite crime against fashion—I mean, who wears mauve velvet aside from some cheesy lounge singer with a pornstache doing a bad rendition of *Mack the Knife*? But other than that, no. They did a military-grade wipe on their systems and weren't carrying any cargo at all."

I nodded. "So that guy had a point. The fact that they were silent running near a place mentioned in the nav log of a different ship—in an entirely different system? That *looks* sketchy as hell, but it's not much to go on. And it sure doesn't constitute a crime."

"Actually, Van, that's not quite true. They were silently running in a volume of space that could reasonably be considered frequented by interstellar traffic. That makes them a navigation hazard, which is illegal under Interstellar Commerce Protocol Five."

I blinked at him. "You're saying we should charge these guys with being a nav hazard?"

"Hey, they sent up Al Capone for tax evasion. Whatever works, right?"

I shrugged. "Let's do it. Draft up the charges."

When I served them with what was frankly a *Hail Mary* charge, their flat cool briefly cracked.

"This is bullshit," Jameison snapped. His two companions added a few even cruder adjectives. I just smiled and shrugged.

"Hey, I don't write the laws, I just enforce them."

"This is, what, a fine? Maybe?"

"That'll be up to judicial. I'm just a—what was the term that little girl used back on Spindrift? The one who wanted to be a

Peacemaker. Cute kid." I snapped my fingers as if trying to recollect something.

Perry spoke in loud, friendly tones. "Van the Space Policeman, I believe. You shoulda seen this kid—dressed like a unicorn, having the time of her life, and—"

"I don't care if some kid gave you a nickname. The charge won't stick," Jameison growled.

"Au contraire. The nickname is sort of a rhyme. That adds considerable weight to my argument," I said, waving a cautionary finger. Then I leaned forward, the smile wiped from my face. "I'll make *sure* it sticks. It's my mission in life. Now, then, Icky? If you would?"

Icky looked mournfully down at her hammer. "I wish you could meet her, but Van, the Space Policeman, says into the cell. You know, for your own protection."

Jameison blanched, and all three of our *guests* went meekly into the brig, each eying Icky's huge hands as they passed by.

The charge was thin but legitimate. And for now, it would have to be enough.

"YOU KEEP MY LIFE INTERESTING, Tudor, I'll give you that much," Gerhardt said as soon as Torina, Perry, and I entered his office.

"Um... you're welcome?"

"I wasn't saying that's a good thing."

"Oh. Okay, sorry?"

Gerhardt sat back in his chair. "Constituting a navigation hazard? You arrested them for that?"

"No, like I said in the report, I actually arrested them for being implicated in an attack on us."

"Implicated how, exactly?"

"When that class 9 attacked us, they were silent-running nearby."

"So sitting quietly in the shadows near the scene of a crime is itself a crime?"

I slumped a bit. There was no getting around it. The evidence linking our prisoners to the attack on the *Fafnir* made *flimsy* look like Stonehenge in comparison.

Gerhardt nodded. "Yes, I thought so. Your prisoners actually have a stronger case against the Schegith for an unprovoked attack on their ship—which I am *not* going to reimburse them for, by the way. You would have had a stronger case if you'd arrested the master of the Schegith freighter."

"I—"

Gerhardt cut me off with a raised hand. "Whatever you're going to say, Tudor, don't bother. It is what it is at this point. You're just fortunate that you *could* legitimately charge and take them into custody for constituting a navigation hazard, or you'd be facing a wrongful arrest action right now."

He drummed his fingers on his desk. "Do you see what I mean by interesting?"

"Kinda, yeah."

Gerhardt sat forward again. "All of that said, the involvement of the Seven Stars League actually *is* interesting, and the *only* reason I'm not just dismissing that charge and throwing this case out. If they'd been smart, they'd have said nothing at all and just be on their way now. But claiming diplomatic immunity kickstarts a process that must now run its course."

"What do you mean?"

"We have to retain these prisoners in custody while the matter is referred to the closest League consulate, which is in the Epsilon Eridani system. We've done that. What should have then happened is for the consulate to forward their diplomatic credentials, whatever they are, and confirm they have said immunity. We would then release them to the League's custody to dispose of their case, which again probably would have just involved letting them go."

Torina narrowed her eyes. "But?"

"But, the League is instead sending an envoy here to deal with the case in person. I could understand that if the charges were especially serious, like murder. But constituting a navigation hazard? That should have been handled by some junior League consulate staffer as on-the-job training."

"So we've kicked over a rock and potentially exposed something the League doesn't want us to see," Perry said.

Gerhardt nodded. "And what makes matters worse is that they could have just made this all go away by doing nothing at all. So now I'm curious as to how this is going to play out."

He leaned back again in his seat. "The League envoy will be here in about one standard day. Don't leave Anvil Dark, Tudor. I want you here when they arrive." He gave a thin smile. "I can't help feeling that this is somehow going to end up being about you."

"You mean their Satrap and his whole *wanting to arrest me* thing."

"Indeed. Let's just hope their case for doing that isn't any stronger than"—he waved a hand at his terminal, which was displaying my report—"this one."

SINCE WE HAD a day to kill, and since I didn't want to just sit around fretting about whether I was going to find myself being extradited to the Seven Stars League, I decided we needed something to do. I spent a few hours helping Icky and Zeno make repairs to the *Fafnir* and doing basic maintenance, then decided to go see Bester, the Guild's archivist. The term that Zeno's mother, Tendothir, had used to describe that mysterious war—The Clearings—was crying out to be investigated.

Accessing Bester's archives was one of the strangest aspects of working for the Guild, and that was saying something. The so-called open archives were freely available to Peacemakers to peruse, but the secure or closed archives required Bester to give explicit access. It was access he charged a strange price for—some token with deep personal meaning to the inquirer.

"I hope we don't have to do many more of these archive searches, because I'm running out of meaningful trinkets," I said as we walked into the archives. This time, it was a die-cast model of an F/A-18 Hornet fighter similar to the one my father had flown. When I was fourteen or so, I'd tried to alter it so that it had the same tail insignia as my dad's jet, and I managed about what you'd expect from a fourteen-year-old. The tail fins were crudely painted over and awkwardly lettered with something that looked more like shitty graffiti than aircraft markings. But it still meant a lot to me, so I expected a correspondingly deep level of access.

Bester slowly looked up as Perry, Torina, and I entered. "Hey, Bester."

He stood—again, slowly. Bester resembled a big, anthropomorphic sloth, right down to a slow and deliberate manner. I had learned to be patient with him.

"Hello, Van." He paused. "Torina." He paused again. "Perry."

I really didn't want to engage in small talk because small talk with Bester was a drawn-out affair. But he was also a good source of gossip around the Guild, because pretty much everyone liked and trusted him. I mean, he came across as a big, gentle, lumbering teddy bear, and how could you not love that?

"What can I do for you today?" he finally asked after we exchanged a bit of rumor that didn't end up being particularly interesting, at least not to us.

I explained what we were looking for. He pondered it for a while.

"That's going to require access to the closed archives—"

"Way ahead of you, Bester," I said, putting the little Hornet on the counter. He blinked at it a few times, then picked it up in a beefy, hairy hand.

"Cool. F/A-18 Hornet, right?"

It was my turn to blink. "Um… yeah, it is. I'm surprised you recognize it, being an Earth aircraft and all."

Bester answered by slowly pulling out a data slate, tapping at it, then turning it to me. "I've got a thing for heavier-than-air vehicles," he said.

I stared at the picture. It depicted an aircraft I recognized as a B-25 Mitchell, an American medium bomber of Second World War vintage.

I looked at him. "Okay—"

"That's mine."

"Yours."

He nodded.

"You own a piston-engine American bomber."

He blinked. "I do."

"You own an airplane back on Earth."

He smiled a languid smile. "No, it's on my homeworld—duh. I fly it whenever I get the chance. I actually wanted a P-51 Mustang or a Supermarine Spitfire, but—" He gestured at his own bulk, which was probably a tight fit in the relatively spacious B-25.

"How—?" I started, then shook my head. I shouldn't be surprised, really. The number of Earthly things I'd encountered out in known space was shocking. Earth didn't realize it, but it was already an honorary member of known space, only waiting for the discovery of twist technology to graduate to full membership.

Of course, I also had a sudden image of Bester the anthropomorphic sloth sitting in the cockpit of his personal B-25 and wearing aviator shades and a sheepskin jacket—

"What's so funny?" he asked.

"Uh—sorry, just woolgathering there," I said, shaking my head. "Anyway, if we could get access to the closed archives—"

"For this, absolutely, full access," he said, holding up the model of the Hornet.

Bester led us behind the counter, through a set of blast doors, and into a series of compartments containing everything from advanced organic memory modules to moldering tomes and dusty old scrolls—which, now that I thought about, were printed on animal skins that would also make *them* organic memory modules, wouldn't it?

Bester handed us over to an AI-controlled librarian, who took our queries and helped us find the records we were looking for. I found myself eyeing the many books and scrolls and sheafs of yellowed paper, wondering what fascinating information treasures might be languishing on the ranks upon ranks of shelves. Someone could spend a lifetime digging through it all, though, and probably not even get halfway.

We steadily collected a variety of archives, mostly data modules, but also some hardcopies. Once we'd exhausted the AI's catalog of things potentially linked to The Clearings, we plunked ourselves into cubicles and started poring over what we'd gathered.

For the next few hours, we shuffled documents, swapped out memory modules in readers, and drank coffee brought to us by Icky from the *Fafnir*. We ended up requesting more archival items, based on references we found, and examined them, too. Finally, when my and Torina's eyes started to glaze over, we sat down to compare notes.

"I found a whole lot of nothing," Torina said.

I nodded. "Same. An awfully conspicuous amount of nothing, in fact. Every time I thought I had an interesting lead, it wandered off into a black hole of missing or redacted data."

"The digital stuff is all the same," Perry said. "There are big gaps where data is either missing or corrupted"—he made air quotes with his wings—"but an awful lot of that corrupted data looks suspiciously like it's been overwritten with random noise."

"So it's a cover-up," Torina said.

"Yeah, seems so. Someone doesn't want anyone to know what the significance of The Clearings is. The culprits are the Seven Stars League, this Guild, or both," I said.

"And/or someone else entirely," Perry pointed out.

I rubbed my eyes. "True enough. Which means I guess we've hit a dead end."

"Actually, I did manage to glean one useful fact, taken as an aggregate of a few bits and pieces that apparently slipped through all the redaction and obfuscation. There were a lot of deaths. Like, potentially the entire population of planets," Perry said.

Torina stretched. "Must have been one hell of a war."

"Yeah. But what I don't get is why it's covered up at all. It was a war that took place well outside known space," I said.

"Even so, it still involved the League and the Guild. Whatever role they played is probably the reason for all the redaction," Perry said.

I nodded. "I know. Which leads to the next question. Just what the hell were we doing out there?"

I woke the next morning to find a message from Gerhardt waiting for me on the terminal in my cabin aboard the *Fafnir*. The Seven Stars League envoy was four hours away.

I clambered out of bed, intent on showering and getting dressed, but Perry appeared at my door. He entered and closed it.

"I wanted to corroborate this before I said anything, but it was definitely the Galactic Knights Uniformed involved in The Clearings," he said.

I stripped down, not particularly concerned about doing it in front of Perry, put on a bathrobe, and grabbed my shower kit. "It took you this long to get corroboration?"

"I had to make some discreet inquiries, and do it in a way that I wouldn't risk triggering anyone's interest."

"Okay. But we already knew that, right? Tendothir explicitly said that the Galactic Knights were involved."

"Well, sure, but to her that would just be a name. I wanted to see if I could learn anything more *about* their involvement."

I grabbed my towel. "And did you?"

"I think our new old friend B was involved, seemingly because of her medical expertise."

That stopped me. "Huh. Well, if these Galactic Knights Uniformed are as secretive and compartmentalized as they seem to be, she probably won't be willing to offer much up."

"Still worth asking her. Probably Groshenko, as well. I mean, you are part of the organization, Van. And whether the GKU likes it or not, thanks to those sinking fish in the Solar System, you're now involved in The Clearings—whatever they are. So they either keep you in the dark and risk you blowing the lid off something out of ignorance, or they read you into it enough that you don't."

"I'm getting the sense you're advising me to just drop any further investigation for now, at least until we can talk to B or Groshenko."

"I am. And if you've got another trinket around, you might want to give it to Bester to make sure he keeps all of this to himself. He is a bit of a gossip."

"Yeah, I noticed." I stared at my locker. The only other memento I'd brought with me was a copy of a Captain America comic signed by Stan Lee. It dated from a burst of obsessive comic book enthusiasm I had when I was twelve or so and had pestered Gramps into taking me to a weekend geek convention in Sioux Falls.

I nodded, as much to myself as Perry. "Okay. First, shower and breakfast. Then, Bester. And then, we'll go and spend some quality time with the envoy from the Seven Stars League."

"They seem nice," Perry said.

"Compared to a radioactive badger? The envoy is a *delight*."

"Probably a lot less... glowy, too."

I smiled, then began looking for my toothbrush. "That's one of the reasons you're so valuable to me, bird. You're just packed with *science*."

6

When I arrived in Gerhardt's office with Torina and Perry in tow, the Seven Stars League envoy was already there.

"And this must be Peacemaker Tudor," the man said. "Tell me, how does it feel to be a wanted man?"

"I've always been somewhat handsome, but it was my sophomore year of high school where the mustache *really* paid off with the girls. See, I'd gotten into this old show called Magnum, and—" I stopped, then chuckled in a self-deprecating manner that was complete and utter horseshit. "Ahh. I misunderstood. Well, let's start with the basics. It's a pleasure to meet you. And you are?"

"Marcus Kells, Deputy Ambassador for the Seven Stars League to the Eridani Federation," he replied with oleaginous ease.

I nodded with matching sincerity. Kells was a middle-aged human who was gangly but soft—*skinnyfat*, to quote Perry. His eyes were bright but empty of anything resembling emotion—the eyes of a snake, if that snake was trying to sell you a timeshare in Orlando.

He wore a natty suit with a cravat that could have been taken out of a Dickens novel. Neither of us offered a hand to the other to shake, which was fine, because I didn't want his aroma of mid-level bureaucracy rubbing off on me.

"Ah. Mister Kells, to what do I owe the pleasure?"

"You arrested three of my deputies under false pretenses, thereby adding another crime to the list that we would like you to answer for. And, to that end, I have just provided your Master Gerhardt with an extradition request." He turned to Gerhardt. "So, if you can just approve it, I will take Mister Tudor here into custody, retrieve my wrongfully imprisoned deputies, and be on my way."

Gerhardt pursed his lips for a moment, then stood and walked to the door, then opened it and looked at it.

Kells frowned. "Is there a problem, Master Gerhardt?"

He closed the door and shook his head. "Well, for a moment I was concerned that I had somehow wandered into your office. But that's my name on the door, so it appears I was wrong." He leveled a hard stare on Kells. "This *is* my office, which means I am going to ask you to sit down."

"I really don't have——"

"Time?" Gerhardt nodded. "Very well, then. We'll arrange for you to take your deputies into custody and make a speedy departure. I look forward to seeing the disposition of their case."

Kells bristled. I exchanged a look with Torina, who returned an impressed nod.

"Master Gerhardt, perhaps there is some misunderstanding. I have provided you with a valid extradition request for Tudor. You are obligated to honor it, under the Peacemaker Charter, to which the Seven Stars League is a signatory."

Gerhardt nodded. "You're right. I am," he said, then handed over a data slate.

"What's this?" Kells snapped.

"A list of individuals potentially implicated in various crimes conducted in known space. I believe there are ninety-seven of them. I would like them extradited into our custody, in accordance with the Charter you are a signatory to, so they may be questioned."

Kells reddened. "There are... two of the most senior members of our civil service—"

"Potential fraud involving misappropriation of funds," Gerhardt said.

"—and three of our planetary governors—"

"One for his connections to a drug cartel operating out of a bogus mining operation in Wolf 424—which also happens to be where your three deputies were taken into custody—and one for—well, you can read the potential crime yourself. It's not the sort of thing I like to say aloud in polite company." Gerhardt looked at Torina with a flash of archaic gallantry. "It's unseemly. My apologies."

Torina batted her lashes and gave him a thankful nod, as if he'd just squashed a cockroach on the way to cross her foot.

Kells, watching the sidebar with growing rage, cleared his throat and tossed the slate back onto Gerhardt's desk. "This is an *outrage*. You're offering trumped-up allegations against some of our most respected politicians and bureaucrats just to protect this man," he said, stabbing a finger at me.

Gerhardt's face didn't change even a fraction. "Would you like to see the evidence? It's all there on the slate. In each case it provides a legitimate prima facie case against each of those ninety-seven individuals. Now, I suspect that we'll quickly dispose of most of them—at least the ones labeled persons of interest, once they provide a satisfactory explanation for their—"

"Why do you want to protect this man?" Kells asked, again pointing at me.

I couldn't resist. "Not polite to point."

Kells fired a glare at me. Gerhardt gave me a hard look, then turned back to Kells.

"This is not a matter of protecting anyone. Rather, it has been customary for signatories to the Guild Charter to trust the Guild to police itself. In turn, we refer cases back to signatories like the League to deal with. That means that to the extent that Tudor is guilty of anything, we will deal with it, just as you will presumably deal with these cases—some of which we referred to you years ago. But if those ancient customs are no longer in effect—"

Gerhardt offered a shrug. "Well, then we're into a brave new world of law enforcement in known space, at least with respect to the Seven Stars League, aren't we?"

I could only stare at Gerhardt in wonder. He'd managed to weaponize bureaucracy in a way that would have made George Orwell proud.

Kells leaned on Gerhardt's desk. "I want to speak to the rest of the Masters."

Gerhardt stared coolly right back at him. "Extraditing a Peacemaker would require a consensus by all of us available at any time. As far as this matter is concerned, that means I *am* the Masters."

Kells made to bluster some more, but Gerhardt cut him off. "We are well aware that Tudor tends to tread the boundary of what's expedient and what's actually legal. We will ensure that he is properly dealt with."

"I want him censured, and I want it done publicly."

Gerhardt steepled his fingers. "Any shame that attaches to him attaches to this Guild. Again, we'll ensure he is dealt with. Of course, we do have the matter of your extradition request—and ours."

Kells straightened, his expression venomous. "I am withdrawing it and will leave the whole affair in your... *capable* hands."

"Very well. I'm likewise rescinding our request so that you can deal with the individuals named within it appropriately."

"What about my three deputy envoys?"

"They will be returned to your ship within the hour."

Kells took a moment to bathe the room and all of us in it in the searing glare of his frustrated rage, then stalked out.

Torina, Perry, and I looked at one another but said nothing, and waited for Gerhardt to break the silence. I braced myself for some sort of censure, charges, or whatever it was he chose to do in the wake of the League envoy's ire.

"I've spent my life dealing with guilty people," he finally said, staring at the door. "And those four are guilty as sin."

I cocked my head at that. "Four?"

"The three you arrested, and the good Envoy Kells. By turning this into a diplomatic incident, they overplayed their hand. You're getting too close for their liking to—*something*."

"We call that being *over the target*," I said.

He turned from the door to me. "Exactly. And I want to know what that *something*—that target—is, whether it's merely a faction within the Seven Stars League that's up to no good, or if it's the

League itself. I'm leaning toward the latter, which means that the security of all known space is at risk."

He glanced back at the door, then returned his gaze to me. "Are you familiar with the Guild title of Justiciar?"

I thought about it, then shook my head. "Sorry, no."

Perry spoke up. "It's an archaic title dating from the Guild's early days, when each Master was named to the Guild by one of the original seven Charter states. The Guild was basically seven different factions, each under a Master who supposedly represented the interests of known space as a whole, but—well, let's just say it didn't work out."

"It did not. The Guild was essentially nothing but a forum for each state to air its grievances, accuse one another of wrongdoing, and make a lot of inconclusive noise. What it didn't do was administer justice," Gerhardt said.

"So what changed?" Torina asked.

"The Galactic Knights, that's what changed. They were a subset of powerful individuals across all of the Charter states who wanted to restore and maintain stability across known space."

"Mainly because they wanted to make money. Instability and unrest breeds volatility, which makes markets unpredictable. These people wanted to smooth that out, so they found willing people within the Peacemaker Guild and cultivated them. Over the course of a hundred years or so, they managed to reengineer the Guild into what it is today," Perry added.

"That's not really advertised anywhere, is it? I mean, I've been with the Guild for a few years, and I've never heard this particular origin story before," I said.

Gerhardt shrugged. "Go back in anyone's history, and I'm pretty sure you'll find what's popularly believed or known and what really happened are two different things."

I had to nod at that. After all, the popular notion of the birth of the United States was all about a gloriously patriotic fight for freedom from tyranny—and it was. But it also involved a lot more bickering over taxes and excise duties and similarly mundane stuff than many people realized.

"So what's a Justiciar, then?" I asked.

"As the Galactic Knights—a name that itself is a clever bit of marketing, by the way—as they began to exert more and more influence over the Guild, the entrenched power structure fought back. One of the ways they did that was by creating positions that only reported to a specific Master. It was a way of both symbolizing and rewarding loyalty to that Master. I don't think the title has been used for, oh—"

Gerhardt turned to Perry, who immediately replied. "Over one hundred and forty years. There was a schism among the Masters back then, and they started naming their own Justiciars, until the Galactic Knights got things back under control."

"There's another bit of Guild history that doesn't get much press," Torina noted.

Gerhardt smiled. "You mentioned kicking over rocks and revealing unpleasant things. Well, the Guild has some rocks of its own." He turned back to me. "All of which is to say that the title of Justiciar is still on the books, so I am going to use it. Tudor, you are, effectively immediately, my Justiciar. That means that you report to me, and no other Masters."

I'd figured that that was where this was going, but I had to raise an objection. "Isn't that just going to paint a big—hell, a *bigger* target on me and my crew?"

"It does kind of single us out since the title hasn't been used in over a century," Torina added.

But Gerhardt shook his head. "It is widely known that you're pursuing an ongoing case that involves Crimes Against Order. Outside that door, that's the reason I've given you this title. The other Masters have all agreed to it for that reason, since it allows them to foist the whole sordid affair of that case onto me."

"You deliberately caught the hot potato," I said, which just earned me blank looks from Gerhardt and Torina.

"It's—never mind. The point is, they didn't want to have to deal with a case of Crimes Against Order, so you stepped up."

"That's right. Inside this room, however, your mandate is broader than that. I want you to find out what the League is up to. With the tension building among three of the most powerful factions in known space over the planet called Landfall, the recent attacks by the Sorcerers and their coconspirators on Unity, and your ongoing Crimes Against Order investigation—"

Gerhardt sat back. "I can't help feeling that these are all symptoms of something much bigger and more dangerous that's squirming beneath a much bigger rock, one covering all of known space. We need to kick it aside and see exactly what it is we're dealing with, Tudor."

He sat forward again. "You will have increased access to Guild resources, including a larger operating stipend. There are also several other Peacemakers inside this particular circle of knowledge, people whom I trust, and therefore you can, too—Lunzy, Lucky,

K'losk, Alic, and Dugrop'che. You may, of course, choose to extend your trust to others, but I'd be wary about that, Tudor."

I caught his look. He wasn't coming out and *saying* there were corrupt and subversive elements lurking inside the Guild, but he didn't have to.

Still, it was like Perry landing on the crashed ship and causing it to plunge into the frozen lake. Having to deal not just with the Sorcerers, Group 41, whatever fragments remained of the Fade, the Seven Stars League, the enigmatic Galactic Knights Uniformed, and on top of all of that, the corruption and menace *inside* the Guild—it hit me like a sudden avalanche, leaving me feeling momentarily overwhelmed.

Gerhardt must have noticed. "Having said all of this, Tudor, I believe you and your crew should take a break before proceeding with this investigation. Since you're a Justiciar now, it's only fitting that you have your Moonsword upgraded accordingly. Go to Starsmith, have your blade enhanced, and have the bill sent back here to me, to my attention."

That sudden feeling of being buried under the weight of circumstances abated. Starsmith was one of very few places I felt genuinely safe, thanks to the unimaginably powerful aegis of the strange being called Matterforge. If it didn't want someone or something entering the Starsmith system, then it wouldn't. It was as simple as that.

I nodded. "Thank you," I said and turned for the door.

"Tudor."

I turned back.

"There's still the matter of your censure. I did tell Mister Kells that you would be dealt with appropriately. So, consider yourself dealt with appropriately. But——" He leaned forward, his gaze boring into mine. "As my Justiciar, you represent me out there. Do *not* make me look bad, Tudor."

I paused, giving his words due consideration, because he was giving *me* consideration. "Wouldn't dream of it."

7

WE ARRIVED at Starsmith to find Linulla in seclusion. Another Conoku smith named Gekola greeted us at the entrance to their underground warren of laboratories, storerooms, and dwellings.

"I don't want to disturb him if he's on some sort of retreat. I'm hoping to get an upgrade done to my Moonsword, so if another smith—"

"I'm sorry," Gekola said, raising a claw. "Once a Starsmith has begun working a blade, they must be the only one to continue working it."

"Oh." Well, that was inconvenient. I didn't want to complain because a phrase like *in seclusion* implied something cultural or spiritual, and I certainly didn't want to rain on that sort of parade. But it struck me that there were more practical issues that arose from that. Apparently, it occurred to Icky, as well.

"So what happens if a Starsmith kicks off?" she asked.

Gekola looked at her. "Kicks off?"

"Yeah. Kicks off. Croaks. You know, dies."

Zeno hissed something to her in a whisper, but Gekola merely nodded. "In such a case, then there is a provision for another Starsmith to assume crafting the blade in question."

"But—"

This time, I cut Icky off before she provoked a diplomatic incident of her own. "That's fine, Icky. Don't worry about it."

I turned back to Gekola. "So when should we come back?"

"There is no need for you to come back. Actually, Linulla is in seclusion for reasons related to you, Peacemaker Tudor."

I blinked in surprise. "Me? What about me?"

"I don't know. Our people normally go into seclusion, a ritual named Rites of Cleansing, for matters related to spiritual impurity. It may be that Linulla is preparing himself for some task he intends to undertake for you."

"That would imply he knew we were coming," Zeno said with suspicion.

But I waved her off, too. The bizarre entity called Matterforge apparently existed not just on the surface of a star, but also across time. It generally didn't reveal much about what it knew, but it sometimes offered snippets, like it had to me, suggesting Peacemakers I could trust. Presumably, that had been based on what those Peacemakers were *going to do*, at least from my perspective as a limited being stuck crawling through one successive moment of time after another. Maybe it had revealed to Linulla that we were on our way here for reasons that required his *spiritual purity*.

Which was quite the timesaver.

"In any case, Linulla asked that you be brought to him when you arrived. The rest of his family is awaiting your companions—apparently the one named Icrul in particular. They seem quite enthusiastic about seeing you," Gekola said.

"That's because she's a big—and I do mean big—kid herself," Perry said.

Icky scowled. "Am *not*."

GEKOLA TOOK me to meet with Linulla, who was staying in seclusion in a remote part of the maze of underground tunnels and chambers that was the Starsmith Forge. He gestured me into the room, but rather than follow me in, he merely closed the door behind me with a pointed *click*.

I found Linulla sitting on a stone dais in a barren, unornamented room. I'd once toured a gold mine in South Africa during a hacking conference, and although it hadn't taken me even close to the fearsome depths of the deepest mines, it had still been an eerie experience. With nothing around me but rock, revealed by the lamps on our hardhats, it was as though I was floating in a sea of darkness. I'd felt isolated from the world by megatons of rock bearing down above and around me in silent oppression.

This chamber had a similar feeling, albeit on a smaller scale.

I hesitated, then started forward. Linulla sat bathed in the only light in the chamber, his carapace a sculpture of shadows and light.

I stopped a few paces away. "Linulla?"

My voice both rang with echoes off the stone walls but also fell flat, as though truncated by that same stone.

"Van. Please, a moment," he said.

I waited. It seemed to me that Linulla was doing something, but whatever it was, it was purely internal and known only to him.

Finally, he relaxed. "Van, I'm glad to see you. I need you here so that I can complete my Rites of Cleansing."

"Okay. I'm glad to help, but… why?"

"Because you are the source of my spiritual impurity."

That caught me short. I stared for a moment, then shook my head. "Me? How?"

He made a soft clicking sound that I'd learned was the Conoku equivalent of a sigh. "Actually, that's unfair. We're both responsible for my spiritual impurity."

"With my sincere apology, Linulla, I don't understand—"

"For the past months, every work I have undertaken has contained a flaw upon completion. Not a serious flaw, and generally not enough to affect the functioning of the work, but a flaw nonetheless. And that is an affront to a Conoku. We strive for flawlessness in everything we create. We do not achieve it, of course, because perfection isn't possible, but to create things that are actually subpar is—it is unacceptable."

"These flaws are related to this spiritual impurity?"

"They are."

"And that's somehow related to me?"

"It is."

"Okay. Well, first of all, I will accept any and all responsibility. Secondly—how?"

"You asked me to perpetrate a falsehood."

I stared, aghast. A falsehood? How had I—?

But then it hit me. I had asked Linulla to create duplicates of two of the Vanguard satellites orbiting Earth. In other words, forgeries.

Linulla nodded. "You know what I'm talking about."

"I—oh, Linulla. I do. The Vanguard satellites." I sighed in disgust. "I shouldn't have asked you—"

"No, you shouldn't have, but neither should I have agreed. I convinced myself I was doing it for a greater good, however, which is a dangerous thing to believe. How many terrible things have been justified in the name of a *greater good?*"

"Many."

"Indeed. In any case, I further convinced myself that doing it for this greater good would absolve me of any spiritual taint. But I was wrong. Our—" The translator failed on the next word. "I'm sorry. The term refers to that part of ourselves that isn't flesh. Our minds, our spirits, the essence of who we are."

"We use different terms back on Earth. The one I'm most familiar with is *soul.* Anyway, I get the idea."

"Soul. Yes. Whatever it is called, it was not deceived by my belief in the rightness of what I was doing, even if I'd managed to deceive myself."

I shook my head. "Again, Linulla, I'm so sorry. How can I make this right?"

"By joining me in this vigil. This chamber is kept utterly empty, because only in utter emptiness is there true perfection." He paused, then added, "You won't need to sit here on this hard stone for long. It's—I need contrition, Van. Even a moment of it, if genuine, will relieve me of this cultural and spiritual burden. It's painful to me, and even more so coming from a friend."

"Ouch."

"My thoughts exactly."

"Shall we begin, Linulla?"

He regarded my face for a long moment, seeing something that made him click his pincers in approval. "We already have."

WHAT I NEEDED TO DO, it turned out, was sit quietly on my ass for a couple of hours, the unyielding stone creating more and more aching discomfort in said ass the entire time.

If I'd been into Zen meditation, I might have been better equipped. Instead, it took all my willpower to not fidget, scratch an itch on my nose or neck or back, shift around to lessen the strain on one cheek or the other, or openly show my discomfort. Linulla managed to sit as still as the stone giving me so much grief, which was an advantage to an exoskeleton, I guess. When it came to things intended to be mindful and meditative, the vigorous exertion of Innsu was more my style.

And then I stopped fighting it. The fidgeting, the movement—I stopped. I let it pass by like a wave—not because I'd achieved some higher state, but because of Linulla. He was here because I had been weak. He was here because I used some but not *all* of my faculties to find a solution.

I knew in that moment that he was a good friend. And I could learn to be a better friend.

As this settled into my awareness, Linulla began extending his legs, creaking to life with the deliberate movements of a waking machine.

"The ritual is complete, Van."

"It is?"

He laughed, then turned his bulk to face me. "It is."

Still, Linulla abruptly announced that the Rite of Cleansing was complete. I took his word for it, since nothing had noticeably changed. Well, nothing external to me, anyway. Inwardly, I was beating myself up for suborning Linulla into forgery in the first place and decided to take it as a lesson—the *greater good* was all very well and fine, but like the road to hell it was a potentially dangerous path paved with good intentions.

When the vigil was complete, we rejoined the others. We found Icky and Zeno immersed in a seething pool of Linulla's kids, while Torina and Perry had returned to the *Fafnir*. When I got her on the comm to tell her I was back online, I could hear the questioning tone in her voice, but I put her off by saying I'd tell her about it later.

Torina did, however, suggest a good idea.

"It struck me that the Conoku are pretty long-lived, so I asked Gekola if he knew anything about The Clearings. He didn't, but based on the general region of space, he suggested looking into something called the Downward Spiral. Perry and I did some digging but didn't find much. It seems to be a more or less colloquial term used to describe a group of races downward from the galactic ecliptic relative to known space. Whatever they actually called themselves wasn't clear, but they got labeled the Downward Spiral partly because of where they were—downward, a spiral, the Milky Way galaxy—"

"I get it," I said.

"You're smart, Van, and don't let anyone tell you otherwise. Ever."

"Does that include you?"

"Don't be ridiculous. It's a natural reaction for me to call you a goober."

"A term of affection, I assume?"

"Naturally, dear. Anyway, it's also because they apparently collapsed into bickering, then backstabbery, and eventually war. And that's all we've been able to find out. You might want to ask Linulla. He could know more."

I did, and he did—a little more.

"I once dealt with a merchant who claimed to be trading with a race outside of known space that he said was a remnant of the Downward Spiral. I was intrigued and made a trip to the location he'd specified, an orbital in a distant system called The Torus."

"That's so generic," I replied. "The Torus? Let me guess, it's shaped like a—wait for it—a torus?"

"A very good guess. It's also a violent, lawless place."

"I've been to Spindrift and Dregs, so I'm used to that."

"No, you aren't. Even in those places, there is some nominal order, at least. If nothing else, you have jurisdiction in them. No one has The Torus in its jurisdiction. The only law there is *might makes right*."

"Charming. There's no central authority at all?"

"None that I could ever discern. So if you go there, take my advice—carry every weapon you can, and do not ever, under any circumstances, back down. If anything, take the opposite stance. If anyone gets in your way, remove them by force."

I frowned. "First of all, harsh. And second of all, it doesn't sound like a very safe place at all."

"It isn't. I lost a claw in a fight on my one and only visit there, about eighty years ago. That was when I was young and adventurous."

I smiled. "If I see it, do you want it back?"

"I appreciate the offer, but I grow them back well enough," he said, waving all of his very much intact claws." Just do me a favor and bring both of *your* claws back. Or... hands, actually. In any case, you know what I mean."

"Yeah, I get the picture."

"Now then, fetch your Moonsword. I may have addressed my spiritual impurity, but the Rite of Cleansing isn't actually complete until I have crafted a—well, not a perfect work, of course, but as close as I can get."

THE NEXT UPGRADE had nothing to do with the Moonsword as a weapon—it didn't make it sharper or any more stabby. It instead gave it another functionality I was pretty sure I'd come to appreciate.

"It will essentially function as a data siphon that can intercept and, to an extent, decrypt said data, then retransmit it to a nearby device, such as a data slate. It's going to take me about a week to complete it, because there are several intermediate steps that— anyway, it's going to take me about a week."

I thanked Linulla, and we prepared to get underway. That mostly entailed disentangling Icky from Linulla's kids. On our last trip to Earth, she'd discovered an old copy of the Twister game in my bedroom, one I'd gotten for Christmas when I was probably eight or nine years old. She'd thought it had something to do with superluminal travel through space but was even more excited to find out it involved putting your hands and feet onto colored spots and trying not to fall down.

While Netty did the *Fafnir*'s preflight checks, I had to go find Icky, who'd wanted to get a last game of Twister in with Linulla's kids. I found her in the middle of a game and just took a moment to watch. I had to smile. I suspected the game's inventors never imagined it being played by a massive, four-armed ape and a seething clump of anthropomorphic crustaceans.

"Right foot—claw, whatever—blue!"

I let it go on for a little while longer, then interrupted. Icky had to literally disentangle herself from the three—no, make that four of Linulla's children playing with her. It turned out that having six or more limbs made the game a *lot* more complicated.

"Icky, we're going," I called.

She looked at me from under one of her arms and between two segmented, chitinous legs. "Be right there, boss—woah!"

Someone lost their balance, and the whole gang of them fell into a tangled heap of laughter.

"If and when you manage to extract yourself from that mess, Icky, I'll see you back at the *Fafnir*."

"You should play with us sometime, Van. It's a lot of fun!" She rubbed at her shoulder, a tolerant grimace on her features. "Bit pinchy up in here, though. I'd guard your buns."

I cast a critical eye over a pile of muscle and hard, jagged limbs, imagining my tender self underneath it. Buns included.

"I've been guarding them all my life. How about a raincheck?"

"Does that protect you from pinching alien hooligans?"

I thought it over. "By proximity, yes."

Icky began to stand, laughing. "Then consider this rain check issued. For the safety of your buns."

8

"WELL, that's definitely truth in advertising," I said as we approached the orbital called The Torus.

It was just that, a torus, a massive, ring-like structure similar to the imagined space stations that would, according to science fiction, one day orbit Earth. This one was huge, though—nearly five kilometers across, with three rings stacked atop one another. Spoke-like constructs extended from the inner side of the rings to a cylindrical hub that had to be at least a klick across all by itself. A rough mental calculation told me that this single orbital probably had more internal space than Crossroads, Spindrift, and Anvil Dark combined.

We approached The Torus with tremendous caution. Linulla had gone to great lengths to emphasize the hazard of the place, which apparently included an almost complete lack of any decent traffic control. Ships were pretty much on their own until they reached a terminal control zone that extended around the station for one hundred klicks. Even then, the sole control within that tiny space was an AI that assigned berths. And even *then*, if more than one ship wanted the same berth, because it was closer to some part of The Torus they wanted to access, a bidding war would erupt on the spot. Apparently the listed docking fees were only a minimum, and if you wanted to add a surcharge on top of them to get your preferred spot, you could.

We had no preference and simply waited for the AI to assign us a berth.

I sat back, stretched, and glanced at Torina. "When you don't know where you're going, any berth will do—"

The *Fafnir* abruptly accelerated hard to one side, and the collision alarm blared. I tensed and sat up in time to see something about class 9 or so whip past just a few hundred meters away.

Netty immediately spoke up. "Sorry, everyone. I assumed that ship would alter course to avoid us, but it never did."

"So, what, he was just going to crash into us?" Zeno said.

"More like dick-waving, forcing us to make way, or— yeah, crash into us, I guess. Tells us a lot of what we need to know about this place," I replied, my heart hammering out a machine gun beat in my chest.

"Torina, shoot a missile up the asshole's tailpipe," Icky snapped.

Perry looked back at her. "While I approve of your nomenclature, not sure that's a great way to announce our arrival here if our aim is to be lowkey.."

She shrugged. "I'm telling you, these people only respect force."

"Let's keep firing lethal ordnance as something we can escalate *to*, if need be," I said, but when Icky began to protest, I added,

"Still, tag that shithead's engine bell with a firing solution. Just in case."

"One can only hope the plasma doesn't cook off this entire area, given Netty's accuracy as a weapons officer," Zeno intoned.

Torina gave Zeno a long look. "Easy there, sunshine."

Zeno's whiskers lifted. "Happy to lift the mood."

A few minutes later, we were assigned a docking port. Netty carefully moved us toward it, keeping our velocity low so we could abruptly maneuver, if need be. It was a hair-raising experience, sharpened by the fact I'd got used to reasonably orderly docking procedures, even at a relatively wild place like Spindrift. At least I'd come to think of Spindrift as *wild*, but I was quickly coming to realize that it had nothing on this place, The Torus.

———

WITH NOWHERE IN particular to go, we just exited the *Fafnir* and started walking.

I'd taken Linulla's advice to heart. Torina and I both wore our b-suits but covered them with loose-fitting civilian clothes to avoid any hint of being a Peacemaker. It was the same reason we hadn't been broadcasting our Guild credentials with our transponder data. We had no legal jurisdiction out here, nearly sixty lightyears from the nearest system recognized as part of known space. Trying to pretend we did would just end up attracting attention for no good reason. We likewise let Perry do his own thing, flying top cover among the pipes and ducts and conduits that snaked along the overheads, and left Netty in charge of the *Fafnir*. Most of the aliens out here were species I didn't recognize, aside from the occasional

Yonnox or Gajur, but I did see a few humans. Overall, it meant we didn't unduly stand out in the crowd.

Well, except for our being armed to the teeth. I felt a little conspicuous that way, with The Drop bouncing on one hip. If I'd had the Moonsword, I'd have had it prominently displayed as well. Torina had taken it a step further, with her holstered handgun hanging from her waist and a coil gun, a rifle-sized mass driver, slung over her shoulder. I'd worried it might be overkill, until I saw the fearsome arsenal on display in the crowd milling around the docking concourse.

I glanced at a squat, hulking alien in a pressure suit carting around something that reminded me of an AT-4 anti-tank weapon, then shrugged. "Okay, I take it back. All this firepower really isn't out of place."

"Told you," Torina said, patting the stock of her coil gun.

"What, you were expecting this? Have you been here before?"

"Nope, not at all. But Linulla was pretty clear. Besides, it's more of a *faux pas* to show up underdressed for the occasion than over-dressed."

"I prefer to be——" Icky began, but I put a hand on her meaty shoulder.

"Pants-free. I know, girl. I know."

"Just saying. Like my spirit. I like to *roam*," Icky enthused, and to my alarm, managed to wiggle her booty,which was about a meter and a half wide on a slim day.

"I—um, of course you do. You're a VW bus away from your final form, Icky. Hey, Perry, how about you? See anything noteworthy?"

You mean aside from a tank division's worth of firepower?

"Yeah. I mean— anyone specifically watching us, that sort of thing. You know. Tradecraft. You're good at that, bird."

Van, this place makes Dregs look like a suburban neighborhood in Des Moines. Everyone is constantly watching everyone else, waiting for someone to make a move. I swear we're one sneeze away from an epic firefight. Note to self, keep Icky away from the snuff.

"That's a standing order. If I ever want to glisten again, I'll roll myself in coconut oil."

Boss... why?

"Other than smelling like a pina colada? It's just supposition. Now then, if you do see anything—"

I will dive behind the hardest of hard cover and then let you know, you got it.

Given that it was about eight klicks around the circumference of this ring of The Torus alone, we settled on stopping into the first place we came across that resembled a bar, restaurant, or similar meeting place. That turned out to be a place called—

"*The One-Eyed Yak*? Seriously?"

I stared at the 3D holographic sign, which sure enough depicted a yak—one of those hulking, shaggy, ox-like things native to central and southern Asia.

I changed course toward it but had to stop when a dour group of thuggish, vaguely reptilian aliens in ominously black uniforms marched past, escorting someone in a flamboyantly ornate palanquin. I noticed that the crowd gave them a wide berth, so we did, too.

"How badass do you have to be to cause *this* lot to make way for you?" Torina muttered.

"No one even blinked at me," Icky said, a touch hurt.

I glanced around, taking in a throng of heavily armed, brutish aliens all fidgeting nervously and obviously not looking at the palanquin. Torina and I did the same, though I kept an eye on it sidelong. They marched away and the crowd resumed its wary milling.

Looks like there is some order here, after a fashion, Perry said.

"Yeah, private security forces if nothing else," I said as we resumed our way toward *The One-Eyed Yak*.

It turned out to be a bar reminiscent of every fantasy tavern I'd ever heard described, right down to rough wooden tables, brimming mugs of something foamy slopping around, and all the patrons trying their best to keep their backs toward a wall. A hulking figure behind the bar did, indeed, resemble a yak, and it was missing an eye. Nearby, a human male was helping to sling drinks. He was fifty-ish, with pale skin, a pornstache, Willie Nelson braids, and a beaded headband, and he sported a grubby sweatshirt emblazoned with LET THE BEATZ DROP in graffiti-style balloon letters.

I shook my head. "I have *got* to meet this guy."

Torina and I wended our way to the bar. As we walked, a doughy creature with oversized anime girl eyes stepped in front of us. It uttered a rapid-fire string of sibilant squeaks and chirps, like an angry snake arguing with an even angrier squirrel. I pointed at my ear and shook my head.

"Sorry, no translation."

The alien loosed another string of hissing chitters. I turned to Torina.

"Are you getting any—"

She didn't even glimpse at me, though. Instead, she lashed out with a side kick, then spun back and chopped the side of the alien's head. It staggered back, and she pressed in, driving out a sequence of punches that dropped it to the floor, where it stayed—gasping, I guess, though it really just spasmed in rhythmic shudders.

I gaped at her for a moment, then tensed, bracing myself for an attack—

Which never came. Instead, the bar patrons around us offered nods and grins, in the case of species I recognized, inscrutable reactions in the case of those I didn't, or just ignored us completely.

I turned to Torina. "Um, darling—?"

She leaned in. "You didn't see the arm behind its back. Heluva blade there."

"I could see both of its arms, and they were—ah, unarmed."

"No, I mean the third arm that's literally behind its back." She made a point of giving the creature a contemptuous look as we stepped around.

"Pretty sure that was a test as much as anything else, Van, and not one intended to sound out our diplomatic skills. Remember what Linulla said, the only law here is strength."

I looked around again at the crowd. When I did, a few of them quickly looked away.

"That's more like it," Icky said.

Zeno gave a long, slow sigh, patient as the tide. "It's like prison."

"Exactly," I agreed.

Torina gave me a questioning glance, and I shrugged. "They say that if you ever get sent to prison, on the very first day make a point of picking a fight with the biggest, baddest sack of belligerence in the place. It's supposed to establish that you're either tough or crazy as hell."

"Or get you killed," Torina added.

"There is that."

We reached the bar, and the human wearing the BEATZ sweat-shirt ambled over to stand opposite us.

"Welcome to *The One-Eyed Yak*, dudes. You enjoy our little greeting committee?" His voice had a California surfer-dude thing going on, like Michelangelo—the *Teenaged Mutant Ninja Turtle*, not the Renaissance artist.

I narrowed my eyes on him. "*Your* greeting committee?"

"Yeah, totally. It's a little service we provide to our patrons. Mxszeet gets in your face, and you either beat the hell out of him and establish some badassed cred, or you don't. And if you don't, then you totally shouldn't be here in the first place, man."

"And you consider that a *service?*"

The man leaned forward, his graying braids brushing the bar. "Between you and me, man, half the people in here would gut you for your shoes. Trust me, culling the herd of candyasses saves lives. A beating, you can survive. A blade or a bolt? Nope."

"What about the other half?" Torina asked, her words glacial.

He gave a crooked grin. "They, pretty lady, would watch and enjoy. Dinner and a show sorta thing, am I right? Anyway, what's your poison?"

"Just to be clear, you don't literally mean poison, right?" I asked.

The man laughed. "Ain't good business killing my customers, dude."

I glanced back at the doughy alien, who'd clambered back to his —feet, I guess you'd call the pseudopod things on the bottom of his flabby body.

The bartender shrugged. "Things are complex here, and the learning curve is steep."

Icky leaned forward, her eyes bright. "Van, can I have a pina colada?"

"In a minute. Information first, then drinks."

Zeno chimed in. "At the least, we can expect some kind of lower intestinal distress from anything on the menu. At best—"

"A taste explosion like visiting the Caribbean?" Icky asked. "I checked my slate. That's what pina coladas taste like, according to the entry."

Zeno regarded the dirty glasses with suspicion. "Oh, there'll be an explosion."

I held up a finger. "Guys? Let's discuss this topic... how about never?"

Torina snorted, then turned a megawatt smile onto the bartender. It was... impressive. Her attention had a kind of weight to it, drawn from her beauty and that diamond focus she brought forth with such ease. "You're not from around here, are you?"

The bartender regarded her with surprise, then turned back to me, a feral intensity on his face. "You worked that out? Yeah, I'm from—well, depends. Technically, I'm from the back of a broken-down VW van about ten miles outside Monterey. But if you believe in the *rules*"—he made air quotes—"then I'm a citizen of California, US of A, Earth, all that shit. Or I was, anyway. Now I'm just a wandering child of the universe, all Skrilla, part killa."

"Skrilla? Is that your name?"

"Don't wear it out," he said, grinning.

"So you're the owner of this fine establishment?"

He nodded toward the hulking, one-eyed alien. "Me and my business partner over there. He's the strong, silent type, though. Ain't that right, Rotan?"

The yak-ish alien said nothing.

Skrilla smiled. "See what I mean?"

Torina and I introduced ourselves, and some of the tension drained away. Skrilla poured us each a couple of fingers of bourbon, which he had behind the bar because of course he did, then leaned on the counter.

"So. I'm thinking… *cop*," he said.

I peered at him over the rim of my glass. "What, you want to become one?"

He laughed. "Coy ain't just something you find in a pond, am I right?"

"Torina and I are just tourists."

"We're here to take in the scenery," she added, waving an elegant hand. "Breathtaking."

"Lots of better scenery to see elsewhere, dudes. The only reason people come here is business, or to… get away from it all."

"So which was it for you? Business, or getting away from it all?" I asked.

"Eh, a little from column A, a little from column B. It was either this or stay where I was, living with my old lady in Orange County."

I smiled. "Really? Orange County, or a star system dozens of light-years from Earth. Those were your alternatives."

"You've never met my old lady."

I laughed. I liked this wildly improbable guy who could have been a poster child for Woodstock if he had another ten years on him.

"Long way to come just to get away from an old woman," Torina said.

Skrilla stared at her, then laughed. "You're adorable, pretty lady."

"By old lady, he means girlfriend," I said to her. "Or wife."

She raised an eyebrow. "Really. So does that make me your *old lady*, Van?"

Skrilla immediately leaned in. "Don't do it, man. It's a trap."

"Of course not. I'd never use that kind of insensitive language. You're my *squeeze*," I replied, flashing a grin. Before Torina could strike back, though, I turned to Skrilla. "Seriously, what brought you way the hell out here from Orange County?"

"Taxes, man. Taxes and *rules*." He made the air quotes again. "You can't go anywhere on Earth where you don't smack face-first into both. When I got abducted, it was the best thing that ever happened to me."

"You were abducted?"

"Was there any probing involved?" Torina asked.

"I hope so," Icky said, peering around for a pina colada she didn't have.

He grinned. "Only a little. And yeah, abducted, as in taken against my will and all that shit."

That piqued my curiosity. "Who abducted you?"

"They never did introduce themselves. Mean bastards, though. No sense of humor at all."

I pulled out my data-slate, called up the hand-drawn sketch of the Sorcerer Tony Burgess had given us and showed it to Skrilla. He nodded.

"Yeah, that's them." He looked at me. "I was right when I said cop, wasn't I?"

"Let's go with investigative journalist," I said. "Can you make a pina colada, by the way?"

"Can I? Of course. I'm a Calfornian."

"Two then, please. And make one the size of a depth charge," I told Skrilla.

"For the big one?" he asked, casting a gimlet eye on Icky's bulk.

"We prefer the term *thicc*," I corrected.

"So do I, my man," Skrilla said, somehow out-skeeving everyone around us which was no small feat.

Zeno gave a matronly sigh. "While I approve of you being open to lovers of all sizes and pants status, I'm sort of Icky's… advisor."

Skrilla looked wounded. "Just sayin', I appreciate the—

"Skrilla?" Zeno asked, her tone cooling down.

"Yes, uh, ma'am?"

Zeno leaned over, her whiskers twitching. "Wipe those filthy glasses and behave while you make our drinks, you randy old goat."

"What she said," I agreed.

In answer, Skrilla lifted a leering brow at Icky, then turned and began making cocktails with surprising alacrity.

Zeno grinned. "I've always been a great wingman. Especially for Icky."

Perry turned, slowly, to regard Zeno, his beak dropped in astonishment. "I'll have a bourbon, Van."

"You don't drink, bird."

"I know. But after these revelations I'm going to start."

"Can't say I blame you. It's a touch spicy in here for me right now, but I'll drink your bourbon and tell you all about it. I'd like info first, though, before we have our impromptu HR meeting about topics like—"

"Sex and going potty, Van," Torina added, helpfully. Her eyes danced with wicked glee as Skrilla finished shaking the pina coladas to frothy perfection.

"Going... potty? Are we seven years old?"

"Icky's sense of humor is," Perry quipped.

I looked up, letting a breath trickle out before laughing at the absurdity of—everything. Then I took Torina's hand in mine and watched as Skrilla doled out the drinks before topping off my bourbon. Icky tilted hers up and began making noises like a sasquatch on molly.

"Good?" Skrilla asked.

Icky' eyes watered, and she slammed a hand—then another—against her face. "*Cold.*"

I nodded sagely. "Brain freeze. Rub your tongue across your palate, hard."

"Front to back?" Icky asked, still holding her face.

Torina shrugged. "Don't look at me. I'm not entirely sure about her inner skull structure." She cast a glance at Icky's drink, which was reduced by half. "The girl can put it away, though."

Skrilla beamed. "Another satisfied customer, right Rotan?"

Rotan said nothing, which had zero effect on Skrilla's sunny outlook.

"We'll definitely be back," I told Skrilla, as I assessed Icky's condition, which was improving by the second.

"Small sips, you barbarian," Zeno told Icky.

"Whiskers knows what's up," Skrilla said in approval.

When the glasses were empty, we disengaged from Skrilla—but not before Torina did some probing of her own. Her subtle questioning of Skrilla was a masterclass in dancing around the topic—

our investigation—while leaving the wayward beach bum just shy of genuine suspicion.

I looked at Torina with even greater respect, then took her hand again because it fit so well. I put my glass down with an air of finality. "We've got more sightseeing to do. Pleasure meeting you, Skrilla."

"Yeah, sure, anytime, dude. Anytime."

I started to turn away, but stopped and glanced back. "Any attack planned for when we leave? I like to be ready, just in case."

"Not by me. As for the rest of this riff-raff—" He shrugged, then grinned. "You have a nice day, officer."

I grinned back. Only one table of patrons made any moves toward us on our way out, and half-drawing The Drop was enough to get them to sit back down. The bar was crowded with people all packing firepower, so a single shot could trigger a firefight and leave lots of people hurt or killed. If appearing to be okay with that made me seem a little crazy, that was fine. Crazy seemed to be a sort of armor around here.

On the other hand, if he'd called my bluff—

I eased out a breath as we exited the place. Fortunately, he hadn't.

BACK OUT IN THE CONCOURSE, Perry performed a quick sweep for anything resembling trouble outside *The One-Eyed Yak*. Since things were calm, we pushed on, taking the measure of everyone and everything. After three steps, Icky stopped, leaned to the left, and released a thunderous belch that filled the air with the subtle fragrance of a car air freshener designed by someone with clogged sinuses. It was… memorable.

"You okay?" I asked.

Icky hiccuped. "Never better. I *like* the taste of pine."

"Sure, let's go with that," I agreed, letting my eyes scan the crowd, which was still a robust collection of people who *matched the description* for any and all crimes.

"He was taken by the Sorcerers. The natural question is, why didn't they chip him?" Torina said, as we ambled along, weaving through the throng.

"Good question. Maybe there's a certain threshold number of brain cells that have to *not* be burned out smoking weed, and below it, the subject is not, shall we say, a good candidate."

"Smoking weeds?"

"No. Weed. Technically, marijuana, an Earthly plant which you can smoke, and end up feeling relaxed and euphoric—or so I've been told."

And hungry. Don't forget the munchies, Perry put in.

"And I suppose you've got a lot of experience with weed, bird?"

I've got my wing on the pulse of pop culture, Van. Had a Bob Marley poster in my parts locker back in the 90s.

"If I find out you played hacky sack at any point, it's going to damage our friendship," I murmured to Perry.

I have limits, boss. I call that 'The Patchouli Line'.

"Glad to hear it."

Torina pointed. "There's a tech bazaar. See, that sign over there?"

I followed her finger. "The one that says Tech Bazaar?"

"I worked it out all by myself." After a smug wink, she began pulling me toward our target.

We wandered into a sprawling marketplace full of gadgets and bits and pieces—mostly scrap, but it could be repurposed or used as spare parts. In that sense, it was kind of a high-tech junkyard. But there were shiny new odds and ends stored in clear cases behind a long counter. They weren't what caught my eye, though. What did was the proprietor, a tripedal, artificial being—a synth.

I stopped and pretended to be interested in—a bin of something or others, I wasn't sure what. "Torina, see who's behind the counter?" I said, keeping my voice quiet.

She picked up a random object and studied it. "I do. Similar to the other synths we've seen, but also different. Think they're related?"

"How could they not be?"

I frowned and watched the synth sidelong as it served other customers. It had the same pale, waxy skin as others of its kind we'd encountered, with gaps through which metallic rods and tubes and sliding actuators were visible. It had two unblinking, doll-like eyes and, instead of a mouth, a round, bronze wire-mesh grill.

The synths were a wildcard in our investigations. We assumed they were connected to our various bad guys, particularly the Sorcerers, but hadn't found any hard links and weren't sure if they were minions, or partners, or even in charge of it all, for that matter.

"Only one way to find out. Perry, keep a close watch out for anyone behaving suspiciously out there."

That would be everybody.

"You know what I mean."

I don't see anyone showing any particular interest in that shop you're in, at least not yet.

Torina and I made our way up to the counter, pausing to examine and discuss various things as we went. The synth paid no noticeable attention to us until we stepped up to the counter, at which point it clattered toward us on its triple legs. It seemed to see-saw between moving with a smooth, fluid grace and bouts of herky-jerky hesitancy, as if there was an internal conflict with its operating systems.

"Greetings to you welcome to the Tech Bazaar is there anything I can help you with today."

The voice emanating from its grill was flatly mechanical, offering not even a hint of emotion. I found that strange. Perry and Netty were both artificial intelligences but were capable of a full range of emotional responses. These synths, on the other hand, almost seemed built to emphasize their artificial, machine nature.

I smiled at it. I thought about playing this obliquely but decided to hell with it. I wanted to see what sort of reaction I could get from it. "Maybe. I've been informed of a business opportunity, but to realize it I have to contact—" I turned to Torina. "I keep having trouble pronouncing. The Pulo—Puli—"

"Puloquir?"

"Right. The Puloquir."

"They are difficult to contact being located in The Deeps you must go there to contact them however I can provide a comm device that will facilitate your interaction with them."

"That would help, of course," I replied, keeping my tone in the region of neutral but buoyantly hopeful. I didn't trust the synth.

Not yet.

"The Deeps. I keep hearing about these Deeps, but it's hard to sort out what's true and what's just tales," Torina said. She introduced herself into the conversation seamlessly. We were merging into a team—operating without cues as an effective duo, and damn if it didn't feel good.

"The Deeps are a volume of space downward from here relative to the galactic ecliptic which are significant by the relative lack of stellar bodies. This necessitates long periods of travel which if not properly accommodated by planning and preparation can result in hazards to ships and their crews including exhaustion of fuel and supplies notably food and water."

"Okay. So where around here is a good place to obtain provisions for a long flight? And I will take that comm device, thanks," I said.

The synth, which I noticed had the word Occupant stenciled on its chest, scuttled off to a cabinet and retrieved a small and rather antiquated-looking device from it. It struck me that I wasn't even sure if bonds were usable currency out here, but it turned out they were. If anything, they seemed to have value as a hard currency the way US dollars did back on Earth.

"As for provisioning and generally obtaining foodstuffs of reasonable quality the establishment called Pulsar on Level Two Ring Section Five is highly recommended the establishment called The Comet's Flare on Level Two Ring Section Nine is not."

I handed over the bonds to cover the purchase of the comm device. "Why do I get the feeling you're getting some kickback from Pulsar to recommend them?" I asked, smiling.

"Such corruption is irrelevant I merely state facts as they have been presented to me since I do not consume organic matter for sustenance I have no particular—"

Occupant paused. "I believe the vernacular is *no skin in this game* is it not?"

"Actually, it is." I took the comm device. "And let me say thank you. Truly. Appreciate the help."

"You are welcome to return any time to conduct more commerce."

We left.

"You're not seriously going to plug that thing into the *Fafnir*, are you?" Torina asked.

I gave a soft snort. "I'm not even convinced it works, or if it does, if it actually has any relation to the Puloquir. I was more interested in seeing what our synthetic friend back there had to say."

"Okay, and?"

"And, he seemed just a little too easy to deal with, don't you think? Everything we've heard about the Puloquir is that they're a vicious, warmongering race that creates immortal AI-controlled weapons and then turns them loose. I mean, I know Occupant, if that's really his name, probably can't be emotional, but he wasn't even evasive."

It's a good point. He was happy to recommend Pulsar over The Comet's Flare, suggesting he's capable of being discriminating, but he didn't seem at all fazed by you asking about the Puloquir, Perry put in.

"Which means either he has no problem with the Puloquir—I mean, he even keeps their tech on the shelf," I said, holding up the device we'd bought. "Or that the Puloquir really aren't as big a problem as they've been made out. I want to know which," I said.

"So what's the plan?" Torina asked.

"Well, we've come all this way, so we might as well go see for ourselves. We'll gas and provision up to the gunwales here, then go for a trip into The Deeps."

I looked at the comm device again.

"And see who, or what, is out there, and if it's got anything to do with our investigation." I activated my comm. "Netty, get ready to point us down. We're going into The Deeps."

9

I wasn't sure what I expected from a region of space that went by the ominous name of The Deeps. I knew it was empty, of course, but in the back of my mind I'd assumed a somehow sinister emptiness, a void with some sort of malignant nature to it.

But it wasn't. It was just a void, a whole lot of empty space.

"Van, we've got sufficient fuel to twist to the next star further in, back to the Torus, and maybe—just *maybe*, two more hops. Without additional fuel or a means of refueling, we simply can't go any further," Netty said.

"Well, we can, we're just not getting back," Perry put in.

I sniffed. "Of all the places I want to spend the rest of my life, on board this ship with you guys might make the top twenty. But that means there's nineteen more I'd prefer—no offense."

"Actually, being stuck aboard this ship with you guys definitely would not make my own top twenty—no offense," Zeno replied. "Top ninety? Maybe."

"You have a top ninety?" Perry asked.

"Sure. I like making lists while I wait for my noodles to reheat."

"Okay, Virgo," Netty chirped.

Zeno grinned, sending her whiskers up in a bristling arc.

"Twisting again, boss. Lonely out here," Netty reported.

"Fire it up. Further in, Netty, and clear the solution. Something about all this—" I gave a small shake of my head, searching for the word.

"Yeah," Torina agreed, taking my hand.

After leaving The Torus, we twisted to two star systems, each successively further into the yawning void. The first was a red dwarf star surrounded by some rocks. The second—the one where we currently were—was another red dwarf star, surrounded by some more rocks, but with a lonely ice giant thrown in for good measure. Netty figured it was probably a rogue planet that had fallen under the influence of the red dwarf's gravitation, so it was no more native to this desolate region of space than we were.

I sat back. "This isn't the right approach. Just casting around blindly out here, it—"

"Van, we have a contact. A class 12 ship has just twisted in uncomfortably close to missile range."

I saw the icon pop onto the tactical overlay. "Any sort of ID on it?"

"Class 12 mass but an unfamiliar design otherwise. And now it's accelerating straight toward us."

"I guess we can assume they're not just planning on dropping by for a visit," Torina said.

I sat up. "No, I'd say that's a safe bet. Okay, Torina, power up the weapons and let's all go to battle stations."

We spent the next couple of minutes suiting up, clamping on our helmets, and readying ourselves for the encounter with the approaching ship. So far, it hadn't actually demonstrated any hostile intent, so I had Torina stay at weapons hold. We didn't activate the fire control scanners, either, but did pound the crap out of the other ship with our active scanners.

We got no reaction. The class 12 just drove straight on toward us.

I frowned. "Okay, let's try talking. Netty, open a broadcast—"

A warning sounded. The other ship had just illuminated us with its fire control system.

I cursed. "Okay, Torina, weapons—"

Something lanced out of the approaching ship, a coherent beam of energy that flashed past us. Another followed, slamming into our port side, detonating REAB modules and turning armor to glowing slag.

"Holy shit! What is *that?*" Torina spat, even while opening fire with our lasers. They seemed downright anemic in comparison to whatever the hell the other ship was shooting at us.

"You know those plasma cannons we took off the Iowa because we couldn't get them to work properly? I think this is them, or something like them, anyway, working properly," Zeno said.

I started hurling the *Fafnir* through a hard series of jinks while veering away, trying to open the range. We weren't far from a twist point, but the enemy's weapon packed enough punch that it wouldn't take many hits to cripple us.

"How the hell are those shots so accurate? At this range?" Icky asked from aft, where she was already doing frantic damage control.

Another shot landed. Alarms sounded, one of the scanner arrays went dark, and the particle cannon went offline.

"Why aren't they missing? We're way the hell outta range!" Torina snapped.

"They're using some sort of twist effect to reduce the effective range to nearly zero when they shoot that thing," Perry replied.

"But how——?"

"Doesn't matter," I cut in. "Netty, fastest possible course out of here——"

Two new contacts appeared on the overlay. Both barely registered, flickering in out and out of resolution. One streaked away from the other——a missile?

Another shot from the fearsome weapon flashed past us, missing by what felt like meters. I glued my eyes on the gravitational data, waiting, willing it to flick to the green parameters that would let us twist.

The firing stopped. Our attacker had abruptly changed course and now seemed to be trying to race back out to a twist point. The ghostly missile contact, which had apparently been targeted on him, closed inexorably in. At the last moment, the bogie erupted with streams of point-defense fire, but they just groped blindly. And a few seconds after that, the missile detonated, its blast somehow focused like a shaped charge, ripping our tormentor in two. A moment later, it vanished in a colossal secondary explosion.

I slumped back in my seat. "Holy shit."

Torina gave a soft grunt of agreement. "If this is common gear out here, we might want to rethink this, ah, excursion."

I hit the comm. "Unknown ship, whoever you are, thank you. At the risk of sounding cheap, I'd love to buy you a beer."

The comm lit up with a familiar face. "I don't drink beer. Make it a single malt scotch and we'll call it even."

It was B, our enigmatic Peacemaker doctor and apparent member of the even more enigmatic Galactic Knight Uniformed.

I just stared, finally shaking my head. "B. Huh. Fancy meeting you out here light-years from anywhere. Did you just happen to be in the neighborhood?"

"What are the odds of *that?*" Torina muttered.

"Impossible to calculate. Too many variables," Perry said.

Torina would have shot him a glare if her helmet hadn't prevented it. But I was with her. Regardless of how incalculable the odds that B just happened to be in this desolate system partway into The Deeps, they were definitely beyond the reach of any math we could do.

"Coincidences aren't real," I said, grinning.

B just quirked a brow and both antennae. "Of course, I'm not here by accident. I followed you. You might want to look into some upgrades. You're leaking spoor like a wounded buck."

That meant some serious stealth, which we saw through at the last moment and only, I'm sure, because she launched a missile. Which had also been stealthed. And had then tracked its target with military precision and detonated in a focused blast with the viciousness of a massive, shaped charge.

And she was a doctor.

"So you followed us all the way from known space?"

"Oh, that part was kind of by accident. I saw you arrive at The Torus, so I got curious about what you were up to and ended up saving your bacon, so to speak."

"Okay, why were you at The Torus?"

She sighed. "Because I really am out here for a good reason. I've got an appointment with some triplets."

"Ships? Stars? That fancy three-level spa run by empaths?"

"Oooo, the Feelgood Three? I wish. No, actual babies. And that's where I have to go now, which means my escort duties are over and you're on your own after this, Van. Unless, of course, you'd like to watch my six and come along."

"To where?"

"I'm sending the nav data to Netty now." She grinned. "I'll even give you a present for helping me out."

I laughed as Icky and Netty confirmed we weren't leaking any air so I could pull off my helmet. "*You* give *us* a present. I think we're the ones who owe you, B."

"Indulge me."

"Does this present come in the shape of a bottle?"

"Only if that bottle can hold incandescent plasma. Anyway, I really do need to get going. Are you able to keep up?"

I glanced back at Icky, who nodded. I turned back to the comm.

"Lead the way, killer. We'll be right behind you."

As NEAR as I could tell, B really had been at The Torus on entirely unrelated business. She'd seen us arrive but hadn't intended to have anything to do with us until she noticed the class 12 that attacked us rushed to depart right after we had. Intrigued, she tagged it with a tracker—how, she wouldn't say—then followed along behind.

"I wasn't sure what their intentions were, so I thought I'd keep an eye out, at least until I had to break off and come here."

Here was a star system back up from where we'd been, relative to the galactic ecliptic, so closer to both The Torus to coreward and known space to spinward. Known on Earth by the poetic name WDJ0551+4135, it was apparently a stellar oddity—a white dwarf star more massive than Sol. The stellargraphic data Netty displayed said that the star was actually formed from two smaller white dwarfs, probably a binary pair, that had slowly spiraled into a collision with one another, merging into one big white dwarf.

But the star wasn't the reason we were here.

That would be an Earth-like planet that once hosted a thriving civilization which, in an eerie and sinister echo of current human civilization, had obliterated itself in a thermonuclear war, and not a polite exchange of nukes. This war was *filthy*, with no less than four rounds of hypersonic warheads arcing between continents, each successive wave ringing the planet like a bell.

While turning cities to slag—and the world into a tomb.

"Shame, too. They seemed to be doing so well," B said. "Cultural anthropologists said they were probably only a few decades away from discovering the fundamentals of twist mechanics. Instead, they got stuck in that Great Filter people talk about back on Earth, flash-fried themselves into oblivion."

Gloomy silence hung over the comm for a moment. This race, which had called themselves the *slo'tan*, could have been twin to humanity in terms of cultural and technological achievement. Now, all that remained of them was an electromagnetic ghost, an expanding sphere of radio-frequency emissions that would slowly fade into the faint microwave hiss of the cosmic background.

"Anyway, that's not the reason we're here. Or not directly, anyway," B went on. "That big ship orbiting the planet is."

I saw it on the scanner. It was massive—nearly two klicks long and one across the beam. It hadn't originated in known space, so it had no meaningful transponder broadcasts, just a location beacon.

"Who are they?" I asked B as we both fell toward orbit around the war-ravaged planet.

"Reclamators. Think of them as reverse mercenaries. For a fee, they travel to planets like this one, scoured by war, or just on the brink of being habitable, do whatever terraforming's needed to make 'em habitable, and stock them with new life."

"They sound like the Synergists of Arminsu-el back home," Torina said.

B nodded. "Kinda. These folks do it on a bigger scale, though—planetary, instead of regional, which is more the Synergists' thing. And they're not quite so, um—"

"Flower power?" I suggested.

"I was going to say crystal and patchouli crew, but yeah. What the hell was that all about, anyway? That whole hippy thing back on Earth? I missed most of it, kinda caught the end of it. Mind you, Woodstock was a blast," B said. "Bit thin on hygiene, but still… "

I smiled at that. "First of all, hippies were before my time, thank you very much. I'm a child of the nineties, so grunge rock and the early days of internet porn are more my thing. Second, you were at Woodstock?"

"Yup. Even got to meet Hendrix in person."

"Uh—how about your, um—" I pointed at my head.

B laughed. "My antennas? Had them covered by a big-assed rasta hat. I think that's what made Hendrix notice me, in fact. Well, that, and the fact it's all I was wearing."

"Uh—I have so many questions."

"Which I'm not gonna answer. Girl's gotta have her secrets, right?"

Torina, Zeno, Icky, and even Netty all responded together, variations on *Yup*.

I glanced at Perry. "We're outnumbered, bird."

"Did you just assume my gender, Van?"

"I assume you're a gander. Sorta."

B cut in. "Time for us to go, kids. I've got clearance for both of us to dock with the Reclamators' ship. You can find me once you're aboard. I've got those triplets waiting for me." She looked at another screen, her eyes flashing with intensity. "According to the report, they won't wait long. See you there."

AT FIRST, I thought these Reclamators were actually machines. They vaguely resembled old timey diving suits but were covered in sleek armor and had an extra pair of arms, like they were made for a Wu'tzur. It turned out, though, that that was just a container, and that in their natural state they were really fluid blobs of extraordinarily complex matter that seemed to somehow combine both organic and inorganic life—protoplasm crossed with amorphous silica, as B put it. Moreover, they were tardigrade levels of tough, being able to endure almost any environment that wasn't close to absolute zero cold or fusion plasma hot without much trouble. It made them ideally suited for reclaiming environments that would be instantly lethal to most other species.

B described them as we were docking. "Oxygen atmosphere? Check. Chlorine, methane, ammonia? No problem. Crushing gravity or zero-g? Both good. Radiation that would render you and me down to sterile sludge? If they had eyes, they wouldn't even blink them."

They were still a little unnerving, though, because of that resemblance to ancient Earthly diving suits. They were somehow charming and vintage and fuzzed with an air of danger, all at once. There was a steampunk quality to their suits, right down to the brassy fittings and polished bolts.

"I've got even money on them versus a kraken, boss," Perry quipped.

"Same. That's exactly the vibe I'm getting."

And then we were greeted, and their alien sense evaporated with a simple handshake.

"I'm Caretaker," he said, pumping my hand three times with vigor. "Always nice to see humans. Hey, how'd that whole World War Two work out?"

"You were on Earth during that?" I asked.

"Yeah. We were collecting some DNA samples when that whole Pearl Harbor thing happened not that far away. I'd liked to have stuck around to see how it all turned out, but duty calls and all that."

"Well, we won."

"*We* being—?"

"The Allies. The Americans and British, Russians, Canadians, French—"

"So those—oh, what were they called—led by a short guy with the bad haircut, had a mustache on his philtrum that resembled what you call a caterpillar—"

"The Nazis? Yeah, they lost."

"Good. They were scum," Caretaker said, then gestured for us to follow him. He clumped off in his bulky suit, with the rest of us following along behind in bemused wonder.

The corridor opened up, becoming a catwalk traversing among huge transparent tanks of water that were alive with myriad bizarre creatures. I gaped at something the size of a killer whale but with a Cthulu-esque cluster of writhing tentacles around its mouthful of row after row of serrated teeth. Another tank was jammed with—

"Are those jellyfish? Like, Earthly jellyfish?" I asked.

The Caretaker stopped. "Indeed they are. It turns out these little guys will thrive in nearly any ocean—well, water ocean, anyway. They're really beneficial, too. They do a good job of moderating the acidity of water, which helps us by stabilizing environments we're repopulating, keeping things predictable until we get a self-supporting ecosystem."

"Huh—"

A squeal of delight cut me off. Icky, Zeno, and Torina had carried on to the next set of tanks. Icky had just seen the creatures populating one of them and had apparently fallen in love.

"They're adorable! I so want one!" she said.

I'm not sure what was cuter—the sight of a hulking, hairy, four-armed alien squeeing like a little girl over a new kitten, or the creatures that had prompted it. And they were pretty damned adorable. The best description I could come up with was a seahorse crossed with a teddy bear, with the eyes of a puppy. It was like someone had mined the imagination of a nine-year-old girl for the cutest things possible, then stuck them all together into one bundle of *d'awwww*.

Icky was practically dancing with glee. "Look at them! I wanna take one home and—"

A sudden flurry of motion cut her off. One of the larger teddy-seahorse-puppies, which had been placidly drifting by a smaller one, abruptly lunged and tore its more diminutive cousin into ragged chunks, then gulped them down amid a cloud of gore.

A long moment of silence lingered.

Torina finally glanced at Icky. "Still want one?"

"Yeah—no. I'm good. I'd be afraid to fall asleep anywhere near one in case it, you know, suddenly grew legs. Stars and plasma, that's—"

She paused as the larger creature, apparently satiated, resumed its languid drift, little eddies of carnage swirling in its wake.

"That was *nasty*," Icky finished.

"These *kozidnits* are always a problem. We have to plan for some, uh, losses while we're transporting them because of their, well, frisky nature."

"*Frisky*? You consider that *frisky*? I'd hate to see what you consider *unusually violent*," Torina said.

I exhaled slowly, watching the tank with a gimlet eye. "Remind me to never let these guys suggest a pet."

We carried on, passing amid more tanks full of spectacular and terrifying wonders.

"So all of these creatures are meant to be introduced down there, on the planet?" Zeno asked.

"They are. Each one of these species is selected for its resistance to ionizing radiation," the Caretaker said. "And although you can't see it, every one of these tanks is infused with microscopic creatures that on Earth you'd call—ah, plankton. But we've engineered these plankton to take up radioactive isotopes and heavy metals in their carbonate shells, so that when they die and sink to the bottom, they take them with them. We estimate the oceans will be back to normal environmental background levels of radiation in about two hundred years—give or take."

We walked a little farther, then B came up on the Caretaker's comm unit. "We've started delivering the babies, in case you guys want to be around for the blessed event."

"We'll be right there," the Caretaker said, picking up the pace. When we reached the other end of the colossal space enclosed by the ship's hull, I paused and looked back at the ranks of water tanks stretching off into the distance, each chock full of alien life— including the jellyfish, who were certainly alien out here.

It gave me another of those moments, a flash of unreality and wonder. I found myself suddenly wishing that everyone on Earth could see this. What a difference it would make to the way humanity viewed the universe—and itself.

But that made me think of the people who'd exterminated themselves with nuclear fire just a few hundred klicks beneath us, and I sighed, turned, and followed Caretaker, wondering how many bones—and stories—lay underneath our feet.

WE ARRIVED to find that B was finished and the happy event had come and gone. We found her cleaning herself up in a medical facility while the new arrivals were cared for in a separate compartment.

I smiled through the transparent partition. "Look at those beautiful bouncing—baby—uh—" My smile faded when I realized I had no idea what I was looking at, aside from there being three of them, and they were uniformly horrifying. They resembled those pill-bug things you find under rocks back on Earth, but unlike a roly-poly as I called them, these had zero charm.

"They'll grow into themselves," B said. "Once they hit what humans would call puberty, they'll blossom into—" She paused, then shrugged. "Okay, they're going to remain ugly as sin, at least to you and me. The point is that they're healthy. Even better, there's one of each sex, which is rare amongst their people."

"People? They're, like sentient?"

"Oh, yes. There's a cadre of them aboard this ship. They're called the Sindithik, and they'll be supervising the reclamation efforts for the next couple of hundred years," the Caretaker replied.

"Let me guess—they're radiation resistant," Torina said.

B nodded. "You could use them as reactor shielding and the only negative effect they'd suffer would be boredom. That said, they were originally a spacefaring race, so they've genetically modified themselves to add more mass and structural integrity to their bodies to resist gravity. It also makes their births more difficult."

"And they have three sexes," I noted.

"Actually, it's four, but only three of them are involved in reproduction. It makes for a, let's say *complicated* social and cultural situation, but interesting as all get out. We could learn a lot from them about relationships."

I turned to Caretaker. "Well, please pass our best wishes on to— uh, the mother, or whoever it was who gave birth to them."

"I most definitely will."

We started back for our respective ships, chatting with Caretaker on the way.

"Is there anything we can do to help, Caretaker?" I asked.

"With the planet? It is appreciated, Van, but this is… it's what we do. It's our purpose, and we understand, via B, that you have a purpose as well. She thinks highly of you, by the way."

"I—thank you," I said with what I hoped was a humble tone. Compliments are harder to take than insults, for some reason, and Caretaker exuded a kind of earnest truth that made his comments even more direct.

By the time we reached the *Fafnir*'s airlock, we'd established a good rapport with him. More to the point, we now had not just a reliable source of information out here on the edge of The Deeps, but a neutral one. There was apparently a general understanding that the Reclamators were hands-off, to the point that even pirates and other miscreants gave them a wide berth.

We bid Caretaker farewell and were about to depart, when B stopped me.

"I've still got that present for you, Van."

"The one that involves superheated plasma."

She smiled and nodded. "Consider it a *get out of jail free* card."

I opened my mouth, but she just raised a finger and cut me off. "Cast off the *Fafnir*, move a few klicks away, then wait. I'll join you and transfer my little present."

Mystified, I did as she instructed once everyone was aboard. She sidled her ship up to within a few meters of the *Fafnir*, then revealed her gift to us—a missile.

"It's bleeding edge tech from Unity, called a Deconstructor. Compared to our off-the-shelf missiles, it has better acceleration, a full-power burn time at least thirty percent longer, far better AI guidance, and a directional warhead—so you don't have to waste all that destructive power by blasting it in every direction. It's what I used to help you with your new friend yesterday," she said.

"I have so many questions, but I'm not going to bother asking them because I know I won't get any answers. So I'll just say, holy shit, thank you."

Zeno, our weapons expert, spoke as we did a quick spacewalk to load the missile into the *Fafnir*'s magazine. "Well, I have many questions, too, but I'll give it a close examination to get my answers."

B's voice crackled over the comm. "Don't get too inquisitive. The onboard AI's going to be watching and if you try to do anything more than basic maintenance—and I'm sending you the manual, by the way—it'll wipe itself. I reassured my Unity contacts that we would *not* try to do any reverse engineering."

I made a mental note of how B had phrased that—not *our* Unity contacts, but *my* Unity contacts. I had no doubt that the actual contact was between the GKU and Unity, but B was canny enough to avoid even hinting in that direction. It hit me with the stark realization that this *secret organization* stuff was full of potential pitfalls, and that I'd better start being more careful about what *I* said.

Zeno sighed. "Well, shit. This is like putting a zamfo cake in front of a P'nosk'un and telling them they can't eat it."

"Think chocolate cake and kid, respectively," Perry clarified.

I smiled as we closed the magazine access panel. "Kinda figured that from the context. Don't worry, B, we won't screw around with it. We'll just shoot it at some deserving target."

"Now you're talking. Like I said, *get out of jail free.* That Deconstructor will pretty much erase anything up to class 12, and has a good chance of crippling anything up to class 15 or so."

As we returned to the *Fafnir*, I switched to a private channel B had told me we could use for secure communications the first time I met her. "Straight up, B. Was this really an accident? I mean, is there really any chance we just *happened* to cross paths way the hell out here in the space boonies?"

The reply was all B.

"There's always a chance."

"B—"

"Van, let me put it to you this way. Out here, there are only three types of people—allies, enemies, and the dead. My advice? Always try to be the first one."

10

WE WERE able to purchase fuel for both the fusion and the twist drives from the Reclamators, which meant our next hop didn't have to be back to The Torus. Instead, I decided to head back for known space via another pair of lonely red dwarf stars about fifteen light-years apart. From the second of them, we could twist as far as Spindrift, if we wanted. I had no particular expectation that we'd find anything unusual or even interesting at either of them, but since they both lay just outside the nearest coreward border of known space, why not?

The first one came up dry, surrounded by nothing but more rocks and ice. The second, though, the closer of the two to known space, was anything but dry.

"What is that? A ship?" I asked, eyeing the scans. Whatever it was, it was orbiting the red dwarf amid yet another group of asteroids. We might not even have noticed it if it weren't broadcasting what amounted to a NO TRESPASSING signal in various languages, including several our translators could recognize.

"It could be. Mass-wise, it's about a class 11, but it would be an unusual design. We'd have to get closer to be able to tell," Netty replied.

I nodded. "Okay, then. Let's take a look."

As the drive lit, Torina sat back and crossed her arms. "No trespassing might mean it's some sort of marker buoy. Maybe someone owns this system."

"Or claims ownership, anyway," Perry added. "Always dodgy this far out."

I took the hint. "I get the sense you guys are urging caution. I hear you. I just want to get close enough to see the bear, not poke it with a stick."

We flew on. We had enough time to actually stand down for dinner while Netty did the flying, so we ended up having a bit of a feast. As suggested to us back on The Torus, we'd stocked up on provisions before heading into The Deeps but hadn't depleted them much. That meant we had some stuff with a shelf life that wasn't going to keep. So, waste not, want not and all that.

Torina watched Icky shovel food into her mouth, then sighed. "I keep telling myself that someday I'm going to get used to that. But I never do."

Icky looked up, chewing. "Get used to what?"

"That event horizon you call a mouth, where stuff disappears from the universe, never to be seen again."

Zeno glanced at her sidelong. "You think this is bad, you should see what it's like when she eats noodles. She makes sounds like the *Fafnir*'s waste reclamator."

Icky glared around the table. "Hey, I've got feelings, you know."

"Icky, do you deny that you're an, um, *enthusiastic* eater?" I asked her.

She'd just shoveled in another mouthful and replied through it. I think it might have been, *What do you mean?*

Perry, perched nearby, spoke up. "You know, sometimes I watch you guys eating and so obviously enjoying it that I think, damn, it'd be nice to be able to do that. But then I see that"—he pointed a wing at Icky and her smacking mouthful of food—"and realize that, nah, I'm good."

"I have a delicate palate, bird," Icky managed around about five hundred calories of food.

"But of course you do," Perry oozed.

Icky smiled, displaying a train wreck of food and teeth, then cut her eyes at Zeno in triumph. "Toldja."

Zeno's whiskers twitched. "I—" She sighed, took a generous swig of her drink, and stared straight ahead.

"Van, we're close enough to our bogie to get a clear image," Netty interrupted.

I stood. "Let's go see who's telling the universe at large not to walk on their lawn, shall we?"

We settled into our seats as Netty put up a high-resolution image of the *bogie*, as she'd called it. It was a spindle-shaped construct, maybe a hundred meters across at the middle and tapering to clusters of antennae or sensors at either end. A toroidal tube girdled it where it was thickest.

"Any hits at all, in any databases, Netty?"

"Nothing. There are some secondary scanner returns from that tube around its middle that suggest it might be filled with a fluid, though probably not water. That's about it."

"Okay. Let's try to get a little closer. Torina, keep your finger poised above those fire control scanners, but keep them dark for now. We'll try being friendly."

I activated the comm. "Unknown ship—or whatever you are—this is the *Fafnir*, a Peacemaker ship from—"

An alarm sliced off my words. We'd just been illuminated with powerful targeting scanners—strong enough that they actually induced some fringe interference in our own returns. At the same time, ports opened on the spindle-shaped hull, revealing guns of some sort.

Lots of them.

"Van, I'm counting fifteen weapons of unknown design, and by counting, I mean staring down the muzzles thereof," Netty said.

"When they say *No Trespassing*, they really mean it," Zeno said.

I nodded, rotating the *Fafnir* and doing a hard braking burn. "I don't need to be told twice," I said, then glanced at Torina. "You know what? It's too dangerous to keep fussing about out here without some hard intel."

She returned an enthusiastic nod. "You're thinking the Schegith?"

"Well, we were told that they've crossed swords with the Puloquir, at least. That means they have some experience out here."

"Shall I set course for Null World?" Netty asked.

"With all due haste, my dear. The sooner we're not staring down those fifteen guns you mentioned, the happier I'll be."

B's words rang in my mind as we deflected our trajectory back out to a twist point.

Out here, there are only three types of people—allies, enemies, and the dead.

Indeed. And while her advice to try and stay in the first group was sound, I couldn't help thinking the latter two were by far the more common.

————

WE ARRIVED AT NULL WORLD, the Schegith home planet, to find it aflame with a planet-wide lightning storm.

"That is one *hell* of a show," I said, watching the coruscating flickers and flashes scrolling beneath the *Fafnir* with awe.

"Null World has almost no water to make clouds, so where the hell is this coming from?" Torina asked.

"Ooh, I know this one," Perry said. "Null World's prone to planetary dust storms that fill the atmosphere with fine, conductive particles. Combine that with a well-timed flare from the star to dump charged particles into the planet's magnetic field, and you end up with something like the aurora borealis back on Earth, except way, *way* more powerful. Electrical discharges, instead of just pretty, shimmering lights in the sky."

"So is it dangerous?" I asked.

"Oh, hell yes. That flash, right there? Think a lightning bolt the size of Iowa—the state, not the ship."

I scowled. "So we're stuck up here in orbit until it subsides? When's that going to be?"

"These storms can last for days," Perry replied.

I crossed my arms in annoyance. I really wanted to tap into Schegith's knowledge, whatever it was, about the Puloquir, The

Torus, The Deeps, all of it. I wasn't keen to do it over the comm, though. I supposed we could head back to Anvil Dark and return here when the storm was done. We did have some battle damage to repair, but none of it was especially critical, and I didn't want to lose the momentum we'd gained in our investigation. We'd already gleaned everything Bester could suggest from the Guild's archives at Anvil Dark about the region coreward of known space, and I had no particular business there otherwise—

"Van, I have an idea," Zeno said.

I turned to her. "Shoot."

"I've been playing around the numbers, and I did a quick-and-dirty simulation. If we fire the particle cannon at full power, in continuous fire mode, we can create an ionized pathway through the air along its beam. With the way the beam is polarized, it should carry any discharges away from the *Fafnir*."

"Like a lightning rod."

"Exactly."

Icky frowned. "That's going to be hard on the particle cannon, don't you think? It's not meant to fire continuously like that."

Zeno nodded. "We'll almost certainly burn out the accelerator, and might wreck the thing entirely."

Torina curled her lip. "You don't ever get something for nothing, do you?"

I sighed. "No, you do not."

"The good news is that there's another particle cannon down that sinkhole on your farm back in Iowa. Of course, we'd have to retrieve it, refurbish it, then mount it on the ship. That'd take a couple of days, at least," Zeno said.

I narrowed my eyes at the spectacular display below. Was it

worth sacrificing the particle cannon? Given its short range, it wasn't a weapon we used very often, but when we did, it often proved decisive. On the other hand, replacing it would cost us nothing but time —well, that, and the need to use the *Fafnir* to sling the replacement out of the sinkhole. And I couldn't help the nagging feeling that there might be surveillance assets watching the farm.

Of course, if we had a distraction—

I sat up. "Let's do it. Netty, prepare to deorbit. Zeno, configure the particle cannon into our lightning rod. Everybody else, hang on and hope we don't get flash fried on the way down."

THE RIDE DOWN through the planetary lightning storm was every bit as exciting as it had promised to be, and then some. The tunnel of ionized air created by the particle cannon drew repeated blasts of electrical discharge that walloped the *Fafnir* with thunderclaps like missile detonations. At the same time, turbulence stirred by the searing lightning bolts heaved and flung us up and down, side to side, and back and forth. I'd become used to the *Fafnir* as a rocksteady ship plying her stately way through the void, not a flying machine buffeted by gusts of wind.

Two thirds of the way down, the particle cannon finally faltered and died with the blare of alarms. By then, we'd passed through the worst of the electrical storm, which had been mostly confined to higher altitudes. We plunged the remaining distance to our landing site just outside Schegith's underground lair amid only a few, desultory flashes. I'd been prepared to remain grounded here for a few days by the storm, but at least we'd be able to enjoy Schegith's hospitality and lounge around the sprawling underground lakes collectively known as the Undersea. But by the time we landed, Netty noted that the storm was already beginning to abate.

"So we could have just waited a few hours, instead of burning out the particle cannon?" I said, glaring at the sky. "Of course, why not."

"But then we'd have missed that thrilling ride down from orbit," Torina replied with a smile.

We still winced under a couple of good flashes and blasts from the heavens above as we hurried into the shelter of Schegith's subterranean digs, then the big doors closed behind us, sealing us in and the storm safely outside.

ONE OF THE Schegith met us and demurely asked us to *follow this one, please*. We did and were led into a new series of tunnels and chambers we hadn't visited before. I noticed several other Schegith busy doing—stuff, I wasn't sure what, which was a far cry from when we'd first come here. Then, it had only been Schegith herself, the creature that led her race while also giving it its name. There was some sort of group identity to the Schegith that I'd never really been able to wrap my mind around. But it worked for them, so that's all that really mattered.

Our guide led us to an expansive hall that opened up both to the sides and above, the ceiling being vaulted like that of a cathedral. Along each side were row upon row of shelves inset into the rock, at least a dozen of them stacked atop one another. Only the first couple were within easy reach, with the remainder apparently being reached by mobile platforms not unlike the scissor lifts used back on Earth by people working on high ceilings, maintaining overhead wires, that sort of thing. I was surprised to see even more Schegith here. Just over two years ago, we'd rescued that last half-dozen from digital servitude under our identity-thieving Sorcerers. That brought the total of the race to seven, but I'd seen at least twice that many just in our walk from the entrance to this hall.

"Someone's been busy having baby Schegith," Torina said with approval.

Icky ran a hand along the rock. "This was only recently annealed, too. I think all this"—she gestured up and around—"is new stuff."

"It is," a familiar voice said. I followed it and found Schegith herself reclining on one of the scissor lift things, clad in a white garment that draped her massive, slug-like frame.

"This is the Chamber of Memory," she said as we approached. "This one had it built in order to hold the memories and experiences of this one's people. That way, if calamity should ever befall the Schegith as it almost did, there will be records of who and what they were."

We stopped in front of the lift and looked around. Most of the shelves were empty, but down at this end, near the back of the big chamber, the shelves were arrayed with increasing numbers of items —books, boxes, cases, even scrolls and things like rolled maps. But it was a mural depicted on the back wall of the Chamber of Memory that caught my attention. I pointed it out to the crew.

It was the *Fafnir*.

The mural, using some cunning tech, was three-dimensional in a way that made me feel like I was actually standing in front of the

Fafnir herself. The ship slowly rotated so that she would, over the course of a minute or so, be displayed from all angles. Beneath it glowed a string of characters that, without translation, would be unintelligible. The translator, though, offered two possible means for it. One was *friend*. The other was *savior*.

"That's really something, Schegith. I… am not sure what to say, other than thank you," I said, nodding toward it.

"It is unnecessary and even incorrect to thank this one. Gratitude is properly offered in the other direction. This one, on behalf of the Schegith, gives you thanks for the crucial role you played in restoring the people."

Another Schegith, who'd been examining a terminal set into the wall between two of the shelves of artifacts nearby, lumbered over to join us. "This one echoes the sentiments of Schegith," he said, and I immediately recognized the voice.

"You're Schegith's cousin, the one with the battlecruiser who's helped us out, ah, on more than a few occasions," I said.

He inclined his head in a slight bow. "It is good to finally meet you in person, Van Tudor."

I nodded back with a gravity I felt the moment demanded, which was considerable. I wasn't sure what to call him other than Schegith's cousin because, again, in some way I just didn't get, this was a race of distinct individuals who all nonetheless went by the same name. That would make it awfully confusing taking roll call or determining who owed what taxes, so there was some component to Schegith communication that we just couldn't discern.

"Have you come to visit this one's people purely for socializing, or is there some other purpose, Van Tudor?" Schegith—the actual leader of the race lounging on the lift—asked.

"This one presumes there is a specific reason, since you dared to descend through the winnowing," her cousin ventured.

"The winnowing—oh, the lightning storm. Yeah, that was really something. Made for a spicy ride."

"You are fortunate. This winnowing was short-lived. The worst instances can last for standard weeks, even months," Schegith said.

"Well, we did want to speak with you. It's been suggested to us that you have some knowledge of the Puloquir," I replied.

At the mention of the word, both Schegith and her cousin visibly tensed, ripples of muscular contraction shivering through their bodies. I glanced at Torina, but she was mystified as I was.

"The Puloquir. That is a dark word that hasn't been spoken here for a very long time," Schegith said.

"Oh. Sincerest apologies, Schegith. I meant no offense—"

"It is not a matter of offense. It is rather one of contempt. This one has encountered few people deserving of such… judgment. The Sorcerers who sought to enslave this one's people are one. The Puloquir are another. They are—"

The translator choked on the next word. I cocked my head, meaning to ask for clarification, but Perry beat me to it.

"Think about all the worst aspects and excesses of the Nazis, Van. Then think of something worse than that," he said.

"Really? I… that's hardcore, Schegith."

"The Puloquir are cruel beyond measure. They believe that only from such wanton cruelty can evolution and progress occur," Schegith said.

"So they're xenophobes," Torina put in.

"Xenophobe implies that they only direct their brutality and hatred toward other species. They are no less cruel and destructive amongst themselves. They believe that this is how only the strongest of thought, deed, and will can prevail, and the race as a whole grows and improves."

"What massive douchebags," I said.

Schegith shuddered with what I'd come to learn was laughter. "Douchebags," she repeated. "Yes. That is a good word. They are that."

"Okay, they're terrible. Can you actually tell us anything useful about them?" Icky asked.

I heard Zeno whisper a rebuke, but Schegith didn't seem to be bothered by Icky's characteristic bluntness.

"Yes, this one can provide various schema describing the Puloquir, their vessels, and their weapons, as observed by the Schegith during conflict between the two peoples. But this one urges you to tread with great care. If you confront the Puloquir, you will confront evil itself."

"I think we could say the same thing about the Trinduk, and especially the Sorcerers," Torina said. "Makes me wonder if the two aren't somehow connected."

"Oh, I'd be awfully surprised if they weren't. Mind you, it doesn't sound like either group would appreciate the other very much, so if I had to guess, I'd say it's probably an *enemy of my enemy* thing, at best," I said.

Zeno shrugged. "Doesn't matter how much they hate one another if they hate us more."

"That's true to a point. Don't underestimate how easy it can be to lever cracks open in a relationship once you find them," Perry said.

I felt a rush of excitement but had to dial back the sudden

enthusiasm to link the Sorcerers and the Puloquir. "First, we don't *know* that they're in cahoots. Second, let's concentrate on learning what we can about the Puloquir so that next time we head out into The Deeps and surrounding region, we're better prepared."

"This one will provide all possible assistance. The Schegith archivists are at your disposal, Van Tudor," Schegith said.

I thanked her profusely, whereupon she suggested that we return in seven weeks to receive everything that the Schegith could pull from their archives about the Puloquir, which were apparently extensive. Clearly, the two races had fought at least one major war, and perhaps several. I agreed but with a frown.

"Seven weeks? That's a specific time frame," I said. "Why?"

Torina and Zeno both got it before I did. Torina gave a knowing smile.

"You're not smoking your pipe anymore," she said.

"And you're wearing that white garment. And, if I'm not mistaken, you're somewhat more—trying to be diplomatic here—fuller-figured," Zeno added.

"Oh, sure, I tell someone they're looking *fuller-figured* and it's insulting," Perry muttered.

I looked from one to the other, my brows raised in a question. "What am I missing here? To repeat, what's the big deal about seven weeks—?"

I stopped at the looks I was getting from Torina and Zeno. Even Icky was grinning. I shook my head. What the hell—?

"Psst, Van, Schegith is pregnant," Perry hissed.

I blinked. "She—" I turned to her. "You're—"

Schegith, her cousin, and a couple of other Schegith nearby shuddered with laughter.

"Yes, Van Tudor, this one is about to welcome new life, who will be this one's heir. And it would be good for you to join in that welcome, for my offspring will bear a unique name. They will be Schegith Haadrake, an old word of the people that refers to a great and powerful beast."

"Which we would call a dragon. So Schegith the Dragon. That's a damned fine name," Perry said.

Schegith looked at me. "A fine name, and a fine way to honor those considered to be true friends."

11

WE SPENT a full day on Null World, taking some time to just relax on the shore of the Undersea while the last of the winnowing faded away. When we were clear to leave, Schegith's cousin brought us a data module containing the preliminary results of their dive into their archives for stuff about the Puloquir.

"It is somewhat scant but will hopefully be enough to provide you with a start, at least," he said.

I accepted it with gratitude, then we boarded the *Fafnir* and launched. I'd intended now to head back for Anvil Dark to effect repairs, and then to Earth to retrieve a replacement particle cannon, but as soon as we opened up the Schegith data another possible course of action presented itself.

Galactically, almost straight down from Landfall, the super-earth where we'd been sent by The Quiet Room on our satellite-killing mission, the Puloquir maintained an outpost. The description given in the Schegith data—which was admittedly more than ten years old now—described it as a spindle-shaped station similar to the one broadcasting the NO TRESPASSING message we'd recently encountered. The Schegith had also given us some potentially useful intel regarding Puloquir weapons, though the information was dated at best.

Much like fish, intel starts to stink after a few days. In this case—it was years. I chose to proceed with a healthy sense of cynicism.

"Still, at least it gives us an idea what we're up against. Missiles for long-range firepower and rapid-fire mass drivers close in seem to be what the Puloquir prefer," Zeno said after reviewing it.

"Which suggests that that class 12 that B so fortuitously saved us from wasn't a Puloquir ship," Perry noted.

"Well, shit. Looks like they were just another sundry group of bad guys who decided to start shooting at us. I'm starting to lose track of who wants us dead."

"Look at this way, Van. If we weren't making a difference, no one would care about us."

"There *are* more than a few Peacemakers who spend their entire careers doing the equivalent of giving out parking tickets. They don't want anything to do with the tough cases," Netty added.

I sighed. "I hear you, but I'm telling you, some days the idea of just handing out parking tickets has a certain appeal."

Torina smirked. "You'd get bored in no time."

I felt myself smile. "Does my dangerous lifestyle excite you?"

"Not really."

"I'm crushed."

"It's the stability that excites me," Torina said.

"Did I mention I save my receipts?"

Torina put a hand to her chest. "Go on, big fellah."

"Wait until I show you my budget software. Now then, before my love has a minor cardiac event, let's gas up. I'm thinking Spindrift."

"On the way, Van," Netty said. "Then to the Puloquir outpost?"

I gave a single nod. "If it exists."

"It will," Perry said.

I shot him a glance as Netty did the nav calculations. "What makes you so sure?"

"Based on everything we've heard about the Puloquir, do they sound like a race that would give up territory?"

"The bird's got a point," Icky put in.

I nodded. "He does. Well, last time we just took a look at the bear. This time, let's poke him with that stick I mentioned."

Icky tapped her hammer. "Thought you'd never come around, boss."

THE OUTPOST WAS VERY MUCH THERE. It was, as far as we could tell, identical to the last one we'd encountered—spindle-shaped, sensor clusters at its tips, a fluid-filled ring around its middle. It wasn't broadcasting anything this time, though. In fact, it wasn't generating any real emissions at all, so we only found it because we were looking for it.

It was located amid an astronomical oddity on the edge of the star system, yet another further different red dwarf star with a name composed of letters and numbers. Three small planetoids, each about the size of the Earth's moon, were locked in a mutual orbit around their collective center of gravity or barycenter. They did their stately dance in the cold darkness of the system's margin, so far away from the star that it was just a dim point of ruddy light. The Puloquir outpost apparently orbited them, treating their collective mass as a single body. It was actually more complicated than that, as Netty pointed out, but it was close enough.

We got suited up and made sure our helmets were at hand but didn't depressurize the *Fafnir*, at least not yet. When I was sure everyone was ready, I turned back to the instruments.

"Okay, let's try something different. I'm going to broadcast a challenge again, but this time, Torina, let's go active with the fire control scanners. If these guys are going to just shoot at us anyway, I'd rather trigger it sooner instead of later."

I activated the comm, announced our identity, and then, just for the hell of it—because we didn't actually have legal jurisdiction here—added our Peacemaker credentials. At the same time, Torina flicked on the targeting scanners. Our fire control system immediately offered targeting solutions, but we just waited.

Sure enough, the outpost responded by hammering us right back with targeting scanners. A moment later, an alarm sounded.

"Multiple missile launch signatures," Netty announced.

I watched the overlay, seeing how the missiles began to track and trying to formulate the best response. While I did, Icky called out.

"Helmets!"

We grabbed and fastened our helmets in place, then each gave a thumbs-up. Icky hit the cabin pressure controls, depressurizing the ship. Then she unstrapped and moved to her damage control station aft.

I turned my attention back to the overlay, bracing myself for a salvo of missiles implacably homing in on the *Fafnir*. And there was —a barrage of exactly two. The outpost had launched six more, but two of these seemed determined to attack a rock about a thousand klicks to port, another a spinning chunk of ice ecliptically high above us, and two more some distant star system to spinward. The last had been coughed out of its launcher but hadn't lit its drive. Its tracker had locked onto us and blipped furiously away, but at its present fifty meters per second or so of velocity, it would take days to reach us.

"Netty, what the hell is going on?" I asked.

"No idea. Maybe some sort of elaborate deception?"

"If it is, it's subtle as hell, because I'm definitely not getting it. Zeno, any ideas?"

"It's a shitshow."

"Superior conclusion, Zeno. I was hoping for something a little more informative?"

"I'm with Netty. I've got no idea. I mean, it looks like six of the eight missiles they launched failed, which suggests they didn't initialize properly. And that rate of failure is… unheard of."

"Huh." Missiles that were *up the spout*—that is, ready to launch— were normally fed continuous, real-time targeting data by the fire controller, a process called initializing. It meant they had the most up-to-date tactical picture when they launched, which gave their internal tracking systems a baseline to work from. Until their own relatively short-ranged terminal guidance kicked in, it was the only way they knew how to fly toward their target. But if they were initialized with bad or corrupted data—

On a hunch, I turned to Torina. "Shoot down any incoming missiles, but hold off on firing anything at that outpost."

"Why?"

"Because I have a feeling there's trouble in paradise over there, and I want to know what it is."

"And what if that's the deception?"

I curled my lip. "Pretend you've fired a bunch of malfunctioning missiles to—what? Draw us in? If they want to destroy us, why not just fire a bunch of missiles that are, you know, actually a threat?"

"You're the boss. I just hope I don't live to regret this—wait. Scratch that. I hope I do live to regret it, as long as I'm alive," Torina added.

When the two missiles actually attacking us reached terminal guidance range, only one of them locked. The other just kept wheezing toward us. But without a lock, the avionics package only knew to attack the volume of space where we were—which at this point was a space the size of earth.

A single burst from the point-defenses shredded the sole attacking missile before it could even get close. Its surviving companions continued their fruitless attacks on rocks and ice and that distant star system.

"I'm telling you, whoever lives there better watch out. In about two hundred thousand years, that missile is going to come right down their throats," Perry said.

"If it isn't picked off by enterprising scrappers," Zeno countered.

"I hope someone does. Nice payday there," Perry said.

We coasted inward, ready to light the drive and start maneuvering if more threats appeared. The outpost did peel back armored panels and reveal ominous guns, just as we'd seen previously. I slowed our approach at that, but none of them fired. And a few minutes later, the tracking scanners that had lit us up abruptly died.

"Van, there's a ship launching from the outpost. Unfamiliar design, roughly class 4, similar to a standard workboat," Netty said.

"Someone's getting out of Dodge," I muttered, and Torina looked at me.

I held up a hand. "Sorry, just an expression."

"Dodge? You mean, like a 78 Charger RT? That's a sweet ride," Icky said.

I started to turn, but Icky was still aft. "Uh, Icky? You're suddenly an expert in classic Earthly cars?"

"Hey, ever since I saw that car of your cousin's, I've come to appreciate them as the fascinating machines they are. All those mechanical parts—they're so needlessly, gloriously intricate!"

"Needlessly?"

"Yeah. I mean, just drop in a fusion cell and call it a day. But no, there are all those valves and cams and gears and things that wear out and shatter. And don't get me started on the lubricants. They all *wear out* and it's such a magnificent mess, I can't help but love it."

I was struck by a sudden image—Icky, wearing sunglasses, her voluminous hair all wind-blown as she cruised down the Pacific Coast Highway in some vintage convertible. In truth I needed to see that. I made a note to buy her a convertible at the soonest opportunity and keep it on the farm for her initial cruise.

I yanked my attention back onto the overlay. The outpost's targeting scanners were still dark. In fact, its emissions were falling off, as though the whole facility had been taken offline. In the meantime, the fleeing workboat wasn't doing a very good job of fleeing, since it had only briefly lit its drive before cutting it again, and now coasted away at a paltry klick or so per second relative to the outpost.

"There is definitely something wrong here," I said, frowning at the overlay and various displays.

"It's like something catastrophic happened aboard that outpost," Perry agreed. "Which might be the case. A serious radiation leak from a reactor, an internal explosion—who knows, even a mutiny. Any number of things might have gone south."

"Yeah. I don't want to waste the opportunity to get some hard intel, though." I flicked my attention between the workboat and the outpost for a moment, then made a decision.

"The workboat can wait. Let's go take a close look at this outpost."

"You sure about that, Van? If they are trying to lure us in… " Torina said, letting her voice trail off into ominous possibilities.

But I shook my head. "I don't think they are. We're close enough that they wouldn't need to do anything fancy, just try and overwhelm us with firepower. If anything, though, that station seems to be in the process of shutting down."

"Again, you're the boss."

I gave her a look of thanks, but her term drove home the point that being the boss meant their lives were in my hands.

I only hoped I hadn't gotten this all wrong.

I HADN'T, though, or at least it seemed that way. The outpost remained dark and silent. That made it seem all the more sinister as we slid to a stop a few hundred meters away, but it might as well have been just another of the dumb rocks whirling around the nearby star.

"Van, there is virtually no internal space in that thing," Netty said. "At this range, I can reliably scan the interior, and it's full to the brim with machinery, weapons, and magazines. I don't even think Perry could get inside there without being cramped."

"Whoever's in that workboat must have been somewhere," I replied.

"Yes, but not necessarily inside. If they were a maintenance crew here to do repairs, they might have been living and working out of their ship. That's not uncommon in known space, for crews doing maintenance on things like nav buoys."

"It might also explain why this all seemed to go so very wrong for them. If this outpost was suffering some major malfunction, that might explain why they were here in the first place. Then we showed up, and a team of techs decided to scram before they were able to repair whatever failed," Perry offered.

"All very good points, although I note that our friends out there still don't seem to be in a hurry to scram, as you put it. They still haven't lit their drive," I said.

"Maybe it's non-serviceable, too. Murphy's Law in action."

"Who's Murphy? And what law is he responsible for?" Zeno asked.

"No idea, and his law basically says, *anything that can go wrong, will go wrong*," I replied.

Icky's voice crackled over the comm. "I'd call that the first law of being a spaceship engineer-slash-fixer-upper."

"Van, I have to admit to having a new worry," Zeno said.

"What's that?"

"Well, if we're right, and there something went catastrophically wrong over there, and we're parked close enough to walk—"

I stiffened. "Oh, shit. Right. We need some distance in case it goes boom."

"Van, I've got the best scans I'm going to get, but I do have a suggestion before we, as you guys put it, scram. That medial torus is again clearly filled with some fluid that's denser than water. We should try to take a sample, if we can," Netty said.

"It could potentially help us understand these Puloquir better. We already know they live in liquid methane-ammonia. Maybe that ring full of fluid is their equivalent of living quarters," Perry suggested.

"Which would explain why there's no internal space in the spindle-part of the station. Yeah, good catch. Now, is there any way we can take a sample without having to do an EVA to get it?" I asked.

"Let me guess—you want the bird to do it," Perry said.

"Nope, I don't want anyone going over there, if we can avoid it. At least no one irreplaceable. Netty, could Evan do it?"

"He's not meant to detach from the exterior of the ship, but if we give him a standard EVA maneuvering unit, he should be able to, sure."

"Okay, let's do it. Netty, get him configured, then back us off as far as you can while still being able to control him. Maybe we'll be able to find out if anyone's home."

It took a couple of hours and some careful maneuvering, but Netty was able to steer Evan, our outdoor version of Waldo, who did routine maintenance and repairs, to the fluid-filled ring on the exterior of the ship. He was well-suited to the task, being designed to cling to surfaces while he worked. With a cutting torch, he opened a hole in the ring, then collected a sample of the fluid inside it in an evidence vial. Once he'd secured it, Netty had him maneuver his way back to us.

The outpost remained ominously silent throughout.

Once we had the sample aboard, Evan stowed in his little hangar outside, and as the workboat departed, we kicked the drive and accelerated away from the outpost.

I left Netty to match course and speed with it, a process which would only take minutes. In the meantime, we examined the contents of the vial. Evidence vials were specifically made to stay thoroughly hermetically sealed but could be accessed for analysis through a cleverly designed cap. We placed ours into the analyzer, a device that gave us a basic suite of tools to test and study samples in the field. It wasn't even close to the abilities or precision of a full lab, but it would do.

Operating the analyzer was Perry's job, so we waited while he ran samples of the viscous, cloudy, pinkish fluid through various tests. After the analyzer indicated it was finished, he put the results up on the main galley display.

"It's mostly liquid methane and ammonia, which is no surprise and seems to support that ring being some sort of living space for the Puloquir. It also contains small amounts of liquid organic hydrocarbons and a few more complex compounds, but that's not the really interesting part," Perry said.

I looked at the data. I wasn't a chemist, so the various chemical names and corresponding numbers didn't mean much to me. I finally shrugged. "Okay, what's the really interesting part?"

Another series of clunky chemical names appeared, with more numbers associated with them. They didn't mean anything more to me than the last set had.

"That first set of data is what I think is probably native Puloquir oceanic mixture. This second set is characteristic of organic life. I think this is, uh—well, the best way to put it would be Puloquir soup."

Icky grimaced at the pinkish stuff. "Ewwww."

"You can say that again, big girl," Torina put in.

I frowned at the fluid. "Are you saying that cloudiness and those little bits I see floating in there are... um, people? Or, actually, Puloquir?"

Perry nodded. "I'd say so. It's not for sure—I mean, we really know nothing about the Puloquir, so there could be another explanation. But based on what little we do know, yeah, I'd say that we're looking at the decomposed remains of some number of Puloquir, suspended in their native ocean medium."

"Which means there's probably nothing alive over there," Zeno said.

I nodded. "That's how it would seem. Okay, then I really want to take a look at that workboat now. Netty?"

"We've matched velocity, and I've positioned the *Fafnir* three hundred meters away, to its port side."

"Okay. Torina, grab our flexi-cam. We're going to take some pictures."

NETTY BROUGHT the *Fafnir* to within one hundred meters, then Torina and I crossed to the Puloquir workboat. We remained tethered to our ship, just in case the workboat started to maneuver, but I suspected that wasn't likely. Once we'd plunked ourselves on the workboat's hull, I found a spot to clamp our flexi-cam. It was another investigative tool, a camera with a flexible fiber-optics cable, that passed through a drill bit and could be fed into an enclosed space. The drill was part of it, and once I had it secured, I activated it. Its diamond bit began to spin, chewing into the Puloquir hull.

"Wouldn't it be faster to just cut our way in?" Torina asked.

"It would, but I don't want to risk decompressing their ship—if decompressing is the right word for an atmosphere made of liquid." I watched the bit sink into the hull plating. "Who knows? As miserable a bunch of assholes the Puloquir have been made out to be, if we can rescue a few of them, it might earn us some goodwill."

It took another five minutes for the bit to finally penetrate. We fed the optical cable inside, using the controls on the camera to move it around and scan the inside of the ship.

It was not a pretty sight.

This fluid wasn't as murky as the stuff we'd sampled from the ring, but it still wasn't exactly clear. We saw bulkheads, structural members, panels, all the things you'd expect to find in a ship, just all immersed in fluid. It was like examining the interior of the *Fafnir* if she were filled with water. It didn't take us long to find the crew, though, and that's where the *not a pretty sight* thing came in.

We just watched in silence, slowly moving the camera to take in the horrific scene.

There were three of them, each about two meters long, vaguely resembling Moray eels with arms. They were sunken and emaciated, which might have been natural for them, but I didn't think so. They looked diminished, like they were supposed to be more robust than this but weren't.

"Netty, Perry, can you guys tell what killed them?" I asked.

Netty replied. "We've been comparing the imagery with the preliminary data Schegith gave us. We don't know for sure, of course—I mean, there are lots of variables—"

"Best guess, please."

"It looks like they've suffered some sort of wasting effect, either a disease, or even starvation," Perry replied.

I looked at Torina, her own eyes wide behind her visor. "Everything we find out just raises more questions. We need to retrieve those bodies and bring them back to some real expertise."

"You want to go in there?"

I sighed. "Yeah. I mean, it's just another atmosphere, right?"

"I… guess. Can't help but feel it's like taking a swim in a pool full of corpses, though."

"You'd swim in the ocean, right? It's full of corpses, and I don't just mean microscopic creatures," Perry said.

"That's different."

"How?"

"Let's just say there's a certain corpse to water ratio that's acceptable, and no, I don't know what it is. But I know when it's been exceeded, and... yeah, this definitely exceeds it."

It took us a full day to work our way through the Puloquir airlock —or fluid lock—get aboard, enter the gross horror show of gore-flecked fluid, get the bodies into sealed body bags, then return them to the *Fafnir*. Only Torina and I actually entered the Puloquir ship to minimize the amount of decontaminating we'd have to do.

The three bodies had begun to decompose, bits of them floating around us as we bagged the aliens for their last trip. The flesh—rubbery when they were alive—sloughed right off them, making gathering the Puloquir into a macabre kind of game, where we were forced to decide how much to save and how much to leave behind. Everything was *slick*, and I gave Torina ample moments to take deep breaths. She's hardcore, but this was a hideous version of graves duty well beyond anything she'd seen on Helso—or in space.

When the third bag sealed, I turned to Torina and pointed to the lock, feeling a rush of relief that had a physical weight to it.

"How are you?" I asked her as we stood in the Fafnir's airlock being scoured clean some moments later. The corpses were contained and under the control of Perry and Zeno, but for added precaution, Torina and I were being blasted with every form of decontaminant the ship had to offer.

Torina's face was pale behind her glass. "I don't know how you did it."

"Oh, that's easy. I imagined puking and screaming in front of you, reached deep inside myself for stubborn inspiration, and swallowed my gorge about every thirty seconds while we swam through that ocean of alien soup. Naturally, I squinted into the distance and worked my jaw muscles, too, because that's what badasses do."

She smiled at me, the expression going from wan to warm. "Thanks."

"All part of my relentless pursuit of masculine perfection, as long as it doesn't involve crunches. I have limits."

She snorted with laughter as the last blast of hot air dried our suits, and then… we were done. Free. We'd survived, sort of, unscathed, and now we could begin deciphering what the Puloquir endured on their way to a death that was lonely and vile.

Entering the *Fafnir*, we stripped off our suits and stood in mute thanks, letting the stale ship's air bathe us in a welcome touch. Torina still looked sad, but only just.

I touched her arm in unity. "It was haunted, that place. Sort of."

She grimaced. "Yeah. I mean, we're around death all the time, but somehow, the way they went out—"

"Right. Like… a violation."

Being immersed in the Puloquir fluid had been somewhere between *unpleasant* and *horror show*, the fluctuation being tied to just how many chunks of dead alien bumped against my face mask at any moment. Showered and changed, we both returned to the cockpit, color returning to Torina's cheeks as Zeno handed us both hot coffee.

"So what do you want to do about the outpost, Van? And that ship?" Perry asked.

"We'll leave the outpost alone. We might assume there's no one alive on it, but we don't know for sure. As for that ship, though—"

I turned to Torina, and she just nodded, flicked the lasers from

STANDBY to ARMED, then opened fire. None of us said a thing as the searing beams of coherent energy tore the Puloquir ship apart. And none of us said anything when Torina kept firing, bombarding the wreckage, rendering it down to glowing dust and gas.

Perry dipped his beak in approval. "Right, then."

When it was done, and still with almost no conversation, we set course back to Anvil Dark, our thoughts and fears keeping us silent as the stars raced away in the night.

12

"So this is how you found them?" Gerhardt asked, his gaze locked on the scene behind the transparent screen.

I pointed at the bags. "Yeah. *Just* like this."

We'd offloaded the three bodies when we'd returned to Anvil Dark and handed them off to the Guild's biomedical division for examination. The three bodies were now each ensconced in a clear, rectangular tank filled with the closest approximation to the Puloquir ocean medium that the medical techs could manage. Various cables hooked to sundry probes and analyzers trailed from them, leading to machines filling with data. It was all very Frankenstein's Lab, but with the specter of death—and the unknown—hanging overhead.

One of the techs behind the screen turned to us. She was a Gajur, wearing essentially the utility version of a b-suit and helmet. "Preliminary results suggest that they starved to death. We've identified a number of microorganisms, but none of them fit the profile of a pathogen, so it probably wasn't the result of disease."

Gerhardt nodded. "Anything else?"

"Well, yes? Maybe?" The tech moved to the closest tank and pointed at the Puloquir's back. "There's what seems to be a nerve-nexus right there, although some of it is... missing."

"Missing? As in decomposed, or missing some other way?" I asked.

"I suppose it could be the result of decomposition—maybe something that was particularly prone to it, the way that eyes decompose before skin, which decomposes before bone. But—"

She shook her head. "But I don't think so. It looks more like there was some tissue removed. If I had to guess, I'd say either a wound, or the result of some sort of surgical procedure."

"Fatal?" Gehardt asked.

The tech shook her head again. "We're not sure. Like I said, these are preliminary results. Again, though, if I had to guess—yes, I'd say it would be a fatal wound—"

One of her assistants interrupted her and handed her a data slate. She scanned it, then said, "Huh."

I exchanged a look with Gerhard. "Huh?"

"Yeah, huh. According to these data, these Puloquir were also badly dehydrated."

"But they live in—ah, fluid," Gerhardt protested.

The tech nodded. "They do, but if that's their atmosphere, then it's not necessarily what they need to drink. Humans breathe air but drink water, after all. In fact, most species based on typical DNA require water, but these Puloquir are biochemically different. For all I know, and until we learn more about their biochemistry, they might have needed to drink liquid mercury to sustain their life processes. Whatever it was, though, they weren't getting enough of it."

Gerhardt looked at me. "So the question is whether this was done to them deliberately, or if it was just the result of a terrible accident."

The tech spoke up before I could. "If it helps, their systems show extreme stress and chemical residue from what I'd say is a lack of sleep, or whatever the equivalent is for them. Some sort of down-cycle or recuperation time, anyway. These people didn't just starve to death. They were driven to exhaustion and their own demise."

For whatever reason, my mind made an immediate connection back to the identity chips, which were a different sort of machine-induced slavery, but slavery nonetheless. "Anything mechanical in them that could do that? Like a chip, or a unit that hijacks their nervous system?" I asked.

"Nothing ceramic, metal, or crystalline on any scans. And no evidence of nano-devices. We'll keep looking, though."

Gerhardt nodded. "Thank you. As soon as you have anything more, send it to both myself and Peacemaker Tudor—"

"There is one other thing, actually. We think these Puloquir were young—barely mature, in fact, based on what we could glean from that Schegith data you shared with us. To the extent we can say its equivalent, if these were humans, they'd probably be no more than five or six years old."

Both Gerhardt and I just stared.

The tech nodded. "I know, right? That's—"

Gerhart crossed his arms. "What kind of parent lets their five year old fly off in a starship all alone?"

"If you're asking me, I'd say the kind that doesn't have a choice," the tech said.

Gerhardt turned to me. "Tudor, do you think this is connected to your ongoing case of Crimes Against Order?"

"Well, we have no evidence that it *is*—"

"That's not what I asked you. Do you *think* it is?"

Was Gerhardt, the by-the-book stickler, asking me what I was *feeling* about this? If so, he was starting to soften up, even beginning to take on the shape of a normal human being instead of a walking procedures manual.

I finally nodded. "Yeah, I think it is. Like I said, we've got no evidence to link this to our case, but it—well, it has that feel to it."

Gerhardt nodded. "I agree. This is now becoming a very complex *system* of crimes, well beyond what any one team can handle. I'd like you to call in a Peacemaker you trust—your choice. You'll remain the lead investigator, but I want two of you on this case now, and I want you to work closely together. I'm not losing Peacemakers to whatever this is."

"No need to call, I'm already here," a new voice said. It was Lunzy.

I gave her a raised eyebrow. "Were you like, waiting around the corner, so you could make a dramatic entrance?"

"No, actually, Torina said I should join you here and talk to you. She's concerned that this is all getting to be too much for you alone, Van, and came looking for some help. The dramatic entrance thing? Well, that just happened to work out. To be candid, I coulda used some theme music."

Perry opened his beak, and an ominous chord filled the room. "How's that?"

"Atmospheric, bird. Well done."

Gerhardt offered the ghost of a smile. "You've got a good Second there, Tudor. And AI."

I smiled. "I do indeed."

Lunzy cast a gimlet eye on the dead Puloquir.

"So, who are we questioning first?"

ACTUALLY, *first* we addressed the issue of ship repair. The *Fafnir* had taken more of a beating than I'd realized. That plasma cannon our class 12 ambusher had been shooting at us was a brutally effective weapon, especially since it could somehow apparently use a twist effect to reduce its effective range to nearly zero. Zeno analyzed every scrap of data Netty collected during the firefight and had only one thing to say.

"I want one."

"Too bad B destroyed that class 12 with one of those Deconstructor missiles. If we could have got our hands on that weapon intact—" Icky started, but Zeno held up her hand.

"I don't want one that badly. Or, to put it another way, if B hadn't shown up when she did, I highly doubt we'd be having this conversation right now. It sure was lucky, Van, that she *did* just happen to show up, though, wasn't it?" Zeno said.

Her suspicion regarding B, who she was, and what her motivations were might as well have been flashing in neon. I just shrugged. "Yeah, we're lucky she just happened to be at The Torus, saw us, and figured we needed some top cover."

"Yeah. Lucky."

I was going to eventually have to pull back the veil on the Galactic Knights Uniformed, at least as far as my crew was concerned. Groshenko, B, and Perry had all emphasized the need for utter secrecy, but any more incidents like that happy coincidence in The Deeps was going to blow the lid off it anyway.

Fortunately, Zeno and Icky both got distracted with the repairs, then went back to the schematics of our own flakey plasma cannons —the ones we'd removed from the *Iowa*—to try and figure out where we were going wrong with them. In that sense, I was with Zeno. Considering the increasingly dangerous and implacable foes we seemed to be facing, I wanted one of the damned things, too.

"As I SAID, it's essentially a data siphon. It now functions as an antenna that can intercept transmissions, decrypt them, then retransmit them to a nearby device, such as a data slate. And it will do so in a way that appears to be random background noise to anyone who might attempt to detect its emissions," Linulla said, then clacked several claws at once in a rhythm. "I rather enjoy being sneaky, and thus, I wish to impart stealth to you as well."

"You're... ah, sneaky?" I asked with a diplomatic cough.

Linulla turned his ponderous carapace with surprising delicacy. "Surely you don't think of me as anything less than—Perry, what's a good word here?"

"Furtive."

"Thank you. Furtive," Linulla concluded with a triumphant click.

"I, ah… of course, friend. You're the picture of stealth, and it makes sense that you would pass it on," I managed.

The air filled with Linulla's version of laughter, followed by no less than ten of his children joining in.

"I'm enjoying light banter with you, Van. I'm a shelled block and I know it, but as to the blade? She is mystery itself."

I smiled, abashed, as Linulla handed the Moonsword to me, hilt first.

With repairs to the *Fafnir* complete, we made the journey from Anvil Dark to Starsmith to pick up the Moonsword. I stepped away to make sure I had clear space around me in his cavernous forge, then studied it, still grinning from the aftereffects of Linulla's humor.

As to the Moonsword, there was *nothing* funny about it. The hilt was a few centimeters longer, and the cross guard had been made a little bulkier. The blade itself seemed no different, until I noticed a fine, golden strand embedded in the center of the blade, from its base to its tip on both sides. I experimented by swinging it a few times and found that its weight and balance had also changed a little. Not that I got into a lot of tense, cut-and-thrust sword fights with it, but I would have to spend some time exercising with it to adjust to its new feel.

Linulla demonstrated how it could intercept data transmissions, either directly, in the air, or through what back on Earth we called TEMPEST emissions, the electronic emanations leaking from a system even if it wasn't actually broadcasting anything.

"Its decryption capabilities are formidable but not limitless. Heavily encrypted traffic, so-called military grade, are beyond its capabilities. But it can still intercept and retransmit them to a data slate to be recorded and decrypted later," Linulla said.

I nodded, admiring the blade. "This thing really is the Swiss Army knife of things with blades, isn't it?"

"Sure."

I glanced at Linulla. "You have no idea what a Swiss Army knife is, do you?"

In answer, he reached into a pouch on the utility harness draped over his chitinous frame and extracted a Swiss Army knife, one of the big, elaborate ones that could pull a cork, turn a screw, pick your teeth, probably cut glass or change a spark plug, quite possibly travel through time—oh, and cut things.

I smiled at it. "I stand corrected."

Icky, who'd been watching from nearby, turned to Perry. "He keeps adding stuff to that sword and you're gonna end up redundant, bird."

Perry lifted and lowered his wings in a shrug. "When Linulla upgrades it to include a scintillating personality, I'll start worrying."

___

THAT CONCLUDED our business at Starsmith—except it didn't. While the rest of the crew busied themselves with sundry things—Torina liaising with Lunzy, who was still back on Anvil Dark, about the nitty-gritty of our case, Zeno fussing over the plasma cannon schematics, and Icky playing more damned games of Twister with Linulla's kids—I asked to speak with Linulla privately.

"Van, if this is about the matter of that forgery and the Purification that it necessitated—"

"No, it's not. I mean, I am still really sorry about that, but that's not it. I find myself with a metric ton of questions about this case I'm buried in, most of them really complicated and probably linked in ways I don't understand. I've got about a dozen different ways I can proceed from here, but I don't know which is the best one. Hell, I don't even know if *any* of them are any good, or if there are things I'm just missing."

"You want to talk to Matterforge."

"Yeah. I need some insight, and when it comes to insight, he—it —whatever—is about as insightful as it gets."

"Yes and no. Matterforge's insights can be almost epic in scope, or so specific as to be almost useless. Anyway, it's not like I can just summon it. The best I can do is take you to the comm and let you try to contact it. I'll warn you, though—it rarely responds."

I shrugged. "Still worth a shot."

Linulla took me to the remote chamber hosting the comm terminal used to contact Matterforge. Its display depicted the star, Struve 2398-A, a simmering red dwarf given to occasional flares of emission that had scoured the surface of the Starsmiths' planet to barren rock.

Linulla made to activate the comm, but it was already showing an open channel.

"Van Tudor," the voice spoke, every syllable rich and alien.

Linulla just nodded, then left.

"Um… yes, it's me. Uh, hello there, Matterforge. I gather you were expecting me."

"You state the obvious but are still surprised."

"Well, yeah. Even obvious things can still be surprising."

"Yes. I have not had much interaction with your species, so your psychology is still largely opaque to me. In any case, you have come to me to seek insight into matters you are pursuing."

"That's right. Since I happened to be here at Starsmith anyway, I thought I might as well see if you were up for a chat. See, here's the situation—"

"You do not need to explain. I completely understand the situation facing you."

"You do?"

"As I said in our previous interaction, I experience time and space as a continuum, not discrete instants and locations as you do."

"So you could tell me what's going to happen? With some… accuracy?"

"It is not that straightforward. I can only describe to you what will currently happen, which the act of explaining will change, and that would lead to an irreconcilable loop of cause and effect and cause and effect."

"Ah. Well, I guess that answers one of the big questions then."

"Which is?"

"Whether we really have free will or not."

"That is a question?"

I shrugged. "To my people it is."

"What would be the alternative?"

"It would be called determinism, I guess. That everything that's going to happen is predetermined."

"Randomness is inherent in the fabric of space-time. Quantum effects cannot be predicted. That alone renders such an idea invalid. That your species would even struggle with this is… truly fascinating."

I couldn't help smiling. "The insects surprised you, eh?"

"You are not insects. But I see your point, and once again, am mildly surprised by your nuance. Humans are... layered."

"That's a generous term. I thank you on behalf of my world."

"How interesting. I have considered the history of your species and now see how such conclusions could be drawn."

"You've considered the history of my species? Like, all of it? Just now?"

"Yes, I have."

"Coulda used you in college on test days, but that's irrelevant now."

Matterforge's replies had a sense of acceptance about the mundanity of our universe—a fact that gave me pause. Even a being that lived on the surface of a star and could see across time and space had limits, I guess.

But I wasn't here to discuss the philosophy of existence, the nature of religion or any other existential questions with Matterforge. And, true to its nature, it already seemed to know that.

"That said, you are now seeking to understand the circumstances that surround you and how you should best act to deal with them," it said.

"That's right. Anything would be helpful."

"Again, I cannot suggest things to you that, from your perspective, have not yet happened."

"Because of that cause-effect-cause loop thing. Yeah, I get it. And I'm actually kind of glad, knowing that the future—well, the future as I understand it—isn't fixed. But if there's anything from the past or present that might help—"

"If you would seek to understand more about the species you

know as the Puloquir, then you must know that they are fleeing. Flight, and the fear that provokes it, dominate their psychology."

"Fleeing? Fleeing what?"

"To answer that, I will describe to you another species, one that from your temporal perspective no longer exists. It, too, was forced to flee by another species, known only to them by a term whose meaning in your frame of reference would be 'Tenants.'"

"Tenants?" I immediately thought of apartments and leases and my own former digs in Atlanta. "I'm assuming you don't mean a rental situation gone bad."

Silence.

I sighed. Okay, real estate references were wasted on Matterforge. I chose to press on, and we'd keep lease agreements and taxes out of it. "Regarding these... Tenants—"

"They are, from your perspective, clever and deceitful, but as parasites go, they are also inferior. The most successful parasite does not kill its host."

"So these Tenants are... something I should be pursuing."

"I do not suggest you do anything with this information. I am only stating that it is ultimately relevant to understanding your situation."

I opened my mouth to press for more but closed it again. Deep in my mind, I'd been hoping that Matterforge would just give me answers in a neat package, ready for action and justice. I'd been hoping it could complete the puzzle, but that was naive.

This job required big boy pants, and I wore them as a matter of course. So did my crew, with the exception of Icky, who merely wore the responsibility but refused the fabric.

"You are considering the maturation of your role as a captain and commander."

"I am. It's difficult not to, given my responsibilities for the lives of people I care about. And those I don't know, but am morally obligated to… preserve. Thank you for what you could give me. I'll use it well."

"I had no doubt about that. Your morality is not in question."

"But something else is?"

"Yes."

"May I ask what that is?" I pressed.

After a small pause, filled with the song of stars, Matterforge spoke.

"Your survival."

13

WE WERE on our way back to Anvil Dark to plan our next move, when Lunzy pinged us with a request to talk. Netty opened a secure comm link to her.

"Hey, Lunzy, what's up? Any leads at your end?"

"Oh, you might say that. Watch this," she said, touching a control.

The display changed to an image of three humanoid aliens with long, slender necks and oversized eyes—the classic image of the gray aliens of which Earthly pop culture was so enamored. Instead of being all *Close Encounters of the Third Kind mysterious*, though, these three were on a rant. It came across as weirdly incongruous, since the gray aliens of pop culture were generally portrayed as aloof and inscrutable.

"This broadcast is a warning, see? To the Peacemaker named Tudor, and everyone who associated with him. He is *dead*. They are *dead*. Their friends, *dead*. Their families, *dead*. The same goes for anyone who cavorts with the carnal beast named Belowasc Gerti, who will answer for her sins," one of them grated.

One of the others spoke up. "*Dead*. Everyone *dead*."

The third shot the one who'd just spoken a hard glance. "What's that? *Everyone* dead? That makes no sense—"

The transmission abruptly cut off, and Lunzy's image reappeared.

"Okay, that was kinda like *E.T.* crossed with *Goodfellas*, and if anyone doesn't know what that means, look it up. Who the hell are those guys, anyway? And who's Belowasc Gerti?" I asked.

"To answer the second question, that would be B," Perry said.

Torina sniffed and shook her head. "Was that real? Or was it some local theater group practicing a really shitty play?"

"I think they're real," Lunzy replied.

"I think they're dumbasses," Icky said.

I had to smile at her. "Thank you, Icky. Succinct as ever."

"As for who they actually are, I'm not sure. All I can tell you is that transmission originated somewhere near that location you just visited, The Torus."

"Huh. Small universe, isn't it?"

"Sure seems that way sometimes. Oh, and by the way, you are now officially the Peacemaker with the most public declarations from bad guys about how horrible you are and how you're going to pay for it," Lunzy said.

"I take it you're including the Satrap of the Seven Stars League in that," Torina said. "Which means you're kind of saying a head of state is a bad guy."

"Do you have a problem with that, Torina?"

She shook her head and smiled. "No, not at all. Just making sure we're on the same page here."

"If you'd like to know who they are, I can tell you," Perry said, and we all turned to him.

"Really?" I asked, now fully curious. "Hit me, bird. Who are these idiots, and more importantly, why have they declared a *public* war with us?"

A still image from the video message appeared on the display in a split screen with Lunzy. "Friends, I give you three of the fifty-three remaining children of Jacomir the Douchebag."

Torina smirked. "Is that an official title?"

"Okay, I took a bit of creative license. Anyway, these deep thinkers, who tout themselves as The Lowfangs, are the eldest children who've not gotten themselves killed. Jacomir's kids have an astonishing gift for dying in stupid ways, just like their father."

"How did he die?" Zeno asked.

"Challenged a country boy to a knife fight back on Earth. It didn't end well."

"So now we have this blood feud from 1943, Earth years, to add to the schedule? I think the Puloquir take priority, Van, them being in crisis and all," Netty offered.

"Agreed. And we're not going to ignore that, because it's our duty. That said, this broadcast came from near The Torus, eh? I wonder—"

I pondered the still from the video for a moment, then had Netty put the metadata for it up. "Netty, can you extrapolate that back to a location on a star chart?"

She did. The image split yet again and now also displayed a map of the surrounding galactic region, one location highlighted with an icon.

"Okay, now, based on the data Schegith gave us about the Puloquir, highlight every location that's tied to them in some way."

She did. One of those locations corresponded exactly with the origin point for the broadcast from Jacomir's dissolute kids.

I sat back. "Well, what do you know."

"Good catch, boss. Netty and I both missed that," Perry said.

I nodded toward the still image. "You were probably stunned by their looks. They were, to quote my Aunt Beatrice, *dipped in ugly*."

"Like half-boiled chickens. I've never thought Jacomir's brood had a good look," Perry replied.

"Hey, some bird-on-bird anger. I can hardly wait," Icky said.

"Netty, is there any bounty or bonus for bagging those three, ah, entrepreneurs?"

"Funny you mention it. They're actually listed as pirates on the bounty slate for miscellaneous, shitty little reasons, so there is a standing payout on them. Fifty thousand bonds each."

"Each?"

"That's what it says."

"That's a substantial bounty. There must be more than just *shitty little reasons* for it," Torina said.

"I'm not sure what to tell you, aside from, there it is."

"Van, I'll do some digging, see what I can find out about these assholes on this end," Lunzy said.

"Much appreciated. There's something about a high bounty on those buffoons. Either there's more to them than than the bounty slate is letting on, or someone out there *really* wants these guys taken out. I'd like to know which, because the last thing I want to do is, you know, underestimate them."

"Underestimating bad guys is never a good idea," Lunzy agreed. "I'll let you know what I find out when I find it out."

She signed off.

I turned to Torina and Perry. "Fifty thousand a head for as many as fifty-three kids? That's a cargo pod full of bonds."

"Remember that some of those morons are inevitably dead, Van. Which is why that bounty makes so little sense. We're not dealing with criminal masterminds here."

"But we are dealing with yet another element tied to the Puloquir," Torina noted.

I nodded. "So it would appear."

I stared at the image of the three aliens. They were linked to the Puloquir. They were also linked to B. And B was prominently linked to us.

Which was great, but we were still missing any connection to the Sorcerers, the shadowy mercenary outfit called Group 41, and our identity theft case. I was sure there was one—I mean, seriously, there *had* to be—but I couldn't see it.

Yet.

"Perry, Netty, start doing some digging of your own about these Lowfangs, the heirs to the Jacomir Dynasty, and the Douchebag throne. I want to know how they're connected to the Puloquir and... anything and everything else. Compare notes with Lunzy as you do because we're going hunting."

LUNZY, working through contacts she'd made over the years, was able to start shedding some light on the region of space surrounding The Torus, bordering The Deeps on one side and known space on the other. It soon became clear that a region outside known space wasn't necessarily *unknown* space, as in *here there be dragons*. Rather, it meant that most of the major interstellar agreements and protocols that applied to known space simply didn't extend that far. It was more like the European Union back on Earth—many European countries were part of it and cooperated within its framework for things like travel and trade, but some didn't. That didn't make them any less European, just not part of the thing called the EU.

That included the Charter that enabled and gave jurisdiction to the Peacemaker Guild in known space. Even then, though, it turned out there was a hodgepodge of very narrow agreements with some of these outside powers. For instance, we had an extradition agreement in place with the Karunda Hegemony, a trio of races occupying a dozen star systems spinward of The Torus.

"It dates back to some kerfuffle about four hundred years ago, when the architects of a failed rebellion on one of the Hegemony's planets fled into Ceti and Eridani space. The Hegemony wanted them back, and we were happy to hand them over," Lunzy said over the comm.

"In exchange for something, no doubt," I said.

"Got it in one, boss. It was an extradition agreement right back, in case anyone we wanted for a crime went and hid out in their space. It's still in place, though there's no record of it being used for over three hundred years."

I turned to Perry. "Do you know all this? All these legal details?"

"I do now. Lunzy sent me an upload of all the bits and pieces.

There isn't a lot, but it potentially gives us some standing out there, in some systems, at least."

"How much standing?" Torina asked.

"Less standing on one foot and more standing on one toe."

"It's something, at least," I said. "Anyway, thanks, Lunzy. We're about two hours out of Spindrift, where we gassed up, and we'll be twisting to the origin system for the Jacomir triplets' broadcast in… oh, another three hours or so. Keep us posted."

"Will do."

I started to unstrap, since there wasn't much point to sitting in the cockpit staring at the instruments for three hours. But I stopped myself.

"Netty, Perry, do we have any idea how *much* is out there?"

"How much what?" Netty asked.

"Things. Stuff. People. Civilizations. I mean, up until not that long ago, I'd been focused only really on known space. But then we started dealing with Unity, and now there's The Torus, and this Hegemony, the Puloquir—so how much is out there? Is the Milky Way wall-to-wall civilizations? Do we even know?"

"We know the volume of space for about five hundred light years round known space reasonably well. It's mostly empty," Netty said.

"So most of the galaxy is probably pretty empty then, too?"

Perry spoke up. "We've got anecdotes, mostly, in the archives, suggesting that to spinward, there are more inhabited systems for potentially another thousand light-years or so. Beyond that is just too far for us to have made any meaningful contact with anyone."

"What about to anti-spinward?" Torina asked.

"We're pretty sure there's nothing."

"Nothing? Like no one at all?"

"That's how it seems, yeah," Perry replied.

I frowned at that. "Do we know why?"

"There's nothing in any archives that we can access. It seems like once you get past Unity's space, there are just a whole lot of empty star systems. In a few of them, there aren't even any lingering relics or ruins. Only fallow worlds and untapped resources."

I let that settle as the reality of a lonely, vast universe began to take shape in my mind. We unstrapped and went to the mess, but my thoughts lingered on that yawning gulf to anti-spinward. Why hadn't any civilizations formed out there, since they seemed pretty common in these parts?

Or if they had, what had happened to them?

OUR DESTINATION SYSTEM, where the menacing broadcast from Jacomir's brood had originated, was under the control of the Hege-mony. It wasn't exactly a thriving system. It reminded me of Wolf 424 back in known space—ostensibly under the control of the Eridani Federation but mostly treated as an open system and not all that well regulated.

Of note, the system contained a moon not too different from Titan, Saturn's big moon, that had once been a home to the Pulo-quir. Methane-ammonia seas sprawled across its rocky surface, the Puloquir having lived in their depths. It wasn't clear if any Puloquir remained there, still lurking in the toxic abyss, but the planet had virtually no value otherwise so nobody really cared if they did.

"Doesn't that seem a little shortsighted? I mean, the Puloquir want to beat the shit out of everyone, even themselves, right? So you'd think you'd want to know if you had someone like that living in your backyard pool," I said.

"Maybe if this was a busier or more populated system, they would be. But neither of the two rocky planets here are even remotely habitable by any species that isn't fireproof or infused with antifreeze, which leaves the two gas giants and their moons. And they're all just more airless rocks. So you've got some mining going on, probably a bunch of smuggling and other shady dealings, and that's it," Perry said.

I shrugged. "I don't know, I just have visions of a fleet of those Puloquir *sinking fish* emerging from those stinky oceans someday and laying waste to every surrounding system."

"Complacency is another of those universal constants," Zeno added.

"Hey, if it doesn't happen, then it's not a problem. And if it does, then they'll deal with it," Icky added.

I shook my head and sniffed. "Yeah, *that's* never gone wrong for anyone before. Passivity is a decision, of a kind."

"We learned that the hard way on Helso," Torina said, her eyes looking off into the distance as she sifted memories.

"We won't do it again, dear. Promise," I told her.

When she looked at me, her eyes came back from wherever they'd been, a warmth to her expression that said my promise mattered. That was good, because I meant it. Someday, I knew, I'd have to prove it.

We coasted in-system, slurping up all the data we could with passive scanners. Both gas giants had mining operations orbiting them, slowly chewing and grinding up their smaller moons for valuable ore. There was another operation on the inner rocky planet, which must have been a hell of a place to work considering it orbited nearly half again as close to the system's star as Mercury did to the Sun. And that was it.

I pondered the tactical overlay. "Okay, so if I was a trio of nasty assholes bent on avenging my scumbag dad, where would I be?"

"Well, what do we know about them?" Torina asked.

Perry shrugged his wings. "Aside from who they are and that they exist, not much."

"I think it's safe to say they're probably bullies, though, right?" Zeno asked.

I glanced back at her. "I'd say so. What are you thinking?"

"Well, I've crossed paths with more than a few bullies in my time. The best defense against them is to stand up to them, no?"

I thought about the bar, *The One-Eyed Yak*, on The Torus. Skrilla's ringer, the one who'd challenged us when we'd entered, had definitely fit the mold of a bully. For that matter, so did most of the rest of the clientele, who only left us alone because we were packing guns. If they'd sensed any weakness in us, I had no doubt they'd have seen us the same way sharks view blood in the water.

"So they won't go where people are going to call them on their bullshit," I said, leveraging Zeno's thinking.

"That's right. So if they're here, they're probably somewhere that's somehow vulnerable, where there's some weakness they can exploit."

I nodded. It made good sense. Back on Earth, drug dealers and other miscreants would sometimes perpetrate home takeovers, basically making themselves at home in the house or apartment of someone who owed them money or was otherwise unable or unwilling to stand up to them. We needed to find a place like that here.

I turned to Perry. "Is there any way we—?"

"Can find some place in this system that's on shaky ground so these assholes can lord it over them?"

"You're way ahead of me, bird."

"I'm way ahead of most sentient beings, Van, but I don't like to brag about it. It's unseemly."

"Yes you do. You brag about it every chance you get."

"Hurtful, but fair. I do like to brag about it. Anyway, Netty and I have been looking at all the data we've collected here, everything Lunzy's sent us, and everything else we have in the archives. Thanks to a lot of analyzing and cross-referencing and other work—you're welcome, by the way—we've identified a mining operation working the fourth moon of the inner gas giant that's on the skids."

"Bankrupt?"

"Bankrupt-ish, anyway. Based on a prospectus filed back in known space, where they were looking for investors, and the production data they've filed since then with the Hegemony, they're falling *way* short of their targets."

"That's some good detective work, bird. But it doesn't mean they're in trouble. They could have tons of cash, for instance."

"According to Hegemony open source news, they declared themselves bankrupt."

"You could have just led with that."

"Yeah, but my way makes us sound way more clever."

"Sounds like just the sort of place these assholes we're after would go," Zeno said. "They put up some cash to give themselves a stake in it, then effectively take over."

"Um, I'd like to point out that this is all just speculation. We've got absolutely no evidence of any of this," Torina put in.

I tapped the screen, selecting a point of ingress for Netty to follow. "True. But it gives us a place to start, right?"

WE APPROACHED the mining platform cautiously, ready to run headlong into the sleazebag triplets and have to fight it out. But the platform, which was automated, was devoid of any ships.

"Van, the platform's docking AI is querying us," Netty said.

I narrowed my eyes at the comm. "Open the link."

Torina shot me a glance. "Are you planning on actually going aboard?"

"Nope. Or not yet, anyway. I just want to try something."

"Okay, I've got the link established. The AI is asking to assume terminal control of the *Fafnir*."

That was standard practice even for many stations and orbitals back in known space. The last few hundred meters would be controlled by the station's docking AI, in the same way a harbor pilot would board some big ship back on Earth and guide it into the dock. That wasn't why I wanted the link, though.

"Perry, see if you can do a hack across that data link. Let's see if we can root out some sort of log of ships coming and going to and from this platform," I said.

"On it, boss."

We waited. It didn't take long, only twenty seconds or so, which didn't surprise me. An automated mining platform likely wouldn't have military-grade IT security—although, if it did, that would tell us something, too.

"And there you go," Perry said, the display over the tactical overlay filling with data. We scrutinized it.

"So up until about six months ago, there was routine traffic, empty ore carriers arriving with things like helium-3 fuel—for the platform's reactors, I guess. Then they'd load up with ore concentrate and head back out."

I pointed at the screen. "Then we have a break, here, of nearly a month. And since then, there have been eighteen visits—" I nodded. "Yeah. This ship, right here. The one that made fifteen of them. It's just listed as a registry number, no manifests, no records of cargo offloads, nothing."

"Probably not tourists out for some sightseeing," Zeno said.

"No, probably not." I sat back and rubbed my chin. "So what we need is a spot to stake this place out, where we won't be seen."

"Van, I have an idea," Icky said.

We all turned and listened to what she had to say.

14

"I AM JUST NOT USED to being this close to something and not actually docked with it," I said, glancing up. The hull of the mining orbital stared back at me through the canopy, only two meters away.

Icky had suggested a simple and elegant solution, that we just snuggle as close as we could to the platform and put ourselves in its sensor shadow. It was essentially the same thing we did the very first time I visited Torina's home system, when we hid in the shadow of a big freighter to approach Helso unobserved. What remained of the *Fafnir*'s stealth coating would help suppress our signature even more. Even heat wasn't a problem, since the platform was still processing ore brought to it from the nearby moon by robotic ore haulers, so it radiated a much stronger thermal signature than the *Fafnir* did.

So we waited.

And waited.

"How long are you planning to hang out here, Van?" Icky asked, a full day plus a few hours into our stakeout.

"Hey, this was your idea."

"Yeah, well, it seemed like a good one at the time. But this is booooring."

"We could teach you a new card game. There's one called Crazy 8s you might like."

She scowled. "I suck at card games."

"That's because you have absolutely no poker face. You get a bad draw and you pout. You get a good one and you *woo-hoo*."

"Which wouldn't be so bad if you, you know, put any effort into being a little deceptive about it. Next time, try *woo-hoo'ing* when you get a terrible draw," Torina said.

"Why would I woo-hoo about shitty cards, though?"

Torina smiled. "Never mind—"

"Van, there's a ship inbound," Netty said. "It twisted in about fifteen minutes ago, but after some futzing around, it's adopted a trajectory that will bring it right here."

We all sat up. "Stats?"

"Class 9 or so in terms of mass. At this range, I can't say much more."

"Okay, we've got about—" I looked at the display. "About three hours before they get here. Let's grab all the passive data we can during that—"

I stopped, tilting my head. "Netty, what's this platform"— I jerked my head upward, at the hull nearly close enough to touch— "doing scanner-wise? It should be active, right?"

"It is, continuously, to help as a navigation aid. And I see where you're going with this. You want us to try and hack into it again and eavesdrop on its scanner data."

"Actually, I want to try something else entirely," I said, climbing out of my seat. "I've got that spiffy new update to the Moonsword, so I might as well try it out."

———

IT WORKED LIKE A CHARM. The Moonsword was able to glean nearly *all* of the data-processing residue leaking from the platform, then retransmit it to the *Fafnir*'s comm system where Netty and Perry teased out the scanner information. It meant we didn't actually have to hack the platform's network, which might be detected. Moreover, Linulla's upgrade had a built-in firewall of sophisticated design, so we didn't have to worry about malware oozing across the link, either.

"I like it," I said, placing the Moonsword on the galley table. "It means we can listen in on things without having to give ourselves away."

"As long as whatever you're listening into is, like, no more than ten or fifteen meters away," Perry noted.

"And not properly hardened against residual emissions," Netty added.

"Nothing's perfect, and you're all ruining my moment. Let me bask in the magnificence," I said.

Torinal lifted a brow. "Done basking?"

"In fact, I am. What can you tell us about that ship *now*, Netty?"

"Class 9, a standard configuration from a Tau Ceti shipyard back in known space, but up-armored. Looks like a laser battery, a missile launcher and point defenses."

"That's a lot of firepower for some corporate mining ship," Zeno observed, her tone dry.

"No shit. Ladies and gentlebirds, I believe we might have found our newest frenemies," I said.

Torina quirked her lip. "Frenemies?"

"Yeah. Friends who are also enemies. Only in this case, I use the term *friends* with the greatest of irony."

Even with our particle cannon inoperable, we still had a considerable firepower advantage over the approaching ship. As long as they didn't detect us, we could let them close to point-blank range, then open up and probably demolish them in a single volley of mass-driver and laser fire. But I didn't want to just kill these assholes. I wanted answers, and answers needed working mouths and lungs and things.

"Torina, how's your dead eye feeling? Think you can disarm those guys without blasting them to bits?"

She studied her own tactical data, including the targeting solutions our fire-control system was now spitting out. "I make it—oh, let's say seventy-five percent yes."

"And the other twenty-five percent?"

"That would be *blown to bits* territory. If you want better than that, we'll have to go active on our own scanners, because the system mounted on this mining platform sucks."

I nodded. "Okay, then. Torina, you have control. When you're happy with the range, go ahead and light 'em up."

She nodded, and we resumed waiting.

When they were twenty minutes out, I started paying close attention to the approaching icon. They hadn't gone active with their scanners yet, so they hadn't seen us. If we were lucky, they wouldn't, and would just assume it was another routine trip to their hideout aboard the platform—

"Uh, Van, hate to rain on your parade, but I feel compelled to point out that we don't *know* that Jacomir's kids are aboard that ship. If they're some innocent party, and we start shooting at them——" Perry didn't finish the sentence.

"I know, and it's a good point." I looked at Torina. "I guess that once we illuminate them, we'll have to wait for a reaction before we start shooting."

She nodded.

Ten minutes out, Torina brought the weapons online. I released my master safety to WEAPONS HOT, giving her the scope to fire at will. We then went through our now-standard pre-combat operating procedures—suiting up, putting on helmets, depressurizing the cabin, and getting things ready for damage control.

Five minutes, and the class 9 just kept boring in, in no particular hurry.

"Okay, Netty, on my mark, move us clear of the platform. Give me at least a klick," Torina said.

"Will do."

She let another minute pass, then gave the word. "Netty—now."

The thrusters rumbled, pushing the *Fafnir* away from the platform. At the same time, Torina flicked the active scanners on. To the class 9, it would have been the equivalent of coming around the corner on a dark highway, straight into the high beams of an oncoming car.

I have to admit, their reaction to our sudden appearance was *quick*. The class 9 spat out what I thought were missiles but turned out to be drones, each mounting a small mass driver. It dramatically increased their firepower at short range, which meant I wasn't going to let them get to short range, at least not until we'd dealt with the drone threat.

"Torina, make those drones your priority—"

She opened fire, turning one of them to vapor and fragments.

"—targets."

She glanced at me. "Sorry, was I supposed to wait for your orders?"

"Of course not, dear. Proceed at will," I said, starting a series of rapid jinks through all three axes but still not closing on the approaching ship. Torina, in the meantime, reduced each of the drones to slag and debris with methodical, relentless precision.

Perry made a tongue clicking sound. "They launched those things too early. If they'd waited, we'd have had a problem."

"They're afflicted with the dirtiest of words—potential," I said, now applying thrust to bring the range down. Again, I didn't want to kill them. They were of no use to me dead.

Torina coolly took out their laser with another trio of shots. It responded with a salvo of missiles, but Torina swung her attention to those while we closed to effective mass-driver range. Zeno took control of it and, with one neat shot, blasted their missile launcher, a turreted affair, to scrap.

"Nice round, Zeno," Netty said.

"Thanks. I've been practicing."

"For how long?" Icky asked.

"A century. Or so," Zeno said, nose wrinkled in laughter.

As we swept past the other ship, Zeno then carefully targeted their drive bell, pounding a mass-driver slug through it and forcing their engine into a shutdown. They opened up with point defenses and managed to land a few hits on us that did superficial damage and managed to make some impressive noise.

Quickly, I spun the *Fafnir* around and reversed course, an easy maneuver since we hadn't built up a lot of velocity. Torina took out their annoying point-defense battery, while Zeno lined up careful shots that blew off their thruster assemblies with the inexorable progress of an advancing tide.

And that was it. The class 9 continued coasting toward the mining platform but would miss it by a comfortable margin.

I turned to Torina and Zeno. "Superior shooting. Really. Well done."

"Next time, I might try writing my name in mass-driver impacts on their hull," Zeno said, switching the weapon back into safe mode.

Icky poked her head into the cockpit. "What, was that it? We took three or four plinking hits that barely scratched the armor, and we're done?"

"Sorry you didn't get to do a bunch of damage control, Icky. By which I mean I'm not sorry at all," I replied.

"Yeah, sure, but… boooring."

"That's okay. For our next performance, we're going to board them. How'd you like to grab your hammer and come along, cover my back?"

She brightened behind her visor. "Violence up close. This is *way* better than cards."

———

AFTER MATCHING velocity with the other ship, we decided to do a double entry. While Torina and Perry broke in through the midships airlock, Icky and I would make our entrance. After some thought, I decided to go right for their cockpit.

I puffed thrust from the maneuvering unit, pushing away from the *Fafnir*, then reversed it and stopped myself directly in front of the class 9's prow. Another puff brought me right onto their canopy.

"Going in through the screen door, Icky. Get it? Because of their forward display screen?" I asked, snorting at the power of a dad joke in combat.

Icky, following behind me, sighed. "Don't quit your day job, Van."

I grasped a stanchion, drew the Moonsword, then plunged it into the top of the cockpit with a smooth motion. No air vented when I withdrew it, so their ship was depressurized, either by choice or battle damage. A few more cuts with the almost supernaturally sharp blade loosened a chunk of hull plating big enough for Icky to fit through, but she didn't charge right in. Instead, clinging to the hull beside me, she threw in a dazzle bomb. It detonated with a blinding flash across a big chunk of the EM spectrum, and *then* she went in, bellowing a battle cry that would have turned a pirate's guts to water. The Lowfangs wouldn't be able to hear it, of course, but who was I to dampen her enthusiasm?

I followed her into the ship. Vapor from the dazzle bomb obscured the cockpit, which was empty. Icky was already shoving her way back aft, still shouting her head off, apparently able to breathe and bellow at the same time, not unlike some lead singers in hair metal bands. Again, I followed, only to stop abruptly short when she did, then she punched out with her hammer like a battering ram. I saw a suited figure flung backward, then something sparked off the bulkhead beside me.

Someone was shooting.

I would have intervened, but the flaw in my plan made itself immediately clear—there was only slightly more corridor than there was Icky to fill it. All I could do was stay behind her while she—did whatever the hell it was she was doing. Whatever it was, it involved a great deal of shouting and punching and thrashing. She looked like a woodchipper that sprouted legs, and every blow of her hammer spalled debris or sparks or both.

An unknown voice came on the comm in broadcast mode. "A dress up sailor who weighs less than my balls!" it snarled, and I dropped to the deck so I could look between Icky's tree-trunk legs and get a tiny bit of situational awareness. I saw a Lowfang brandishing a knife at Torina and hissed in a breath.

"Yeah, that's a mistake," I muttered.

The Lowfang might have been a damned fine street-and-bar knife-fighter, but he was against Torina, a master of Innsu. She blocked his strike easily, then slammed him back against the bulkhead, whereupon Icky swung her hammer and stove in his head in a shower of gore.

"Dammit, Icky, we want them alive, remember?" I snapped.

"Oh, uh—yeah, sorry boss."

I braced myself for more action, desperately seeking a way around Icky as I did, but it was over. Torina had one of the Lowfangs immobilized, and Perry sat on the other's chest, looking down into his face.

"Go ahead. Make your move. You'd just better hope this spiffy hyper-alloy beak of mine won't punch right through your visor. And your bones. And this deck, too, shithead." Perry leaned down with a mechanical leer.

I finally pushed past Icky and glowered down at our two prisoners, then at the third and his crushed skull. "Anyone else want to end it out here? Dead or alive, you mouthbreathers are paying my bills."

The two returned looks so venomous they should have come with poison warnings, but they offered no further resistance. I knelt beside one, settling in for a brief chat.

"Hey there, handsome. In case you haven't figured it out yet, I'm Van Tudor—you know, the guy you said was going to be *dead*, my friends *dead*, my family and pets *dead* and all that. And you're under arrest—in case you hadn't figured that out yet, either."

"On what charge?" he snarled.

"Threatening a Peacemaker for a start. Piracy, for another, since you seem to have an outstanding warrant or two for that. And being an asshole. While technically it's not a crime, it *is* reason enough for me to let my staff work out their frustrations on you."

I stood. "Netty, can you contact who or whatever passes for the legal authorities out here and let them know what's happened?"

"Already got them on the comm, Van. They're bitching mightily about us being outside our jurisdiction and in theirs."

"Leave that to me, Van. I've already got the relevant agreements and such queued up," Perry said.

I had to smile. Damn, but I had a good crew.

Icky returned from checking engineering, having verified the ship's reactor was scrammed and we weren't about to blow up. She was grinning from ear to ear behind her visor.

"See, now *that* was fun. We've gotta do more of this sort of thing, Van."

"Only you, Icky, would consider close-quarters combat an amusing pastime."

She shrugged. "Everyone needs a hobby, right?"

TORINA SMIRKED AT THE COMM, which had just translated the message from the magistrate and named me Space Policeman Van Tudor.

"Space Policeman?"

"Hey, the translator's doing its best. It doesn't have a linguistics matrix for his language so I'm translating on the fly," Netty said.

I grinned. "Space policeman. Van, the space policeman. I like that."

"Why not space *cop?*" Perry put in. "Throw some cheesy synth-pop music on it, have some gravelly voiced guy reading the beginning credits out loud while each of you gets a freeze frame—"

He changed his tone to said gravelly voiced guy, and at the same time began thumping and twanging the theme from some 70s cop show. "Space Cop, starring Van Tudor. Also starring Torina Milon. And Zenophir. Special guest rug, Icrul—"

I reached over and squeezed his beak shut, cutting him off. "You watched a lot of old TV, didn't you?"

"It wasn't old when I watched it."

"Uh, Perry, what was that music, anyway? I kinda liked that," Torina said.

I glanced at her. "You do? Really?"

"Yeah. Very upbeat, tells you things are going to be happening—"

"Um, excuse me—I hate to be the voice of, you know, sanity here, but we do have that magistrate out there waiting for us to get back to him," Zeno cut in.

"Right you are," I said and turned back to the comm. Its screen held the image of an alien who reminded me of the creature in the old movie *The Thing From Another Planet*—which was the actor James Arness in a rubber suit. I had no idea what to call him otherwise, because the translator was, as Netty noted, struggling to keep up. It occasionally gave up entirely and just sounded the alien's natural language, which sounded like a dog howling at a distant siren, with only a little more inflection. The name of the race was probably buried somewhere in there, but it was clear that until the technology had more to work with, it was as good as it was going to get.

"Have you had an opportunity to review the legal brief we sent? I think our case for extradition is pretty clear—"

"I have, and am say all makes to be orderly." The creature leaned toward the imager. "Frankly, I care very much of nothing, have great pile of broken cases on my sit-table. I receipt your legal state and grant approbation for you to seal up villains—"

He ended on an ululating wail.

I glanced at Perry. "That's the best we can do?"

"Sorry, Van, it's a complex language based on tones and harmonics. You're lucky our poor translator manages as well as it does."

I turned back. "Thank you. We'll finish collecting evidence, then be on our way."

"Accept thanksgiving"—wail—"is at you."

The screen flicked off. I stared at it for a moment, then shook my head. "Does everyone else think he's okay with us just finishing up and leaving? Because that's what I think, but gotta be honest, I'm not one hundred percent on that, and I'd hate to start a war."

Everyone looked at one another, shrugging and nodding. Perry turned to me.

"I think he summed up his position pretty well, Van. He has no interest in adding to the great pile of broken cases on his sit-table. This is a veteran cop, close to retirement. He's a rumpled suit away from being a TV trope."

"Okay, then. Torina, I'm going to let you and Icky interrogate our prisoners back there. Zeno, you, Perry, and I will cross back to their ship and gather all the evidence we can find. Netty, is it feasible for us to tow that ship back to Anvil Dark?"

"Structurally, it's reasonably sound. I don't see why not, although we'll have to make two mid-flight refueling stops instead of one, probably Spindrift and Procyon."

"Sounds good. I'll let you work out the rigging needed and we'll get to that once we're finished with the rest of this stuff." I stood. "Okay, everyone, you've got—"

"Um, excuse me," Icky said, shaking out her quasi-mullet with a great deal of flair. It was blue, it was long, and it flowed back from her forehead with the magnificence of a third baseman's hair in 1983.

We all stopped and looked at her.

She fixed her stare on Perry.

"You didn't really think I was just going to let the bird's *guest rug* crack go, did you?"

By sealing off the cockpit, where I'd cut a gaping hole through the hull, we were able to repressurize the Lowfangs' ship. Once Perry had confirmed atmospheric integrity and no airborne toxins, we shucked our helmets. I immediately wished we hadn't.

"What *is* that? I'd say something like dirty socks, but dirty socks are potpourri compared to this. I thought you said there were no atmospheric toxins."

"There aren't. None of these gaseous chemicals occur in concentrations high enough to be a health hazard."

I grimaced. "Tell my nose that—but quickly, before it slumps over dead."

"That smell has to be coming from somewhere. That is, unless it's the smell of the Lowfangs' themselves—and if it is, it's another good reason to never date one," Zeno said.

I smirked at her. "*Were* you considering dating one?"

"Girl's gotta keep her options open, right?"

We traced the smell to a series of five small containers, each about the size of a five gallon gas can and fastened to the bulkhead in a cramped compartment just ahead of the ship's engineering section. Four were intact, but one had been punctured by a stray fragment, probably from one of our mass-driver rounds.

"I think they're pressurized sample containers. They're designed to contain a specific atmospheric environment, to keep things like medical and scientific samples pristine," Perry said.

That reek had intensified, from wince-inducing to eye-watering. "So that damaged one is leaking whatever atmosphere it contained. And you're *sure* this isn't hazardous, Perry?"

"Not in these concentrations, like I said. If you tried to breathe this mix of gasses at their regular pressure, then yeah, your lungs would basically melt. But at these levels, they just stink," Perry replied. "That's my scientific judgment. You're welcome."

We examined the intact containers, but they told us nothing. We opened the damaged one but found it only contained some organic sludge.

"Oxidizing atmospheres are actually extremely toxic for some species—as toxic as you'd find, say, chlorine," Perry said.

"You know, I'm having trouble imagining these Lowfangs as the scientific-enquiring types. Whatever these samples are, I'd be willing to bet they're not part of some noble quest to advance our understanding of the universe."

I nodded. "We need access to their computer archives, or what's left of them."

"Van, you're the resident hacker, but it might be more expedient if I did this," Perry said.

"Expedient is good. The less I have to breathe in this funk, the better. And while you're doing that, I'm putting my helmet back on."

15

THE LOWFANGS HADN'T EVEN TRIED to wipe their data stores. Perry was able to crack into them easily enough, then download their contents—which triggered his firewall several times.

"I swear, these morons have a museum of malware in there," he said, finally disconnecting from the data port. "There were viruses and things I haven't seen in years. Some of them brought back old memories."

"How wistful of you, Perry," I said.

"Didn't mean it wistfully. I mean that some of them literally triggered memories I haven't accessed in quite some time. Reminds me that I've got to think about purging some of that old stuff."

"Well, as you wandered down malware memory lane, did you find anything useful?"

"The vast majority of it is trash, or of no obvious value. We can hand it over to Guild intelligence, see if they can extract anything useful from it. I did glean a few potentially interesting tidbits, though. For one, this ship seems to be one of many registered through such a convoluted series of shell corporations and fronts that it makes a hedge maze look like a straight line. Unfortunately, most of it means nothing to me because none of these sundry mercantile houses, guilds, communes, corporate fronts, collectives, or co-ops have any presence in known space. It would be like taking Zeno to Earth and expecting her to be able to understand the Dow Jones 500."

"So that's a dead end."

"For now. But if we can start working out who's who in the zoo out there—*out there* being the region beyond what we've come to know as what is or was Puloquir space—then this information could prove very useful down the road."

Zeno stepped into the compartment, the grungy galley and crew habitat. "I can't find anything else of particular interest. The power plant's safely scrammed and the antimatter containment is sound, so we aren't going to blow up anytime soon."

"I'm good with not blowing up, thanks," I said, then turned back to Perry. "Anything else?"

"Yeah, two things. It's not definitive, but I think those sample containers back there might have something to do with that parasitic race your star-child friend Matterforge mentioned to you, the Tenants."

That made me frown. "Why would these lowlifes have anything to do with the Tenants?"

Perry raised his wings. "Hey, I'm just the messenger. I don't know. Maybe they were transporting them for someone else."

"Yeah, the idea of these guys carting around parasites—that sound you hear is my skin crawling," Zeno put in.

I nodded. "I thought the messenger was taller than you, but—never mind. You said two things, Perry. That's one."

"You're going to *love* this one. These scumbags have been to Earth. Well, maybe not these scumbags in particular, but based on what I've been able to discern here, some of Jacomir's spawn have been there."

I found myself bristling at that. There seemed to be an awful lot of aliens screwing around on my home planet, and it pissed me off.

"Where on Earth?" I asked.

"A place called Gettysburg."

"Gettysburg—Pennsylvania? As in, the battlefield?"

"That's what I thought for a nanosecond or so, but nope, not that Gettysburg. This would be Gettysburg, South Dakota."

"There's a Gettysburg in South Dakota?"

"And one in each of South Carolina and Ohio as well, yeah."

"Huh. Okay, so what the hell were these guys, or their brethren, or... or whoever doing in Gettysburg, South Dakota?"

"Something involving a cache of weapons left in the area when a Yonnox ship was forced down near or into a pond somewhere along State Road 107. Which is a good place to hide things, if you ask me. Most of the Upper Midwest is a good hiding place, because who's going to go there and look around?"

I crossed my arms. "Be flippant about it all you want, bird. But I'm starting to get the sense there's a lot of alien tech scattered around Earth, either put there deliberately or left there accidentally. Eventually, someone's going to stumble onto some of it. And can you imagine someone like Stalin having access to fusion technology or particle beams?"

"No, no, can't imagine that at all, Van."

I frowned. "You denied that awfully quickly, bird—"

"Anyway, Van, I'd recommend we haul all of this back to Anvil Dark and let the techs there sort it out. Especially those sample containers, which are going to have to be opened under tightly controlled conditions."

I nodded, and we prepared to head back to the *Fafnir*. As we waited for the airlock to cycle, I glanced down at Perry.

"The Soviets supposedly had a flying saucer, you know."

"Huh. Quite an… allegation."

WHEN WE RETURNED to the *Fafnir*, Torina and Icky had finished their interrogation of the Lowfangs. Unsurprisingly, it didn't offer much of use.

"They're either brilliant actors, consummate liars, or dumber than a bag of rocks. Maybe all three."

"I get the sense you're leaning toward the latter," I replied.

"Well, you go look into those dull, sullen eyes and tell me. They're mean, short-tempered, and stupid, and that's what they'd put on a dating profile."

"The lowlife apples don't fall far from the tree. Jacomir had a reputation as a moronic brute, too," Perry said. "One moment. Checking Tinder to see if their profiles are active. Ahh."

"You're joking, right? Please tell me these idiots are—"

Zeno coughed, getting our attention. "If I… find out… those mouth-breathing turd buckets are dating, while I'm single… there will be problems."

"It was a joke. Apologies, Zeno," Perry added hastily.

Zeno cast a baleful glare at him. "Carry on."

"Now that we know they're hopelessly single, can I assume you got nothing from them?" I asked.

Icky shrugged, rolling her massive shoulders with Gallic insouciance. "Just a bunch of bullshit about how they're the victims, persecuted by this—" She glanced at Torina. "What was that name again? Something Berti?"

"Belowasc Gerti," Torina confirmed, nodding, then turning to me. "Apparently also known as B, the same mysterious, traveling doctor who fixed your knee and delivered alien triplets—oh, yeah, and just happened to be nearby to save our asses with some advanced military hardware from Unity."

I smiled at the memory. "Okay, then. Well, I guess we need to decide on our next move—"

Torina held up a slim hand. "Wait a second, mister. There's an interstellar gulf of ignorance about this B character that I think you've actually crossed." She leveled her flat gaze on me. "Who the hell is she, Van? How is it that she keeps popping up? And why are these Lowfangs connected to her?"

I sighed and glanced at Perry. He lifted his wings, if barely.

"B is an agent for… another group, a very covert one. And that's really all I can say about it—firstly because I don't really *know* much more than that, and secondly because this group thrives on secrecy to do what they do. So the best I could give you is hearsay and conjecture, and I'd rather not do that."

"Van, I'm your Second. If something happens to you, I'm supposed to take over, right? But how do I take over things that I know nothing about?"

I opened my mouth, not sure how to proceed. But Perry intervened before I could start talking.

"Torina, can we have all the details of your family's banking information, including access codes and authorizations?" he asked.

"What? I—no. No, of course not."

"Why not? All that money would be really useful to us."

She gave a slow sigh. "Look—"

"Or could it be, Torina, that despite having access to your family's money, an obvious benefit to us, it could actually do more harm than good? Like, someone could steal it from us, or Icky could get captured and shaved down until she reveals it—"

"I swear, bird, I'm gonna use you for spare parts," Icky snapped.

Perry aimed a kiss-blowing sound at her, then turned back to Torina.

She, in turn, looked at me. "Van, do you genuinely believe it's better for us to not know this stuff?"

I gave her a level look. "For now, I do, yes. But when the time comes that I think you need to know it—which isn't going to happen until *I* learn more—I will fill you in. I'm asking for your trust, not simply because it's me, but because I've earned it."

She sighed again. "Okay, fine. So Jacomir was somehow connected with B—"

"They were involved," Perry said.

"Involved—? Oh, as in romantically, you mean?"

"For various definitions of the word *romantically*, sure."

"Okay, well, that actually explains a lot. They definitely have a grudge against this B, which they're extending to anyone *they've* linked to B in their tiny, evil brains," Torina said.

"Which raises another question. If everything about B and her secret organization is so… secret… then how the hell did these Lowfang clowns even know you and B were connected?" Zeno asked.

"An excellent question, and one I intend to pursue. In the meantime, though, we have a decision to make."

"Where to go first," Torina said.

"I know this seems cut-and-dried, but I have a suggestion, Van. You're Gerhardt's Justiciar. You should bring him up to speed on everything you've learned and get his input about how to proceed, even if it's *do what you think is best, Tudor*."

"It's a good point. Gerhardt's invested a lot of trust in you, Van. I think you'll want to make that investment worthwhile," Torina agreed.

"Okay, then. We'll go see Gerhardt, bringing him the gift of lowlife assholes," I said.

"Something like a cake might be better," Perry said drily.

"How about a bottle of twenty year old Scotch?" Icky asked, earning a round of stares from us.

"Do you *have* a bottle of twenty year old Scotch?" I asked her.

"Yeah. Remember that little tussle we got into at Spindrift, at that bar?"

Torina grinned. "You mean the one where you broke a table with a Gajur?"

"Yeah. I grabbed a bottle off a table to bash in a head or two but ended up keeping it 'cause I've heard you talk about how good the stuff is. Oh, and by the way? It's not. It tastes the way hatch sealant smells."

"You were going to use a fine bottle of liquor as a weapon? Icky, you are a barbarian," I said, then cocked my head at her. "Wait. Are you saying you cracked the bottle and tasted it?"

"Yeah."

I looked at Torina. "A used bottle of fine Scotch as a gift?"

She shrugged. "You have to admit, it's so *us*."

I SETTLED into the seat facing Gerhardt's desk, Perry to my right, Icky and Torina to my left. He'd waved us in when Max had ushered us into his office but was absorbed reading something on his desk terminal. We waited.

He finally turned to me. "It would seem that the intelligence you collected from the Lowfangs' ship is a bit of a treasure trove, Tudor." He nodded at the screen. "I just got a preliminary assessment from our Intelligence Director. She says that bits and pieces of it have already filled some gaping holes in our overall understanding of connections between known space and the region coreward of us, and that's after only a few hours of work."

"I'm glad it's useful, sir."

"More than useful. We've been looking for ways to deepen our understanding of how the underworld out there is linked to the underworld back here. Based on this, it's starting to sound like it's just one big underworld, and we're only seeing part of it."

"That's great, but is there anyone out there we can work with on this? The one local magistrate we dealt with—to the extent we could actually understand him at all—didn't seem even remotely interested in working with us."

Gerhardt shrugged. "A good question, and one that I can justify deploying some agents to explore, now that we have some hard connections to follow up." He tapped at the terminal, then gestured at it. "In the meantime, in your report, you note that these Lowfangs have had some sort of dealings back on your homeworld—"

He peered at the screen. "At Gettysburg, South Dakota. Does this have any significance for you, Tudor?"

"Well, they say about places like that you can watch your dog run away for three days."

"What?"

"It's flat."

"And that is significant how?"

"It—isn't. I was just—" I gave up and shrugged. "It's not important. Anyway, no, I've never been there, even though it's not all that far away from my home in Iowa. All I know is that it's a tiny little town of about twelve hundred people out on the great American flatlands. Oh, and that a Yonnox ship was either forced down or crashed there, and that the lowlife Lowfangs referred to it as a weapons cache. I find that intriguing."

Gerhardt nodded. "For obvious reasons, insofar as we don't like the idea of advanced weaponry lying around where just anyone can stumble on it. There's also the implications of them being the offspring of Jacomir, a well-known, albeit dead, miscreant. Why are these people interested in Earth?"

"That's what I'd like to find out. I have some contacts back on Earth who may be able to help."

Gerhardt pursed his lips, then nodded again. "Alright. Go back to Earth and find out what you can. But"—he leaned forward—"I am mindful of the fact Earth is your homeworld, and you'd reasonably feel protective about it. If you can't establish a clear connection between the Lowfangs and this potential weapons cache, and our Crimes Against Order case, I will need you to move on, Tudor. It must take priority."

"I understand. And, to be honest, I'm not at all convinced there really is any connection between that case and the Lowfangs. The Sorcerers are many things, but they're not stupid, and getting someone like them involved would probably cause more trouble than it would be worth."

Gerhardt actually uttered a rare laugh. "Lowfangs. It's not a name to really inspire fear, is it?"

"Fear of having your ankles bitten, maybe," Torina offered.

"I like having my ankles bitten. A courtship ritual isn't complete without it," Icky put in, matter-of-factly.

A thunderous silence fell over Gerhardt's office as we stared back at her, not sure where to take the conversation from here.

"That's kinda hot," Perry said into the quiet.

"I know, right?" Icky enthused.

After a long moment of recovery, I finally spoke up.

"Um, given that we've had firsthand experience with translation lately, Icky—just to be clear, what do you think the word *ankles* refers to?"

She lifted a foot at least five sizes bigger than mine and pointed. "Right there, duh. Don't be weird with your people-sex stuff, Van. It's uncivilized."

OUR RETURN to Earth was blissfully uneventful. We detoured via the *Iowa*, just to check up on her, and found everything in order.

Then we pushed on, staying in high orbit until night fell over Iowa. At about 2 a.m. local time, we grounded the *Fafnir* in the barn and sent a message to Tony Burgess that we needed to speak with him. I assumed he'd reply in the morning, since it was the wee hours in Wisconsin as well. But the comm chimed with an incoming call from him while I was still walking from the barn to the house.

"Tony? I didn't expect you to call right back."

"Are you kidding? I get a call from a guy from outer space, I answer it, regardless of the time. What's up?"

I explained the situation to him as I unlocked and stepped into the farmhouse. Perry had already flown around it, scanning, alert for trouble, but he detected nothing out of the ordinary. I started to wonder if we were being *too* skittish, but I glanced toward the cornfields, remembered the Fade shuttles descending, and decided we weren't.

"Yeah, okay—Gettysburg, South Dakota, have there been any UFO incidents there or in the area, got it. I'll do some digging and get back to you as soon as I—"

"Tony, in the morning would be fine."

"What, I'm just going to drift back to sleep after this? Again—a call from a space guy, remember?"

"Space *policeman*," Perry put in. "He prefers Space *policeman*."

———

WE DIDN'T HAVE to use the *Fafnir* to retrieve Tony Burgess from Wisconsin, but sent her workboat instead. We still hadn't named the little craft, which was becoming a point of contention among the crew. The workboat seemed a little flat, but we couldn't seem to reach any consensus about what we *should* name it.

"I still like *Worky McWorkface*," Icky said as we lifted, but I shut her down.

"I wish I'd never told you about that. No, we are not going to name this workboat *Worky McWorkface*."

"But—"

"No."

"Aw."

We flew on toward Wisconsin. I'd brought Torina and Icky, the latter against my better judgment, because if something went wrong —well, because Icky would be part of it. But we'd been having problems with the workboat's drive, and the last thing I wanted was to get stuck somewhere because we were broken down. Sure, Netty could come rescue us with the *Fafnir*, but the more we flew these ships along any profile that wasn't essentially straight up to or down from orbit, the more we risked being spotted. And I couldn't help thinking that there might be parties on Earth actually keeping an eye out for us.

We met Tony at our usual spot, near the lake outside Appleton. His two UFO-logist cohorts were with him—Marla, spookily intelligent and utterly humorless, and Myron, who believed the "gubmint" was behind everyone, everything, and every rock. They'd spent the night digging into their voluminous files, most of which were filled with crazy, for nuggets of actual information related in any way to Gettysburg, South Dakota.

Tony handed over his tablet. "We found—"

"Three incidents in 1983, two CE One in April and a CE Two in May," Myron said, with grave authority.

I looked from him to Tony. "CE?"

"Close encounter," Tony said.

"With aliens," Myron added.

I nodded. "Yeah, I figured that. So, like that movie *Close Encounters of the Third Kind*—?"

"Pfft, that was nothing but gubmint propaganda, trying to make aliens look all mysterious and benevolent," Myron groused. "Good lighting, though. I did like the purple and pink. Kinda disco."

Tony stuck his hands in the pockets of his combat jacket. "Myron believes that aliens exercise control through a shadow government—"

"That we call the Illuminati, but it's really a cabal of aliens who've replaced the head of every central bank around the world with either clones or androids, and that's how they control it all," Myron cut in again, then gave me a defiant look. "Go ahead, deny it."

"Uh—well, the aliens I know do not have their shit anywhere near enough together to pull something like that off." I curled my lip. "The heads of central banks? Really? Not presidents and prime ministers and such?"

"Oh, please, they have no power. It's the central banks that call the shots. The CEOs of large corporations, too. And billionaires. Everyone worth more than a billion dollars is an alien plant. I mean… it's obvious, how can people not *see* it?"

I stared at him for a moment, then nodded. "Okay, then. So back to"—I was going to say reality but caught myself—"to the matter at hand. What's a CE 1 or a CE 2?"

Marla answered, her voice flat and more mechanical than Netty's.

"CE 1, a person sees a UFO within 150 meters. CE2, an encounter with a UFO in the sky or on the ground leaves physical evidence such as scorch marks or indentations on the ground, hard radar returns, and so on. CE 3, the encounter reveals visible occupants inside the craft. CE 4, the encounter involves an abduction of a human with experiments being performed on said human inside the spacecraft. CE 5, the encounter involves direct communication between aliens and human observers."

Torina grinned. "So this meeting is all of those, except for a CE 4?"

Icky leaned in. "We could take care of that with some probing," she leered, and Myron stepped back a pace. Tony looked nervous. As for Marla—

She looked… intrigued.

So, not humorless, then, Perry told me in my ear bug.

I shot Icky—and Perry—a glare to head off any further discussions of probing. "Anyway"—I turned back to Tony and his 'Truly Aware' compatriots—"what happened in 1983? The thumbnail version, thanks. We'll take a copy of this stuff, too," I said, nodding at Tony's tablet, then handing it to Icky. She extracted a data slate and worked to get the two devices paired up to upload their information.

Myron gave me a wary look, then pointed at Icky. "That's not going to—"

"*She's* not going to do anything, no," I said. "Trust me, Myron, we have no interest in probing you." I frowned as my thoughts briefly touched on the idea, then recoiled like bare flesh from a hot stove. "Seriously. *No* interest. Really."

I turned back to Tony. "Anyway, back to 1983—"

"Yeah, there were two sightings of lights. One early in the month, just lights hovering around a small lake. A short time later, a second sighting, only this time there were flashes, and noises like thunder. And then, in early May, some kids discovered burn marks where the grass wasn't growing back in, same area," he said.

I glanced at Torina. "What do you think?"

"Sounds like a fight. A raiding party, maybe, after something that was already there, like that mysterious weapons cache mentioned in the Lowfangs' data?"

"Or maybe the weapons cache was a result of the fight—something was hidden in that lake, or crashed in it," Icky suggested.

I nodded. "Well, whatever it is, there's only one way to find out the truth. I guess we're taking a trip to scenic Gettysburg, South Dakota."

"I have one request," Torina said. "We don't drive."

I hesitated. I'd actually been considering driving, just Torina, Perry, and me. I figured it was about an eight hour trip, but again, the less use we made of the ships, the less likely we were to be discovered. If we really needed the *Fafnir* in Gettysburg, Netty could have it there in minutes. But sixteen hours of round-trip driving *was* an awful lot.

And sixteen hours on the road in the upper midwest was only surpassed, in boredom, by driving across Kansas. In any direction. For any amount of time longer than thirty minutes.

Tony gave me a wide-eyed look of disbelief. "Why would you drive? Hell, if I had something like your ship, I'd fly it everywhere!"

"Might be a little impractical to go grocery shopping. But yeah, I think driving is probably out."

We thanked Tony and his co-conspirators for their help, but we couldn't disengage until I'd promised them another flight in the *Fafnir*, this time to somewhere beyond the Moon. I reluctantly agreed, thinking we could take them for a flight out to the *Iowa*. I put them off this time, though, blaming a tight schedule.

We lifted, spun the workboat around, and accelerated back toward the farm in Iowa. It wasn't a very long flight, even at subsonic speed—we avoided supersonic travel as much as we could, at least in the lower atmosphere, because even the best tech couldn't conceal the boom of shockwave-displaced air. A line of thunderstorms over the Wisconsin Dells necessitated a detour south, but I didn't otherwise expect any trouble—

Until we were passing over I-90, north of Madison, Wisconsin.

"Uh, Van? We've just been lit up," Torina said.

I tensed, ready to fling the workboat into evasive maneuvers and call Netty for help. But Torina stopped me.

"They're not targeting scanners. Not conventional ones, anyway." She peered at the copilot's display. "It's a radio-frequency signal, coming from directly astern."

I switched the master display to a rearward view. It resolved two small objects closing on us. When I zoomed in, I instantly recognized the shapes.

"Shit. Those are F-16's, jet fighters. Probably Wisconsin Air National Guard. You're detecting their radar emissions."

"Radar. How quaint." She shrugged. "But they won't get any returns from us, so—"

"Uh, actually, that's not quite true," Icky said, from her seat in the back of the workboat's cockpit.

I gave her a hard look. "What do you mean, not quite true?"

"Well, this tub's still got some problems we haven't had the time to properly fix."

"The drive, yes. Or are you about to tell me the cloaking system isn't working, either?"

"It's working fine—or it was, anyway, up until a few minutes ago."

"So they can *see* us?"

Icky glanced up from her rudimentary engineering panel. "This is what we get for buying a refurbished workboat. Remember how I said, *hey, let's buy new*, and you guys were all, *nah, that's too expensive, let's just get something*—"

"Okay, I get it."

"You get what you pay for, Van."

"Again, I get it. No more coupons or second hand ships." I glanced at the workboat's stripped-down version of a tactical over-lay. The two F-16's were fourteen klicks back but closing fast.

I considered our options. If we just flew on to the farm, we'd give away the whole show. Without the stealth tech that normally concealed us from Earthly sensors working, we could be tracked no matter where else we went—including into orbit. We needed some-where we could truly hide so we could fix the stealth—assuming it *could* be fixed—and only then head back to the farm.

"Van, are they likely to fire at us?" Torina asked. I noticed her fingers hovering near the weapons panel. The workboat only mounted a pair of lasers in a single battery, and relatively low-power ones at that. They'd be more than enough to blast two F-16's out of the sky, but that was the last thing I wanted to do. These two pilots were just doing their job, investigating an unexplained contact in Wisconsin airspace.

I shook my head. "Probably not, at least until they get a good look and try to encourage us to land. But if we don't, then—"

I zoomed out the overlay, looking for inspiration. I found it almost immediately and wheeled the workboat through a hard left turn. The F-16s accelerated to supersonic speed, aiming to cut us off as we turned. The only way to avoid it was pouring on thrust and going supersonic ourselves, which meant we'd be rattling windows in Madison as we swept overhead.

"Uh, Van, where are we going?" Torina asked.

"For a swim."

16

Icky pointed out the canopy. "What's that over there?"

"It's called Milwaukee," I said.

"Oh—and that, over there? Those big towers."

"It's called Chicago."

A moment of silence, then, "What's that—?"

"Icky, please, just look at the map."

We now had four pursuers. A pair of A-10 Thunderbolts from the Indiana Air National Guard had joined in the fun, and although not exactly a high-performance aircraft, their mere presence off to our south and east precluded us from going that way. Even worse, another pair of Wisconsin F-16s were now inbound. If an F35 showed up, we'd have a regular family reunion.

I put the workboat into a shallow dive, aiming for Lake Michigan along a course that would pass roughly midway between the Wisconsin towns of Racine and Kenosha.

"Icky, tell me again that this workboat will work fine submerged in water."

"It's airtight, Van, it'll be fine. Well, as long as we don't go too deep."

"Could the—what did you call them? The National Guard? Could they have submersible craft of their own in—Lake Michigan, right?" Torina asked.

"Well, Myron probably thinks they do, but no. To the best of my knowledge, the US doesn't keep submarines prowling the Great Lakes. The only threat would be Canada, and they're too polite to want to invade us."

Perry spoke up, doing his best Canadian accent. "Sorry, eh. We have to invade."

"Darned nice people. Don't think they'll invade," I quipped, watching the scans.

"They might if they keep losing the Stanley Cup to teams in the USA," Perry deadpanned.

We raced toward the shoreline. The F-16's—four of them now, in two pairs—tried just as fast to keep up. I had no doubt they were collecting radar and maybe visual imagery the whole way. Of course, there could also be a gazillion phones on the ground recording us as we swept overhead. No matter how we did this, it was going to very definitely be a thing.

"Perry, have you guys heard anything yet?" I asked.

His voice hummed out of the comm. "Not yet. I could ping the media if you'd like, though."

"No thanks."

"Oh, in case you're interested, in 1994, hundreds of people saw some UFOs over Lake Michigan, but on the other side, around Grand Rapids, Michigan."

"Okay, and?"

"And, well—nothing, really. I did say in case you were interested."

"I wonder who they were," Torina said.

"Probably some hapless aliens with wonky tech whose bones might be waiting for us down there," I murmured, my eyes boring into the screens as I urged the workboat on.

We flashed over the shoreline. The two closest F-16s were only ten klicks behind us. The A-10s weren't much further away, only fourteen klicks to the south.

"Icky, maximum safe velocity to enter the water?" I asked.

"A lot less than this."

"Can you be a *little* more specific?"

"Uh—" She paused a moment, thinking. "I'd say no more than twenty meters per second or so."

"Noted. Brace for impact."

I applied reverse thrust, decelerating the workboat hard, all the while practically praying that the drive didn't just cut out. Assuming we survived the impact, the ensuing rescue would definitely lead to some awkward questions.

I watched the display. "Perry, we enter Lake Michigan in about twenty seconds. I doubt we'll have contact again until we reemerge. If you don't hear from us by midnight, come looking."

"You got it, boss."

The water loomed close. The two F-16s on our tail shot past overhead, unable to decelerate as fast as we could. At the last second, I slammed the workboat into full reverse thrust, angled it down, then cut the drive and dove into the depths of Lake Michigan.

The water closed over us like a thunderclap, and in the following silence, I heard Torina exhale, long and slow.

"Yeah," I said, then felt her hand in mine, and she squeezed my fingers. We said nothing as silvery streams of bubbles raced away and the lake wrapped us up in our descent, the daylight fading to rust in seconds.

WE ENDED up sitting on the bottom of the lake, at just under a hundred meters depth, for nearly four hours while Icky worked through the problem with the stealth system. I was glad we'd brought her, considering how long it took. Torina and I would have struggled with the workboat's schematics and *still* probably not managed to fix it.

Once she brought the system back online, we lifted and flew on thrusters only for another four hours, heading generally north and east, toward the middle of the lake. I assumed that the area where we'd disappeared would be being watched and didn't want to just resume the show if Icky's repairs didn't hold up.

"This is scenic. Sort of like being in a car wash that's four hundred miles long," Torina said, staring at the spray flecking our front view.

"No rainbow colored soap. Bit disappointing," I replied, waving my hand at the iron gray water droplets dotting our image.

"This lake doesn't look friendly," Icky observed.

"Because it's not. And it's not really a lake. It's more like an ocean, at least in temper. Some howlers come across here. I'm sure the bottom is a popular place for wrecks," I said.

Netty chimed in, "More than you know. We're getting returns every few miles, and the style of craft spans several centuries. We just passed a forty-two foot pleasure craft, stuck bow first in the bottom. I'm guessing she went down in the past two years."

I grimaced. "Like I said, a lot more violent than a pond. Okay, kids, we're about—there we go. Lifting out now. All I see is commercial aircraft. We're good."

The workboat emerged over the Wisconsin shoreline north of Milwaukee, then we kept heading northwest until we'd nearly reached Eau Claire, before turning due south toward Pony Hollow and the farm. It took us a long way out of our way, but it struck me as prudent to not follow the same route we'd tried earlier in the day. I finally grounded the workboat behind the barn, cut the power and sank back in my seat.

"Honey, we're home," I said.

We dismounted, leaving Netty to lift the *Fafnir* and retrieve and stow the workboat once it was fully dark. I headed straight to the kitchen and a couple of shots of bourbon.

"Well, that was way more complicated than it needed to be," Perry said as I plunked myself down in the living room.

"Tell me about it. I had visions of getting stuck on the bottom of Lake Michigan," I said, letting my head loll back and closing my eyes. But I sighed and opened them again.

"How much press did we get?"

Perry shrugged. "Surprisingly little. And Tony and his friends helped cover for you by immediately and very publicly insisting that it was all a government cover-up. He even got quoted on CNN. Remind me to tell him thanks for the cover. Are we all set to head off to Gettysburg?"

I closed my eyes again. "Tomorrow. I've had enough Close Encounters of *any* kind for one day."

WE FLEW a spiral pattern centered on Gettysburg, scanning the ground beneath us for anything that hinted at extra-terrestrial origin or even just seemed anomalous. We got a hit just east of State Road 107, about six and a half klicks southwest of the town, roughly midway between two small ponds on either side of the road.

Once we'd confirmed it wasn't just a scanner ghost, we grounded the *Fafnir* in the closest decent cover we could find, another shallow pond about two klicks from the anomaly. We were in a patch of low ground and surrounded by a stand of poplars. It wasn't *much* in the way of cover, but it was the best we were going to do in what was otherwise billiard table-flat countryside. This time, we left Icky with the *Fafnir*. Zeno was more of a human size and could easily pass as one, at least from a distance.

I checked myself over. I'd strapped on The Drop and the Moonsword, as well as a couple of water canisters, a first-aid pack, and a small, portable ground sensor. I wore my b-suit, with my coat over top. Torina and Zeno had donned the b-suits as well and also sported long weapons—Torina had her coil gun and a goo gun, while Zeno lugged both a boarding shotgun and a second goo gun. It wasn't likely we'd run into anyone as we snuck across fields of sorghum and canola through the gathering darkness, but I wanted to be prepared just in case. At worst, between The Drop's stun function and the two goo guns, we should be able to do a non-lethal takedown on anyone with whom we *did* happen to run afoul.

Once we were all satisfied we were ready, I turned to Perry. "Okay, bird. Fly and be free," I said with a dramatic wave.

"Freeeeeedommmm!" he said, flinging himself skyward to take up his top-cover position. It was times like this that I appreciated the fact he looked, from any distance, like nothing but a bird, a big raven or a raptor. Having his keen awareness watching out while we crept among crops made me feel a lot more secure.

"What a perfect end of the day," Torina said as we broke out of the trees and into the full splendor of a vista that was literally mostly sky. The sun glared red through stacks of clouds on the horizon, some piling into thunderheads. We'd checked the weather, and although there was nothing but a chance of rain in the forecast, I asked Netty to keep on top of it. I was a kid of the prairies, so I knew how quickly *a chance of rain* could become *damaging storms, large hail, and tornadoes* at this time of year.

"So all this stuff is edible?" Zeno asked as we pushed our way into a field of canola.

"Not as-is, but yeah, these crops are all grown for food of some sort or another," I replied.

"And it goes on and on in every direction for such huge distances. We have to work hard at cultivating any fertile land on Helso," Torina said, pushing aside canola. "Here on Earth, it just seems to be all around us. What a bounty."

"That's the plains. Or some of them," I said, choosing a path forward.

Torina and Zeno kept up a running chatter as we picked our way through the fields. I stopped them when I finally recovered the anomalous signal with the ground scanner. By then, the sun had set, leaving only a roseate smear, horizontal and fading fast.

I winced at the thin whine of mosquitoes and waved them away —a pointless effort since they just flew right back in. They tormented Torina as well but seemed to have no interest in Zeno whatsoever.

I waved my hand again, studying the scanner's display. "Okay, two hundred meters straight ahead of us. Perry, can you see anything?"

"Wheat, sorghum, wheat, canola, wheat—did I mention wheat?"

I aimed my mouth at the vox pickup and pointedly sighed.

"Sorry, boss. Nope, there's nothing down there, be it visible, near UV, or even into the mid-infrared. Well, aside from you guys, of course. You stick out. Quite a lively image."

"I can live with that if there's no one out here," I replied, then turned to Torina and Zeno. Despite Perry's lack of anything definitive, we couldn't rule out tech that might be stealthed and happened to be at ambient temperature. We decided to split up and approach the anomaly abreast, weapons ready, spaced about ten meters apart. Torina and Zeno accordingly moved left and right, then gave quick whispers over the comm when they were ready.

"Okay, let's go," I said, and we started creeping forward, an unspoken shift in our movement taking hold. It was showtime.

I gripped The Drop in my right hand while keeping the scanner in my left, watching its display. The signal, weak and sporadic, slowly got closer. I stopped us at one hundred meters, again at fifty, and once more at twenty-five, just to take a moment to watch and listen. Aside from a fitful night breeze and the pervasive whine of the damned mosquitoes, though, we heard nothing. We were alone with the prairie.

And three hundred million mosquitoes.

"You guys hold about ten meters back. I'm taking a look," I said, and we resumed our way forward.

I crouched as I covered the last ten meters or so, The Drop raised. Still nothing. Steeling myself, I pushed on and walked until I was on top of the anomaly.

There was… nothing.

I sighed. "Whatever it is, it must be buried—" I started, but cut it off with a yelp as the bottom fell out of the world and I plunged into blackness.

BUT NOT VERY FAR. I ended up with my head at ground level, staring at sorghum stalks from less than a meter away.

"Van! Are you okay—?" Torina said, her tone wavering as she ran toward me.

"Yeah, I'm fine. You're not gonna believe this, but I found a hole."

Two shapes appeared against the sky, towering over me.

"Hi. Catching my breath. Bit of an *oof*," I said, looking up at them.

Zeno crouched down. "This seems to be a false cover—a platform made of some sort of wood, covered with earth."

I nodded. "Yeah. Not sure why they decided to go with wood, since it, you know"—I plucked off a handful of soft splinters—"rots."

"Wood has the advantage of not being easily detected. Metal might create a magnetic or electrical conductivity anomaly that could give away the show," Perry suggested. "I'm getting a vibe that this is intentional."

"A *vibe*?" I asked.

"Yes. Vibe. I'm not ready to use the term *resonance* because it's a bit——"

"Crunchy, even for you?"

"Crunchy, that's it," Perry agreed.

"Are we talking about food, or subterfuge?" Zeno asked.

"Subterfuge. Crunchy and food in the same sentence introduce the possibility of peanut butter with gravel in it, which is an abomination," I said, as Zeno and Torina helped me out of the hole. I then knelt, pulled out my flashlight, and shone it into the space beneath.

Zeno grunted, then propped me up. "Crunchy peanut butter is just… peanutty."

"And as an American, I demand more convenience in my food. Thank you for your concern."

Zeno exhaled. "Lazy, but right. Hmph. What do you see down there?"

"Um… there are stairs under here—more wood, and not in very good shape. And they seem to go down to——"

I pushed my head further into the hole. "A door. So there's a buried room or something down here. I'm liking the mystery, if not the angle to get in."

Zeno stepped around me, knelt, then grabbed something and gave an experimental tug. The wooden platform I'd broken through moved. Together, we were able to heave it up and off of the opening it concealed, revealing the stairs that descended about four meters to another door, this one of heavy wood reinforced by strips of some dull alloy.

"Well, that's ominous," Torina said,

I nodded. "Yeah, it is." I touched my comm. "Perry, we need you."

"Of course you do," he said, landing beside the opening. "Hey, you found a hole."

"How good are you at finding booby traps and things?"

"One hundred percent, but I assume you mean *without* setting them off."

"That'd be nice, yeah."

We waited while Perry scanned and investigated the stairs and the door. He discovered a microswitch concealed beneath the bottom edge of the door—which would open when the door did, breaking the circuit. It was small, subtle, and well-placed.

"A trap or an alarm, or both," Zeno suggested.

Once we knew about it, disarming it was easy—just slide something under the door and keep pressure on it while opening it. There was even a small notch on the bottom of the door that corresponded to the switch's location, probably for that very purpose. It left me seething.

"Bastards. There are twelve hundred people living a few klicks that way, in Gettysburg, and hundreds more in the surrounding area, on farms. If any of them had stumbled on this—if some *kids* had stumbled on this—"

Torina's eyes glittered like flint in the night gloom. "And who, finding a mysterious door in the ground, could resist opening it, yeah. *Bastards* is right. Van, this—cache, or whatever—is a crime in itself."

"It is."

"We're not going to let it go if we find out—"

"Who put people at risk? Hell, no."

She touched my arm, a brilliant smile lighting her face. "Good."

We opened the door and found a small concrete room about three-by-three meters. Wooden shelves lined the walls and were packed with boxes, cases, cylinders—containers, dozens of them. Zeno, Perry, and I spent a few minutes investigating, while Torina crouched at the top of the stairs keeping watch.

"Memory cores over here," Zeno said, peering into a square wooden crate.

"Yeah, power cells, probably for coil guns, down here," Perry added.

I opened a flat case and nodded. "And here are three coil guns to put them in. Heluva kick on these, too. Look to be almost armor-piercing, not just anti-personnel."

"That's a weapon of war," Perry observed. "These aren't really off-the-rack, if you know what I mean."

I raised a brow. "That they're—what *do* you mean? These are from a state entity? Stolen?"

Perry pointed a wing at the bounty ahead of us. "Sure as hell didn't get them at WalMart."

Torina *tsked*. "Statistically, they would have come from a Dollar General. Lots more of them."

"If I see a Dollar General in space, I'll know we're not in space. We're in Tennessee," I said. "Okay, this is a *lot* of firepower."

It was a trove of small arms and equipment, including weapons, their power cells and ammo, data cores and slates, portable comms and hand scanners, and a large case that contained a brutish, shoulder-launched weapon that resembled an American Javelin anti-tank missile. Zeno identified it as an Eridani military weapon, a surface-to-orbit missile called a Reach. A separate case held five of its missiles.

I moved to the middle of the room and turned around, taking it all in. "There must be—shit, hundreds of thousands of bonds worth of gear here."

"That Reach is three hundred and fifty thousand on its own, plus another hundred for each of those missiles," Zeno put in.

"Okay, so probably more like a million bonds of advanced tech and weaponry, stashed in a hole in the ground in South Dakota, with nothing but some dirt and a booby-trapped wooden door preventing anyone from coming along and screwing around with it," I said.

I tried to imagine some farm kids finding this stuff, pawing through this gear—assuming that the door didn't blow them up, that is. Or some criminals getting wind of it and getting their grubby hands on those coilguns. Or the government finding that surface to *orbital* missile launcher. And who knew what was on these data cores and slates?

And were there any more caches like this scattered around the country? The world? Were there vaults like this one in Afghanistan, say? Somalia? What sort of horrors could terrorists unleash with stuff like this?

"Needless to say, we're seizing every bit of this. There's way too much to lug back to the *Fafnir* on foot, even if we did a half-dozen trips. We're going to have to risk bringing her here." I checked the time. We still had a good six hours of darkness left, which should be plenty—

"Van, a sporadic contact just came on passive scanners to your southwest, ten klicks and closing fast," Netty cut in. "*Very* fast. Not a casual visit."

I snapped out a curse and led Zeno and Perry back up the stairs. We looked to the southwest, saw nothing—then saw a dark shape that quickly grew, and that was all I needed to see.

"Everyone, back down into the hole!" I barked.

Zeno hurried back down the stairs, Torina and Perry right behind her. "Netty—" I started, about to tell her and Icky to lift and prepare to engage whatever the hell was coming but caught myself. Did I really want to give the good citizens of Gettysburg and environs a late-night battle between two spacecraft in the sky over their town? We hadn't even yet seen what fallout might come from our desperate race across Wisconsin and into Lake Michigan aboard the workboat. I'd be happy to knock that off the front page, but an alien space battle over South Dakota wasn't how I wanted to do it.

I dove down the stairs, then turned back, The Drop raised and pointed back up them.

A few seconds passed, then something swept overhead with a rush displaced air and the unmistakable rumble and whine of thrusters.

Then... nothing.

I crept back up to the top of the stairs. As soon as I did, something slammed into the ground a few centimeters to my right, showering me with dirt. I looked up and saw more dark shapes silhouetted against the stars. Not ships this time, but figures descending on triangular parachutes of some sort.

That was all I had time to take in before I was engulfed in a fusillade of gunfire.

I YELLED for the others to come back to the surface, taking two hits as I did. My b-suit stopped them both, but I was going to have some nasty bruises.

"Take them out before they land! They get down in these crops, this'll get a lot harder!" I snapped, then dodged to one side of the hole, raised The Drop, and fired. I wished I'd brought a long gun but was stuck with the big sidearm and tried to make the best of it. Torina and Zeno had coil guns and now took up fire positions. Like a lethal metronome, they both began snapping out methodical shots.

In seconds, I was embroiled in one of the most intense firefights I've had the pleasure of attending. The descending figures poured automatic fire down at us, beating the earth with a hail of rounds that churned dirt and debris like we were rearranging the landscape.

Zeno stood, aimed, and fired, and was rewarded with a hideous scream that will never leave my memory.

"I'd say that's one down," I muttered as Torina drew aim and fired twice. She grunted in pain as a round slammed into her side, spinning her with a cry.

My rage bloomed, dark and poisonous. Torina recovered, took a knee, and began firing again even as my second shot took an invader in the skull—the wet snap that followed was satisfying and grotesque.

Perry turned into an angel of vengeance, shredding one of the parachutes and sending the wearer earthward so fast they didn't have time to scream. In blazing succession, Torina and Zeno were both hit—again—then I took a pair of rounds on my b-suit before every descending chute was close enough to hit without long guns.

"Finally," I said as our collective hail of fire began to punch into each target. Torina and Zeno fired in unison, and our opponents went limp in their harnesses. One abruptly wheeled his chute back toward the southwest at a height of maybe a hundred meters, but he must have caught a favorable night breeze and swept off in that direction, gaining velocity as he went. By the time I lost sight of him, he was hundreds of meters away.

The other four all landed nearby with heavy thuds, either dead or dying. The fact that they might be alive was… unacceptable.

I spoke in a level tone. "Shoot to kill. Center mass past forty meters, headshots in close. Leave no doubt."

I drew down on a target and put two rounds in him, sending a mist into the night. With a strangled, wet cry, I heard him *thump* into the earth, but I was already moving toward the next fighter, who was struggling against the ropes of his chute.

His struggle ended suddenly when Torina's sidearm cracked with grotesque finality.

"Dead," she said, her eyes hooded and mournful.

I looked over her shoulder at the mess. "I'd say so."

Wincing and limping from our various impact wounds, we retrieved the bodies and their chutes, then unceremoniously dragged them back to the hole, down the stairs, and dumped them in the hidden room. It took us twenty minutes of sweaty, gasping exertion, while Perry was back in the air keeping watch. With every step, I expected the unknown ship to reappear and douse us with point-defense fire. I was glad for Icky and Netty to lift the *Fafnir* to a few thousand meters and orbit over the top of us, giving us further security. But if that ship did come back, and we did destroy it, we'd have no chance of doing anything about the wreckage.

When we'd dumped the last body, I pulled back and sucked down about a gallon of water. Torina yanked off one of our attacker's helmets.

It revealed the face of another of Jacomir's evil brood.

"How many of these assholes did that guy spawn?" Zeno asked, one arm dangling limply at her side.

"Too many," I snapped, putting away my water. "We've got to move. Icky, come on down here. We need to load all of this stuff onto the *Fafnir*, then get the hell gone. All due respect to the law enforcement around here, but I hope they take the night off."

A few moments later the *Fafnir* descended with smooth efficiency, disgorging Icky to stare, wide-eyed, at the carnage we'd created.

Despite being a blue simian-esque alien with all the femininity of barbed wire, she managed a fairly good pout. "You never let me have fun."

I pointed to a corpse. "That... was not fun."

Icky sniffed. "For you."

I tilted my head. "Fair. Now that we've discussed our feelings, you ready to lift?"

She flexed all four arms, smiling. "Ready, boss. What am I taking aboard?"

I smiled up at her, wiping sweat from my eyes. "I'll help. Let's start with the things that go *boom*."

WE *ALMOST* MADE IT. With Icky and Waldo able to lend a whole bunch of powerful hands, we were able to load the contents of the vault into the *Fafnir* in less than fifteen minutes. I contemplated just leaving the bodies here but immediately dismissed the thought—they had to come with us too, along with all their gear, which included their bulky chutes. And looking at their chutes reminded me of the one that had sailed off to the southwest.

I looked that way. "Damn. Okay, we've got to go hunting—"

"Uh, Van? Turn around," Torina said.

I did, right into twinned flares of LCD glare. Headlights. A vehicle was approaching along a rough dirt track that passed about fifty meters south of the bunker. The lights wobbled as it bounced over the uneven ground, giving us maybe a minute before it got here. It wasn't enough time to get the last two bodies loaded aboard the *Fafnir*.

My mind raced. I could think of only one way to deal with this, though.

"Okay, everyone on the ship, then close it up. I'll handle this."

The others knew better than to argue. This was my homeworld, and these were my people. If we had any chance of avoiding something tragic, I had to be the one to engineer it.

I clasped my hands behind my back, keeping The Drop concealed. I'd already set its underslung beam emitter to the maximum safest stun setting. I had a faint hope that I might be able to talk my way out of this—*see, officer, I was doing some night time skydiving with some friends, and I got separated from them. Yes, I'm telling the truth, and this really* isn't *the thinnest coating of bullshit scraped over yet more bullshit you've ever seen—*

The vehicle was a white SUV with no obvious police markings, so just some curious civilian, then? It slowed, then turned off the track to direct the glare of its headlights squarely onto me. I jammed one eye closed to protect my night vision, squeezed The Drop in a death grip, and waited.

The passenger door opened. A pause, then something flopped out of it and thumped into the dirt. It was a body.

Shit. This was already taking a wildly unexpected turn. Without even thinking about it, I pulled The Drop from behind my back. Before I could raise it, though, the driver's door opened and a voice called out.

"I think I found something you lost."

It was a woman's voice, strikingly resonant and melodious. A tall figure stepped out of the SUV and around the open door, then walked toward me. I could see both of her hands, held out to her sides. She stepped out of the direct glare of the headlights, surrendering the advantage of having them glaring into my eyes. As she did, spillover light caught and illuminated her.

Three things triggered my senses, and all at once.

First, she was indeed tall—probably a little taller than me, in fact —of middle years, potentially anywhere from forty to sixty.

Second, she was wearing a black leather jacket and denim trousers, but beneath that was what I could swear was a b-suit.

And third, I knew her. I had a picture of her in the *Fafnir*, in fact, one taken at the farm decades ago with my grandfather, with Perry photobombing in one corner.

It was Valint. My grandmother.

She smiled.

"Hello, grandson of mine. We've got a lot to discuss."

17

DAMNED right we had a lot to discuss, starting with, *where the hell have you been all my life, Gram?*

But we weren't going to have that conversation in a sorghum field in South Dakota only minutes after a firefight that saw five aliens killed. Valint uploaded a set of nav data to my data slate, then climbed back into her SUV.

"Meet me there, as soon as you can," she said and drove back up the dirt track the way she'd come.

Stunned, I managed to say, "Okay."

And that was that. I just stood, gaping at the two red taillights bouncing away.

"Van?"

I turned. Torina stood beside me with her coil gun ready. Perry landed on the ground in front of me.

"Perry says that was… your grandmother," Torina said.

"Yeah."

"Are you okay?"

"I—" I started but wasn't sure where to go with that sentence, so I just shook my head.

"Let's just get the hell out of here before anyone else shows," I said, then headed back to the *Fafnir*.

"Van, I had no idea she was even still alive," Perry said.

I turned and looked back and down at his amber eyes. I actually believed him. Even if he had 'known' she was alive, it could have been trapped behind a memory lock and simply inaccessible to him. So I just nodded.

"I believe you, Perry. Now, let's go."

AFTER LOADING the last body aboard the *Fafnir* and doing her best to cover the vault, Icky boarded.

Into the night, we lifted. I saw a trio of vehicles racing down State Road 107 toward the turnoff into the fields, but we didn't bother waiting around to see what they did. If they *did* investigate the scene of the fight, I had no doubt they'd find the hidden vault, but that's all they'd find. We'd emptied it of its contents, meaning they'd be faced with a small, buried concrete room. And that, I suspected, would lead to thoughts of survivalists and old Cold War-era fallout shelters. It would be another mystery that would probably eventually find its way into the conspiratorial archives of the Truly Aware.

Speaking of whom—

An email from Tony Burgess was waiting for me when we arrived back at the farm, saying we needed to talk. It was just shy of

6 a.m., and although I felt like I'd run a marathon—and been hit by a speeding truck right before the end of it—I called him on the secure video connection I'd given him. Only I could initiate calls on it. It was as encrypted as I could manage without requiring alien tech at his end, and since it originated from the *Fafnir*, it should be untraceable by any Earthly agent.

He answered immediately.

"Van. Holy shit. The UFO world has been blowing up."

"Let me guess—an alien spacecraft was tracked across Wisconsin, before vanishing into Lake Michigan."

"With about a hundred thousand images posted to social media, yeah. What happened?"

I offered a tired shrug. "Even outer space tech malfunctions sometimes."

"Well, I've had about a hundred calls from everyone from other UFO-ologists to CNN. Seems that since I live near the sighting, I'm somehow supposed to be an authority on it."

I rubbed my eyes. "Great. What have you told them?"

"I played dumb. But Myron thinks that we'll have the men in black lurking behind every bush around Appleton now. And I can't say I really disagree with him."

I gave a tired nod. It was a good point. Like it or not, Wisconsin was going to be a hotbed of UFO interest for the next while. More worrisome was the fact that any number of aliens currently lurking on Earth would have ample opportunity to see the images in the media. I had Tony forward me a few, and sure enough, they depicted what was clearly a class 3 workboat sailing across a blue Wisconsin sky dotted with puffy clouds.

So it wasn't really the attention of the men in black that

concerned me. There were far more dangerous parties out there that might turn their attention to Wisconsin, like the Sorcerers.

Netty interrupted. "Van, I thought you'd want to see this. I managed to get the radar tracking data the Air Force collected after the cloak on the workboat failed."

"How?"

"I know a toaster oven at Volk Field Air National Guard Base."

"Netty—"

"What, it's okay for Perry to be a smartass?"

Despite everything, I couldn't help smiling. "You're right, Netty. Sass away, friend. Just keep it to small doses, please. Oh, and thank you."

While Tony waited, I examined the radar data. We'd first shown up on radar just a smidge eastward of a due north track from Madison. I breathed a sigh of relief at one small mercy, anyway. Thanks to the thunderstorms over the Wisconsin Dells, we'd been forced to the south, then turned back west roughly over the village of Fall River to resume our way back toward Pony Hollow in Iowa. It meant our sudden appearance on radar made our course look as though we'd come from the east, roughly from the direction of Milwaukee. If the cloaking system had failed even five minutes earlier, our southwestward track from the Green Bay-Appleton area would have been easy to see.

"Okay, the good news is that we weren't obviously coming from your neck of the woods. So, for the time being, just keep playing dumb," I said.

Tony grinned. "Actually, the Truly Aware are all over this. They got Myron on the local news and he went off on a rant about government cover-ups and things—which, incidentally, I think he

248

actually believes. In his mind, you guys really are still part of some big conspiracy."

"But he'd be inside of it—part of it."

"Yeah, but he's convinced that you're not showing him the whole picture, so now there's a conspiracy inside the conspiracy. It's conspiracies all the way down. Anyway, it's exactly what people would expect from us, which is what we want, I think?"

I nodded. "I'll leave this in your hands, Tony. Please try to gather as much information about our, um, sighting over Wisconsin as you can in the meantime. Who knows, it might end up containing something useful, something we can use."

Tony gave a thumbs-up and signed off.

I went to bed, but not for long. All I could do was toss and turn, thinking about Valint. I finally gave up, rounded up the crew, and told Netty to get ready to take off. It was time for a family reunion. We were heading to Valint's ship, where I would ask pointed questions.

And I would have *answers*.

THE ONE OBVIOUS thing missing on Valint's ship, the ominously named *Stormshadow*... was Valint herself. I turned to our greeting party, a Fren-Okun named Golont, who sported a belt, two side arms, and the air of a mortician. Despite his demeanor, he anticipated my question, and wasn't unwilling to speak.

"Valint will be with you shortly. Please, make yourselves comfortable."

"But—"

Golont turned and walked away, closing the door behind him. I stood glaring at it.

"Van—?" Perry started, and I wheeled on him.

"What?"

"Uh—was just going to suggest sitting down."

"I don't want to sit down. I want—" I had to stop and take a couple of breaths.

"Van, another ship just twisted in a short distance away. It's B," Netty said over the comm.

I forced myself to sit down. "Great. My *living* alien grandmother, and a woman who's a cross between Florence Nightingale and James Bond." I turned to Perry. "You know, farming corn back in Iowa seems pretty appealing right now."

"Don't forget sorghum. It's sweeter," Perry offered.

I gave him a tight smile. "Thanks, bird. Who was the—did you see a snake as we came through the lock? Lot more silvery than most of the ones I've seen back home, but—"

Perry spoke up in a tone that told me he'd been speaking to another AI. "That's Woodvale, handles a lot of the ship repairs. You've met Golont and his sparkling personality, and Bunn is the ship's AI. She's nice, known her for years. And then there's Striker."

"I sense some hesitation on your part regarding Striker?" I asked.

Perry lifted his wing an inch. "No, I've known him for… a long time. He's been with Valint for more than a century. He's a bit of an acquired taste, unless your family had a few Edwardian manservants underfoot at the country estate."

"That stiff?" I said, snorting with laughter.

"He prefers the term *proper*."

I felt a clunk and a tremor through Valint's ship as B's docked. A few minutes later, the door opened. Valint entered in all of her towering glory, followed by what must have been her combat AI, a strange, six-legged contraption resembling a—velociraptor? An ostrich? Something ostrich-like, anyway, with four extra limbs and a vaguely canine head.

Weird. I tried to imagine what my reaction would have been to seeing *that* tapping on my kitchen window back in Iowa the night I pushed the button on that mysterious remote control. I doubt the encounter would have gone as smoothly or free of hysterical screaming as my first meeting with Perry had.

The reunion was brief, polite, and had all of the danger you'd find at a Methodist pancake breakfast.

"Hello, Striker," Perry said.

"Hello, Perry. Long time no see."

"Yeah."

And that was that.

B followed Valint and Striker into the compartment carrying a small case, but I stood and held up a hand. B hung back, her brows —and antennae—raised in inquiry.

"B, I'd like a few moments alone with Valint, please."

B hesitated. Valint just kept her attention on me.

"Of course. And you'll get them. But there's something we have to do first. Business before pleasure, as it were," she said, offering a smile that I didn't return.

B came into the compartment, muttering, "Wow, tension, meet knife."

She placed the case down on Valint's desk and passed her thumb over the latch, which clicked. Before she opened it, though, she turned to me. "Van, this is for GKU eyes only, got it?"

"Sure, yeah, fine. Now, if I actually knew who was in the GKU and who wasn't, that might matter," I said.

"Just assume no one's in the GKU unless you know that they are for certain."

I glanced at Valint. "So I guess you are, what with being alive and all."

I didn't expect Valint's cool, composed expression to change. I was a little surprised when it did, becoming one of uneasy discomfort. I took a darker delight in that than I should have, then immediately felt a little bad for it.

B opened the case. "Behold a Tenant, in all its glory."

The open case revealed something like a gelatinous millipede some thirty centimeters long, a lurid, electric blue with no discernible head, eyes, or anything else. It was motionless behind a clear barrier, though whether a live specimen or a dead one I wasn't sure.

I shoved aside my preoccupation with my grandmother, determined to get on with business—a business upon which a lot of lives could turn. Despite a visceral revulsion at what amounted to a big blue worm, I leaned toward the creature in the case. "I don't see any sensory organs. At all."

"That's because there are none," B said.

"How does something evolve with no sensory organs? More to the point, how does something with no sensory organs develop sentience? Because as far as I've been able to understand, these things are sapient, right? Or sentient?"

"As far as we know, yes," B said.

"Okay. So if they're sentient, they must have chosen to come into space? How does a race without the ability to sense its surroundings develop a yearning for the stars?"

"Another excellent question," Valint said. "One to which we have no answer. In all my time out here, this is only the third intact example of a Tenant I've ever seen."

She glanced at B. "How much did this set you back?"

"Thirty thousand to a gatekeeper in Aquila. A class 9 had some sort of complete systems failure. The crew was dead in seconds. When the ship was recovered and the bodies examined, this... thing... was pulled out of one of them. And yes, the crew were all Puloquir."

"In Aquila? How?"

"I don't know. I can only tell you where they were going."

"And where was that?" I asked, expecting a horrifically distant and mysterious place, like the galactic core or something. But B sniffed and shook her head.

"From here, not far at all. In fact, just little ways, uh"—she glanced around, then pointed at a spot on the deck—"that way, I think. According to the nav data, they were going to Charon. You know, Pluto's moon."

I straightened. Pluto, where someone presumably connected to the Sorcerers had been illegally mining osmium, a critical component in the identity chips. Was this the link that brought it all together under the aegis of one, big case?

Valint caught my reaction and nodded.

"I think, Van, that we should go do a pass by Charon and see what's going on there." She took a breath. "We'll take the *Fafnir* and leave your crew here to get some rest, and B can tune them up

—blood panels, vitamins, all the usual stuff to keep them fighting fit."

B nodded. "My pleasure. I'll bill you later."

Valint gestured toward the door. "Shall we?"

I suddenly had about a dozen things I wanted to say, but I held my tongue, nodded, and led the way back to the *Fafnir*. I'd waited decades.

A little longer wouldn't hurt.

WE UNDOCKED from the *Stormshadow* and set course for Charon, but a full minute into the flight I hadn't yet said anything not actually related to operating the ship.

Valint, in the copilot's seat, finally turned to me.

"Well?"

I glanced back. "Well, what?"

"Well, you have a thousand things you want to talk to me about."

"Oh, I'm sorry, are we through the business and transitioning into familial issues? I'll confess, the shift was abrupt—"

"Van—"

"Because I just seem to be along for the ride here," I went on, my voice flat. "I'm a piece on the big chessboard, being moved around by players I still don't understand, except that one of them is my *grandmother*."

"Van, look—"

"Who isn't dead, as it turns out, but somehow managed, in a stunning coincidence, to show up in the same sorghum field in the wee hours of a South Dakota night that I happened to be there, running down a cache of alien weapons." I turned to her. "By the way, did you know they were there all along? Where any kid could have stumbled on them? I mean, what little boy or girl wouldn't be thrilled to have their very own alien coil gun? Who needs arms and legs and siblings, right?"

This time, Valint said nothing.

I looked back ahead, at nothing. "I'm done now."

Valint sighed. "I guess this means no grandmother of the year nomination."

It was my turn to stay silent.

"Van, look—yes, I knew about that cache of weapons. But it wasn't just unguarded. There was a surveillance bug that you never found not far away, keeping an eye on it. It would have alerted someone in Gettysburg if anyone showed any clear intent to try and break into the cache, so they could intervene. Trust me, there was a whole process in place."

"Would have been nice to know that. Why not just get rid of it and save all the trouble?"

"Because it belonged to *someone*, and we wanted to know who. Which means you managed to uncover in a few days what we were working at for months—that it was Jacomir's brood behind it."

"Okay. So how did we, and you, and they all happen to end up converging on the place all at the same time?"

She sighed again, and this one was bitter. "I had another bug at your meeting place with those UFO nuts from Wisconsin. When I learned that you were heading for Gettysburg, I decided it was time to reveal myself to you. I was on my way to do just that when Striker saw your firefight, and that one of the Jacomir offspring had decided that discretion was the better part of valor. I figured I'd save you the trouble of finding him—not to mention help you get the hell out of there."

"So you've been spying on me."

"I spy on lots of people, Van. It's what I do."

"I'm… lots of people?"

Valint turned in the seat to face me. "You know, I'm willing to indulge your bitterness and anger, but only to a point. After that, it starts to wear pretty thin—"

I turned to face her with a glare, alien or not, Peacemaker or not, my grandmother or not. "Excuse me, but in the past twenty-four hours I've learned that my own grandmother, who I have never before met in my entire life, is alive, and that she's been spying on me instead of actually interacting with me, which is especially hard since she is the only family I have in the universe, except for Carter Yost and his father, my uncle—"

I took a breath, holding back what was becoming ungovernable. "Which begs the question, is he your son, too? Are you Carter's grandmother? And does *he* know about you?"

I dreaded the answer. If it turned out that Carter and Valint actually had a relationship, I wasn't sure where to go with my anger. Or me, for that matter.

We held locked gazes for a moment, then Valint slumped back with a rueful smile. "You know, it's funny. I've fought the worst that the galaxy has to offer for decades. I've almost died repeatedly doing it. I've seen things that would freeze the blood of any decent person. I can kill a man almost instantly with one hand—but when it comes to this whole family thing, I admit it, I suck. I'm no good at it."

She stared up at the overhead. "That's my way of saying that

I'm sorry I haven't been in your life, Van. Hell, I was barely in Mark's. And when he became a Peacemaker, we saw even less of one another. We loved each other, but we both put duty before the things we wanted." She shrugged. "So I suck at being a wife, a mother, *and* a grandmother—if that makes you feel any better."

We flew on in silence for a moment. I was struck by a wistful, almost desolate tone to Valint's words. I recognized it, because I'd heard it often enough before—

From my father, right before he walked out the door to a deployment, or signed off from a voice or video call while he was away. It was a tone I hoped to never hear again. I'd spent years burying that memory. That... echo.

I sat back. I'd come to terms with my father's dedication to his career, which was important not just to him but to many other people. And while I was still seething about Valint spying on me, remaining just out of reach without me even knowing she was there, I'd been a Peacemaker long enough to know why. There were some *very* bad people out here. And that meant I should try to look at her not as my grandmother, but as another Peacemaker doing their job. From that perspective, her actions made perfect sense.

Hell, if I'd never become a Peacemaker, she'd have never revealed herself to me. To do otherwise would just expose me to unnecessary risks, thanks to those same bad actors.

I turned to her. "Does Carter know about you?"

"In general? Yes. Have he and I ever met? No. That doesn't mean I haven't tried to get him eaten by aliens for a couple of decades now. He always manages to escape with his skin intact, though."

I smiled. "That's Carter, always landing on his privileged feet."

"Van, I won't have a lot of involvement in your life either. I can't. There are things going on in the GKU that are going to prevent it."

I nodded. "I know. I guess it's just——" I glanced at her and sighed. "Don't mind me. It's been a trying couple of days. I guess that's why I was, well, such an asshole about it all."

"Oh, I think you're entitled to a little assholery. Which means I'm sorry about that *wearing thin* comment a moment ago."

"So what should I call you, anyway?"

"What do you mean?"

"I called Gramps, Gramps. Should I call you Gran?"

She sat up, smiling. "Do I look like someone who wants to be called Gran?"

"How about I stick with Valint?"

"That sounds good to me."

18

IN THE END, I decided I'd rather get to know this remarkable—woman, is how I thought of her, even if she wasn't human. The alternative was to hang onto bitterness and recrimination, and life was too short for that. Better to have Valint as part of my life occasionally, than not at all.

My grandmother was not human, but in the galactic sense, she was close, being a Hu'warde, and our species could make babies with minimal scientific intervention. With a single-dose fertility drug, babies weren't just possible—they were *likely*. The prevailing theory, according to Valint, was that her people and humans shared some common ancestor, and therefore most of their DNA. Who that ancestor had been, where they'd come from, and the circumstances of the split were an enduring mystery.

Perry was happy about the fact that Valint and I had subsided from angry recrimination to quiet chatting. He poked his head into the cockpit. "Does this sudden lack of palpable tension mean you two have made up?"

"We're... on our way to making up, let's put it that way," Valint said, giving me a questioning glance. I nodded.

"Good. I've gotten all caught up with Striker in the meantime—which actually took less than a millisecond-ish, so we've spent the rest of the time gossiping," Perry said. "Talking shit, as the kids say."

"I can't help noticing that you seem to have a less strained relationship with Striker than you do with Hosurc'a," I said.

I swear that Perry's face somehow darkened, despite being made of immutable alloy. "That's because Hosurc'a is an AI—an artificial imbecile."

"What have you got against him, anyway?"

"Oh, he knows what he did," Perry said, then withdrew aft.

I stared at where he'd vanished. "I have *got* to find out just what is up between those two."

"Does it affect their performance?" Valint asked.

I shook my head. "Nah. It's just prurient curiosity."

She grinned, and so did I, the last of the immediate tension dissipating. It was timely, too, since we were close enough to Charon that Netty detected a sporadic scanner return from the little moon that wasn't just rock or ice. In addition, we didn't detect any sign of activity on Pluto, mining or otherwise.

"Shall we go take a look?" Valint asked.

"We've come all this way. Netty, go active on the scanners. If we're going to provoke something, I'd rather do it at a distance."

Data sluiced back with the scanner returns. Valint and I both watched as it popped onto the tactical overlay.

"A ship, or what's left of it, it seems," Valint said.

I nodded. "Netty, can you match it to anything?"

"I cannot. Whatever it is, or was, doesn't correspond to any known ship design. I don't think it's been on Charon for long, though. In fact, it's still giving off a power signature, suggesting a reactor is still operating in low-power mode."

Netty kept collecting data as we approached Charon, but it didn't reveal much more to us. The wreck was about a class 10 or so in terms of mass, but even that wasn't certain because of damage. When we were close enough we could get visual imagery, we could see that part of the hull, from amidships back, seemed to be more or less intact. Everything forward of that was just crumpled wreckage.

We did a pass by the wreck site, giving it a good once-over. Aside from it, we saw nothing of note. And while we could see the scarring of the illegal mining on Pluto hanging in the blackness nearby, a pale half-disc in the wan light of distant Sol, there was no actual activity. We were, as far as we could tell, alone.

"We should go down there, take a closer look at this," Valint said.

"Just the two of us?" I asked.

"You have something else in mind?"

"Well, yeah. My crew and yours could be here in a few hours. For, like, backup."

Valint shrugged. "I'm used to working alone. If you'd rather stay up here and keep watch—"

I unstrapped my crash harness. "What, and disappoint my grandmother by looking like a wimp?"

WE LEFT the *Fafnir* in an awkward orbit. Charon was close enough to Pluto, and large enough in comparison, that the barycenter—the point around which the two of them revolved—was at a point partway between them. In other words, they were effectively orbiting each other. Moreover, Charon wasn't large enough to have much of a gravitational pull of its own, all of which meant Netty had to keep doing quick burns with the drive to maintain a halfway stable orbit around what amounted to both Pluto and its moon, while keeping in a position to watch over us.

We left the orbital mechanics in her capable virtual hands and descended in the *Fafnir*'s as-yet unnamed workboat to investigate the wreck. As the rocky surface of Charon loomed closer, Valint looked around the workboat's interior and smiled.

"I gather this was your Wisconsin UFO?" she asked.

"Yeah. The stupid cloaking tech that's supposed to keep it hidden conked out while we were heading back to Iowa."

"I assumed it was something like that—unless, of course, you decided to play a *UF-oh shit* stunt."

I frowned. "A what?"

"You haven't heard of that? Sometimes aliens visiting Earth decide to have some fun with the locals—go hover over a field some-where, turn off the cloak, and fly slowly over a populated area, then zoom off in some random direction and switch the cloak back on so it looks like they vanished, that sort of thing. Your grandfather called it *UF-oh shit* because, that's what the people who saw it happen would say."

"Your grandfather used to give out tickets for doing it," Perry said.

That raised my eyebrows. "There are tickets for that? Or for, well, anything? Since when do the Peacemakers give out tickets?"

"They don't, but the assholes doing it didn't know that. Mark would make them pay a fine on the spot which, of course, went right into his bank account."

"What? So he was shaking down these aliens for cash?"

Perry shrugged. "They brought it on themselves. Play stupid games, win stupid prizes, as your grandfather put it."

I had to chuckle. "Yeah, that sounds like Gramps. I love that hustle."

I let Valint, the far more experienced pilot, take the controls while we did a low pass over the wreck site. Netty still couldn't identify the ship, so we wheeled around and settled down on a field of ice about a hundred meters from the wreck.

We dismounted and stepped onto the perpetually frozen surface of Charon. My helmet's heads-up told me it was a chilly minus two hundred and twenty Celsius, which really wasn't much different than the usual temperature of space not near a star. Somehow, though, it *felt* a lot colder. The ice under my feet squeaked through the soles of my boots, occasionally crunching as I stepped into ruddy-brown deposits of tholins, organic macromolecules that originated on Pluto. My b-suit was more than capable of keeping me warm, but I swear I could feel the chill seeping up into my feet.

"Perry, make a note. This place is ripe for a ski resort."

"Boss, I'm thinking that skiers might go orbital. You know, physics."

"Perry, scratch that idea. We'll stick to timeshares."

"Attaboy. We'll sell that swamp planet one week at a time," Perry enthused.

We contended with the low gravity at every moment. Our steps were long bounces, with maneuvering units close at hand in case we inadvertently hit too hard and bounced back spaceward. Striker scuttled deftly along on his multiple limbs, which could grip irregularities in the surface, while Perry puffed along on thrusters overhead. It took us a few minutes of careful movement, but we finally made it to the intact part of the wreck without mishap.

"I find this tedious, and beneath me," Striker stated in the tones of a British curmudgeon.

Valint looked at me, shaking her head ruefully. "He's always been a touch elitist."

"I certainly am not. I'm merely cognizant of my worth," Striker protested.

Perry laughed. "Do you get dental and vacation?"

"I don't nee—Valint, a question. Are *all* of your relatives such ruffians?" Striker asked, affronted to his digital core.

She paused, then answered. "Yes."

"Hmph." Striker hopped delicately ahead while Perry sent me the equivalent of a raspberry in my ear bug.

"Lonely out here," I managed, looking back at Sol, which was just a hard, bright spark, like a distant flare of a welding torch. Its pale light barely touched the wreck, but between our suit lamps and thermal imaging, we were able to find what seemed to be an intact airlock. It wasn't a standard design, but we didn't want to just cut open the hull either. As far as we could tell, the interior beyond it was still pressurized, or at least part of it was. So instead we opened up the access panel and, guided by both Perry and Striker, fiddled with the circuitry inside. It took us a while, but we finally got the airlock to cycle open.

I made to enter but stopped and grinned at Perry.

"It's so nice seeing you and Striker getting along like this."

"You seem unduly interested in the relationship between Perry and me," Striker noted, his tone one of British bemusement.

"That's because the only other combat AI I've seen him interact with is Hosurc'a, and they seem to have some baggage."

"Ah, yes, the legendary feud."

I blinked through my visor. "*Legendary* feud? What—"

"Tick-tock, Van. We going inside, or did you want to savor the outdoor ambience of Charon a while longer?" Perry snapped

I deliberately widened my grin but sensed not to push and clambered into the open airlock.

"These bulkheads are covered with traces of frozen methane, ammonia, and other volatile organic compounds," Striker said.

Valint and I both spoke at the same time. "Puloquir."

I turned to Perry, who was prepared to cycle the lock closed. When it did, it would no doubt flood with the fluid that comprised the Puloquir atmosphere. "Go ahead."

The outer door closed. A moment later, sure enough, liquid gushed into the airlock and quickly filled it. The murky fluid reduced our vision to just a few meters and dramatically limited the use of things like thermal imaging. I drew the Moonsword, while Valint extracted a wickedly curved dagger from her harness, which she unfolded into an even *more* wicked double blade, one protruding from her clenched fist in either direction.

"That's rather stylish," I said, eying her blade.

She sniffed. "I detest anything that's… let's say contractor grade. I prefer playing the game with style."

"Game?"

Valint's eyes danced. "Years into this life, and you don't think that?"

"I—okay, fair. I might not use the term game, but it's a lot more than just a job."

"Van, I think I can give us a clearer view of this place," Perry said. "Just gimme a second."

We waited, bemused, then a window popped open on my heads-up. It was a detailed, grayscale rendition of the interior of the airlock.

"Nifty, bird. How'd you manage that?"

"Remember my ultrasound digging system? I just reconfigured it to act as a sort of sonar."

"Clever."

"I have *got* to get one of those installed," Striker said.

Valint sighed. "I'll put it on the list. Doubtless, you'll want to enter some seedy establishment owned by someone with an eye patch, or some other unsavory calling card."

I chuckled. "Combat AIs, am I right? They're all gearheads with a penchant for the underbelly of society."

"Penchant?" Perry asked. "Easy now, Jean-Claude."

"Just flexing my cultural wings, bird."

Striker opened the inner door, and we made our ponderous way inside. We pushed off bulkheads and swam more than we walked because of the combination of low gravity and buoyancy. It didn't take us long to search the intact interior, which had been sealed off with pressure doors. Not much was intact, and that included the data archives, which must be buried somewhere amid the wreckage of the forward hull. We did find two Puloquir, though.

One was very much dead. The other, though, was sealed in

some sort of plastic-ish sack, from which tubes and cables sprouted. They led back to a panel in the bulkhead marked with symbols we couldn't readily decipher. Instead, Valint used a small hand-scanner to gather what data she could.

"This one is still alive—just."

"Dead, or in some sort of suspended state?"

"Believe it or not, Van, I don't know much more about the details of Puloquir physiology than you do."

I touched the sack. As soon as I did, noise crackled across several comm channels.

"You—"

I tensed. "Hello? Can you hear us?"

"I—"

"I'm Valint, and this is Tudor. We're both members of the Peacemaker Guild. Can you understand us?"

"I—" A pause. "Yes."

"Who are you? What's your name?"

"I—" Another pause. "Gringzet-in. Daughter. Of Divine Voice —of Tlol-nik Brood."

"Gringzet-in. Okay. Can you tell us what happened, Gringzet-in? To your ship? Your crew?" I asked.

"Rejected. Other broods—collaborating. Breeding."

"Breeding? They're breeding? Or they're breeding something else?"

"Tenants."

I couldn't help glancing at Valint. Perry had pulled back to encompass all of us in his ultrasound effect, so I could see a clear image of her from the back in the inset window on my HUD, but couldn't see her face.

"They're breeding Tenants?" Valint asked.

"Yes. Stop. Must stop."

"Okay. Look, we want to get you out of here, but—"

"No. Find their essence. Know truth. Post-Body Core. Seven Stars know. Some are friends—"

Silence.

"Gringzet-in?"

Nothing.

"Her life signs are fading—to zero. She's dead," Valint said.

"Wait. So, if we'd shown up here two minutes later, we'd have found her already dead?"

"I don't think so," Striker said. "I've been looking over this panel she was hooked up to and analyzing whatever emissions leaking out of it I can. I think she was in some sort of suspended state that was canceled when we showed up."

"That suggests that what she told us was so important it was worth her life to say it to us, instead of waiting until we could get her back to a full medical facility," Valint said. "A sort of Hail Mary, to quote your sports cultures."

"Doubtful she'd have lasted that long," Perry added, and there was real regret in his tone.

"That's not really the point, though. If she—or another Puloquir—rigged her up like this deliberately, she'd function as sort of a distress log."

I nodded. "Yeah. So what was she telling us that was so important she was willing to die to say it to us?"

WE SPENT some time picking through the wreckage for data cores and other archival materials but didn't find much. When our air supplies crept down into the yellow, we returned to the workboat, recharged, then recovered the Puloquir bodies inside fluid-tight body bags. Once that was done, we returned to the *Fafnir* and, ultimately, Valint's ship, the *Stormshadow*.

B was still aboard, having put Torina, Zeno, and Icky through a battery of tests and having prescribed some supplements, changes in diet and, in Icky's case, a couple of lifestyle choices.

"Wu'tzur are naturally omnivorous. She needs more vegetable matter in her diet," B said.

Icky scowled. "I hate salad. I mean, you use more energy chewing it than you do from digesting it. And my back six molars have to be flossed, every time."

"First of all, that's not even remotely true. Secondly, your body is telling you need more veggies, my dear."

"*Six* molars?" I asked.

"Actually, twelve, and no, you can't see them, weirdo."

"Wasn't gonna ask. Pleased you floss that much, though," I told her.

"Thank you. I like the *goblurmut* flavored floss. Refreshing."

"What's it taste like?" I had to ask.

"Mint. Duh."

"Perry, you did a stint as the *Fafnir*'s waste reclamation AI. You should be able to shed some insight on her diet, by the way," I said, studiously avoiding Icky's mouth. I had no idea how many teeth were in there, and I wasn't sure I *wanted* to know.

He glanced at Striker, then at me. "Sorry, Van, no idea what you're talking about in front of the other combat AI—thank you very much."

We took some time to review the playback of our encounter with the dying Puloquir that Striker and Perry had both recorded. When it was done, I turned to the group.

"Okay, unless Seven Stars means something else, that would seem to point at the Seven Stars League, right?"

"Meaning they're somehow involved with the Puloquir," Torina said.

"Technically, what she said was *Seven Stars know*. That really only implies that they have information about something," Striker pointed out.

"Okay, so what about this Post-Body Core?" I asked. "Does that mean anything to anyone?"

A pause, then B raised her hand. "I know who they are."

"They? And who? So it's a group of people, not a thing?"

"It is not. The Post-Body Core is a secretive group of bioengineers who believe that organic physical bodies are an unnecessary evolutionary constraint. They advocate for a sort of, ah, post-physical body renaissance, whereby we replace organic life with mechanical. Outwardly, that's all they are—a wacky fringe group of esoteric researchers."

"How about inwardly?" I asked.

B shrugged. "We really don't know much more than that. There's really nothing illegal about espousing some sort of weird belief, so aside from knowing they exist, we've never really invested much more effort in digging into them."

I sat back in my seat, stunned. "Are you shitting me? We're chasing down a bunch of murderous scumbags who steal peoples' identities and install them in machines, and *no* one thought to mention this Post-Body Core to us?"

"Have to admit, it sounds like the possible connection would be obvious," Torina put in.

B shrugged. "I don't know what to tell you, Van. No one was really taking this Post-Body Core seriously."

I stood, clenching my fists. "You know what the problem is? Everything's compartmentalized. Right hand has no idea what the left hand is doing because everything's hush-hush. How much further along in our investigation might we be if someone had bothered to tell us about these assholes? Might we even have solved it by now and saved a mess of lives?"

"There's no way to know——"

"Yes, exactly," I said. "There's no way to know, because everybody's playing their bullshit spy games and keeping it all to themselves. It's no wonder the bad guys always seem to be one step ahead of us."

B opened her mouth but closed it again. I could tell from her expression that she didn't think I was wrong, so really, what was she going to say?

"Mark my words, B. Secrets are gonna kill one of us, sooner or later."

A moment passed in silence. I leaned onto the back of the comfy seat I'd been sitting in just a moment ago.

"I want to know *everything*. Every last thing about the Post-Body Core, and anyone and anything even remotely connected with them. And I want to know who knows it."

Valint shifted uncomfortably. "Van, some of that material is——"

"I know what you're going to say. It's *classified*."

"For good reason——"

"That's no longer valid, and here's my promise to you all," I intoned. "I want it *all*, before I leave here, or my next stop will be Anvil Dark, where I will reveal absolutely everything I know to Master Gerhardt and let him decide how to proceed." I spun on B and Valint. "And I mean *everything*. No aces held back, B. Nothing. And as for you, Valint—gran—don't you think we've had enough shadows between us? When is a secret more important than... this? Than us? Than being prepared, *together*, for what comes next?"

B and Valint exchanged a look. Valint shrugged. B sighed.

"If you want to know more about the Post-Body Core, talk to The Quiet Room," B finally said.

"The Quiet Room. The bank. Why them?"

"Because they came to us asking what you just did—to have us share everything we know about the Post-Body Core with them. They had some reason to launch an investigation into them about fraudulent use of research grant money."

"So you informed the bank about them, and that was that?"

Valint leaned forward. "I get that you're pissed, Van, I don't deny you have good reason to be. You're right, this should have been brought to your attention. And as an aside, B and I will make sure that you have access to anything we think will help you in your investigation going forward."

She sat back again. "But there's only so much Guild to go around. And strictly financial crimes eat up huge time and resources, which means we have to let other things slide. It really is a zero-sum game."

"So, when it comes to things like fraud, embezzlement, and the like, unless it's a case we can open and close quickly, we tend to hand it over to The Quiet Room. They have their own investigatory arm, so they do the legwork and then bring cases back to us, or just go straight to whatever jurisdiction is relevant," B added.

"Okay, fine. I need to know that when I get to The Quiet Room, we aren't just going to be stonewalled, though. You know, because things are *classified*."

B nodded. "I'll give you an access code to a non-descript account. Go to Procyon, deposit fourteen point seven bonds into it, and wait."

"So, a dead drop."

"Pretty much. Tell them that the next deposit will be, oh, say, twenty-seven point two bonds, so we can reset it."

Icky was staring at her as she spoke. "Wait. You're not really a doctor, are you?" She grinned. "So I don't really have to follow that *eat more veggies* thing, do I?"

Perry shook his head. "*That's* what you took away from all this, Icky?"

19

WE DID AS B SUGGESTED, traveling to the by-now familiar moon of Outward in the Procyon system, where The Quiet Room maintained one of its major branches—or possibly its actual head office, though no one was really sure. With Torina and Perry in tow, I deposited the exact amount of bonds that B had specified, then we waited, lounging in the plush waiting room off to one side of the bank's lobby. I amused myself by watching whoever entered to see if I recognized anyone. I didn't, though, and then a voice interrupted me.

"Peacemaker Tudor?"

I hadn't even heard them approach. It was Chensun, Dayna Jasskin's lithe and pale assistant.

I stood. "Hello there."

"You just made a deposit."

"I did."

Chensun nodded, once. "Please follow me."

They—because I still wasn't sure if Chensun was male or female, or if the concept even applied to their race—led us through a labyrinth of corridors to a small meeting room. We'd barely seated ourselves before Dayna Jasskin came in.

"Van, it's good to see you, even if the circumstances are somewhat unusual," she said, taking a seat.

"You mean the secret-squirrel dead drop?"

She smiled and nodded. "It may seem a little hokey, but it's simple and gets the job done."

"The job being dealing with especially sensitive subjects, which is why I assume we're here, in a room with walls that block all EM radiation," Perry said.

"Something like that," Dayna replied.

I looked around at the unremarkable, off-white walls. "Isn't your whole facility secure, though? Isn't this a little redundant?"

"There's secure, then there's really secure—and then there's this. With that door closed, we might as well be inside the event horizon of a black hole as far as information getting out is concerned. Well, except whatever you carry inside your head, of course. Which brings us to the reason for this particular visit, which I assume you're carrying inside *your* head right now."

"I am," I said, then went on to explain what little we knew about the Post-Body Core. When I was done, Dayna turned to Chensun.

"The Post-Body Core is ostensibly a loosely organized group of bioengineering researchers located in eleven different systems. They believe that the natural course of evolution for all sentient life is to develop the ability to make machines, and then use those machines to replace their organic bodies. They believe that this will result in an immortal race, which is a prerequisite to explore beyond the confines of this galaxy."

"They're not wrong. If you ignore the Magellanic Clouds, it's two million light-years to Andromeda, the next closest galaxy. Depending on drive efficiency and flight parameters, that represents at least decades, and quite possibly several centuries of objective travel via twisting," Perry said.

"Even subjectively, it involves years of travel, given the limitations of twist technology. And that ignores the fact that there are no meaningful, intermediate sources of fuel," Chensun replied.

"So, what, we all ditch our bodies, implant ourselves in machines and then go flying off to other galaxies?" I said.

Chensun nodded. "Yes. That is exactly their aspiration."

I turned to Dayna. "Okay, fine. I'll even grant that it makes a sort of sense. But you guys aren't involved because you're into some sort of scientific debate."

She gave a thin smile. "No, we're not. We administer a research grant and fellowship program established as a legacy by a wealthy, philanthropic Eridani family, the Dayzun. They disburse research funding to causes they deem worthy, leaving the details—and the due diligence—to us."

"And someone from this Post-Body Core group has been cooking the books, lining their own pockets, that sort of thing," Torina said.

Dayna nodded. "But that's not the worst of it. Shortly after we started our investigation, it became clear that there was a lot more to the Core than it first appeared."

I stuck up my hand. "Ooh, ooh, I know, pick me. They're a bunch of vicious, filthy criminals, aren't they?"

"How *did* you guess."

"Hey, if I've learned anything during my years as a Peacemaker—it's that someone who comes to your attention for any reason also ends up being a vicious, filthy criminal." I smiled at her. "Present company excepted, of course."

Dayna offered a genuine smile. "Nice save, Peacemaker. Anyway, yes, the Core is implicated in a range of crimes—notably piracy, and quite likely murder. Once that became clear to us, we suspended our investigation and referred it to your Guild."

"Okay. Pretend I don't know anything about this case—because I don't. What's happened since then?"

"As far as we can tell, nothing. Or, at least, nothing that's been shared back with us."

I sighed. "Yeah, it figures. Don't suppose you remember who you referred it to specifically, do you?"

I braced myself for it to be someone disastrously disappointing, like Gerhardt, or even Groshenko. Or, for that matter, Valint. But it was none of them.

"Yes, we referred it to Master Yotov."

I sat back in relief. "Well, there's your problem."

"Yes, we're well aware of Yotov's status. But we assumed that the case would have been subsequently picked up by someone else in the Guild." Dayna's face hardened. "The fact that you're here, asking these questions, suggests that it hasn't."

I spread my hands in a helpless gesture. "Don't get me started on how much our internal information sharing sucks. I had a pointed conversation with some folks about it less than a day ago, in fact. We've been working a major case of Crimes Against Order, but no one thought to tell us about these guys who want to implant people's identities into machines."

"It is possible that that case, which implicates the Trinduk sect known as Sorcerers, is effectively a test bed for techniques and technology being developed by the Core," Chensun offered, in a rare instance of an actual, original thought. I was surprised, having assumed that they were essentially a living database but not much more.

I nodded. "Exactly. So imagine my unhappy surprise when I found out about this. Anyway, here we are. So the Guild is now on the case. The next step is to run down these Post-Body Core assholes and subject them to a greater force—like me."

Dayna tilted her head at me. "To what end, Van? Please understand I'm not judging, I just want to make sure we're pointed in the same direction regarding our goals."

"Well, again going back to my vast, four-year experience, if I've learned anything it's that flipping mid-level scumbags is the shortest path to success. So that would be my next move—finding said mid-level scumbag and applying the necessary pressure."

Dayna grinned. "I couldn't agree more. Peacemaker, allow me to introduce you to Wixor, the Courier."

She nodded to Chensun, who did nothing discernible except stand there. An image appeared on a screen I hadn't even realized was on the wall behind Dayna. It depicted something close to a panda, although it was too lean and feral-looking. Moreover, its right hand and forearm were mechanical—as were its ears.

"Wixor is well known among the crews who work any and all trade routes between Dregs and The Torus. He's been on our internal targeting list for nearly six years."

Torina turned to Dayna. "Your *targeting* list? Actually, allow me to correct that. *Your* targeting list?"

Dayna shrugged. "The Quiet Room's goals don't always quite align with those of the Guild, or even the various political jurisdictions. We happen upon crimes that Peacemakers don't, and we also prosecute issues that are outside your concern."

"What, exactly, does *prosecute* mean? You're a bank," Torina persisted.

"Before you start thinking we're operating secret prisons or hit squads or whatever, we're not. We do investigations, gather information and evidence, then usually present complete cases to whatever jurisdiction is most appropriate."

"Usually."

Dayna nodded. "Usually."

I decided to interrupt because this conversation was heading in a direction that would lead to an unsatisfying answer for someone, which included me. "So this Wixor—you've investigated him?"

"We have. He's been a bad boy for some time. Now, with this new Guild interest in the Post-Body Core, you've given us reason to initiate a case against him—which gives you your mid-level bad guy to lean on. We're sure that the Core is doing more than just talking about a Post-Body future, and is doing things—profoundly unpleasant things—to help bring it about. We don't believe that would be good for anyone."

"You're not into immortal clients? They'd be customers forever," Torina said drily. "Although I'm told that the true enemy of a bank is—"

"Compound interest, naturally," Dayna said with a grin. "However, we may have done some risk modeling, and may have concluded that, over the long term, immortal clients tend to accumulate wealth, rather than circulating it to the more—well, mortal types, who are more likely to spend it."

Torina sniffed. "So, in the end, it's about money."

Dayna's smile became thin again.

"Ms. Milon, we're the bank. It's always about money."

———

AS WE DEPARTED PROCYON, we reviewed the file Dayna had transferred to us. It painted an unpleasant picture.

"So this Wixor operates a sleeper ship? As in, putting passengers into some sort of suspended animation? Why? Since when do travel times get long enough to make it worthwhile?" I asked.

"When you want to offer absolute cut-rate, discount fares. If your ship just consists of sleeper modules, then even if it would only be a few days of twist-hops, you don't have to offer amenities, food, even space to walk around," Netty said.

"Not to mention you can pack 'em in like cargo modules," Icky noted.

"And to put the vile cherry on top, the people you're transporting are generally going to be the poorest and most downtrodden," Perry added.

I nodded. "Yeah, the least likely to be missed. So let me guess, some of these poor bastards just don't wake up."

"Well, not before they've been sold off to the Post-Body Core, or elements within it."

"Great. Wixor is the equivalent of the old body thieves, who dug up freshly buried corpses and sold them to medical schools as

281

teaching aids. Except these aren't corpses, these are living people." I sighed. "How can this not be linked to the Sorcerers?"

Perry shrugged. "I'd say it probably is, but until we have hard evidence, all we can do is deal with the case on its own merits."

"And hope that it gives us that link," Zeno added.

"Okay, Netty, is there any way of tracking where Wixor's ship of horrors is right now?" I asked.

"His ship, the *Fool's Hope*, was registered departing the Dregs traffic control zone two days ago. His flight plan had him making a run to an uninhabited star system, a waypoint, on the ecliptically down edge of known space. That would suggest his destination was The Torus."

"The *Fool's Hope*? Little on the nose, don't you think?" Zeno muttered.

"I suspect subtlety isn't Wixor's strong suit," I said. "Okay, assume he makes the cheapest possible flight in terms of fuel to get there he can. Can you plot the best place to intercept him?"

A red dot appeared on the overlay.

"Iota Centauri. What's there?"

"Nothing—at least not yet. It's a class A main sequence star, two point five Solar masses, only about three hundred and fifty million years old. It's surrounded by a large debris cloud that will eventually coalesce into larger bodies. Think the Solar System, about four billion years ago," Netty replied.

"Gotta admit, I don't often think of the Solar System four billion years ago. So that's our best intercept point?"

"Using your assumption of the cheapest possible flight, he probably refueled at Halcyon and is now departing there. Iota Centauri is his likely destination for a navigational fix before he continues on to The Torus."

I nodded. Dayna had laid out a generous series of rewards—one hundred thousand bonds for Wixor, and another two hundred and fifty thousand for his employer. The mention of money had prompted another question.

"Does Wixor's employer use The Quiet Room to move payments around?" Perry had asked.

Dayna nodded. "You're in luck. They do, and the origin for the transactions is here." She nodded to Chensun, and the image on the unseen wall screen had changed again, to a location on the edge of our favorite system for shady dealings, Wolf 424.

"Welcome to Point Lonesome, as we call it. There's nothing there but an old twist station, long abandoned. Now obviously, it's not, but we've never found any evidence of activity there."

I frowned at that. "A twist station?"

Perry answered. "Back in the days before the physics of twisting was commonly known, you needed a target to twist *to*—you couldn't just twist to wherever you wanted. At some point—it's not really clear when—twist mechanics were refined to the point where ships could set their own targets, so these twist target stations became obsolete. Some were repurposed, while others were just abandoned. There are no records I can access regarding the Wolf 424 target station more recent than two hundred-ish years ago."

We'd decided to tackle Wixor first, which was why our next destination was Iota Centauri. I wanted to get my hands on the grubby middleman and ask him some questions as pointed as Perry's talons.

Upon arriving at Iota Centauri, we powered down and waited. We were suited up, but without helmets and still pressurized. There was a chance that we'd already missed Wixor, since he'd passed through the system already, so I didn't want us to sit sealed up in our suits if it wasn't necessary. But Netty didn't think that was likely.

"He'd burn more fuel and incur more costs, so unless he had a specific reason to hurry, I agree with you, Van—he's likely to make his trip as cheap as possible. And, assuming he really is heading for The Torus, that means he should be passing through here sometime in the next few hours."

"Yeah, he's a businessman. A vicious, murderous businessman, but a businessman nonetheless," I replied.

"Okay, there's something I don't get," Icky said. "If the banker lady knew where this ship was, then why didn't the bank just grab it themselves? Why pay us all that extra money to do it?"

"If I had to guess, it's because The Quiet Room has a financial interest in Wixor's boat," Zeno said, and we all turned to her.

She shrugged. "Think about it. The Quiet Room knows all about Wixor but has done nothing about him. Meantime, you do some secret spy-dead-drop thing to speak to this woman, Dayna, in what sounds an awful lot like an off-the-books sort of way, at least to me. I don't think she's dirty—quite the opposite, in fact. I think she's been sidelined, kept out of the loop, and this is her way of working around it."

"If that's true, then she's taking quite the risk of attracting the wrath of whoever's trying to keep this covered up," Torina noted.

But Zeno shrugged again. "Maybe, maybe not. Maybe she's

gunning for someone's job and she intends to use what we find to discredit them. It wouldn't be the first time someone was used to further someone else's political interests—in this case, hers."

"You've a devious mind, Zeno," I said, unable to resist a wry smile.

"That's because I'm a devious person. Always have been. I mean, your grandfather didn't sentence me to house arrest for being excessively honest."

I laughed, but Zeno's words made me think. If someone in The Quiet Room somewhere above Dayna was aware of what was going on and trying to keep it hushed up, then there might be more to it than just saving the bank some embarrassment. There might be money changing hands, and not just going into the bank's accounts, but someone's personal ones.

Gramps used to have a saying—get as many fingerprints on the ax handle as you could. It made eminent sense now.

"Netty, while we're waiting, initiate a twist message to our friend B. Tell her to rendezvous with us at Point Lonesome forty-eight hours from now," I said.

"You want to get her involved in this? Why not Lunzy, or Lucky, or—um, pretty much anyone more trustworthy. Which, incidentally, means *anyone* at all, at least as far as I'm concerned," Torina said.

"Wait. I'm getting the sense you're suspicious of B."

"Oh, we passed *suspicious* a long time ago."

I smiled and nodded. "Which is exactly why I want to call on her. First, I want to see if she actually responds and shows up. Second, if she does, then I want to establish that our relationship is a two-way street."

"She did give us that kickass missile," Icky said.

"She did. But just like how Zeno doesn't trust that Dayna's motives are entirely altruistic, I'm actually with Torina—I don't think B's are, either. I want to know where we stand with her—"

Netty cut in. "Van, a ship just twisted in. It's the *Fool's Hope*. Am I good or what?"

"I'd have been even more impressed if you could have narrowed it down to the exact minute, but yes, Netty, you're damned good. How long will it take him to get a nav fix?"

"Not long."

I tapped my chin. He wasn't far enough into the system to prevent him from quickly twisting away. As I pondered the problem, I noticed additional contacts.

"Uh, Netty, why am I seeing three icons?"

She put a zoomed image of the *Fool's Hope* on the screen above the overlay. It depicted the ship itself, an up-armored class 11 fast freighter with a smaller, workboat-like vessel a few klicks to either flank.

"Those are both cargo drones. They seem to be slaved to the *Fool's Hope*, which isn't uncommon. It's a way of extending the cargo capacity of a ship."

"Are they armed?"

"No evidence of it."

I nodded. "Okay, let's avoid targeting those. I have a feeling their cargo may be alive."

"Quick estimate—if he packs his ship and those two pods with as many sleepers as he can, we're looking at between three and four hundred so-called passengers," Perry said.

I turned to Torina. "Hey, deadeye—can you knock out his drive, from here, with the lasers only?"

She studied the tactical overlay for a moment, then shrugged. "It's a definite maybe."

"Do your best, Annie Oakley."

"Yeehaw, babe."

We powered up, Torina bringing the lasers on line. She took her time lining up her shot, making minute adjustments to bring the firing solution's probability as high as she could make it. I had to hold my tongue, worried that Wixor was just going to finish getting his nav fix and twist away again, but not wanting to interrupt her.

After a punishingly long time, she finally triggered the lasers. Their beams, which took a couple of seconds to reach the target, converged on the stern of the *Fool's Hope*. It vanished in a brilliant flare of incandescent vapor that lasted a full five seconds. When it died, the ship's twin drive bells were both left detached from the stern, drifting slowly away.

"Holy shit, deadeye is right. Torina, I've never seen anyone shoot off another ship's drive bells from nearly three light-seconds away. You've *got* to show me how you did that," Zeno said, her voice tinged with something like awe.

Torina smiled. "It's all in the wrist."

"Damned fine shooting, my dear. I think we all owe you a drink," I said, grabbing my helmet.

"Okay, places, people. We've got a scumbag to nab."

20

As WE CLOSED on the stricken *Fool's Hope*, it disgorged a workboat—
a fairly hefty class 4. It immediately began snapping lasers at us,
their coruscating bolts a sure sign of failing systems. The *Fool's Hope*
joined in with a salvo of missiles, but her own lasers stayed silent,
probably because the damage to the drive had scrammed her
reactor.

I worked the *Fafnir*'s side stick, jinking the ship hard to throw off
our opponents' aim. Torina concentrated her laser fire on the workboat, which was also slewing through evasive maneuvers, while periodically switching fire to the oncoming missiles. We were limited in
what we could do since we didn't want to simply destroy the *Fool's
Hope* or her pair of accompanying cargo pods. I was leery of even
doing too much damage to the workboat, in case Wixor was
aboard it.

We took several solid laser hits from the workboat, but none that
did serious damage. Zeno, operating the mass driver, finally put a

slug through it that killed its drive. Unfortunately, a moment later it exploded in a dazzling pulse of light.

Zeno sighed. "Oops."

"Let's hope Wixor wasn't aboard it, or there goes our payday," Perry said.

"Hey, I said *oops*."

"Don't worry about it, Zeno. I doubt Wixor was in that boat. If he had been, it probably would have just tried to bug out. Based on his history, he's not the *go down fighting* sort of guy—"

I was still speaking when a tremendous explosion engulfed the *Fafnir*, and everything went dark.

I BLINKED AT THE INSTRUMENTS, which were stripped down to the essentials, meaning the *Fafnir* had kicked into safe mode. But even as I sat gaping, things started coming back online.

"Everyone whole?" I asked.

One by one, the crew checked in. By the time they had, Netty had most of the ship back up and running.

"What the hell happened?" Torina asked.

"We triggered a mine. That workboat was apparently dropping them between us and the *Fool's Hope*," Netty said.

"Trying to buy them time. Though to do what, I'm not sure," Perry said.

"I hope it's not to—" Torina started but cut herself off. I knew what she'd been going to say.

I hope it's not to kill all his passengers.

"We need to get aboard that ship as fast as we can. Netty, can you take us through these mines without getting us blown up?" I asked her.

"I'll echo Torina here. Maybe?"

"Do your best, please."

"Oh, wow," Icky said.

I glanced back and found her just behind Perry, staring down at the deck.

"Oh wow?"

"Yeah, oh wow." She turned and pointed up, then back down. "Big-assed fragment went right through us—about thirty centimeters behind your head, Van."

I craned my neck to see. Sure enough, something about the size of a baseball had shot clean through the *Fafnir*'s hull, in one side and out the other, passing about the length of my foot away from the back of my head. If the *Fafnir* had just *few* centimeters per second of velocity less, or the mine's orientation had been even *minutely* different—

Just like the possible fate of Wixor's passengers, it didn't bear thinking about.

WE DECIDED to do a contested entry into the *Fool's Hope*, earning the respect of dads everywhere who think that adversity builds character.

Torina and Zeno cleanly shot away its ability to fight back with precision rounds that left the enemy a glorified filing cabinet. Then we parked the *Fafnir* about a hundred meters away. Icky, Zeno, and Perry went aft with a breaching charge so they could secure engineering and make sure the drive and powerplant were safe.

"Ready with that bomb, you maniac," Zeno told Icky, who was twirling the explosive around her hand like a duffel bag.

Icky looked nonplussed. "Why?"

Zeno looked—up, away, to the stars—everywhere but at Icky, who regarded her with a placid grin. "Icky. Please stop playing with the explosive device."

Icky stopped, then held the bomb with something more like care. "I've got it wired so that it—"

"I know. I designed it. That doesn't mean I want it being *twirled*."

"Bombs are a lot less fun than I thought," Icky grumbled.

"So is losing a limb because you fidget like a sugared up second grader, to use a human equivalent. Van, where are you breaching?"

I picked a spot further forward, and with Torina at my side, I readied to start carving the hull. It was more cumbersome than entering through an airlock, but airlocks were also choke points where Wixor's crew could lie in wait for us. Coming in through the hull kept them guessing about where we'd breach.

And the Moonsword was the ultimate can opener.

"Okay, entering in fifteen seconds," Zeno said. I could see her and Icky further along the hull of the *Fool's Hope*, moving a few meters away from their breaching charge to clear its blast. That was my cue.

I plunged the Moonsword into the hull-plating and *pulled*. I could only marvel at how the preternaturally sharp blade so readily sliced through solid alloy. It was like cutting an ice cream cake; it required some effort but not much. By the time the breaching charge detonated and Icky and Zeno swarmed in through the resulting hole, we had a hole of our own. The ship had been mostly depressurized, venting only a puff of frozen air, then I was inside, finding myself suddenly head down toward the floor as the internal gravity grabbed me. I pulled my head back and went the other way, feet-first, and dropped to the deck inside with a fluidity that was becoming second nature. Space was lethal, but space was home.

Icky and Zeno were clearing aft, so I turned and headed forward. Right away, I could tell that this ship wasn't just a standard cargo configuration. The holds were packed with racks of small cubicles, reminiscent of one of those cubicle hotels in Japan where I'd once spent a surprisingly cozy and comfortable night. These were smaller, and when I detoured into one of the compartments containing them and peered into one, I saw a prone body and that was it. The thing wasn't designed to hold someone who was awake —it was strictly a coffin-like container—

"Van!"

I spun at Torina's shout and moved to the door opening back into the corridor. Something sparked off the opposite bulkhead. A slug, fired from somewhere behind us, presumably by crew caught between us forward and Icky and Zeno aft.

"Van, go, keep moving forward! I've got your back!" Torina said, her voice rough with urgency.

I poked my head around the hatch coaming. Torina had taken cover in the next hatchway back and was exchanging methodical fire with two figures sheltering in a cross-corridor sternward, close to where we'd breached the hull. I double-tapped The Drop in that direction, twice—and awkwardly, using my left hand, because of the arrangement of door, corridor, and bad guys—giving Torina an opening to keep up the suppressive fire.

"Heading forward!" I said, then turned and charged up the corridor, switching The Drop to my right hand and keeping the Moonsword ready in my left.

I hit another cross junction, took cover, and hesitated. I should clear the short corridors going left and right, just to make sure I didn't pass any potential hostiles and let them get between Torina and me. On the other hand, Wixor and control of the ship was on the bridge. Then again—I was here, I was heavily armed, and I was getting pissed.

Anger, in proper doses, is a fine medicine.

The corridor ended about five meters ahead of me, making an abrupt turn to the left. This was as far forward as it went. I charged up to the corner, just as someone leaned around with a freakin' howitzer.

Okay, it was a boarding shotgun, but suddenly staring into its muzzle it was like gaping down the barrel of an artillery piece.

"Shiiiiiii—"

I didn't think, just flailed out blindly with the Moonsword while snapping out one, two, or maybe three shots—I didn't count—in that general direction. The Moonsword connected, neatly shearing off most of the gun's barrel. It fired an instant later, but not with a tight blast of flechettes. Instead, with the barrel truncated just a few centimeters ahead of its chamber, it produced a spectacular blast like a small grenade that flung flechettes in ragged spray. They pattered against my b-suit and visor, none of them with enough energy to do more than just bounce off. I thought I heard alien swearing—always a good sign—but my chili was cookin' and I had one direction in mind.

Foreward.

I kept charging, shouting, barreling around the corner and into whoever had just shot at me. I crashed into whoever it was, getting a brief impression of a man, except chunks of him were metallic as brightness and light caromed about in my view, creating a chaotic melange of silver and shadows. Another enemy stood right behind him, a slug pistol raised. I let my momentum barrel the first into the second, his shot vanishing somewhere into the overhead, then laid into them with The Drop, pistol-whipping it against my opponent, and the Moonsword—

The Moonsword.

If I'd only had The Drop, I'd have been in trouble. These two—men, I guess—were halfway to being full-on, movie-style Terminators, with limbs or parts of them, sections of face and skull, and some of their torsos having been replaced by gleaming alloy tech. They recovered swiftly from my charge and started lashing back at me in coordinated strikes that would have quickly pummeled me into a b-suited sack of hamburger.

But I had the Moonsword, and it could slice through metal almost as easily as flesh. They struck, I blocked and parried with Innsu-honed technique and cut them. I struck out, they tried to block in turn, and I cut them. Neither of us did *anything*, it seemed, and I cut them. In seconds, the corridor was Jackson Pollock'd with spatters of blood and other fluids, the deck was slick with gore and bisected alloy components that scraped and rattled underfoot. One fell, then I drove the Moonsword into the other's skull. The point punched cleanly through, embedding itself in the blast door behind him. I yanked the sword back and he slumped to the deck.

"And... scene," I said, flicking the blade to clear it of blood.

They both remained down amid a scene that wouldn't have looked out of place in some gritty European torture-porn flick. Breathing hard, I held up the blade. It glittered back at me, entirely clean of blood. It struck me that the orgy of violence had been so quick and intense that I hadn't even kept track of my swings, as evidenced by cuts in the adjacent bulkheads. I wasn't sure if anyone had ever managed to hit themselves with their own sword, but shuddered briefly as my imagination painted a vivid and bloody picture of what would have happened if I had.

I shoved it away and jammed my attention on the task at hand. I turned to the blast door, slammed the Moonsword into it and carved it open.

It took me a moment, letting anyone on the other side get ready for me. I kicked in the chunk I'd cut into an opening big enough to let me through, meaning to immediately dive out of the way of any fire coming through the hole back at me. I was a touch slow, though, and took a potent laser-shot square on.

Except the Moonsword deflected it, so I made a snap decision and lunged into the space beyond the blast door instead. Wixor stood just a couple of meters away, a laser-rifle the size of a light machine-gun cradled on his hip. He fired again, and again the sword deflected the shot into a nearby console with a shower of vaporized metal and sparks.

I slashed at his gun, slicing off the barrel. Then I lifted the tip of the Moonsword and touched it to Wixor's visor. The point actually dug into the transparent material a millimeter or so, sending a spiderweb of cracks away in random patterns.

It was about now that my thinking caught up with what my body was doing. With my free hand, I switched to a general comm broadcast.

"Stand down and surrender, or I'm gonna redecorate this bridge to match the corridor outside, asshole," I snapped.

I saw Wixor glance behind me. He couldn't have seen much of the corridor through the hole I'd carved in the blast door, but it was enough to make his eyes widen. He dropped the remains of the laser rifle and raised his hands.

"Torina, talk to me," I said.

"We're just—sorry, give me a sec."

I waited.

"Okay, we've just finished mopping up back here. Between Zeno and Icky playing the hammer and me being the anvil, we caught the bad guys in a vice."

"Mixed metaphors much?"

"Alliteration much?"

I laughed. "Okay, I've got Wixor up here on the bridge. Get Icky and Zeno to finish securing the ship. You and Perry come on up here and join me so we can start retrieving whatever's left in this tub's data archives.

"That would be nothing. I wiped it all," Wixor hissed.

I grinned at him.

"You'd be surprised how much something we're able to coax out of nothing. But you'll get points for trying, at least."

Perry arrived, eyes flashing. "Boss, lemme have a crack at that drive. Remember the one that was cooked off, that Yonnox ship data?"

"I do. Damn fine work. Perry here—that's him, with the talons—found *everything* on a drive that looked like scrap. He's—"

"Persistent," Perry finished for me.

I smiled, and it was cold as a grave. "Persistent."

DESPITE MY BRAVADO, I really didn't expect to get much out of the archives of the *Fool's Hope*. I was pleasantly surprised, then, when Perry was able to retrieve a large volume of data. Most of it was performance data for the ship, but it included old passenger and cargo manifests and nav logs, which would be useful fodder for our intelligence people. We tried to interrogate Wixor in the meantime, but he stubbornly refused to do anything but demand legal representation. I had Icky haul him back to the *Fafnir* and lock him up.

No sooner had she dragged Wixor away than Perry called to me. He stood on a console, cabled into a data port.

"Van, I just cracked open an encrypted file."

"Okay—and?" Something in his tone made me... uneasy.

"The encryption was an old Peacemaker scheme."

I froze. "Why do I have a feeling this is going to be really bad news?"

"Well, if you're worried that somehow our crypto has been compromised—it was. It's a scheme that was dropped right after Yotov was outed as a villain."

"So our current crypto is still secure?" Torina asked.

"There's no evidence it isn't. But even that's not the really interesting part, and by interesting, I mean unsettling as hell. It's a passenger manifest, apparently covering those aboard those two train car pods out there. If it's accurate, everyone aboard them is Puloquir."

"Well, shit. Where are they coming from? And going to?" I asked.

"As for *coming from*, no idea. That information just isn't in the file."

"Okay. And *going to*?"

"This is where the plot really thickens. Their destination is listed as *Ponte Alus Kyr*."

I saw Torina glance at me from behind her visor. "I thought they were good guys."

"Yeah. So did I."

WE'D HAD ONLY a few dealings with the research facility known as *Ponte Alus Kyr*, mainly in relation to a stealthy satellite we'd recovered shortly before meeting Zeno for the first time. The satellite was a weird amalgam of inorganic machine parts and organic ones, essentially living tissue, but the bio-engineers who'd examined it hadn't been able to tell us very much. Our interactions since had been a few brief, comm-consultations on specific matters of technical expertise and evidence.

While it was a medical facility packed with people who were serious, ethical scientists, there was a vague aura of Frankenstein's lair if you looked hard enough. It wasn't anything outright, but every time I entered one of the sterile, orderly halls, something twigged my senses.

I told Perry as much and his answer was definitive and instant. "It's lawful evil."

"Did you just quote Dungeons and Dragons?"

"Sure did. It's a lawful evil vibe."

"And Tumblr?"

"Boss, vibe's been everywhere for years, not just among the Tumblr crew. It's almost as if you don't pay attention to my emails," Perry said, shuffling alongside me with an air of patient frustration.

"Emails?"

He looked up at me, eyes glowing softly. "Um, yeah. Look, we'll go into our corporate communications policy later. This place kinda gives me—

"The creeps. Same."

All of this added up to a facility that was now squarely in my sights for crimes I'd never thought possible—not among medical professionals of this character. I hadn't really thought of *Ponte Alus Kyr* in the context of the Post-Body Core, probably because I'd just assumed they were good guys, as Torina put it. But I should know better by now, in the wake of Yotov and the other corrupt Masters —the bad guys really didn't always wear black and twirl mustaches. It was especially galling, though, to think that a place I'd considered a valuable and useful ally was actually, to turn a phrase, *a wretched hive of scum and villainy.*

After some consultation with Zeno—who'd entered the bridge of the Fool's Hope with a look of disgust at the charnel house that was the corridor outside—and Icky aboard the *Fafnir*, we decided to slave the two train cars to the *Fafnir*'s workboat. Zeno would then take it, them, and Wixor to Anvil Dark and report directly to Gerhardt. The *Fool's Hope* itself, lacking a functioning drive, was stuck, so we requested help from the Eridani Federation, the closest competent jurisdiction in known space. They agreed to send a transport to retrieve the *Hope*'s passengers, who all seemed to be ordinary people simply taking advantage of a cheap trip out to The Torus.

"Zeno, when you're done at Anvil Dark, come join us wherever we go after we meet B at Point Lonesome. If for any reason you can't contact us or otherwise don't know where we'll be, we'll meet you at *The One-Eyed Yak* on The Torus in four standard days."

"Delicious. I get to fly by myself out to the land that law forgot? I can hardly wait."

"You'll be fine."

"Oh, I know. I've spent most of my life doing stuff in sketchy places on my own. I guess I've just gotten used to doing stuff in sketchy places with you guys."

"Well, first round's on me, Zeno. Sorry to make you drive."

She glanced pointedly out into the gore-splashed corridor. "Meh, I could use some time alone. Meantime, I think you could use some time away from that sword."

She reached up and wiped something from my helmet—something that had gone sticky and dark in the vacuum of the Fool's Hope's interior.

"Don't get lost in the fight, Van," she said, then turned to join Icky in slaving our workboat to the two pods full of Puloquir.

21

I'D SAY that Point Lonesome lived up to its name, but seriously, any random spot in space is pretty damned lonesome. What made this particularly remote spot on the edge of Wolf 424 different was its location relative to the rest of known space. As Netty patiently explained it to me once, twisting doesn't involve a trajectory between two points in space because ships don't actually travel the intervening distance. Rather, it involves geometry. And there is an optimum twist geometry that relates any two points, that includes things like the gravitational effects of intervening masses such as stars, as well as the effects of time, and it very rapidly became clear to me why it took a super-powerful AI to figure it out.

All of which was to say that Point Lonesome wasn't close to the optimum geometry for traffic arriving from or heading to other well-traveled places in known space, like Spindrift or Tau Ceti. It didn't mean we couldn't twist there—rather, doing so involved a greater distortion in objective time and required us to burn more expensive antimatter fuel. And that's what put the lonesome into its name. Unless there was a compelling reason to come to this lonely bit of space, no one would. It was like the panhandle of Oklahoma—nice, but not really on anyone's list of places to go, unless you just liked to travel.

"It's why we see bad guys just selecting random coordinates in interstellar space for their meetings. Without a large mass like a star nearby, the twist geometry is much more forgiving," Netty said.

We'd actually taken two hops to get here—the first into a favorable twist geometry at Wolf 424, then the second to Point Lonesome itself. It was baked right into the arcane physics of twisting that it was actually faster to make the longer journey.

So here we were. Wolf 424 shone in the distance, while around us was a whole lotta nothing. Or nothing, that is, except for the disused transfer station, which was itself an early compromise way of getting around the whole issue of twist geometry before its underlying physics and the related math were understood. The closest ship was hours of flight time away, a class 8 skimming a gas giant, probably scooping up and concentrating helium-3, either to fuel itself or to sell for a tidy profit. Even in the howling wilderness of space, commerce continued when and where it could.

"Netty, this old station is abandoned, right?" I asked, studying the data on the overlay.

"Supposedly, but your next question is going to be, *why is it powered up then?*"

"Something like that, yeah."

"No idea."

I gave an idle nod. The station was essentially an oblate sphere, with what looked like four comms arrays located at cardinal points around its circumference, plus one each on the top and bottom. If it were abandoned, it should have long ago cooled to the ambient minus two hundred and thirty Celsius or so of the space around it. But it was considerably warmer than that, glowing against the dark thermal background, meaning something was generating internal heat.

"How about transmissions, Netty? Or other emissions?"

"An elevated neutrino count suggests that there's a fusion reactor running over there. Otherwise, no."

"Doesn't look like it's armed, either," Torina said.

"Unless it's going to open up like a pretty flower and reveal a battleship's worth of firepower," Icky put in.

"I doubt that's the case. The station wasn't armed to begin with, and there's no evidence of major retrofitting. I suppose there could be a few point-defense batteries squirreled away somewhere in there, but that would be about it," Netty replied.

"Okay, well, let's poke at it and see what happens," I said, taking manual control of the *Fafnir*. I applied a brief burst of thrust and made a slow approach, starting about one hundred klicks out. Torina had the weapons powered up and locked onto the station, including a quartet of missiles.

Speaking of B—

"Netty, no word from B?"

"Not so far."

"Hmph." Asking her to meet us here had been as much a test of her willingness to respond to our calls for assistance as it was us genuinely wanting her help. If she didn't show up, and it turned out to be a matter of her choosing not to, that told us something, didn't it? That she may only appear when it suited her, and we couldn't count on her.

At about eighty klicks away—basically no distance at all in celestial terms—we were lit up by active scanners, but they didn't have the powerful, spectrum-shifting properties of targeting scanners. Someone or something on the station was looking us over.

To be on the safe side, I broadcasted our identity and my Peacemaker credentials, but we got no response. And by the time I brought the *Fafnir* to a halt about five hundred meters from the station, nothing had otherwise changed. The scanners continued to illuminate us, the station continued to sit there, and that was it.

"Well, whatever's going on out here, it doesn't seem to involve a lot of paranoia," I said, frowning through the canopy at the silent station.

"I'd say the awkwardness and expense of getting here, to an abandoned station that's only listed on old historical charts and has otherwise been forgotten, is how this place defends itself," Perry said.

"Hidden in plain sight. It's often not a bad strategy." I had Netty bring up whatever schematics were available for the station, and noted there were two UDAs, universal docking adapters, whose pattern hadn't changed in several hundred years.

"You know, I think we should just drop in for a visit." I unstrapped from my seat. "Netty, bring us in to dock at the closer of those two UDAs. Perry, Icky, you're with me. Torina, you stay here and keep the motor running in case we have to bug out in a hurry."

"How about me, Van?" Netty asked.

"Uh—you'll stay here with the *Fafnir*, too? Since you, you know, *are* the *Fafnir?*"

"I know. A girl just likes to be asked, though."

I STEPPED out of the airlock and into the station's interior, The Drop raised, the Moonsword ready at my hip. Icky followed with her sledgehammer, which had now been kitted out with a reinforced poly-graphene handle and wickedly keen spikes to pierce armor. Perry came along behind her.

I looked around in thermal, then switched on my helmet lamp. The interior of the station was dark, wasn't pressurized, and there was no artificial gravity.

"No one's home," Icky said.

"Doesn't seem like it," I agreed, looking up the corridor ahead of us, then left and right along the corridors that followed the circumference of the station. I pointed at the first. "This seems to head toward the center of the station. Let's check it out."

I pushed off, sailing along the corridor, occasionally correcting my course with a nudge from a hand or a foot. Icky trailed me a few meters back, giving us both space to maneuver. Perry, though, used his thrusters to pass her, and then me.

"I'm gonna take point, Van. I'm getting flickers of something from up ahead."

"Flickers of—something? Can you be more specific?"

"Quivers on the EM needle, as it were," he said, drifting past me. "Not enough to say anything definitive yet, but the signal's getting stronger the further this way we go."

"I don't know about you guys, but this place doesn't come across to me as empty," Icky said.

"I don't think it's empty. I think it's waiting."

"Waiting? Well, that's more chilling than it needs to be. What do you mean, waiting?" I asked him.

"Just a feeling," Perry said.

"You have feelings now?"

"It's something I'm trying out."

"Like Icky's mullet?"

"Don't be jealous. Three more months and it's gonna be a stunner," Icky preened.

"Three more months and you're going into *soccer rocker* territory," I said, my eyes flickering forward.

"Is that good?" Icky asked.

"If you're European. And it's 1988."

We pushed on, gliding along the corridor. With each passing meter, I braced myself harder and harder for something bad to happen—an ambush, triggering some old security system or awakening some slumbering bots, something. But nothing did, and we reached the core of the station without any strife except the things my own imagination conjured up.

"Hello?"

The voice that buzzed across the comm wasn't Perry's or Icky's. It was female, and that was all I knew. I caught myself on a stanchion as we entered the core, an open, atrium-like cylindrical space that must have spanned the station from top to bottom. Here, at its midpoint, a fusion reactor hummed away, sending power along hefty conduits to the four comm arrays on the exterior, up and down, and to the four cardinal points. More machinery towered above and plunged below the reactor.

"Um, hello—who's this?"

"I might ask you the same question. All I know is that you approached and docked in a ship."

"Perry, who the hell is this?" I asked.

Icky grabbed another stanchion a couple of meters away with one of her smaller hands, while her bigger ones hefted her hammer. "And *where* are they?"

"Who, I don't know, at least not specifically. As to where—well, look straight ahead. They're somewhere in there," he said.

"An AI?"

"Actually, I don't think so. Now that we are close to the source, I can say with a pretty high degree of confidence that we're hearing a stolen identity, who's been plugged into this comm system."

"Whoever was just speaking has it right. My name is Totovar, and I am—or was—a Ligurite."

A Ligurite. I'd only ever known one of that psychically persuasive race, our old and corrupt friend the former Master Yotov.

"Do you remember how you got here, Totovar?" I asked.

"I remember being on my homeworld, literally walking down a street. My next memory is being here, like this. That was… four years, eight months, four days, and three point six five hours ago. But who's counting?"

"Hey, wasn't whatsername, that Guild Master—Yotov, that's it. Wasn't she a Ligurite?" Icky asked.

I opened my mouth to reply, but Totovar beat me to it.

"Yes, Yotov is a Ligurite. She also happens to be my cousin."

We spent some time piecing together what Totovar remembered, and what she'd learned since being plugged in like a glorified battery.

The station, she explained, was a comms hub for the movement of money—shady, sketchy, dirty, and in some cases, outright illegal money. The way she described it almost made it seem like an ATM for criminals. Like the other stolen identities we'd encountered, it wasn't Totovar's conscious mind that was being exploited, but rather the subconscious and autonomous parts of it—for instance, the parts of her brain functions that would regulate things like her heartbeat were integrated into the station's systems in ways that even the researchers back on Anvil Dark studying the problem didn't quite understand.

"Someone out there is way ahead of the curve technologically, compared to the rest of known space," I said to her, as we tried to track down the location of whatever hardware contained her—well, contained *her*.

"Either that, or someone stumbled on some alien tech and they're taking advantage of it," Totovar said.

"Yeah, that's a possibility, too."

"But it's possible to return my consciousness to a new physical body."

"In our experience, it is. It's not a simple or cheap process, but —" Perry and I stopped, near a panel inset into the central core of the station. The lack of gravity was a blessing, because if the station did have a down based on the orientation of the decks, I'd be poised over a good seventy-five meter drop right now.

"I think this is it, Van. The strongest signal leakage that I can tie back to the operation of her, well, brain functions, is right here."

I nodded. One small blessing was that the identity chips, when they were operating, generated a characteristic signal. It was part of the reason we'd kept Totovar talking while Perry tried to zero in on where she—what remained of her, anyway—was installed.

I reached for the latch to open the panel, but Icky drifted up beside me. "Van, wait a sec."

I pulled my hand back. "What?"

"Uh—Tovotar, right?" Icky said.

"Totovar," our stolen identity replied.

"Yeah, sorry, Totovar. You're involved in moving around a lot of money, right?"

"I am. Probably tens of millions of bonds at this point, and maybe some other currencies as well."

"Do you know where it's all coming from and going to?"

"No. I only know senders and receivers to random strings of numbers and letters. Why?"

"Well, I'm just thinking out loud here—"

"Easy, big 'un, don't wanna pull a hammy," Perry murmured.

"Silence, bird, I'm a trained athlete. Anyway, the other, uh, identities we've discovered have been running industrial machines or similar trivial shit, right? But this one's handling money. What'd you bet that the bad guys don't want her falling into enemy hands?"

I frowned at Icky for a moment, then got it and gestured at the panel. "Wait—are you suggesting that this is booby-trapped?"

"To at least surge power through her chip and turn it to slag, yeah. But maybe also to shut down fusion containment on that reactor a few meters below our feet. I mean, wouldn't you if you were a bad guy?"

"Damn. Icky, you're right, and that's a good catch. Can you—"

"Check for it?" She extracted a portable scanner from her harness. "Just stand back and let me do my magic."

I did. Icky began scanning the access panel and the area around it, but slowly, with intricate and precise deliberation. I tended to forget she wasn't just about swinging hammers and smashing things, that when it came to tech she had the care and patience of a watch maker.

While she worked, I turned my attention back to Totovar. "Is there anything else you can tell us about this or what happened to you?"

"Well, since it seems that you really are here to rescue me, I'll let you in on a little white lie—my last memory isn't exactly my homeworld."

"Okay. What is it, then?"

"I was at Drifting City when this happened. I had, ah, *business* there."

"Drifting City?"

Perry, hovering a few meters away, spoke up. "Wretched hive, blah blah. It's another place where bad guys congregate, a literal floating city in the atmosphere of a Venus-like planet with pools of sulfur and winds so hot they boil lead—but not everywhere. Remember how when we took our trip to Venus, we noted that there was a portion of the atmosphere with the right temperature and pressure to support human life? It's like that."

"Yeah, but it wasn't breathable, though."

"On Venus? No, it was all carbon dioxide and sulfur

compounds. But Drifting City's planet has a much higher oxygen content in its atmosphere, so even humans can get by with simple rebreather rigs."

"Huh. So the reason I've never heard of this place before, in the four years I've been doing this is—?"

"It's outside our jurisdiction. Drifting City was established only about two hundred years ago, as an experimental platform on the closest candidate planet to known space. It's too far from any of the major political powers for them to be interested in it, so there haven't been any moves to include it in known space since then. It just kinda sits out there like an independent city-state, doing its own thing."

"Yeah, but I'd have thought it would come up in some briefing or background material or something."

"Would you like to be filled in on all the places where we *don't* have jurisdiction, Van?"

I thought about it. Every waking moment I spent reading intel reports and case summaries was one immersed in just trying to keep up with what was going on across a handful of important locations—Spindrift and Crossroads, Dregs and Halcyon, maybe a dozen or so others. I sure as hell didn't have the capacity to keep tabs on much more, and all those places together probably accounted for maybe ten or fifteen percent of the population of known space.

"Point taken," I finally said. "There's just too much known space for one guy as it is."

"As a great bird once said, space is big."

"Okay, but just how many seedy hubs of sin are there out here, anyway?" I asked.

"More than there are churches, I can tell you that for sure."

"Yup, she's booby-trapped," Icky finally announced. "There are microcircuits built right into the hinges of this access panel, and a grid of wires carrying trickle current embedded in the panel and the plating around it. Open it without disarming it, something's gonna happen."

"Any idea what?" I asked.

"Probably not a little flag popping out with some confetti and the word BOOM printed on it," Perry said.

Icky scowled at him through her visor. "Your circuits get fried somewhere along the way here, bird? What the hell are you talking about?"

I shook my head. "Never mind. Okay, so you can probably guess what the next question is going to be—"

"Can I disarm it?" Icky said.

"Yes."

"No."

"No?"

"No. At least, not reliably. Whoever built it knew what the hell they were doing."

"Shit. Totovar, we may need to have a team of techs from Anvil Dark come here and—"

"I really don't want to wait. There was message traffic generated after you arrived here, aimed down relative to the galactic ecliptic," she cut in.

"Toward The Torus, and The Deeps," Perry said.

"Yeah. Shit. So we've got a window of hours here, tops."

"I'll give you some added incentive. I've got access to all of the message logs. They might just have what amounts to random strings of characters as address identifiers, but they can't truly be random, can they? Otherwise, they wouldn't actually contain any useful information. Anyway, spring me and it's all yours," Totovar said.

I couldn't resist a thin smile. Ligurites were noted for what seemed to be some low-level, latent psychic effect that made the things they were saying sound eminently reasonable, even if they really weren't. Yotov exploited this constantly. That effect didn't apply here, but it didn't stop Totovar from trying.

"The issue isn't whether we want to spring you, Totovar. It's doing it in a way that doesn't get you wiped or all of us blown up," I replied.

"I understand. Rest assured, I don't want that, either. What I want, in fact, is revenge. That means me getting out of here, getting installed in a new body, then finding out who's responsible for doing this to me and making them pay—starting with my dear cousin Yotov."

"I hear you. Enemy of my enemy and all that. So, to that end, is there anything you can tell us about this place, these systems, and that booby-trap that might help us?"

"For instance, can you shut down that reactor down there? That'd be a big help for a start. I mean, there might still be explosives on board this thing, but every source of kaboom we can eliminate is one less to worry about," Icky said.

Totovar was able to shut down the reactor but not before a burst broadcast was emitted from each of the comm arrays. It was just more alphanumeric nonsense, but it probably meant something to someone—which meant any doubt that we were on a clock had been firmly dispelled.

"Tick tick," I said.

Totovar agreed. "Yup."

"Sorry, Van, but this scanner just doesn't have the resolution," Icky said, frustration hardening her voice.

We'd spent an hour now trying to figure out a way to bypass the security grid that had been erected around Totovar's chip. Torina and Netty hadn't yet detected any activity in the region around the station, but its location was working against us. It had, by virtue of definition, been placed where gravitational effects from Wolf 424 wouldn't inhibit twisting, so any bad guys who came to see what was up with their fancy money machine could twist in literally only a few klicks away, if they wanted. And with the *Fafnir* docked, she couldn't even maneuver. The sense of vulnerability made my toes curl in my boots, but time dragged on and we seemed to get no closer to a solution.

"What do you need, Icky?"

"A better scanner. This one's designed to deal with, you know, ordinary spaceship problems, not a maze of microcircuits in a booby-trap." She sighed, a ragged thing that expressed her frustration in great detail.

I swore softly. We had nothing on board the *Fafnir* with the fine resolution required. Even Perry's scanners just didn't have the needed granularity. I'd made about twenty mental notes in the past hour to acquire something with the capability we needed, just so we had it on hand. But that wouldn't help here and now, would it—?

Something tickled my brain. I was missing something. It was

maddening that I couldn't pin down what. But there was something—

I looked around for inspiration. What the hell was it?

"I don't know, Van. Maybe we should just go for it—" Icky started, but I shook my head. My eyes had fallen on the hilt of the Moonsword.

There it was, I thought, drawing the blade. Icky's eyes went wide behind her visor.

"Woah, Van, I'm doing the best I can here—"

"Don't worry, Icky, I haven't gotten that frustrated—yet. I wonder, though." I fiddled with the control recessed into the cross guard, the one Linulla had only recently added.

I held the Moonsword near the access panel. "Icky, you should be getting a signal from this sword on your scanner."

She glanced at it, tapped at it, then looked back at me. "Holy shit. You've been holding out on us, Van."

"Sorry, but this is the first time that new upgrade's come up in the field. How's the resolution it's giving you?"

"Awesome, and then some. With the data from your blade, the scanner's AI can resolve not just the individual microcircuits, but even the flow of current through them."

"Please tell me that's going to make a difference."

She grinned. "It ain't gonna hurt."

It still took nearly two hours of painstaking work to finally access Totovar's chip. Icky had to drill a grid of fine holes between the lurking microcircuits, then establish bridges between them by spot soldering jumper wires. I could only marvel at the fine, precise work she could manage with her smaller pair of hands. I marveled even more at her patience doing it. When it came to most aspects of life, she had the attention span of a six-year-old. When it came to tech, though, it seemed nothing could faze her.

There was a reason that Wu'tzur made such great engineers.

We finally opened the access panel, revealing the identity chip. We scanned it for any connections or circuits we didn't recognize, but it seemed to conform to the exact design of the other chips we'd found. I reached for it but paused.

"Okay, Totovar, you're going to—actually, I don't know what you're going to experience."

"It doesn't matter. I've assembled all the data I can. Now, get me the hell out of here."

"Getting the hell out," I said, grabbing her chip and unplugging it.

It struck me that after all this, wouldn't it be deeply ironic if we missed something—if the act of unplugging her chip actually somehow triggered some sort of security. But it also struck me *after* I had her chip in my hand. Still, being in one piece was a good sign—

"Van, we have company," Torina said.

I tensed and muffled a vile curse or three. After all this, we were still going to have to fight our way out of here?

"Let's go!" I snapped, pushing off the station's core and back toward the corridor that would take us to the *Fafnir*. "Torina, we're on our way. As soon as the airlock seals, kick her—"

"Actually, Van, you can relax. It's your friend, B," Torina said.

"Hello there, Van. Someone call for a doc with an attitude problem?" B said, her voice cutting in over the comm.

I puffed out a breath. "You made it."

"Yeah, sorry about being late. I was attending to a medical issue in the Procyon system. Anyway, here I am. So, what'd I miss?"

"All the hard work," Icky groused.

B laughed. "Right on time, then."

22

RATHER THAN HANGING around Point Lonesome, we twisted in company with B to a refueling depot located in a better-traveled part of the Wolf 424 system. We took the opportunity there to compare notes aboard the *Fafnir*.

"So, we sent Zeno to Anvil Dark with those cargo pods of Puloquir and our miscreant du jour, Wixor," I said, finishing my side of the briefing. B nodded.

"You've been busy. I'm impressed. And on top of all that, you rescued a stolen identity."

"My name is Totovar," Waldo said. As we had with other identities we'd retrieved, we plugged Totovar's chip into Waldo, our otherwise semi-autonomous maintenance bot. It was no substitute for an actual body, of course, but it did at least give her the ability to interact.

"My apologies," B said, her antennae waving.

"You're a doctor. Does that mean you can get me a body?"

"Sorry, I don't have a spare one lying around. But I understand that Van's next stop is going to be *Ponte Alus Kyr*, and if anyone can make it happen, they can."

"That's assuming *Ponte Alus Kyr* hasn't been compromised. That is where Wixor was taking the Puloquir, after all," Torina said.

Icky nodded. "Yeah, kinda hard to imagine they intended to do anything good with 'em," she said, stretching out her legs—an act that took a big chunk of the *Fafnir*'s galley.

"Which is why I'd like you to accompany us to *Ponte Alus Kyr*, B. Your medical expertise might come in handy," I said.

"Not to mention the added firepower."

"That too."

"What I don't get is why *Ponte Alus Kyr* is involved in this. They're a legitimate and well-funded research facility. Why would they take the risk of getting into bed with someone like Wixor?" Torina said.

I shrugged. "That's a very good question, isn't it? If I had to guess, I'd have to say this has something to do with the Post-Body Core, which has something to do with our identity thefts and the Sorcerers, which means it all has something to do with our Crimes Against Order case, and so on and so on and so on."

"It's all one big chain of misery," Icky said.

B nodded. "Well put. Okay, so I guess our next stop is *Ponte Alus Kyr*—" she said, standing, then stopped. "Oh. Right. Almost forgot. I've got something for you, Van."

She extracted a data slate, tapped at it, and offered it over. It was a message from Zeno.

Safe on Torus. Not alone. A mysterious gentleman who'll only say he's "from the Guild" is with me for security. He said he can get this message to you. No need to hurry. Drinking on your tab.

Torina read over my shoulder. "Who's this *mysterious gentleman from the Guild?*" she asked, looking pointedly at B.

B shrugged. "There are a lot of people in the Guild. You expect me to know all of them?"

Torina turned her pointed look from B to me. She didn't say anything, but her unhappiness at yet more "secrets within secrets" bullshit involving the Peacemaker Guild was clearly chewing away at her patience. I was going to have to bring her into the circle of knowledge about the GKU, and if B or Groshenko or anyone else didn't like it—well, it sucked to be them. What I *couldn't* do was have this gulf of suspicion yawning ever wider between us.

I resolved to do just that the next time we were alone and had some downtime. Now was not that time, though, so I gave her a look that I hope said, *Please, just a little more patience.*

She held my gaze a moment longer, then pulled it away.

"Netty, you've got that course to *Ponte Alus Kyr* set to go?" she asked.

"Anytime you're ready," Netty replied.

I decided to lighten the mood a little. "We'd better make it fast. I don't know how long it will take them to grow a body for Totovar, and Zeno can really put away the hooch. And food."

Torina lifted one eyebrow. "That sounds perilously close to fat shaming, mister."

"What? I—what? No! Not at all—"

Perry, standing on the galley table, put his wing across my back. "Van, I'm not exactly the most tactful guy—or, you know, human. But even I know when the time has come to stop digging and just silently contemplate the hole you've made for yourself."

▸

LOCATED in the Zeta Herculis system, the orbital station known as *Ponte Alus Kyr* was, at least technically, a secret. But it was an Area 51 sort of secret, one that wasn't really that secret at all. Area 51 really did exist, in the form of a detachment of Edwards Air Force Base at Groom Lake, Nevada. It was actually a test facility for advanced and secret technology, such as the famous SR-71 Blackbird, the F-117 Nighthawk stealth fighter, and the B-2 Spirit strategic stealth bomber. According to pop culture, it was also involved in research into alien technology from crashed spaceships, which was something I considered utter hokum until I found a spaceship in my barn. Now, I wondered exactly what *was* going on there.

Ponte Alus Kyr was much the same. It wasn't *exactly* a secret. The name wafted through the fringes of the known space version of popular culture, and lots of people claimed they knew what was going on here when practically none of them really did. The space around the orbital was closed and protected by armed warning buoys, all of it enabled through the intersections of a number of interstellar agreements. But we broadcasted our Peacemaker credentials and declared ourselves to be involved in a legally consti-tuted Guild investigation, so the buoys remained silent, and we slid into the *Ponte Alus Kyr* terminal traffic-control zone.

"B made it through as well," Torina said, watching the overlay. "Guess her credentials were good."

I nodded. I wasn't surprised, although I did wonder if she used Peacemaker credentials or something else. *Ponte Alus Kyr* seemed like just the sort of place to be in cahoots with the GKU.

"So, I'm curious, Van. Aren't we here on two sort of incompatible missions? We want to arrange a new body for Totovar—but we also intend to confront these guys about why two cargo pods of Puloquir were being brought here by a criminal. To me, that's a mixed purpose. But then I've never been accused of being subtle," Icky said, wiggling thick fingers at me.

"I don't intend to go in there, accusing guns blazing. Coming here to arrange for a body for Totovar is our official reason, because it links back to our case. I mean, she's a material witness *and* a victim, so it only makes sense we'd want to help her, right?"

"Okay, so when do we get to the confronting part?"

I confirmed that Netty had connected with *Ponte Alus Kyr* traffic control and was aiming us to dock at our assigned berth on the gleaming white orbital, then I turned back to Icky.

"The researcher we dealt with here before, Hoshi, was partnered with a symbiotic being, a Krali'on named Cibilax. I'm planning on getting some quiet time with them. If anyone will have answers regarding the Puloquir and the Tenants, they will."

"Uh, Van, the Krali'on are symbiotes, not parasites. You might want to be *really* careful with your opening lines there so that you're not… misunderstood," Perry warned.

"Way ahead of you, bird. But I got a good vibe from Hoshi and Cibilax when we were last here, so I'm hoping they'll see what I see regarding the Puloquir—that this seems like genocide, one shipload at a time. At least, it does to me."

"And if they just stonewall you?"

"Then we'll be no worse off than we are now. But I hope they can help us, because if we keep finding shiploads of Puloquir like that, then it's a slow drip of massed death, and that only has one unhappy conclusion."

Torina nodded. "They'll be on their way to extinction, like the Eykinao."

I nodded. "Or they'll actually get there, and all that'll be left of them will be a memory."

"So how do you want to do this, Van?" Perry asked.

I smiled at him. "Funny you should ask, Perry, because I've got a specific job in mind for you."

WE WEREN'T MET at the airlock by Hoshi and Cibilax, though. Instead, we were greeted by a human woman whose name tag said Rosen, and a female Gajur named Okalni from Drixis Pharmaceuticals, one of the major partners in the joint venture that was *Ponte Alus Kyr*. B was with them, having docked first, but her attitude was a surprisingly quiet, guarded one. That was all the signal I needed from her to know that something was off here, and that I should be on my guard, too.

"Peacemaker Tudor, welcome to *Ponte Alus Kyr*. I understand that this isn't your first visit here," Okalni said.

I rested my hand on the pommel of the Moonsword. I'd worn it as a sort of badge of office but hadn't bothered to lug along The Drop because I didn't expect to end up in a firefight here. "It isn't, no. We were involved with the unfortunate business around the Eykinao."

"Ah, yes. Unfortunate business indeed. Now, how may we help you this time?"

I noted that we hadn't been invited any further into the station. Okay, fine. If we were going to rest on officialdom—

"You can help us regarding a major investigation we have underway into a serious crime—a Crime Against Order, in fact."

Okalni stiffened slightly. Good. She recognized the significance of the term, and she should, since it was like the cops showing up at your door back on Earth to ask you a few questions about crimes against humanity.

"That does sound serious. How can we assist?"

I glanced around at the open space surrounding us just outside the airlock, at other *Ponte Alus Kyr* staff wandering past. "Um, can we talk somewhere less… public?"

Okalni hesitated an instant. Clearly, she'd hoped that making us obviously feel unwelcome would speed things along. Well, I was about to make myself feel *very* welcome.

She led Torina, B, and me to a small meeting room not far from the airlock. It had clearly been designed with this sort of meeting in mind, one that would happen quickly and didn't involve inviting people deeper into the station. I made a point of thumping down in my chair, stretching my legs out, and smiling. I saw B and Torina both suppressing smiles of their own.

"Alright, Peacemaker Tudor. How can we assist you?" Okalni asked.

"We have an individual on board our ship, a Ligurite named Totovar. She's a material witness to a possible Crime Against Order. She's also a victim of it," I said, then went on to explain her having been physically killed, with her identity installed on a chip.

Okalni nodded. "I've read some briefing material about this. We've assisted you in the past, providing new bodies for some of these unfortunate individuals."

"Mainly through your Flesh Merchants on Spindrift—and yes,

we're aware that they're an, um, annex to your normal operations here."

Okalni returned the Gajur version of a smile. "They're a convenient test bed for some of our work, yes."

"So, rather than working through them, we figured we'd cut out the middleman and come directly here. We need a new physical body for Totovar."

"I see." Okalni sat back in her chair. "That will be both time-consuming and expensive."

I shrugged. "It always is. The Guild will pay."

I caught a glance from both Torina and Perry. I'd probably just committed the Guild to at least one hundred thousand bonds of cost, which far exceeded my authority. But I didn't care. I was Gerhardt's Justiciar, so he was just going to have to back me up.

"Very well, then. We'll make the necessary arrangements," Okalni said, nodding to the hitherto silent woman named Rosen. She nodded back and, without a word, left.

Okalni started to stand, but I raised a hand. "I would also like to speak to Hoshi and Cibilax."

Okalni sat back down. "May I ask why?"

"You may."

Okalni waited, then frowned. I smiled back at her. "Their insight proved valuable the last time we were here. I'd like to tap into it again."

"I see. Well, unfortunately, Hoshi isn't available, I'm afraid."

"I'm willing to wait until she is."

Okalni narrowed her eyes. "You may be waiting some time, unfortunately. She's not currently here."

"On *Ponte Alus Kyr*?"

"That's right."

This was the part I'd been waiting for. I sat up and tapped my comm. "Perry, talk to me. Are Hoshi and Cibilax here?"

"The station logs record them as being present. And yes, I've confirmed that if they'd have left the station, *Ponte Alus Kyr*'s own procedures would require them to have been logged out so there's always an accurate record regarding how many people are here, who they are, and where they are—in case of emergencies," he replied.

I turned to Okalni and waited.

She glared back at me. "Your accomplice broke into our data systems without authorization? That's a serious offense, Peacemaker."

I leaned right into her scowl. "So is lying to a Peacemaker involved in a lawful investigation in a place of Guild jurisdiction—which, I might remind you, *Ponte Alus Kyr* is, and by your own charter. And to add some spice to that, you just lied to me regarding the presence of someone I consider essential to a case of Crimes Against Order. I could arrest you for that right now."

Okalni sputtered a bit. "Essential—how? How would Hoshi be essential?"

I shrugged. "I might consider her a material witness. Or not. I'll make that determination after I talk to her."

Okalni touched her own comm. "Security, please come to the conference room for airlock Three Alpha—"

B laughed. "You're calling your rental cops? Oh, please." She turned to me. "Van, I'd suggest invoking Article Two of Annex A to Interstellar Protocol Five and declaring this entire facility a location of interest."

B continued, her voice shifting smoothly into a threat. "And while you're speaking to your legal counsel about that, we'll be calling Anvil Dark, bringing some forensic audit teams here to comb through all your files, and sealing off this facility to outside access, including comms."

Okalni gaped. "On what grounds?"

B shrugged. "Van said it himself—you lied to a Peacemaker investigating a Crime Against Order. The Guild is going to take a very dim view of that."

Okalni stood. "This is ridiculous. If you think you can browbeat me with your distorted legal opinions, because that's all they are, opinions—"

"Hmm. And I wonder what Ervin Trask's *opinion* would be? He is still the Chair of this facility's Oversight Committee, isn't he?"

I glanced at Torina, who offered a small shrug. I had no idea who Ervin Trask was, but B was running with something here, so I was content to see how it played out.

It got Okalni's attention, that was clear. "You can drop all the names you want—"

"Just like Ervin dropped trou for me when he needed some— let's call it some *work* done, to deal with some age-related issues. He was profoundly grateful."

I glanced at B. "Uh—doctor-client confidentiality—?"

B glanced back. "Interfering with an investigation of Crimes Against Order. I'm sure Ervin would just love to have his pet project implicated in that." She turned back on Okalni.

"So what's it going to be? Do I give Ervin a call, or do we all get out of one another's way here so we can get on with our jobs?"

Okalni dithered a moment, then slumped. "Fine. I'll inform Hoshi that you want to speak with her."

I frowned. There was something about that phrasing, *inform her that you want to speak with her*, not *I'll take you to Hoshi* or *I'll call for her—*

I touched my comm. "Perry, what's Hoshi's current location?"

"Uh—in her office, level two-tango, compartment fourteen —oh."

"What?"

"According to the log, she's been there for nearly seventeen hours. I mean, there's work-a-holism, and then there's that—"

"Thanks, bird," I said, standing and looking at Torina and B. "We need to go. Now."

I headed for the door. Torina followed. B paused, though.

"Oh, and by the way? If you ever feel tempted to somehow make use of the personal medical information I may or may not have just revealed?" She leaned in and whispered something to Okalni.

The Gajur recoiled, aghast. "You... wouldn't dare."

B just smiled, then fell in behind us.

WE RAN into a pair of *Ponte Alus Kyr* security guards shortly after leaving the conference room. They tried to stop us, but I flashed my credentials and a bit of menace.

"Torina, if these two don't get out of our way by the time I finish speaking, you take the one on the left into custody. Oh, and try to not break too many bones this time."

The two guards flinched and withered aside under the double

331

assault of Peacemaker credentials and Torina's dangerous smile. We pushed on, with Perry joining us on the way.

When we arrived at Hoshi's office, the door was closed. The whole facility was designed to be locked down and compartmentalized in case some pathogen or something escaped containment, so the door was stout alloy. I hit the ringer on the keypad beside it, waited a few seconds, then hit it again.

"Aw, hell—I've seen enough." I turned to the two cowed security guards, who'd trailed sheepishly along behind us, apparently determined to at least *look* like they were escorting us.

"Open this door," I said to them.

The two exchanged a glance, then one of them came forward and tapped at the keypad. All it did was sound a thin buzzer. He frowned and tapped again, and got the same result.

"I don't get it. This is my override code. It shouldn't be locked out—"

"Step back," I said, drawing the Moonsword. The man yelped and stumbled back, but I ignored him and plunged the blade into the door.

The other security guard stepped toward. "Hey, you can't—"

Torina intercepted him. "I think you mean that he *shouldn't*. Because"—she looked at me as I drew the blade down, then across, slicing through the substance of the door—"he clearly *can*."

I finished cutting apart the door, then kicked in the loosened section. As soon as I stepped inside, I was hit by the metallic stink of blood.

I saw feet extending from behind a worktable. After hurrying that way, I found Hoshi. She lay in a pool of gore. I couldn't tell if she was alive or dead, but what I *could* tell was that her symbiote, Cibilax, was gone.

B IMMEDIATELY SURGED INTO ACTION. I shouted at the station security guards, who were still standing outside, to declare a medical emergency and get help. That broke them loose, and they both immediately started barking into comms. A moment later, a warning chime began ringing through the station.

Torina and I stood and watched B examine Hoshi. She had a small suite of medical supplies in a pouch on her belt, and she dug into them.

"Is she alive?" I asked.

B activated a medical scanner and touched it directly to Hoshi's forehead. "Um—yeah, she is. Barely. She's lost a lot of blood."

"What happened to Cibilax?" Torina asked, but all B and I could do was shrug. As far as I knew, the Krali'on were physically bonded to their hosts, nervous and other systems intimately connected. For one to be removed, or—

Leave?

I hit the comm. "Perry—?"

"Right here, boss," he said as he sailed into the office and landed on Hoshi's desk with a rattle of metallic talons. When he folded his wings, he saw Hoshi.

"Oh. Ouch."

"Yeah. Perry—or B—what do we know about the Krali'on? Can they separate from their host?"

"Not at will. They share a circulatory system. That's why they're a symbiotic species. They need hosts to leave their home environ-ment, to provide them with oxygenated blood, among other things," B said, injecting Hoshi with something from a spray syringe.

"Well, not as far as we know, anyway. The Krali'on are a secre-tive species at best, and neither they nor their hosts talk much about the nitty-gritty of their relationship," Perry put in.

B glanced up. "Okay, point taken. Let's put it this way. If a Kral-i'on wanted to separate from its host, there'd have to be some measures put in place first. It's like us with b-suits. We can step out of an airlock into the void if we want, but if we're not wearing a suit, we're not going to last very long."

A commotion rose in the corridor. A medical crash team had arrived. We stood back as they worked with B to stabilize Hoshi, then they loaded her onto a gurney and hustled off to the *Ponte Alus Kyr* infirmary.

Watching her being wheeled off, Torina sighed. "I guess if you're going to have a severe medical emergency, then a bleeding-edge—" She caught herself. "Sorry, poor choice of words. A *cutting-edge* bioscience facility is the place to do it."

"Assuming they *want* to keep you alive, that's true," I replied, starting after the gurney.

"You think the station itself is implicated in this?"

"Right now, I suspect anyone who didn't arrive here in the *Fafnir* or aboard B's ship."

"That's a lot of people."

"It is. But let's start with the person we know lied to us. Torina, invite our friend Okalni to another sit down session, if you please."

23

WE MET Okalni in company with the *Ponte Alus Kyr* Director, an earnest if somewhat nerdy human male named Winthrop. He was another immigrant into space from Earth, a man whose accent made him from the United Kingdom, but who'd formerly been a senior executive with a Silicon Valley bioscience spinoff working on neural interfaces. How he'd ended up here was likely an interesting story, but something he said twigged me. He'd been involved in bioscience research on Earth for more than twenty years, he'd said.

"Tell me—do you know Jeanette Ruiz-Rocher?" I asked, cutting him off before he completed his introduction. I watched him closely.

He recognized the name, that much I could tell. But instead of lying—which would have been a huge red flag—he nodded.

"I do. Or, rather, I recognize the name. She made quite a sinister name for herself in the field back on Earth."

"So you're aware that she ended up coming into space and getting herself a sinister reputation out here, as well," I said as we arranged ourselves around a conference table in Winthrop's plush office. "As in, she's still near the top of the Peacemaker Guild's wanted list."

Winthrop gave me a quizzical look. "Are you implying that I should know her just because we happen to have worked in broadly the same field? A field that consists of thousands of researchers back on Earth?"

I smiled. "I'm not implying anything. And if your background had been as a carpenter or a florist, I wouldn't even ask the question. But you have to admit that the chances of you knowing one of several thousand people in bioscience is, well, a lot better than you knowing any one of eight *billion* people on Earth."

That seemed to fluster Winthrop. "I… know of her. And of the disrepute she brought to our field. So I hope you find her and prosecute her, doubly so now that you seem to be hinting that she and I are somehow involved with one another."

I decided to leave it at that. Jeanette Ruiz-Rocher and her accomplice, a vicious Yonnox thug named Kuthrix, were gaping wounds in our investigation. We'd gotten close to them once early on in my Peacemaker career, but they managed to elude us and we hadn't caught even a whiff of either of them since. So they were gone, but definitely not forgotten.

I shook my head. "My apologies. As I said, I'm not meaning to imply anything. But running across someone involved in her field, and from Earth, was just too good an opportunity to pass up to, you know, at least ask the question."

Winthrop nodded. "Which means we can get to matters at hand. This whole business with Hoshi is most unfortunate."

I gave him a hard stare. "She's on the brink of death. So, yeah, I'd say it's unfortunate."

"I didn't mean—"

I plowed on, cutting him off. "What I want to know is why Okalni lied to us about her being on the station. That was a concern at the time—lying to a Peacemaker investigating a crime is obstruction of justice, and lying to a Peacemaker investigating a Crime Against Order is, well, a whole lot worse."

I turned to Okalni. "But you lied about the presence of a person who's nearly dead, quite possibly as a result of foul play. Oh, and a person who I was specifically looking to talk to about that Crime Against Order, so—not to put too fine a point on it—that officially makes you a *person of interest*."

Okalni, looking stricken, turned to Winthrop. "We have to tell them."

I sat up. "Tell me what?"

Winthrop sighed. "Hoshi was involved in some classified work on behalf of… a paying client."

"And I was just conforming to that client's wishes regarding keeping the whole matter discreet," Okalni hurried to add.

I looked from one to the other. "You do realize that you're going to have to reveal who that client is, and what sort of *classified work* you were doing for them."

"Peacemaker Tudor, you must appreciate—"

"Let me put it to you this way. If you don't, then I will declare all of *Ponte Alus Kyr* a crime scene, then bring in teams to dig through every bit of data storage you've got. It's going to take weeks, probably, and you're not going to be doing much during that time except answering repetitive, pointed questions and, of course, incessantly bitching about it all."

I glanced at Perry and waited for him to signal me, maybe by speaking through my ear bug. But he just kept his amber gaze on Winthrop and nodded his head.

"We can totally do that, per Interstellar Protocol Three, Article—"

Winthrop waved a hand. "That won't be necessary. The client was the Security Directorate of the Seven Stars League. And the project involves some specific biochemical research regarding the integration of disparate nervous systems."

I looked at Torina at the mention of the League. She just returned a knowing nod. Indeed. We'd just had some dots connected, hadn't we?

"By which you mean plugging one individual's nervous system into another's," Perry said.

Winthrop nodded. "That's right. They approached us with a research proposal—generously funded, I might add—to study the interactions of specific neurotransmitters in two different species, and how intermediary mechanisms could be developed to allow them to function seamlessly."

"Hoshi was assigned to the project because, being in a symbiotic relationship with another being herself, she had insights into the underlying molecular biochemistry that would have proved useful," Okalni said, but then rushed on. "But that was the extent of it—a rather mundane investigation of some really niche biochemistry. If we'd have imagined, even for an instant, it would lead to this—"

Torina leaned forward, cutting her off. "Did you actually assign Hoshi to the project, or did the League request her?"

"She'd already had some discussions with the League about the project, before they even proposed it to us. But that's not unusual. Researchers are often in informal contact with outside agencies, conceptualizing projects before making a formal pitch," Winthrop said.

"So she was… in league with the League," I said.

Winthrop frowned. "With all due respect, that makes it sound like something illicit and unethical was going on. Hoshi's project consisted of studying some neurotransmitters in different species —that's it."

"Okay, sure. Then how do you explain what happened to her? Or the two cargo drones carrying Puloquir here? Puloquir who were apparently being kept in a state of what amounts to suspended animation?"

Winthrop sank back and sighed. "I can't."

"You had *no* knowledge of that. Like, none at all."

Okalni shook her head. "We didn't. And feel free to examine every record, the minutes of every meeting, all of it, to see if you can find any mention of it. You won't."

"That just means if it happened, it was all off the books," Perry noted.

"Whatever was going on, whatever Hoshi was involved in behind the scenes—*Ponte Alus Kyr* had nothing to do with it, Peace-maker Tudor. I can guarantee you that," Winthrop said, sitting earnestly forward again.

I looked from one to the other, trying to suss out any hints of duplicity. These were scientists, though—maybe somewhat bureau-cratic scientists, but not bureaucratic enough to really have the stonewalling thing down. And they weren't hardened criminals, spinning lies as naturally as breathing. What I saw on both their faces was a stew of shock and worry, tinged with a hint of disgust.

I stood. "We will expect your full cooperation as we investigate this."

"Of course, Peacemaker Tudor. If you need anything at all, just let me know and I'll ensure you get it," Winthrop said.

We left them and swung past the *Ponte Alus Kyr* infirmary to check on Hoshi. It wasn't good.

"She's in a coma," B said. "She lost a lot of blood, but just as damaging—maybe even more so—was the loss of her symbiote. Her body, and particularly her nervous system had established a biochemical equilibrium with him. When he was suddenly taken away, she went into a sort of shock, both physical and mental."

I stared through the window into the room where Hoshi lay, swathed in some sort of inflatable body bandage, hooked up to wires and tubes leading to a plethora of machines. A sterile-suited medical tech was injecting something into an IV and studying the results on a display over the bed.

"Is she going to make it?" I asked.

B shrugged. "No idea. If I had to call it, I'd say she's fifty-fifty for recovering. Even then, I'm not sure what *recovery* will even look like for her. This whole host-symbiote thing is pretty new and novel, even for me."

I nodded. "Yeah, well, I suspect that we're going to have to get a lot better at understanding and dealing with it—and soon."

TORINA POURED herself a cup of cappuccino—her latest Earthly indulgence—and leaned against the *Fafnir*'s galley counter. "So we don't even know if Hoshi was a perpetrator or a victim."

"Or both," Perry pointed out.

Torina nodded. "Or both. The trouble is that even though she was working with the Seven Stars League, she may have been an unwitting pawn."

Icky made a pfft sound. "She was in cahoots with—what did you call it, their *Security Directorate*? How many organizations called things like a *Security Directorate* do you know of that aren't shady, underhanded assholes?"

"She's not wrong," Perry put in.

We all turned to him. He stared back.

"What?"

"You're agreeing with Icky," I said.

"Hey, stopped clocks and all that, right? In this case, though, it's particularly apt. Netty and I have done some digging, and we've found enough sidelong references to the Seven Stars Security Directorate to raise at least some yellow flags, if not actually red ones."

Torina sipped her cappuccino. "Don't suppose any of those sidelong references have anything to do with the Puloquir or the Tenants, do they?"

"No. Or there's nothing even remotely conclusive, at least. Like all intelligence services, the League's Security Directorate is infused with institutional paranoia and a healthy dose of compartmentalization. Their counterparts in the Eridani Federation or Tau Ceti might know more, but good luck prying anything out of them."

"How about the bank? The Quiet Room? They seem to have stuff on everybody," Icky said.

Perry glanced at her. "That's a good idea, Icky. You're on fire today."

"Hey, I'm not just another pretty face."

"That's for sure."

"Listen, bird, why don't you—"

I stepped between them. "And there goes all the warm and fuzzy feelings of goodwill and friendship I'd been basking in. Anyway, talking to The Quiet Room *is* a good idea. Netty, put in a call to Dayna Jasskin. Tell her that I'd like to speak with her, at her convenience, please and thank you."

"On it, boss," Netty replied.

I turned back to the others. "What I don't get is why the Puloquir and the Tenants are suddenly involved with *Ponte Alus Kyr* and the Seven Stars League. Hoshi is the obvious connection, either because she's involved or because she got in the way and had to be taken out—but what is it actually all about?"

I shook my head as my thoughts tumbled along without going anywhere in particular. "Why the Puloquir? Why Tenants? Aren't they direct competition to the Krali'on?"

Torina shrugged. "They do seem to occupy the same niche. But as far as we know, the Krali'on don't leave their homeworld without a willing host. The Tenants, on the other hand, don't give a shit. They just—" She sighed. "We're right back at the same thing again, aren't we? Stolen people. It's always about power, and if that means seizing life in the process, so be it."

"A tale as old as time," Perry agreed.

But I shook my head emphatically. "Not if we can help it. And to that end, we've got a promise to keep. We have to get Totovar her body. And once we do, she can help us."

Totovar, in the form of Waldo, spoke up from the aft-end of the galley where she'd been sitting and listening in.

"Help you how? I don't have much to give, Van. I'm not even sure anyone wants me back, if I'm being truly honest. My people aren't known for their familial bonds, if you get me."

"Actually, I think you can do a lot for us, because what you've got is what you know, and especially *who* you know. And knowing what I know of Ligurites, that's probably a lot of people."

"People are kind of what we do, I suppose."

"Right. So how would you like a job?"

"Go on."

"You get your body, and you come work for me—just for this case. I've got something specific in mind, and it's perfect for you. Do this, and I'll pay you fifty thousand bonds."

Icky hissed through her teeth. "Lotta money there, boss. She's kin to Yotov. You know?"

"And your mother was a scumbag criminal kingpin, but we don't judge you based on that."

Icky blinked. "Point taken. I'll shut up now."

I turned back to Totovar. "I want you to use your contacts—and I know you'll have them—at the Ingano field office. It's—"

"In the Seven Stars League. I know them. What do you want me to do?"

"Simple, really. Go to their office and ask them how long they've been funding the Puloquir Civil War. Then, get the hell out of there and meet us aboard the *Iowa*, our other ship parked near Sol. I'll give you the nav data and key to get in."

Totovar was silent for a moment. "What if you're wrong? What if the Seven Stars League isn't involved the way you think they are?"

I thought about the smear of gore where Hoshi Onwyn had been laying, sprawled near death in her office. "Well, then, you'll get some blank looks at Ingano, and that's about it. Something tells me I'm not, though, and I think I can prove it. But first, I'm going to need to tie a few things together, starting with something I noticed on one of those Puloquir vessels. They used a triple screen data slate, and I've only seen *one* of those in my travels out here. Care to guess where?"

"The League?" Torina asked. "One of their primary manufacturers makes them. Pulsar Netcore, the multisystem group. Nice people, if you like profit and hate giving vacation days to your workforce."

"You're correct, dear," I said, smiling broadly. "And I'm betting the government—or at least the elites—have a heavy stake in Pulsar."

"It's almost like you read their articles of incorporation," Torina said.

"You know, boss, I've got a feeling that there are a lot more Tenants in the Seven Stars leadership than we suspected," Perry said.

I gave him a quizzical look. "Really? Why?"

"Okay, here's where I admit that you humans and your gut feelings are rubbing off on me. I've done a statistical breakdown—specifically, a principle components analysis—of all the data I can envision related to the Seven Stars League, the Puloquir, and the Tenants. There are definitely some trends, but none of them meet the threshold of statistical significance."

I smiled. I knew what *principle components analysis* was and how it was used, having done some statistics work of my own in the past—

mainly while data mining during my hacker days. "Okay, so that means they're not statistically significant."

"No, they're not. But there's enough there for me to—" Perry lifted his wings in a shrug. "Like I said, here's where that feelings thing comes in. There's *almost* enough correlation there to point at something significant, even if the math says there isn't. I just think that's important."

"Okay, so run with this, Perry. How many Tenants do you think are lurking in the Seven Stars League?"

"Um, all of them? In any case, enough of them that they're there for a reason. They can't really get around on their own, so if they're looking for hosts—"

I nodded. "Yeah. They've got to find them somewhere, right?"

"This really sounds like our ID thieves, just a different flavor of them," Icky put in.

"Yeah. There's that, too. One thing at a time, though. We need to find out what's going on in the Seven Stars League. And I'm not anxious to put in an appearance there myself, thanks to our good friend the Satrap with the perfect hair, so sending along someone like Totovar is the next best thing." I sighed out a slow breath. "Hopefully, anyway, we can figure out what they want."

"I know what they want. It's the same damned thing every time," Torina said, her voice hard. I shot her a glance.

"And what would that be, my dear?"

"An empire."

24

Hoshi remained in a coma, but the *Ponte Alus Kyr* medical staff stabilized her, at least. Once it was clear she could travel, B took charge of her, effectively commandeering her case under some obscure but apparently potent confluence of protocols and agreements. I sealed the deal for her by reminding Director Winthrop that he'd promised full cooperation—and Hoshi was being removed from what was more or less a crime scene, for her.

"Since she's very much a person of interest in this investigation, I'd much rather have her at Anvil Dark, surrounded by Peacemakers, thank you very much," I said to him. He grumpily conceded, and B made arrangements for Hoshi to be transferred to her ship.

"We'll take her back to Anvil Dark, and I'll see what we can do there about restoring her bodily functions to some sort of equilibrium. All due respect to the folks here at *Ponte Alus Kyr*, but aside from Hoshi herself, they really haven't got a lot of expertise in this.

Now, if Hoshi was a machine and we wanted to hook her up to organic tissue, or vice-versa, then this place is golden," she said.

I made to turn and head to the *Fafnir*, but hesitated. "So what expertise do we have at Anvil Dark?"

"Not much. But that's okay, I know some people, and there's someone I trust implicitly who would have at least some of the know-how we're looking for."

"What about Totovar's new body?" Torina asked.

"It's going to be another week before it's ready, at least, according to the good Director Winthrop. We'll make a stop here when it is," I replied.

We left it at that, each returning to our own ships. We were returning to Anvil Dark together, partly to help protect B's ship in the event that someone out there *really* wanted Hoshi dead, and partly because I needed to talk to Gerhardt. A lot had happened, and a lot more had to happen as a result. I didn't want to press forward with any of it without his being plugged in, though.

Sometimes it really was easier to get forgiveness than permission. But sometimes it wasn't.

Like now.

WHEN WE ARRIVED at Anvil Dark, I'd intended to go straight to see Gerhardt. He wasn't on the station, though, having gone on some liaison visit to Procyon—which may have meant The Quiet Room, but Max wasn't about to divulge details of the Master's itinerary. It left me stuck in a quandary—I really didn't want to hang around Anvil Dark without reason, but I really *did* want to talk to Gerhardt, who'd be returning sometime in the next two days. I was also mindful of the fact that Zeno was waiting for us at The Torus. I wasn't worried about her keeping herself entertained, but she felt like another point of vulnerability for us, even if the GKU was keeping an eye on her.

Icky made a good case, though, for giving the *Fafnir* some shop time. She still had unpatched battle damage, and her powerplant was rapidly crowding up against its quarterly level 2 inspection.

"And I don't wanna miss out on it and go overdue, 'cause I'm going to have to put that in Gehardt's dumb maintenance log, and I don't wanna give him a chance to complain," Icky said.

I finally agreed, meaning we'd be on Anvil Dark for the next couple of days.

I spent most of the first helping Icky, clad in a pair of grubby coveralls, stripping out damaged hull plates and aligning new ones in place so she could fasten them with a thermal bonding agent—a sort of glue that, when heated to a critical temperature, fused itself to the plates as though they'd been welded. The result was a bond even stronger than the tensile toughness of the plates themselves. Icky joked that if we got the *Fafnir* damaged enough, the bonding agent would eventually completely replace the hull entirely and we'd end up with a more durable ship.

"We'll rename it the *Theseus* if that happens," I told her.

"Why?"

"It's an old—you know what, never mind. Hand me that patch."

We'd just replaced a plate on the ship's upper forward quarter, where the fragment that had passed through the *Fafnir*, just a few centimeters behind my head, had entered. It had been temporarily patched, but Icky figured a few more hours of pressurization and it would probably start to leak. I was manipulating the overhead crane slinging the REAB module that covered it into place when B called via comm.

"Van, Hoshi's out of surgery. I think she's going to make it now."

"That's fantastic. When will she be awake?"

"Woah, there, young man. There's a light-year or two between *going to make it* and *ready to have a conversation*. We had to graft in some cutting edge and very expensive synthetic neural tissue, along with an artificial gland that will provide her body with the biochemical inputs that she would have been getting from her symbiote. She's going to have to be sedated and monitored for any signs of rejection for... oh, at least two or three days."

I cursed inwardly. I had burning questions to ask her, but her health came first. Still, it was a chance to take a break from the laborious drudgery of working on the ship. "Okay, I'm going to come and see her anyway."

Icky was as happy to take a timeout from work as I was, so we got changed—well, I did. All Icky did was fluff her nascent mullet and smile. Then we headed for the Infirmary. Torina was off taking care of some of the business side of operating the *Fafnir*, an ordeal involving the Guild's operating accountants that I was more than happy to leave to her. Perry had been off doing whatever he did on Anvil Dark, but he told us he'd meet us at the infirmary.

"I'll bet there's a secret bar or something where all those AI's hang out," Icky said as we left the hangar bay.

"What would they do there, Icky? Since they don't, you know, eat or drink?"

"I dunno. Watch artificial strippers, maybe?"

"You have a weird mind, girl, but let's file that idea away for a possible investment if we need to, ah… hide some money."

"Filed. Can I pick the name?"

"Sure. Whatcha got?"

"The Jumper Cables."

"That's a cover band, not a nudie bar."

She sniffed. "You have no imagination."

"I do, it's just not weird. Or vaguely lewd," I told her.

"Fair, boss. Fair."

The infirmary wasn't a long walk, just a few hundred meters from the *Fafnir*'s hangar bay through a part of Anvil Dark that wasn't especially well used compared to other parts of the station. We were maybe fifty meters away when Perry's voice suddenly erupted from the comm.

"Van, we're—!"

His voice fuzzed to nothing. I missed a step, hitting my comm. "Perry?"

Nothing. I started to run, my pulse going into combat overdrive within seconds.

"Perry!"

Icky pounded along behind me, her mass shaking the deck with each punishing step. Neither of us were armed—this was Anvil Dark, supposedly one of the most secure places in known space. As we raced along, I desperately sought anything that might serve as a weapon. Icky had extracted a hefty spanner from her tool-harness, and I was about to ask her to hand me something—hell, even a screwdriver was better than nothing.

Rounding a corner, I saw an Anvil Dark Security Trooper sprawled on the deck outside the infirmary, his sidearm a meter or so away. I dashed over, scooped it up, and followed Icky through the open hatch—

—into pandemonium.

Med personnel were kneeling or lying amid toppled and dropped equipment, scattered instruments and shattered glassware. There was blood and body fluids of every color, sprayed about in wild carnage. I stepped over a moaning officer, a wounded tech cinching bandages around a wound with edges that were bone white.

"On you," I told Icky, which was a damned good strategy.

She accelerated—hundreds of kilos of mass heading in a furious line—until I felt her slow. Whatever was happening was here, and we were in it.

And then Icky *roared.*

With an ear-splitting bellow, she charged ahead, the spanner held aloft like Excalibur. When the big girl got going, she was like a runaway train. I took up a position on her shoulder, the pistol raised and thumb on the safety.

Icky's arm moved and the spanner whistled, connecting with something in a grotesque, meaty clank. She forced her way through a hatch, and I was finally able to sidestep and see around her. Hoshi lay in a bed in the next compartment, visible through a window. B and a med tech stood protectively in front of her. Closer at hand I saw what they were protecting her from—a pair of what were obviously synths, humanoids, with slick alloy gleaming from ragged gaps in their pale flesh. Perry had apparently been the only thing holding them back, putting the *combat* in combat AI.

He thrashed his wings, their feathers oriented to expose the razor-keen edges he normally kept stowed, as he put it, using them like food choppers to slash and slice into the synths. At the same time, he lashed out with his talons, ripping and shredding more artificial flesh. Bursts of dazzling, disorienting light and EM noise punctuated his attacks, which seemed to be everywhere, coming from every direction at once.

It was absolute chaos, but I was momentarily mesmerized by Perry's sheer *range* of ability. He deployed his fearsome arsenal guided by the millisecond precision of his AI-driven actuators. If he'd unleashed this coldly incandescent fury on me, I'd been a bleeding heap of flesh on the floor by now.

But the tough alloy bones of the synths resisted his attacks, so he was only delaying them. Icky whaled away on one of them from behind with her spanner, the metallic clang of metal on metal ringing against the bulkheads amid her howls and bellows of fury.

But the Synth struck back at her, slamming a fist into one of her smaller arms. Bone snapped like a dry branch. Icky howled again, pain now edging the raw ferocity of her shouts.

An instant later, the other synth managed to land a punishing blow on Perry, slamming him back against the bulkhead behind him. He recovered—but this had to end. Now.

I stepped past Icky, leveled the slug-pistol at the head of the synth engaged with Icky and shouted, "Hey, asshole!"

The thing turned to face me and immediately started to react, but I was faster on the trigger than it could move to hit me. I fired once, twice, a third time, the shots crashing through the compartment with a contained thunder that rang my teeth like church bells. The first round glanced off the thing's skull, snapping perilously close by Icky, but I dropped the barrel a notch and put the second and third shots straight into its left eye. The glittering orb shattered in a shower of gore and sparks as it toppled backwards in a tangle of flailing limbs.

"So, they do bleed," I mused, whirling to face the next Synth.

The new target recognized me as a threat and spun with catlike quickness, sending silky fluids in a gruesome arc. I danced backwards, Innsu-style, forcing it to come at me while I shifted my aim. Icky immediately picked up on what I was doing, dropped the spanner—right on my toe, igniting a flash of pain through my foot—and slammed her two big, powerful hands around the synth. For an instant, servos and actuators whined against her fearsome strength, but she held the damned thing, her muscles quivering with superhuman exertion.

It gave me my opening.

I jammed the muzzle of the pistol into the thing's right eye, deliberately waited a heartbeat so it knew what was coming—then emptied the magazine into its brain. It went limp, and Icky slammed it backwards with a savagery that was beyond primal. Perry squawked as he was driven back against the bulkhead and momentarily squashed between it and the synth.

"There's a bird back here!" Perry bawled.

Icky pulled the synth's carcass away, then flung it against another bulkhead like a sack of wet grain.

I glanced down at my right foot, the one Icky had dropped her spanner on. "Well, shit."

She turned to me, her broken arm hanging limp, her face etched in pain. "Van, you okay?"

I leaned against a table and lifted my weight off my foot. "I took exactly one wound in all that, my right big toe, from your spanner. But—oh, shit, Icky, sorry—"

"I'm sorry too?"

Perry flopped onto the table beside me. He was intact, if a little bent in places. His golden gaze met mine. "I need a vacation."

"To go watch artificial strippers?" Icky asked, wincing at her arm.

"Exotic entertainers, Icky. Jeez you're lewd—"

He turned to her. "What the *hell* are you talking about—?" he started, but Torina burst into the compartment, armed with a slug pistol and a murderous glare. A pair of Security Troopers and a trio of Peacemakers that included K'losk followed, all brandishing weapons.

"Sorry, guys. You snooze, you lose," Icky said, then hissed as her broken arm swung as she moved.

B appeared, pushing Icky toward a nearby examination room. "Move, sister. Let's get that arm stabilized."

Torina kept her gun aimed at the sprawled pair of synths. "Van, are you okay?"

"No. Grievously wounded."

She shot me a glance full of worry. "How bad is it?"

I pointed at my foot. "Icky broke my toe." I reconsidered. "Excuse me, she *maimed* my toe."

"And?"

"And what?"

"A broken toe? That's it?"

I hissed a breath in through my teeth as pain throbbed through my foot. "Isn't that enough? I thought the choice of maimed would impart a sense of dire straits. For my toe, not us."

She lowered her weapon as Anvil Dark Security took control. Badly injured medical personnel and the Security Trooper whose sidearm I'd grabbed were being helped or carried in for emergency treatment. I decided that my broken toe could wait.

Still, I kicked myself—I should have kept my protective boots on, the ones I wore while working on the *Fafnir*, that could take an impact from a dropped hull plate. Or I would have kicked myself, anyway, if my toe didn't hurt so damned much.

I stood, and Torina gave me a smirk. "You're quite brave, standing on that shattered bone."

I schooled my face into something noble. "If you wanna use the term hero,"I said, schooling my face into stoic bravery, "then so be it."

GERHARDT ARRIVED A FEW HOURS LATER, in the midst of the chaotic aftermath of what had clearly been an assassination attempt on Hoshi. Somebody didn't want her talking, and I suspected I knew who. As I hobbled my way through the lockdown and into the Keel to meet with Gerhardt, it was confirmed—the two synths had arrived with a liaison mission from the Seven Stars League intending to deal with some cases of mutual interest to the League and the Guild.

"But there was obviously more to it than that," Gerhardt said, his voice hard and tight with anger. "Not only was this an obvious attempt to kill that woman, Hoshi, but we've also discovered that someone hacked the station's comm system. Shortly after that, several League personnel dropped by the hangar bay where the *Fafnir* is currently laid up, just minutes after you responded to the attack in the infirmary."

I nodded. "Netty told me. She threatened them with a point-defense battery, and they beat a hasty retreat." Which was a good thing, because if she'd fired the thing, the high-velocity slugs—which had been up-gunned by Zeno, to make them even more deadly—would probably have punched through the armored bulkhead and into the corridors and compartments down-range. Still, go Netty.

"So they were attempting to take you into custody as well. Here. On Anvil Dark." Gerhardt had just sat down, but he stood again, his fists clenched. "And you're my Justiciar, on top of all that. By attacking you, those bastards were attacking me as well."

I sat to ease the pain in my foot. Torina sat beside me. Icky was still in the infirmary having her arm treated, while Perry was down in the AI servicing shop getting his dents hammered out.

"Does the League have *any* explanation for this?" Torina asked.

Gerhardt sniffed. "The two synths were *rogue agents planted in their delegation*, while the attempt to seize Tudor here was them *exercising their just authority to arrest you on outstanding charges*."

"Which is all bullshit," I snapped.

"Indeed it is. And that's why my answer to them was to send Lunzy and about two dozen Peacemakers to arrest the whole lot of them, toss them into the cells, and impound their ship," Gerhardt replied.

Torina smiled. "Oh, the League isn't going to like that."

Gerhardt pointed at his terminal. "I already have a demand from the Satrap's Privy Council to immediately release them all, citing diplomatic immunity, and also to turn over the two synths so that their security breach can be *properly investigated*." He looked up at me. "Oh, and there's another demand to hand you over."

"You're not going to agree to any of that, are you? Especially the *handing me over* part?"

Gerhardt crossed his arms. "Their claim of diplomatic immunity is valid. Their delegation was traveling with an authorized Writ from that Privy Council I just mentioned."

"You're not seriously—"

Gerhardt waved a hand. "Tudor, you're a bad influence on me. Despite the legal basis for their demand, I told them to go to hell."

I exchanged a glance with Torina, and we both grinned. "Seriously?"

He spun the terminal around. His response was still gleaming on the screen.

In light of the egregious nature of the events at issue, I am rejecting all of your demands without condition. Also, go to hell.

He shrugged. "I told you you're a bad influence, Tudor."

My grin didn't last, fading quickly as anger engulfed me. The nerve of these bastards. Never mind trying to grab me. They'd tried to kill Hoshi, injured a bunch of station personnel as well as two members of my crew, and would have killed us, B, Hoshi, and anyone else who tried to stop them if we persisted in getting in their way. And they'd done it all here, at Anvil Dark. It would be like doing a drug deal in the lobby of a police station back on Earth, then trying to injure or kill the cops that tried to intervene.

"Master Gerhardt, I'm officially requesting leave to take a *delegation* of our own to the League to arrest their Satrap. I'm further asking for authority to use lethal force—lots of it," I said, straining to keep the anger—exacerbated by my throbbing foot—in check.

Gerhardt turned to me. "Denied."

"But—"

"But there's something far more important, Tudor. Before he headed off for repairs, Perry wisely decided to try and download what he could from the two synths. There wasn't enough brain circuitry left of one of them—"

"Yeah, that would be the one I shot in the head six times," I said.

"Indeed. But he did manage to download some data from the other one. It was fragmentary and encrypted, but our crypto shop managed to break it," Gerhardt said.

"Must have been shitty encryption," Torina said, but Gerhardt smiled his thin, hard smile.

"The League aren't the only ones infiltrating operatives into other parties," he said.

Her eyes widened. "We've got spies inside the League's cryptographic system?"

"We don't, but Unity does. And they've been providing us with the necessary cipher keys to break the League's encryption. We've developed a mutually beneficial working relationship with them."

"So what did Perry learn from that synth asshole?" I asked.

Gerhardt sighed. "That the League is conspiring with the surviving offspring of your old and dead friend Jacomir to *guarantee their position and objectives through means other than diplomacy.*"

I stared back at him. "Not much of a revelation, considering they just attacked Anvil Dark."

"This is referring to something else, though. Something being planned in addition to their attack here."

"Is that it? It's a big galaxy. They could be planning damned near anything pretty much anywhere."

"They could, but we just received a communique less than an

hour ago from the Schegith. It's a request for you and your crew to attend the naming ceremony for Schegith's child, who was just recently born."

I sat up. "The baby. That's their target? Why?"

"Because Schegith births are rare, and killing the heir would destabilize the Schegith politically. Our working theory is that the Schegith would turn their focus inward to try to deal with a sudden succession crisis—"

"Meaning they'd take their attention off of their new Protectorates, including Helso," Torina said.

Gerhardt nodded. "Which, until recently, was a League Protectorate. They apparently want it back."

"But—why? Aside from wounded pride, Helso doesn't offer much. It's not an especially strategic location, and it doesn't have any resources that aren't more readily available elsewhere."

Gerhardt shrugged. "Very good questions."

I shook my head. "Doesn't matter. The immediate concern is the Schegith." I frowned. "Even then, though, they'd have to fight their way through the Schegith fleet. And it's far from a pushover—"

"Actually, they wouldn't," Gerhardt countered, tapping at his terminal. "Three days ago, pirates launched a succession of attacks on a supply convoy bound for another Schegith Protectorate on the rimward edge of their territory, a planet called Wonder in the midst of being terraformed. They dispatched the bulk of their fleet to assist, meaning that most of their available combat power is two to three days away. Now, Null World has decent planetary defenses, but against a determined attack—"

I stood, muttering a curse as pain flashed through my foot. It sure as hell wasn't helping my mood. "We're ready to fly now. But we're going to need—"

"Help, yes. I'll work on that, get as many Peacemakers dispatched as I can. I'll also speak to the commander of the *Righteous Fury*."

He didn't add anything about the GKU, so I still wasn't sure if he was aware of them, and his reference to the *Fury* was a signal to that effect, or if he just considered the big battlecruiser another Guild asset.

"I'm also going to do something regarding the League that I should have done a year ago," Gerhardt said, stopping both Torina and me as we headed for the door.

"Declare war?" Torina asked.

"A declaration of war would imply that the Guild is a sovereign state, which it is not," Gerhardt replied.

"So, what then?" I asked.

"Buried deep in the Guild's Charter is a provision called a Writ of Repudiation. It allows the Guild to withdraw its services from a signatory state to the Charter and declare that state hostile to the Guild."

"So a declaration of war."

"Something like that."

25

GERHARDT SURPRISED ME. I mean, *really* surprised me. The Writ of Repudiation had never been used, not even once in the Guild's history. Gerhardt hadn't struck me as the sort of guy who was interested in breaking new legal ground, but he lobbied hard for a Writ with the other Masters, and actually got it through.

Which meant that we were now at war with the Seven Stars League.

And that was fine by me. As we eased the *Fafnir* out of her bay, I found myself looking forward to a confrontation with them. They were scumbags themselves, but even more damning were the scumbags with whom they consorted—Jacomir's foul brood, for one. But there were also the Tenants. And if Perry's dire predictions about their infiltration of the League were correct, then we were squaring off against them as much as we were the Seven Stars League.

And on top of all of that, I was still convinced that the League was bound up with Group 41 and the Sorcerers in a massive web of conspiracy that I was determined to start pulling apart.

Our first stop for that was Null World, coming to Schegith's aid.

We left Anvil Dark in company with three other Peacemakers—Lunzy, K'losk, and Dugrop'che, three individuals whom I'd come to trust. As we accelerated out toward the nearest twist point, Gerhardt called us to confirm that the *Righteous Fury* would rendezvous with us at Null World but would be several hours behind us.

"Which means, Tudor, you're going to have to make a judgment call when you see what you're up against. I urge that you be wary, though. I'd hate for the first action under our Writ of Repudiation to be a defeat."

"I'd hate that, too," I said, assuring Gerhardt we'd be aggressive but would stay on the near side of reckless.

OUR SMALL FLOTILLA arrived at Null World, and I braced myself for a wall of warships blocking our approach to the planet, loaded and ready for battle. We all kept our focus on the tactical overlay as it filled with data. I tensed, expecting icons to start popping up like crazy—

But they stopped at—two?

"Uh, Netty, correct me if I'm wrong, but isn't two ships a paltry force to send against Null World—even if the Schegith fleet is otherwise engaged?" I asked.

"I certainly think so. However, one of the ships seems to be a dedicated electronic countermeasures vessel, which has neutralized most of Null World's planetary defenses that actually have line of sight to them. And there appears to be a third ship on the surface."

Torina turned to me. "This isn't a large-scale attack, or an invasion."

"No, it isn't. It's a surgical strike—an assassination." I activated the comm channel our small flotilla was using. Lunzy and the others had already come to the same conclusion we had.

"Van, we need to get down to the surface of Null World as fast as we can," Lunzy said.

"Agreed. So here's the plan—we charge. Just bore in as fast as possible and get to Schegith's aid," I said, even as all four of us started the highest delta-V approach we could coax out of our ships.

"Van, K'losk here. I've been talking this over with Hosurc'a, and we both agree that we shouldn't underestimate that countermeasures ship. It might make it hard for us to engage since both missile trackers and targeting scanners are going to be pretty badly degraded."

I pondered that for a moment. "Lunzy, you still have that active stealth system installed on the *Foregone Conclusion*, right?"

"I made the last payment about two months ago."

"How about we try pitting a ship that can't be seen against one that's trying to blind everyone else?"

"Intriguing. What did you have in mind?"

"Well, let's see just how good those countermeasures the bad guys are using really are."

ALL FOUR OF OUR SHIPS' AIs, along with our respective combat AIs, put their metaphorical heads together and came up with an ingenious plan. While Dugrop'che made a straight run at the enemy ships, which were an armored class 9 backing up the class 8 ECM ship, Lunzy would follow directly behind him, obscured by his fusion exhaust plume. As she did, her ship would generate spurious signals to portray several ships in formation with Dugrop'che, taking advantage of the fact that the spillover emissions from the ECM ship also degraded the scanners of its consort slightly. It wasn't enough to blind the class 9, since the two ships were intended to work together.

But it would probably be enough to maintain the ruse until we reached missile range. And when that happened, Torina's shooting would make it lights out for the baddies.

It meant that until then, the enemy wouldn't be certain of our actual strength and would probably overestimate it. My hope was that that would put pressure on whoever was on the surface, undoubtedly trying to fight through the formidable defenses of Schegith's palatial underground complex. We hadn't been able to establish comms with Schegith, again because of the ECM ship, so all we could do was work with the assumption we weren't too late. The bad guys were still on the surface for a reason, not withdrawing, so we could only hope. The plan had the added advantage of keeping Lunzy hidden until she could reveal herself at a crucial moment.

In the meantime, while Lunzy and Dugrop'che were perpetrating our little ruse, we'd make a run for the surface, in company with K'losk. My crew and I had the advantage of knowing the detailed layout of the Schegith complex, having been there often enough.

It was… workable. Pedestrian. Even solid, if you squinted a bit. I thought it had too many moving parts, and much preferred simple plans that were less likely to foul up. But it was probably the only plan that would have a chance of allowing us to avoid a protracted fight in the space above Null World and get at least some of us down to the surface to help the Schegith. That was, after all, where the decisive battle was being fought.

In the midst of it all, Torina ordered me aft and told me to take my boot and sock off my injured foot. "If we get into some close-quarters dogfight down there, I want you watching my back, not whining about your toe," she said.

I peeled off my sock. "I don't whine. I inform vigorously."

"Oh, you do so, Van. You're an entire whine cellar all on your own."

"Hey——!"

She flashed me a wicked grin. It faded when she examined my toe, which had gone purple and crooked.

"That *does* look painful," she said.

"You should feel it from this side."

I winced and grimaced as she bound my injured toe to the one beside it, then hit it with a numbing agent. The pain immediately subsided.

"That should keep you in the fight at least," she said.

I stood and put some weight on it. It ached, and I couldn't avoid a bit of a limp, but it was much better than it had been. As I put my sock and boot back on, Torina crossed her arms.

"It's not just your boo-boo I wanted to talk to you about, Van."

"Okay—"

She just stared. I sighed. I knew damned well what she wanted to talk about. And she actually had good justification for wanting to talk about it. We were about to slog our way into battle again, including a potentially vicious, close-quarters brawl in the underground tunnels and chambers of the Schegith. If I didn't make it and she did, she had some decisions she was going to have to make, starting with whether she intended to petition to be named a Peacemaker herself. If she did, then Gerhardt would almost certainly support it, and she'd inherit our existing caseload—

—which meant she'd need to know about all the balls we currently had in the air in relation to them, and that included the Galactic Knights Uniformed.

So, I told her what I knew.

"They're Knights, but not the kind in shining armor and damsels in distress and all that, at least as far as I know. They're a cabal, a legacy or remnant of what the Peacemakers were before they actually became the Peacemakers. They're powerful, focused, secretive to the point of religion, and they also happen to be incredibly effective—from what I can tell."

She'd stood listening, arms crossed, nodding occasionally as I spoke. Perry appeared when I was partially done, but made no attempt to intervene or stop me. When I finished, she nodded again.

"Okay, then. It's good to know that," she finally said—and that was it.

"So… no questions, or objections or anything?"

"What would I object to?"

I shrugged. "I don't know. I mean, on the face of it, it all seems kind of sketchy, right?"

"I think every organization that thrives on secrecy, governmental, corporate, or criminal—"

"Or some of all three," Perry added.

She smiled. "Or some of all three. Anyway, I think that any group like that is going to seem sketchy. It's not the sketchiness that causes the problems, though. It's when they become convinced they're above or beyond the law that they get into trouble."

"And the criminal groups might have a leg up on that, but it can end up contaminating any of them," Perry agreed.

I gave him a look somewhere between bemused and surprised. "You seem to be okay with me revealing this all to Torina."

"Why shouldn't I be?"

"Oh, I don't know. How about that whole *sketchy secret* thing we were just talking about?"

"Van, the truth is that the GKU isn't really an organization as much as it's a set of ideals, a shared purpose that at least kinda sorta moves all of its members' efforts in more or less the same direction. I mean, it's so compartmentalized that it can't realistically be a hierarchy, because hierarchies don't work if you don't know who's above or below you. So the policy, as much as there is one, is for members of the GKU to recruit their own people—people they trust to share the common cause and maintain the secrecy themselves.

I puffed out a sigh. "You know, if someone had told me that at some point, I would have told Torina about this a lot sooner. I thought it was a loose lips sink ships kinda thing."

"You're right to reveal these facts—except when you aren't. Only you can really make that determination. Oh, and as for why no one told you, it's because you didn't ask."

"I shouldn't have to *ask*. This is a superb opportunity for growth as a GKU agent."

"A fair point. Alright, then. What other questions would you like me to answer that you haven't asked?"

Torina chuckled, and I shot her an annoyed glare. "Perry tipped his cards, babe. If this organization is as decentralized as you say it is, then you should be using your contacts to get the information you need. Right now, that list seems to be B—which explains why she always seems to somehow be nearby—Groshenko, Valint, and Perry himself."

I turned to Perry. "Do I need to let them know that I've brought Torina into the circle of knowledge?"

"Only if you don't want them to play dumb when she asks them about it."

"Van, we're five minutes from missile range," Netty broke in.

"I think we're done here anyway. Okay, folks, GKU aside, we've got a battle to win," I said and started back to the cockpit.

"I do have one question, Van," Torina said, and I stopped and gave her an expectant look.

"What's a *damsel in distress*?"

I smiled and shook my head.

"Something you are not, my dear. *Definitely* something you are not."

WE SETTLED back into the cockpit just as Dugrop'che opened fire on the two ships attempting to block our approach to the surface. They responded with a barrage of missiles, about half of which started tracking Lunzy's sensor ghosts. We fired a spread of missiles as well, as did K'losk, filling the space between our respectively on-rushing ships with converging ordnance. Then Lunzy showed off her tactical acumen.

Instead of emerging from behind Dugrop'che's fusion exhaust plume as intended when battle was joined, she snuggled the *Foregone Conclusion* up behind it as closely as she could. I marveled at her bravado and skill—the prow of her ship must have been starting to heat up from the bombardment by high-energy plasma particles. But by embedding herself in the slipstream of fusion effluent, she'd made herself so effectively invisible that our scanners only caught her as a flickering anomaly, and only because we were looking for it.

"I have *got* to remember that trick," I said.

"There is a downside. The forward portion of her ship is likely suffering a whole lotta thermal degradation and is going to need substantial repairs. Also she's taking a healthy dose of rads—and by healthy, I mean unhealthy as hell," Netty said. "She might glow after this. She'll need a scrub and a flush."

My admiration for her tactical mastery puffed away. "Wait—are you saying Lunzy's putting herself into—what, *undue* danger?" *And during an op I'm running*, I added silently to myself. I opened my mouth to have Netty open a comm channel so I could tell Lunzy to break off, but she preempted me.

"Well, she *is* flying into the fringe of a continuous thermonuclear explosion, so yes, she's definitely into the pink part of the hazard scale and inching toward actual red. But Lunzy's no fool, Van. She's a wily old spacer, so my recommendation is to trust her."

"Yeah, but—"

"Van, if that were you who'd come up with the idea, one that might decisively turn the battle in our favor—and assuming you weren't just suicidal—would you expect the commander of the op to trust *you*?"

"She's got her ship and combat AIs and her Second aboard the *Foregone Conclusion* with her, Van. They know the risks, too, but none of them have seized control," Perry pointed out.

I agreed. I had to. They were right, I needed to trust Lunzy. By extension, I needed to trust the people working for me, and that extended beyond my own crew, the people with whom I interacted every day. Sure, there was a center of gravity between giving someone free rein—which had let Icky inadvertently end up disabling the *Fafnir*'s most basic security against digital intrusion—and not enough—which was where my instinct to order Lunzy to break out of Dugroph'che's exhaust plume had come from. Finding that center of gravity was, it struck me, probably the hardest part of being a leader.

Leadership was hard, especially since I was so new to it. So I bit down on my instincts and waited to see what Lunzy intended to do, knowing that her skill and bravery were braided together in a way that gave us the best chance to win.

The outbound and incoming missiles flashed past one another. A few seconds later, the enemy missiles started activating their terminal seeker systems. The six that had been riding streams of false data fed to them by their firing ship suddenly realized they were chasing scanner ghosts and began hunting for new targets. The implacable physics of space meant four of them couldn't—even with their fearsome acceleration—change course fast enough to have any hope of catching any of our ships. With four of the enemy missiles taken out of the equation, it left eight to fly into the converging streams of point-defense fire from the *Fafnir* and K'losk's and Dugrop'che's ships. Netty and the other AIs worked as a silent, millisecond reaction-time team, choreographing the fusillades of slugs to optimize their effectiveness for the minimum possible ammo expenditure.

It was a thing of beauty to watch. One after another, the streams of tracers smashed the approaching missiles into whirling scrap. With a full third of their number taken out of the fight by our ruse, not one of them got close enough to detonate.

The bad guys did a pretty good job of taking down our missiles as well, mainly because of the disruptive effects of the EM ship. It also affected the targeting of our other weapons as they came into range, making for crappy firing solutions. Torina tried a few shots using manual aiming, but even her formidable talent wasn't enough to land a punishing hit.

"Okay, K'losk, let's angle ourselves into a descent," I said, directing Netty to configure the *Fafnir* for an orbital insertion and atmospheric entry to the looming, dun-drab surface of Null World.

"I'm right behind you. Well, not as right behind you as Lunzy is behind Dugrop'che, but you know what I mean," he replied.

As we flipped and burned to decelerate, the two enemy ships changed course and slowed to block us. As we'd expected, their job was evidently to run interference on what was happening on the planet below. That further pulled their attention off Dugrop'che—and Lunzy—who were still accelerating and would now flash past them at nearly point-blank range.

With masterful timing, Lunzy rode the incandescent stream of Dugrop'che's exhaust until the last possible second. Then she flipped and lit her own drive, dropping out of the fusion plume and revealing herself just a few thousand klicks away from the two enemy ships.

"Happy *birthday*," Lunzy crowed over the comms.

They'd had their attention split between us and Dugrop'che, so the sudden and unexpected appearance of Lunzy left them wallowing in confusion for a few seconds.

It was all Lunzy needed.

She was close enough that she could target them using optical fire control only, so our opponents' most potent weapon, their ECM emitter, was functionally useless. Laser and mass-driver fire erupted from the *Foregone Conclusion*, slamming into the two ships, searing and blasting chunks out of their hulls. The class 9 took the hits for a few seconds, then detonated in a blinding flash as her fusion containment failed, freeing the miniature star that raged in the core of her power plant. The class 8 just went dark, slowly tumbling as she lost steerageway. A moment later, a workboat detached and began to accelerate away.

"Van, we'll round these assholes up for you. They won't get far," Lunzy said.

"With pleasure. Oh, and Lunzy? You're insane. How much bow do you have left on your ship?"

"Enough that we're having this conversation."

I laughed and shook my head, then turned my focus to the swelling expanse of Null World now filling the left side of the canopy as we backed into orbit.

"Okay, K'losk, looks like we're the next act. See you on the surface."

26

WE CIRCLED our intended landing site amid a howling storm, albeit not nearly as dangerous as the one we experienced previously here on Null World. A class 8 squatted on its landing struts below, taking a few desultory shots at us with its upper laser and point-defense battery.

"I hate… casuals," I said. "Dear?"

Torina silenced it with a carefully aimed burst of mass-driver slugs. That was too bad, because taking an intact class 8 as a prize would have been a damned good haul of cash.

Perry obviously thought the same thing.

"And so, prize money becomes much less salvage money," he said with a theatrical sigh. "I was winning three auctions on eBay, too."

"Better than nothing, and I can spot you some bonds for your loot," I said, then switched to the comm. "K'losk, can you and your team clear out that grounded class 8? I'd rather not have any bad guys come up behind us."

"On it, Van. We'll be on the ground in about thirty seconds," he replied.

Netty handled the landing, while Torina, Icky, and I crowded up to the airlock, ready to bail out. We were, together, a charged particle, filled with the kind of anticipation that fizzed around and through us.

We were veterans. We were pros.

And, we were all clad in b-suits—or, in Icky's case, as close to a b-suit as we could manage, since we were still waiting on one that I'd commissioned to be custom made for her. It meant she was wearing what amounted to a set of oversized b-suit trousers the Anvil Dark quartermaster had scared up, with the rest of her armor in the various bits and pieces Linulla had made for her. Torina and I had likewise strapped on all the armor we could.

We'd also bombed ourselves *up* with weapons.

"Got enough battle rattle?" I asked, idly. Hell, we had all the weapons we could carry, let alone use.

"I carry myself quite nicely, thank you," Perry said with great dignity. His lethality surpassed almost everything—that whole *combat AI quality*—but as a group, we were packing a badass punch. Besides The Drop and the Moonsword, I lugged along a slug-rifle, the same miniature mass-driver that Zeno normally wielded. Torina had a sniper version of the same weapon and her sidearm, and even Icky carted along a slug-pistol on her harness. But she brandished her sledgehammer as her primary weapon, which made her a vision of terror for anyone who had good sense.

Several hundred kilos of fuzzy blue death had a way of… persuading people in combat.

I remembered one of my instructors in my basic army training, a chunky, hairy sack of belligerence we called Rilla, as in *gorilla*. I'd been convinced he was the most intimidating bastard on Earth, and maybe he was—but compared to Icky in full battle rattle, he came across as an accountant or insurance salesman. In boots and bulked up with her armor, she was two-and-a-half meters tall and probably two hundred and fifty kilos of four-armed, sledgehammer-wielding readiness to start smashing heads and breaking bones. I considered giving her a new nickname—the Persuader, of course—but she was Icky, and that was that. Clearing my head for combat, I gave Icky a serious look; the one I reserve for when the blood is about to spill, and got the same look in return. She was ready. We all were.

Icky offered to lead the way. I let her.

As soon as we touched down and the airlock opened, it turned out that *leading the way* to Icky meant charging at full tilt, as she flung herself into a run at the gate leading into Schegith's underground complex.

Icky didn't just attack. She *howled*.

"Bit excessive," Torina said with the primness of a British governess, and all I could do was smile grimly and follow. Despite the toughness of Schegith's gates, they'd been breached with an explosive charge that left desk-sized chunks of debris and radiating scorch marks searing the ground like the points of a star. Torina and I did our best to keep up, but Icky was pounding with the speed—but also all the elegance and grace—of an express train. Perry, fighting the gusting winds and driving sand, dithered along behind.

Once he reached the lee of the gate, though, he sailed quickly ahead, scouting the way.

"Next junction, turn left," he said, the view through his eyes popping open in a window on my helmet's heads-up display. Distant rattles and bangs tickled the air. It was gunfire.

"The left? That's a roundabout way of getting to Schegith," Torina said.

"Yeah. But they probably don't know that. They're either completely blind to the layout of this place, or they only have some vague idea. It's not like there's detailed maps out there somewhere," Perry said.

"Not to mention this isn't the sort of place you can easily insert a spy. I think they believed they had the luxury of time—and they would have, if we hadn't grabbed the data from that synth who tried to kill Hoshi," I said before stopping at the corner, then crouching and peering around it. I'd finally caught up to Icky and cajoled her into more caution, so she loomed behind me radiating aggression that wanted an outlet. Perry had already gone ahead, but I wanted to make sure no one had entered the corridor after he'd gone by.

"Clear," I said, then started forward again, every nerve on high alert.

We passed junction after junction, clearing each as we went. The staccato stutter of gunfire swelled ahead of us. If the bad guys had gone right at that first junction instead of left, they'd have had a straighter shot at Schegith's lair, but they either didn't know that, or had run into some obstacle that prevented it. As it was, it sounded like they were locked in a ferocious firefight, which now raged around the next corner.

"Okay, Van, we've cleared the class 8. Two prisoners. Hosurc'a and I are on our way in to back you up," K'losk said.

We stopped. "Rodger dodger. Perry'll send back the route to you guys." A loud bang, a grenade or something similar, echoed around the corner. "And the sooner you can get here, the better."

Perry had landed beside me. I glanced at him. "Care to do some more scouting?"

"Fly into a firefight? Sure, what the hell. I've got nothing better to do," he said, launching himself into the air and sailing around the corner.

"Hey, how come the bird gets to go join the fight?" Icky complained.

I glanced back at her. "Patience, my dear. You'll get your—"

The image Perry projected onto my HUD snagged my attention. I saw a dozen or so figures, all heavily armed and armored, hugging the walls and sheltering behind stone buttresses. They kept up a steady fire on an open door, where two Schegith returned brief, desultory shots. What was keeping the bad guys pinned down was actually a turret mounted over the door snapping out relentless bursts that ricocheted up the corridor—and toward the corner where we sheltered.

The image suddenly spun crazily.

"Perry!"

"I'm fine, just took a ricochet in my left wing. But if it's all the same to you"—he paused and the image slewed as he suddenly maneuvered—"I'm going to suggest that the time for scouting is past, and we're into the fighting part."

Two of the bad guys at the rear of the firefight had evidently been keeping a watch behind them, and one of them had spied

Perry. He came whipping back into view, shots snapping after him. One blasted fragments out of the corner, some of them pattering against my visor.

He landed beside me and lifted his wing. "Damn. I just had those feathers waxed, too. Oh, by the way, Van—in case it wasn't apparent, I found the bad guys. They're thataway."

"Figured that out all by myself, Perry, thanks."

Icky crowded in, her eyes bright with the fever of unrealized violence. "We ready to go, boss?"

"Icky, if we just charge around that corner, we're going straight into the teeth of incoming fire." I turned to Perry. "Care to do your dazzle thing for us?"

"What? You mean you want me to fly right back at those guys?"

"Uh, yeah."

"A bird's work is never done," he muttered before leaping into the air and sailing away behind us. Then he turned, accelerated, and wobbled a little because of the damage to his wing.

"Okay, kids, on me!" he said, then vanished into a blaze of blinding light and EM noise.

"Icky, go!"

I didn't have to invite her twice.

With a ferocious roar, she charged after Perry. I went next, holding my slug rifle at the high ready, estimating where my first target would be once Perry's dazzle effect ended. Torina followed behind, ready to start delivering accurate, aimed shots like a lethal metronome, her voice even, her breathing easy. Torina fought the same way she argued—with a methodical air of inevitability that I found both calming and unnerving.

Unnerving if you were on the wrong side, that is.

Slugs snapped and whined past us in the hideous music of close combat. Something clacked off one of my vambraces, then a bullet fragment struck the ankle of my uninjured foot. As I switched feet to compensate for the lancing wound, my toe bloomed with pain again. I swore like a Welsh stablehand, and we moved on, dispensing violence with limitless enthusiasm.

Perry's light show abruptly ended, and he launched himself at the face of one of the bad guys in a storm of beating metallic wings. Icky—

Did something I would think about on my dying day.

Still bellowing like a raging buffalo, she raced past one of the armored figures that had been shooting at us from the rear of the group. He managed to put one close range shot into her, then she swung her hammer—

And knocked his head *off*. Literally. Her hammer struck his visor with such force that it snapped his head back to the point his neck broke and skin, muscle, and tendons ripped apart. Blood erupted in a brief fountain.

She just kept going.

I pushed past Perry, who'd knocked his opponent back, had ripped open his visor and was busy turning his face into bleeding hamburger. I lined up a shot on the next guy I saw, squeezed the trigger—

And fired a three-round burst of slugs into him, two hitting and blowing out half of his torso.

I blinked as I hunted for a new target. Right. Zeno had mentioned something about modifying this slug rifle, hadn't she? I wasn't a big fan of automatic weapons-fire, because it was mostly useful for area suppression. If you weren't talking about a tightly packed group of targets, then timed, single shots were far more deadly.

Which Torina was proving to deadly effect with each pull of the trigger. She didn't even attempt to close, instead sniping one target after another from cover behind a buttress. Stuck with bursts of three rounds and not wanting to take the time to figure out how to switch back to single-shot, I pressed in, keeping to Icky's left and well clear of her swinging hammer. I fired a lot of slugs, most of which didn't hit, but it was enough to force our opponents to take notice. More and more incoming fire snapped around me, some slugs smacking into my armor, one managing to blow a small chunk out of my left bicep. Sterile, anesthetic sealing foam immediately flooded the gap.

The turret ceased firing, at least, reducing the volume of fire in the corridor. Instead, four Schegith lumbered around the corner. Two of them wielded long arms of some baroque design, complete with a hand crank that they spun between each shot. The weapons loosed pale bolts of energy, one of which struck a bad guy and just kind of—melted him.

"Shmaltzy," I said, curling my lip at the carnage. All that remained was sizzling fat and a few bones. Sort of.

Perry hooted. "I'll never think of a deli the same way. Good thing I don't eat."

"Good thing I don't drink chicken fat," I said.

"Don't knock it. It's good in shots," Icky said.

"I… I'll stick to whisky, thanks, big girl."

"You're missing out. You *sumbitch*, eat this," Icky roared, and we left our discussion of delicatessens behind as an armored figure rose squarely in my path, his slug rifle aimed right into my face. Before he could fire, Icky's sledgehammer connected on his shoulder, his bones breaking like snapping twigs. An instant later a slug cracked past from behind, blasting his head apart in a violet arc.

"Modern art. I don't get it," I said.

"Fun makin' it though," Icky said, twirling her hammer.

I looked for a new target. There wasn't one.

After a shuddering breath from the adrenaline, I spun around, taking in the battlespace. "I want one alive. Get me one, okay?"

"Got one back here," Torina said, coming forward with her weapon trained on a wounded bad guy. The rest of them seemed to be dead. One of the Schegith was down and motionless, too.

Icky turned to me. "You alright, boss?"

I winced at some impact points that I hadn't noticed until now, probably on their way to nasty bruises. Just what I needed—more pain.

I nodded and snapped out, "Yeah. Fine. How about you?"

She looked down at me and blinked a couple of times behind her visor.

"Uh—not so much, I think," she said. Dark blood flowed from a hole punched clean through her abdomen.

A second later, she wobbled, then toppled over into a heap, her sledgehammer clattering across the stone floor.

"Hello, Hosurc'a. Good of you to finally join us," Perry said.

I glanced back. K'losk and Hosurc'a had just arrived. Torina handed custody of her prisoner over to them, then hurried to join me with Icky.

"How is she?"

I'd called up her med data on my heads-up. "Not great. She's still losing a lot of blood, but I can get to the exit wound. This is bullshit—Icky, you here, girl? Someone hand me the patch kit *now*." I kept my voice firm but loud enough to get the point across. I didn't like Icky's wound. It was a violation. In quick movements, I sprayed the entry wound on her gut, but I couldn't shift her to address the exit hole, which was, I knew, a heluva lot worse.

"Want my muscles?" Torina asked, her lips pressed in a grim line.

"Thanks. Let's try to—damn but she's dense—" I grunted with effort, my arms straining in unison with Torina. We could barely shift Icky at all.

Her pulse went up, her blood pressure down.

"Shit! We've got to get to that wound—"

"These ones will assist," a new voice said. I glanced up and saw two Schegith already reaching down for Icky. They were hefty, powerful creatures in their own right, bracing their slug-like bulk and heaving to roll her over. As I'd expected, the exit wound was far worse, a hole about the size of a saucer gushing blood. I immediately emptied my first-aid spray into it, then grabbed Icky's from her harness while Torina used hers. Even after using the third, she was still oozing blood.

I took in her vitals. They were weakening.

"Can you help her?" I asked the Schegith.

"This one shall," a new Schegith said. It carried a device that looked like a weapon, which it aimed at Icky's wound. When it pressed the trigger, the flesh around the first-aid foam plugging her wound immediately writhed and boiled, then closed tightly.

"She requires immediate care. Unfortunately, we're unfamiliar with her physiology—" the Schegith medic said.

Perry cut in. "I'll send you everything we've got on the Wu'tzur. You should be able to—"

He stopped. If I didn't know better, I'd swear he'd just choked up.

The Schegith placed Icky onto a wheeled litter and carted her away, while Netty helped relay anatomical and other data specific to the Wut'zur. Perry stood, watching as she was wheeled off.

"Perry, you okay?"

"What? Oh—yeah, fine. Minor damage only."

I nodded, leaving it at that.

"She's in good hands, Van," Torina said. "With Netty's data and Schegith medical tech—"

"Yeah." I turned and stalked back to our prisoner, my anger rising like a red tide.

"Has this scumbag said anything?" I asked K'losk.

"The usual bitching and whining. I've sent Horsurc'a to check the others, see if any of them are still alive—" He paused and glanced at the one Icky had decapitated with her sledgehammer. Fluids still oozed from the ragged stump of his neck. "But I'm not holding out much hope."

I knelt and looked at our prisoner. I knew *instantly* this was another of Jacomir's vile offspring.

He returned a defiant look, albeit taut with pain from nasty slug wounds to his shoulder and hip. I was in no mood to piss around with him.

"Who sent you?"

"Go to hell—"

His words collapsed into a wail of pain as I punched his shoulder.

"Let's try this again. Who sent you?"

"Eat a bag of—"

I punched him again, harder. As I did, I realized that K'losk, Torina, and Perry were watching me, as was one of the Schegith. I braced myself for some or all of them to object, but none of them did. K'losk, in fact, just leaned into the wailing groan of anguish.

"Oh, no, be careful, Van. You might hurt him. And you don't want to do that."

I tried again, but our prisoner remained defiant. I resigned myself to accepting it. I really wasn't going to torture the guy.

The Schegith, on the other hand, had a different take.

"Peacemaker Van Tudor, this"—the next word didn't translate, but I got the vibe it was the Schegith equivalent of *asshole*—"will clearly not cooperate. That means he is of no further value. This one will therefore exercise jurisdiction and assume his custody."

I glanced up. "Uh—okay. This is your planet. What do you intend to do with him?"

"Why, consume him, of course."

The prisoner's eyes flew wide. "What?"

"He will be of value to this one as a source of proteins and other sustenance, at least, since he is of no value otherwise."

He looked at me, wild-eyed. "You can't! I'm your prisoner!"

I spread my arms. "Sorry, but you committed this really egregious crime on the Schegith homeworld. As they say, they have jurisdiction."

I stood and stepped back.

"No! I want… asylum! You can't let them do this!"

"I'm curious—do you kill them before you eat them?" Torina asked, her tone the one of someone watching a nature documentary.

The Schegith looked at her. "What would be the point of that?"

Torina nodded.

"Give me asylum! You have to—!"

I shook my head. "I don't *have* to do anything. In fact, there's not much I can do, sorry."

I turned and started to walk away. So did K'losk and Torina. Hosurc'a returned from examining the other fallen and fell in with us, as did Perry.

The man screamed. "*Please!*"

I stopped and turned back. "You pieces of shit were here to kill the newborn child of the Schegith matriarch. In the process, you badly wounded one of my crew, and her survival is still in doubt. And you really, really pissed me off. Why the hell should I do *anything* for you?"

"I'll—" He swallowed and looked up at the Schegith looming over him. "I'll tell. Everything. What you want to know. Just don't let them—" He gasped as the Schegith reached for him. "*Please!*"

His voice had become a shriek. Terror was etched into every fiber of him. There were few things more horrifying than the thought of being eaten alive, and this poor bastard was living those thoughts right now, probably in excruciating detail.

Good.

I wandered back. "Will the Schegith agree to release this prisoner back to my custody?"

"This one will consent."

I knelt back beside him. "Okay. You said everything. So start talking. Those two beautiful birds over there are going to record it all. When you're done, I'll decide if it's good enough for my purposes, and if it's not—well, then, as the Schegith put it, you'll be of *no further value to me*."

The man babbled a bit, then began to talk, ragged chunks of exposition spilling out of him.

It was most enlightening.

———

SCHEGITH HERSELF, the matriarch, lay sprawled on a bed the size of a garage door. Her child, a beautiful bouncing baby—um, larva, I guess, lay with her. Both were exhausted by an ordeal of labor that was almost epic in scope.

"This one has yet another reason to thank you, Van Tudor," she said, her voice slow and tired.

"I'm just glad it all worked out—well, except for Icky, of course. Is there any news on her?"

"This one's anatomists are still attending to her. They are... deeply concerned."

I exhaled, almost sick with worry. If Icky didn't make it—

I thought about Rolis, who'd sacrificed himself so we could escape what was probably a Puloquir killing machine prowling an ancient battlefield. He'd been my first casualty as a commander. My first loss—a person, gone forever, under my control. My orders.

My fault, ultimately.

I knelt and put both hands on Waldo—on Rolis.

"I—don't know what else to say," I said. I tried to stop my voice from breaking but failed pretty miserably.

"How about goodbye?"

If Icky didn't make it—

I took a breath, then cleared my mouth with a swig of something tepid. I spat against the fouled floor with a savagery that expressed all my rage. All the potential loss, hanging right overhead, ready to cast a shadow on the rest of our lives if Icky didn't pull through.

I spat again, and made to swear, long and rich, but I stopped myself. If I couldn't govern my own emotions now—when Icky and my crew needed me—then I didn't deserve the badge. Or the ship, or the sword, or their trust.

If Icky didn't make it, then life would go on, and so would the job. I'd have to dig even deeper to do it, but it had to be done. Icky's loss would only make putting a stop to this many-headed hydra of a conspiracy all the more necessary, wouldn't it? Otherwise, she'd have *died*—for nothing.

What was I going to say to her father? To my crew? To myself?

Bullshit to that, I mused.

Torina stood beside me. I wanted to hug her, and could feel that she wanted to hug me back. But, again, there was that job to do, and simply knowing was somehow good enough.

I asked Schegith to fill us in on what had happened before our arrival. As she did, Perry came on over the comm.

"Van, I'd say that Jacomir's brood isn't just being manipulated, they're also being used. And by that, I mean actually used. They've got comm channel data aboard their grounded ship that links back to the Seven Stars League."

I took a slow breath. "Of course they do."

"There's also a reference in a comm-log fragment to the

Tenants. It has no context, so I can't tell you what it means. For all I know, one of these assholes might have been a landlord and he was complaining about the rent being late. But I don't think so."

"Neither do I. Keep me posted."

When we finished with Schegith, we returned to the *Fafnir* to tend to our own minor injuries and stow our gear. I kept The Drop and the Moonsword on me, though, in case we had to fight again.

And part of me hoped we would, because I wanted someone to hurt—to pay—for every drop of Icky's blood.

27

BUT WE DIDN'T. Our little task force stayed at Null World anyway, Lunzy, Dugrop'che, and K'losk aloft, while we remained on the surface. I wasn't going anywhere until I knew what was happening with Icky, and the others knew it.

The next day was a long one. We could only wait as the Schegith anatomists, as they were called, tended to Icky and did their best to save her. The biggest problem was lost blood. For obvious reasons, the Schegith didn't have a supply on hand. We had some, because it was SOP for Peacemaker's to carry a supply of blood for each crewmember, but it was quickly exhausted. And we didn't have any Wu'tzur handy for a transfusion. Schegith's people were going to try to use a synthetic fluid that would mimic the effects of Icky's blood, but they counseled caution.

"This one does not know if this will work. The product is designed for Schegith, and although this one is attempting to make the necessary changes to it to accommodate your friend's physiology, it is… far from certain."

I nodded, grateful for the Schegith's honesty, even if it wasn't the news I'd been hoping for. Then I returned to the *Fafnir* and had Netty open a comm channel to Gerhardt.

"Tudor, what's the situation regarding the Schegith?" he immediately asked, without any preamble.

I filled him in. He nodded gravely. "I'm very sorry to hear about your crewmember. I know you can get very close to someone, living and working aboard a ship. I also know that's what makes it so hard to lose one of them."

"I haven't lost Icky yet."

"No, you haven't. And I hope she pulls through. But prepare yourself in case she doesn't. You need to be ready for it. You'll also need to be ready to be there for the rest of your crew, which makes it doubly hard for a Peacemaker. If you're not able to keep being the leader despite how you feel, it will only make things *more* difficult for you as time goes on."

"You sound like you're speaking from experience."

Gerhardt returned his thin smile. "In the history of the Guild, there have been four Masters who, on their way to a seat here in the Keel, *haven't* lost at least one member of their crew. I am not one of them."

He hesitated, as though considering where to go with that. I decided to make it easier for him.

"Have any of those four been recent?"

"Yes. Hugo Groshenko is one of them, in fact."

I nodded, unsurprised. If I'd had to guess, it would have been him. Still, it made me curious. "But Yotov isn't," I ventured.

Gerhardt shook his head. "No. She lost... several members of her crew along the way."

Again, I could tell Gerhardt wanted to say more, probably to slag Yotov for being an uncaring despot more than happy to throw her subordinates to the wolves if it would benefit her. That wouldn't have surprised me either. But, always the consummate professional, I obviously didn't want to dwell on gossip, so I pushed on.

"In any case, we've got more hard links between the Seven Stars League, Jacomir's endless supply of kids, and now an attack on the Schegith—who, I might add, are recognized as a sovereign state by the Guild."

"I'm aware, Tudor, and I'll add that to the follow-up diplomatic missive we're sending to the League."

"A diplomatic missive." I thought about Icky, mortally wounded by a slug fired by a League mercenary. They might not have pulled the trigger, but they put the damned round into the chamber. I had to grip the armrests of the *Fafnir*'s pilot's seat, hard.

"How about something a little more, you know, *forceful* than a toothless *diplomatic missive*? How about we start rounding up Seven Stars assholes wherever we find them and throwing them in The Hole? Or better yet, out the nearest airlock for one final spacewalk?"

I was leaning forward and almost growling by the time I was done. Gerhardt kept his tone neutral.

"Tudor, I understand your frustration. However, there are many moving parts to this and, dare I say it, you and your crew are just one of them."

I opened my mouth, but he raised his hand. "The Eridani Federation has already caught wind of the Guild's Writ of Repudiation, which we delivered to the League yesterday. They've reached out to us through the back channels, telling us that they're ready to join any armed efforts against the League. Worse, they seem to be preparing to use it as an excuse to attempt to seize Landfall, the planet contested by them, the League, and Tau Ceti. If they do, that could draw Tau Ceti into a conflict, which could result in war erupting across known space. So we have to proceed carefully here."

I sat back. "What the hell does *proceed carefully* mean? If we're not prepared to hold these League assholes accountable—especially that vacuous, perfectly coiffed Satrap and his twitchy sidekick—then that Writ of Repudiation is just a damned piece of paper."

"I'm well aware, Tudor."

I spread my arms. "Well aware? So what—?"

Gerhardt cut me off. "Before we wander too far down this unproductive road of acrimony, I have new orders for you. They'll be waiting for you at The Torus with your crewmember, Zenophir, who's waiting for you there. Incidentally, she has a message for you. It boils down to, *tell Tudor to get his ass out here and pick me up before my bar tab's worth more than the* Fafnir."

Despite everything, I couldn't resist a fugitive smile. But it was brief. "Orders? To do what?"

"You have a meeting to attend."

"What sort of meeting—?"

"Everything you need to know is at The Torus. You need to be there within three days. Gerhardt out."

The screen flicked back to its default display of sundry comm-system data. I stared at it for a moment, then slumped in the always-comfortable pilot's seat and rubbed my eyes.

It wasn't even four years ago that I'd discovered a spaceship in my barn. But, as the cliché went, I was already feeling too old for this shit.

NETTY FIGURED that if we weren't worried about conserving fuel, we could be at The Torus in just over a day. That gave us almost two days before we had to leave, which the Schegith anatomists told us would be more than enough. If Icky was going to pull through—or not—we would know well before then.

I decided to descend to the Undersea and spend time alone with my thoughts in its dark, cavernous splendor. Torina offered to join me, but I gently declined. I needed some time to mull over what Gerhardt had said about being prepared to lose Icky, so I could be there for the rest of the crew. I needed some solitary time to do the first part of that—preparing to lose her.

I'd only been sitting on some rocks overlooking the vast underground lake for a short while before a soft clash of metallic wings rose behind me. Perry landed nearby, his talons scraping against the stone.

"I take it you didn't get the memo, the one about me being down here alone," I said.

"Actually, I did."

"So you're here anyway, because—?"

"Because it's my job to look after you."

I gave him a sidelong glance. "To look after me."

"Yeah. I mean, I realize that I'm super intelligent, not to

mention charming as hell, but that's not why I'm aboard the *Fafnir*, Van. I'm there to support you."

I nodded. "I appreciate that, Perry. But I don't think this is something you can help me with."

"What, having a member of the crew in mortal danger? A touch presumptuous of you. I mean, if I was good enough to do it for your grandfather—"

I turned. "My grandfather."

"Yeah. Do you think you're the first Tudor to face the loss of one of their crew?"

"Gramps lost someone?"

"Three someones, in fact. Two of them during the same op."

"I... never knew that."

"No, you didn't, did you? That's because *he* was smart enough to not try and do this sort of heavy lifting on his own. And that's why, two days after losing the two members of his crew during the op, he was able to sit down with you and Miryam and that stuffy couple from the next farm down the road for Thanksgiving dinner when you were fifteen."

"The Wallers."

"Yeah. Hey, did you know she had the hots for your grandfather? And that he had to persuade Valint to *not* disintegrate her?"

"I—didn't, no." I looked back at the lake for a moment, then turned back to Perry. "Gerhardt said I had to prepare myself to lose Icky."

"He was right. And after Icky, it's going to be someone else—although it may be Icky again. She's a maniac when it comes to combat. Anyway, it's part of the job, Van. You always have to be ready to lose people. But my point here is, you don't have to do it alone."

I smiled at him. "So stop sitting down here alone, in the dark."

"Moping. Yeah." He waved a wing at me. "This, this right here? This is the picture beside *moping* in *The Big Book of Feeling Sorry for Ourselves*." He lifted his wing toward the rocky ceiling vaulting high overhead. "You should be up there, where the action is."

"Doing what, exactly?"

"I don't know, Peacemaker shit. Does it matter as long as it's productive?"

"No, I guess it doesn't," I said, levering myself to my feet. "I could use a little caffeine at some point."

"Fortunately, I've achieved biological nirvana and don't need your demon bean. Besides, I've got a little job you can do. You can meet B when she lands."

I stopped. "B? She's here?"

"About ten minutes out."

"How——?"

"Lunzy put in an urgent call to her. She apparently owes Lunzy over something or other, so she called in the marker." Perry gazed up at me. "See? *Preparing yourself* isn't synonymous with *moping*, Van. As a great bird once said, *there are always options*."

I started for the tunnel leading back to the surface. I was kicking myself for falling into just the trap Perry was alluding to, equating *preparing myself* to face losing Icky with *resigning myself* to it. Or, as Perry put it, *there are always options*. The lesson was to keep fighting, even if it seemed hopeless—because you might manage a miracle.

Still, I couldn't resist glancing back at Perry as he launched himself into the air.

"A great bird? You mean Hosurc'a?"

"Not funny, Van. Not funny at all."

B LANDED with a supply of Wu'tzur blood and, more importantly, a comprehensive knowledge of Wu'tzur anatomy. Along with that knowledge came—sass, and plenty of it. Her lips were quirked, antennae waving, and she moved with the certainty of someone who knows her shit.

Which, I was coming to know, was standard for B.

"When you've been patching holes in people as long as I have, you'll end up working on pretty much every species there is," she'd said, antennae twitching as she disembarked from her ship. She arrived to find Icky barely clinging to life. The Schegiths' synthetic blood had kept her going this long, but B figured the next couple of hours would be make-or-break. This time, I stuck myself at Icky's bedside, or as close to it as B and the anatomists would allow.

They ended up losing her.

For about four minutes, Icky was technically dead, causing a hum of activity that reached a fever pitch but never turned chaotic. That should have been it, but the Schegith anatomists had a final card up their sleeve, turning something I'd come to think of as profoundly evil to good. They'd been experimenting with reverse-engineering the Sorcerers identity-theft system to better understand it. And while they were far short of determining how to capture higher brain functions as effectively as the Sorcerers had, they'd apparently pretty much nailed the more primal, autonomous functions.

"Is that what I think it is?" I asked.

The red gem on B's upper lip flashed as she gave me a tight smile. "It is," she said, with all the verbosity of a mortician from Maine.

What it all meant was that, when Icky's body finally gave up and stopped functioning, they let the chipped version of her take over, telling her heart to beat, her lungs to breathe. It kept her going for the four minutes they worked to save her.

And save her they did. With the transfusion of B's supply of Wu'tzur blood and some other medical wizardry I didn't really understand, they convinced Icky's body to start working on its own again. Her blood pressure and other vitals came back up, her condition stabilized, and less than two hours later, she was actually awake.

"You get the registration of the class 15 that hit me?" she asked, her voice a dry rasp.

Torina and I laughed, and Torina bent down and gave Icky a hug. Perry hopped up onto a table beside her bed.

"So you're finally awake. Good. I'm tired of you just lounging around like this. You've gotta start pulling your weight," he said.

Icky rolled her head toward him. "Screw you, bird," she said, then gave a tired smile.

Perry reached out a wing, touched her head, and held it there, but it wasn't rigid. It moved.

He moved. He was in limbo, his actions somewhere between mechanical and maudlin, each movement colored with a love and respect that only a true friend would do. Perry stayed right there with Icky, his amber eyes unblinking as machines uttered the song that told us our friend would live.

The world broke apart into gemlike fragments for me as my first tear fell, hot and unwelcome, and rolled down my cheek while everyone pretended not to see.

———

Icky recovered quickly, thanks to some rapid tissue regeneration therapy the anatomists could finally use, now that B had supplied them with the correct Wu'tzur parameters. Again, I beat myself up for not calling B myself, but I vowed to make up for it by getting proactive. I had B provide the Schegith with the requisite bio data for humans and P'nosk as well, so if we ever found ourselves in a similar situation, the anatomists would be able to immediately do more than just try to maintain a flickering spark of life.

No matter how you sliced it, though, it had been a near-run thing. And it had happened because Icky hadn't been properly protected with armor. That was something else I was determined to fix as soon as we got back to Anvil Dark. Schegith herself, though, stepped into the breach for us.

"Your Icrul nearly died to save this one's offspring. The very least this one could do is ensure that that is unlikely to happen again," she said, instructing her techs to fashion Icky a set of torso armor. They only had a day to do it, but it turned out that a cuirass built for her own people was big enough to enclose Icky's voluminous upper body—more than big enough, in fact. With relatively minor adjustments, they were able to rig torso armor that was proof against most small-arms fire, while being almost as light and mobile as something made by Linulla.

It did, however, make her look far more ample out front, which caused her to shoot Perry a glare when it was presented to her.

"One fat joke, bird, and so help me——"

"Wouldn't dream of it. That would be inappropriate," he said.

She gave him a suspicious look, then nodded.

"Besides, it's not your fault—woah!"

He dodged just quickly enough to avoid a swipe of her meaty hand. I stepped between them.

"Gotta be honest, guys, it does my heart good to see you two snarking at each other again. Now, cut the shit."

By the time our latest possible liftoff time neared, Icky was well enough to clamber out of bed and hobble her way to the *Fafnir*. B and the anatomists were impressed with her progress, the tissue regen therapy notwithstanding.

"Those Wu'tzur are a *damned* tough species," B observed as Icky gritted her teeth and walked, unaided, down the corridor toward the exit.

"Tough, but not indestructible," I said.

B sniffed. "None of us are."

We passed through the corridor that had been the scene of the firefight. Chips and cracks marked slug impacts on the walls. The bodies were gone and the blood was cleaned up, but when I mentioned repairs to the walls, the Schegith escorting us shook its head.

"No. These ones will leave those. They are a part of this place now, as much as any carving or inscription would be."

I nodded. There was an elemental wisdom there. The tunnel would remember the firefight in missing chips and chunks of stone. And we were all just the sum of our memories, weren't we?

We found Schegith, who was also on her feet, for lack of a better term—waiting for us at the exit from her palatial underground complex.

"This one wishes to extend profound gratitude to Peacemaker Van Tudor and the crew of the *Fafnir*. You have again rescued this one's species from chaos and possible oblivion," she said.

"Well, let me say thanks in return for saving Icky for us and providing us with some decent armor for her," I replied.

Icky, her face set in grim determination, raised a hand. "Icky is willing to bet that she's even more grateful than Van."

We laughed. And, remarkably, so did Schegith herself, a low, rolling boom of sound that shuddered up from some deep place inside her. Or, at least, I assume it was laughter, because in a different context it would actually be kind of terrifying, the sound being a chorded, damp foghorn noise with *just* a hint of German.

We boarded the *Fafnir* and lifted, B close behind us. K'losk and Dugrop'che had already departed for Anvil Dark, carrying our surviving prisoner from the firefight. Lunzy had stayed in orbit to give us high cover while Icky recovered.

I was a little uneasy about leaving Null World unprotected, but the uneasiness didn't last long. An hour out, a squadron of Schegith warships twisted into the system. They were mostly automated, since the numbers of Schegith were still low and only slowly recovering from their near-extinction as a race. But one look at the sleek cruisers, bristling with weapons batteries, was enough to put my mind at ease. Null World and the Schegith would be fine, and any assault on them was akin to a death wish.

Which meant I could turn my focus ahead, to The Torus and whatever awaited us there.

28

WE'D SENT word ahead to Zeno about Icky in case she somehow got word that the big lump had been shot. When we arrived at The Torus to pick up Zeno and retrieve our workboat, she threw her arms around Icky, provoking a low hiss.

"Glad to see you too Zeno please don't squeeze so hard that still *stings*—"

Zeno pulled back, grinning. "Pain is good. Pain lets you know you're still alive." Her grin turned wry. "Believe me, I know, having woken a few times over the past days *really* aware I was still alive—excruciatingly so."

"Well, while you've been here drinking like a sailor on payday, Gerhardt tells me you have something for me," I said.

"I don't, but Tosk does." Zeno turned and nodded to someone standing nearby in The Torus's docking concourse. He was human, but the most nondescript man I'd ever seen. From his ordinary build to his plain face, he was utterly unremarkable. Even his clothing was bland. I swear that if I even glanced away from him for a moment, I'd totally forget what he looked like.

"Peacemaker Tudor, let's return to your ship, shall we?" he said.

We did, sealing the airlock when Tosk asked us to. I invited him to the galley, but when we arrived, he still didn't speak.

"Um, okay—it's Tosk, right? So what—?"

"When was the last time you swept your ship for bugs?" he asked.

I stared. "What, you think—?"

"Just before we got here," Perry put in.

I turned to him. "Really?"

"It's a basic security function, Van. One of a bunch that Netty and I routinely do in the background. Think of it as us defragging your hard drive while you're working on something else."

"Good to know." I turned back to Tosk. "So what's going on? What are these orders Gerhardt mentioned? All I know is that it involves meeting someone."

"Is everyone here read in?"

I sighed. *Spooks.* I'd had enough dealings with them back on Earth, working as a hacker, that I knew their default setting of incandescent paranoia only too well. "Yes, they are."

"Read into what?" Icky asked.

Tosk frowned at that, but I just shook my head. "Don't worry about it. I trust my crew, so you can trust my crew."

Tosk spent a moment looking doubtful but finally relented, reached into a pocket, and produced a small data module that he handed to me. "You'll find all of the details of the upcoming operation here. It's encrypted with a key that you will receive as background noise in a transmission you'll be getting from Anvil Dark shortly. Have your AIs isolate channels 15-1 through 15-5, extract all of the noise, then use the amplitude values to generate the key."

"Ooh, sneaky," Perry said.

Icky stared from Tosk to me. "Van, who the hell is this guy?"

Tosk frowned again. "I thought you said your crew was all read in on this."

"Don't mind Icky—she was dead for a while, but she got better. Anyway, can you give us the thumbnail version of this operation?"

Tosk again looked warily. I sighed. "Would it help if we all left?"

That provoked another frown from this utterly humorless man, but he finally shrugged.

"Fine. The GKU and the Guild have decided to invoke Plan Heracles. In essence, all available GKU and Guild assets are being activated, including some that are currently dormant. The objective will be the elimination of the leadership of the Seven Stars League."

A LONG MOMENT passed in silence. Torina was the first one to speak.

"Elimination? As in, assassination?"

Tosk shrugged. "Call it what you will. What matters is that the League has become a Threat to Order in known space. And yes, a Threat to Order is a specific thing—it's essentially the equivalent to Crimes Against Order, except instead of individuals, it applies to a sovereign state."

"Like I can murder someone, but it takes a state, to practice genocide," Torina said.

Tosk nodded. "Essentially correct."

I looked at the data module. "So we're going to war."

"If the plan executes as we envision it, it will be a very brief conflict."

"And this plan is called Heracles."

"Actually, that's the mobilization part of it. As I said, it activates all available Guild and GKU assets and brings them together to conduct a specific op," Tosk said.

"Okay, so what does *all available assets* mean? Has this Plan Heracles ever been used before?" Zeno asked.

"Once."

"And? How did that go?" I asked.

Tosk shrugged. "You'll find the details on there, but… not well. The GKU tried to assist a race known as the Termigu, who were being displaced from their homeworld, and two others that they had colonized. Two worlds were located that could provide an environment close to their natural one, but it required some biochemical and genetic alteration of their race to allow them to survive over the long term. And that is where things… went wrong."

"Went wrong *how?*" I asked.

"Unfortunately, the alteration almost worked—emphasis on *almost*. The result was that the remaining population of Termigu underwent a progressive mutation, effectively devolving into the creatures now known as Tenants."

There was another moment of silence. This time, I broke it.

"*What?*"

Tosk nodded. "As you can imagine, it was not the GKU's finest hour."

"No shit! I mean, just to be absolutely clear, you're saying that the GKU is responsible for creating the Tenants? The same parasitic creatures that are implicated in what's going on with the Seven Stars League now?"

"So this is essentially the GKU trying to clean up its own mess," Torina said.

Tosk glanced at her, then turned to Perry.

"This might provide some more answers. File—Original Sin."

29

We arrived at the rendezvous point specified in the uber-encrypted orders for Plan Heracles we'd been given by Tosk. Several ships, including the sleek bulk of the *Righteous Fury*, were already there. Two more arrived in the time it took us to close and dock with Gerhardt's ship, the *Splinter*. It would have been an awe-inspiring spectacle if I hadn't been so furious.

I strode through the airlock into the *Splinter*, the ship's AI directing me forward, Torina and Perry right behind me. When we stepped into Gerhardt's crew hab—which was as spartan as his office back on Anvil Dark—I found he wasn't alone. He had two other Masters with him. One was Alic, newly promoted into the role, a tactical genius hailing from a race already known for their military acumen, the Eniped. I'd worked with Alic before and absolutely trusted and respected him. The other was a pale, angular, and androgynous alien from a race I didn't know. I knew their name was Kharsweil and that, like Gerhardt, they'd mostly sat out the furor around Yotov and the other corrupt Masters. And that was it, I knew virtually nothing else about them.

"Tudor, glad you made it," Gerhardt said, standing as we entered. I strode straight up to him.

"I was just read into this Plan Heracles and the reason it exists, so neatly encapsulated in the Original Sin file stashed away inside Perry. Tell me, how long were you going to let me keep chasing the Tenants before you saw fit to reveal any of this to me?"

Gerhart returned a cool look. "It would appear that the small talk part of this is over."

I refused to ease up. "You named me your Justiciar, then sent me chasing off after the Tenants and the Puloquir—"

"Tudor, please sit down."

"I—"

Gerhardt, who was clearly going to be just as unrelenting as I was, just pointed at one of the seats around the barren table. I glared at it, then sat, Torina taking a place next to me.

I took a breath. "Alright. So if I understand this correctly, the GKU wrote a plan a century ago, Heracles, intended to summon all available assets to participate in a single, crisis-level op. And the reason for that, which was kept neatly compartmentalized away inside Perry, was that the GKU was responsible for creating a race of insidious parasites, the Tenants. Do I have that right?"

Gerhardt nodded. "Substantially, yes."

"Great. So the GKU was fully aware of who and what the Tenants were and has even had some of those assets we just mentioned deployed to try and keep an eye on them—"

"A job they failed at miserably, I might add," Torina stated.

"—but none of this information was shared with me. You left us to start with a blank slate, trying to figure out where to start chasing down the Tenants when you knew about them all along. And now that there's a crisis, because they've apparently infested the Seven Stars League and are threatening to destabilize known space, you've finally decided it's time to draw back the curtain—"

"I don't understand."

I stopped and turned to the speaker. It was the Master, Kharsweil.

"I'm sorry, you don't understand what?"

"Your emotional state. You are clearly agitated. This is because you were not given information you feel entitled to?"

I blinked again. "Information of direct relevance to a case I was assigned?"

Kharsweil turned to Gerhardt. "I'm afraid I still don't understand. Why should this Peacemaker feel so entitled to information that's extremely sensitive?"

I stared for a moment, dumbstruck.

"Are you—" I managed, then cleared my throat. "Is this a serious statement?" My tone was, even to me, dangerously flat.

Kharsweil turned back to me, their expression—to the extent I could understand their alien features, anyway—reminding me of an adult suddenly interrupted by a rudely inquisitive kid. That just stoked my fury.

"I'm sorry, Peacemaker, if I wasn't clear. Yes, I am serious. Frankly, I'm not even sure why you're here. Don't you have a ship to prepare for battle so that when you receive your orders you're ready to play whatever part you've been assigned?"

I sat still for a few seconds, then turned to Gerhardt, intending to cut Kharsweil out of the conversation. But I found Gerhardt looking back at me with a strange expression, one that I found it tough to read despite *his* features being very human. He seemed to be—holding back? Choosing to *not* participate in this aggravating conversation?

But why? Was Gerhardt cutting me loose? Basically leaving me to twist—?

Boss, Gerhardt's AI just told me to tell you, and I quote, you've got this, Perry said, his voice humming in my ear bug.

So Gerhardt *was* cutting me loose, but not because he was abandoning me. Rather, he wanted me to handle this myself for... reasons, I guess.

"So you're saying I should just quietly return to my ship and wait to be told what to do," I said, turning back to Kharsweil.

The Master gave a slight shrug. "I am confident that your contributions will be of some value. But your strategic insights aren't needed at the present, if they ever will be. You are a... gifted amateur, perhaps, but you're not a planner, or a trusted component of a legitimate battle plan. You will be given information as and when you require it. I'm sure you'll appreciate that that only makes good sense from a security perspective."

Kharsweil spoke with all the inflection of a government bureaucrat pointing out where to sign a form. I didn't get the sense it was because they *couldn't* be animated, but rather that they just couldn't be bothered. To them, I might as well have been a newly minted Peacemaker Initiate here to take the coffee order.

So I smiled right back, my face a rictus of polite neutrality. "Is there any of that secret—dare I call it top secret—information you'd care to share with me right now? You know, before we head into battle? I can't help but want to preserve the lives of my crew. Call it my *humanity*, if you will."

They waved a dismissive hand with long, many-knuckled fingers. "Everything you will need to know will be included in your orders. In the meantime, you will need to provide the lockouts for your combat AI in case we require further access to it."

"Ah, I see. Anything else? My banking information? The passwords to my various and sundry porn accounts back on Earth?"

Kharsweil's expression didn't even flicker. "You have your instructions, Peacemaker."

I smiled back again, but this time, I stood with deliberate slowness, then took a step closer to the officious prick. "I do, including the one where you tell me that you want to treat Perry as some sort of digital slave."

"I'm sorry, who is *Perry?*"

"Illuminating," Perry said.

"My combat AI. And the answer—and my *only* answer, I might add—to your instruction is, no, I will not provide my lockout access to you, or anyone else."

"Why not?"

"Did you hear me use the term *digital slave?* It was mere seconds ago, and you were sitting right there. He's a sentient being, not a piece of property."

"It is explicitly a piece of property, one that belongs to the Guild. You seem to be under the mistaken impression that that's not the case—"

"Oh, I'm under no mistaken impressions here, *Master* Kharsweil. I know exactly what you're asking, and I'm explicitly saying no. Unlike you, it seems, I don't believe in locking sapient beings into servitude—which makes you not that much different than the Tenants, now that I think about it."

I finally got a rise out of Kharsweil at that. A look as cold as the void flashed across their face, and I smiled even more broadly. Before they could speak, though, Gerhardt finally interrupted.

"Alic, would you escort Tudor and his crew members back to their ship, please?"

"Certainly," Alic said, his voice grave. He gestured toward the aft exit from Gerhardt's meeting space.

I stood, turned, and followed Alic without a backward glance, Torina and Perry at my back. When we reached the airlock, I turned to Alic to say—something, I wasn't sure what, because the encounter with Kharsweil had only stoked my rage to a new level of incandescence. But he was already opening his mouth to speak to me.

"Van, before you go, there's something you need to know."

"Some*thing*? I suspect there are many some*things*, starting with just what the hell was *that* all about?"

Alic kept his voice low. "That was about introducing you to Kharsweil. The reason they've been out of the picture for as long as they have is that they lost an arm and a leg in a clash with some Yonnox. Their agenda was already pretty inscrutable before that, and now no one's really sure where they stand—including Gerhardt. He wanted you to see that firsthand."

"Superb. *Another* corrupt Master. You're in bad company, Alic."

But Alic shook his head. "I don't think Kharsweil is corrupt—at least, not in the *motivated by profit* sense of the word. I think they're ambitious and want to impose their view of what the Guild is supposed to be."

"Which is what, exactly?"

"Very much a top-down, *do as you're told and don't ask questions* kind of organization. And something more like the GKU was when it was first conceived—much less neutral and focused on just enforcing the laws everyone else agrees to and—"

"Making the laws, instead," Torina put in.

Alic nodded.

I sighed. "And I thought Gerhardt was the procedure-driven asshole."

"That's what Kharsweil thinks, too, and Gerhardt wants to keep it that way. And that's why he didn't leap to your aid back there. In fact, he and Kharsweil are probably talking about what a—oh, what was the term Groshenko used to use. A loose battery? Launcher?"

"Cannon?"

"Right, that's it, a loose cannon. Gerhardt wants to remain Kharsweil's ally for as long as he can, so he can try to get inside their thinking."

"Which means Van is going to be spending more time being hung out to dry, as it were," Perry noted.

Alic nodded. "I'm afraid so. But if it makes you feel any better, Gerhardt thinks you can handle it. Moreover, you've got allies, Van. Me, for one. And Groshenko, who still wields a lot of power in the Guild. And on top of that, you're not only Mark Tudor's grandson, but you've made quite the name for yourself in the Guild on your own merits."

"You wouldn't think so, the way Kharsweil was talking. He treated Van like some low-level grunt," Torina said.

"That was for effect. He wanted to put me in my place," I replied.

Alic nodded, then reached into his tunic and extracted some-thing—another data module. "Anyway, you've got something more important to worry about."

I took the module and sighed. "So how do I decrypt this one? Determine the chemical composition of someone's belch and use that as the key?"

"Hey, that's not a bad crypto scheme. Gotta keep that in mind," Perry said.

Alic shook his head. "It's not encrypted. It's some intelligence we just received about the next Tenant incursion. Gerhardt wants you to take point in dealing with it. It's all on there." He backed away. "Anyway, I need to get back. Take care, Van."

"Looks like I'm going to have to," I said, then gripped the data module and turned to the *Fafnir*. As we passed through the airlock, Torina spoke up.

"Van, I have a question."

I glanced back at her.

"*What* porn accounts back on Earth?"

"Really? *That's* what you took away from all that?"

TORINA STARED at the *Fafnir*'s cockpit display for a moment, then sank back. "*Helso*? They're planning to attack *Helso*? Why?"

"Good question," I said, giving Netty the commit command. As soon as I'd read the intelligence summary given to me by Alic, I'd had Netty calculate the fastest possible course back to Torina's homeworld—which was also a place I'd started considering a second home of my own. As if I wasn't frustrated enough—

"Van, we'll arrive at Helso without sufficient fuel to make another twist. We'll have to gas up there," Netty said.

"It's not a serious concern for me. Helso will not, under any circumstances, fall out of our control."

"Good to know," Torina said, following that with a searching look.

She left the next question unasked. I knew what she was getting at. If we twisted to Helso and found ourselves grossly outmatched, we'd have no way to escape. But I truly didn't care. Helso was one of the few places in known space I'd die to protect.

That said, I did have a crew to think about. I turned back to Icky and Zeno.

"Listen, guys, we—"

"Van, I know what you're going to say," Zeno cut in. "Just shut up and fly."

I gave her a grateful look. Icky, however, just switched her gaze from me, to her, to me, then back to her.

"What? What was Van going to say?"

Zeno sighed and explained exactly what I'd been thinking, that this could end up being a one-way trip. Icky's reaction was to simply nod, then shrug.

"Yeah, what she said. Shut up and fly."

I turned back to the instruments, noting that Netty had already plotted a course to take us clear of the assembling GKU ships before we lit the drive. I noted that two ships had fallen into company with us—K'losk and Lucky, the latter of whom we hadn't seen in months. I hadn't realized that either of them were connected to the GKU and wondered how many other Peacemakers were members of the secretive organization. I was about to find out, though, it seemed, since Plan Heracles summoned *all* available assets from the GKU.

"Ahem."

It was Perry. I shot him a glance. "You rang?"

"I notice you didn't ask this sentient being if I wanted to go on this dangerous little jaunt," he said.

"Uh—" Shit. He was right. "Perry, I'm sorry. If you don't want—"

"Nah, I'm just yanking your chain, Van. My place is at your side, *duh*. But given good Master Kharsweil's attitudes about this stuff, you should probably strive to be more consistent. Otherwise, he might use it against you."

I nodded. "You're right. Good catch, bird."

"Although it is nice to be asked."

I turned back to the flight controls. Three ships. That was all the Masters were prepared to release for this mission to Helso. If the Tenants attacked in anything like force, we'd be hard pressed to do anything more than offer ourselves as a glorified speed bump.

We needed more firepower. Since Helso had become a Schegith protectorate, we'd already put in a call to them for help. But their fleet was still mostly out of position, and they were understandably reluctant to strip too much defense away from Null World, in light of recent events. In fact, that might even have been their plan—to pull the Schegith away from their homeworld, when it was the real target. Still, Schegith did agree to detach what she could, which meant two Schegith destroyer-class ships were on their way to Van Maanen's Star.

But it was going to take them over a day to make the trip, and I had a feeling we didn't have that long.

We needed firepower—

I turned around again. "Icky, what's your dad up to these days?"

She returned a blank look, then understanding dawned and she nodded.

"Why don't I ask him?"

I WATCHED the tactical overlay intently. So far, aside from a freighter just about to fall into orbit around Helso, the only three icons depicted on it were the *Fafnir*, K'losk, and Lucky. There was no sign of Icky's father, but there was also no sign of any Tenant ships—which we assumed were going to be warships of the Seven Stars League.

Torina came back into the cockpit. "My father's going to call for the planetary defenses to be activated," she said as she slid into her seat. "But Helso's not exactly a warmongering planet, so they're pretty basic."

The worry in her tone was unmistakable. I got it. In the space of a few hours, she'd gone from thinking of Helso as safe, to her world being on the verge of a grim, fiery fate.

I brought up the obvious. "Helso doesn't only have to rely on its own defenses, Torina."

"Yeah, we're here to kick ass and take names, and I'm all out of chewing gum," Icky said.

Everyone turned to her. I gave her a quizzical smile. "I think you're mixing your terminology there."

She shrugged. "You know what I mean—"

"Van, three ships just twisted into the system. They're all class

13 frigates, all registered to the Seven Stars League's Self-Defense Force."

"Self-Defense Force my ass," Zeno muttered.

"I hear you, Zeno," I replied, studying the data. It didn't paint a pretty picture.

Zeno sighed. "Any two of those things has all three of us at least slightly outgunned. All three together, though—"

"Have us heavily outgunned, yeah." I frowned at the overlay for a moment. I could feel everyone's eyes on me. I knew Lucky and K'losk were waiting for me to announce our intentions.

I took a deep breath. "Netty, how long until we're in missile range?"

"At their current delta-V, and assuming we don't move too close, about forty minutes."

"Okay. So, one thing at a time. Give me a comm channel, please —space-standard, plus any allocated to the League for their use."

"You're on," Netty said.

I took another breath. "League warships, this is Peacemaker Van Tudor. You have entered space that is under the protection of the Schegith, as well as the Peacemaker Guild—"

"This remains a Seven Stars League protectorate, so we claim full right of passage," a voice snapped back. At the same time, the display lit up with the image of a middle-aged human with iron-gray hair and beard. He was wearing a sinister uniform.

"Actually, sir, Helso ceased being a League protectorate nearly—"

"We don't recognize that—"

The man abruptly stopped, wincing as though in pain. It only lasted a second or so, then passed. He resumed his icy glare.

"The League does not recognize any change in Helso's status," he said.

I glanced at Torina to see if she'd noticed the man's strange behavior. She nodded.

I turned back. "All due respect, but that's up to the people of Helso. And they've made their position clear—"

"We are here to assert the protection of the Seven Stars League. If you interfere, you will be treated as hostile and—"

Again, that wince.

"—and... and dealt with accordingly."

"Well, it seems that we're at a bit of an impasse. There's a Schegith fleet on its way here. Why don't you heave-to until it arrives, and then we can resolve this, you know, amicably."

"I'll say it again. We are proceeding to Helso. If you attempt to interfere—"

Again, that wince, followed by a hissed intake of breath.

"What the hell's the matter with him?" Icky muttered.

Van, it's like he's fighting something that's forcing him to speak against his will, Perry said in my ear.

I nodded. "Excuse me, sir, but are you alright?"

He scowled. "This conversation is over—"

"Uh, actually, before you go, I have a question. Who am I talking to?" I asked.

"I am Ur-Commander Killian of—"

"No, I mean who am I really talking to? Or should I say, *what* am I really talking to?"

Killian glared back for a moment, then gasped and almost cried out. Then his face cleared and went slack.

"Do not stand in the way of our righteous quest for justice, Peacemaker," he said.

"Ah, okay. Well, hello there, you ugly little Tenant, you. Nice of you to actually speak up and… blather on about justice?"

"If you attempt to stop us from exacting our vengeance, we *will* destroy you."

"Yeah, you know as well as I do that we're not going to just stand aside and let you bombard a planet full of innocent people or whatever fiendish shit you have planned here. So why don't we dispense all the posturing. Just come out and say what it is about Helso that pisses you off so much?"

"Nothing is forgiven."

"Which means?"

"The one responsible for our mutacide originates here. We do not, will not forget or forgive. And if you try to prevent our finally realizing justice, that will not be forgotten or forgiven either—ever."

I cut the comm and turned to Perry. "Mutacide?"

"Uh, killing through mutation, I guess? I mean, it's a made up word."

"Aren't all words made up?" Icky asked.

Perry turned to her but just stared a moment. "Mark your calendars, folks. Icky got me there."

I looked at Torina. "They think whoever's responsible for their… mutacide is on Helso? Who could that possibly be?"

"Van, there are seven million people living on Helso. Believe it or not, I don't know every one of them."

I nodded and activated the comm. "If you have a legitimate grievance, if someone perpetrated a crime against your people, we could talk—"

"There is nothing to talk about."

"You're threatening the lives of seven million people because of the actions of one? How is that any more fair or reasonable than what was done to you?"

No answer.

"Van, the League ships will be in missile range in thirty minutes."

Nothing else on the overlay had changed—no sign of any help from the Schegith, or of Icky's father. All that stood between the Tenants and the deaths of seven million people were three outgunned Peacemaker ships and thirty measly minutes to figure out how to stop them.

30

"Okay, that file, Original Sin, makes it clear that the GKU assumes responsibility for what happened to the Termigu—what they're calling mutacide, which I guess refers to them being mutated into Tenants. But the Tenants themselves are blaming someone here at Helso. Both of those things can't be true," I said.

"Actually, Van, they can, if whoever in the GKU was specifically responsible for the screw up with the Termigu came from here," Perry replied.

I nodded. "Good point. So how do we figure out who that is?"

"More likely *was*, since it happened so long ago," Zeno noted.

"Another good point. Perry, there's nothing in that Original Sin file that even hints at who it might have been?"

He shook his head. "Sorry, Van. The file doesn't name any individuals."

"Oh, for—"

"Even if it did, then what? We find this person, or their descendants and, what, hand them over to the Tenants?" Torina asked. With each passing moment, both her anxiety and anger ratcheted up the scale another notch or two—understandable, given the circumstances. And mine wanted badly to keep pace, but it wouldn't do any of us any good if we just gave in and charged at the League ships, guns blazing, or something equally futile.

I shook my head. "No, of course not. But if we could at least convince the Tenants we'll try to help them realize some justice—"

"It's the GKU that should be facing this, not us," Torina snapped. "They're responsible, so they—"

"Sorry to interrupt, but several ships have just broken Helso orbit and are accelerating on an intercept trajectory with us," Netty put in.

I touched the overlay, pulled Helso into the center of the display, then zoomed. Sure enough, five ships were accelerating away from the planet, each a class 8. As the data filtered in, it quickly became clear that while they were fast, if standard freighter hulls, they'd been heavily upgraded with both armor and weapons.

"Who the hell are *they*?" I asked, looking at Torina. She returned a blank shrug.

"Netty, open a broadcast comm—"

"No need. There's an incoming comm message from one of the ships," she said.

The screen lit up—with an image of Torina's father.

"Uh... Mister Milon. Fancy meeting you out here."

Torina's composure cracked. "Dad, what the hell is going on?"

"What's going on is that we're tired of being a protectorate, relying on others for our defense. It was that sort of thinking that almost got us wiped out by a bio plague. So we've decided to take matters into our own hands and build up a protective fleet of our own." He waved behind him at the ship's interior. "Allow me to present my missile freighter, the *Feisty Daughter*."

"But—when? How? Why didn't you tell me—?"

"We decided not to tell anyone until we had the ships fully operational. Most of Helso doesn't even know, at least not yet. This is solely an initiative of the leading families. We conceived of it, and we funded it."

"Not that I disagree with your motives, but you're not exactly warriors. I mean, do you guys have *any* military experience?"

"We have a military consultant who's been very helpful. He was the same one who helped us procure these ships and has provided an advisor on each to act as the executive officer until we're ready to do this on our own."

"Well, I hope that's now, because you've got three big-assed warships inbound," Icky said.

"Oh, we're well aware. Incidentally, our advisor recommends that you fall back and link up with us, so we fight as a single, unified force."

"Can't argue with that," Zeno said.

I agreed. Netty plotted a trajectory back into the Van Maanen's Star system, to a rendezvous with the Helso flotilla. As we lit the drive and started sunward, Torina asked her father, "Who was this military consultant? Do you mean a mercenary?"

I tensed, bracing myself to find out it had been Group 41, and this was all a massive trap.

"I think you know him. It was Petyr Groshenko," her father replied.

I relaxed. But that immediately sparked another question in my mind. Groshenko was GKU, after all.

"Tell me, did you reach out to him, or did he come to you?" I asked.

"He came to us. Why?"

I looked at Torina. "He knew, or at least suspected that the Tenants might try this."

"Which means he probably also knows who the Tenants are after—who they're not going to forgive," she replied.

I nodded. "Netty, call up Groshenko, please."

"We have precious little antimatter fuel remaining, so it's going to be a brief twist comm, maybe a minute or so, if you want to maintain a decent reserve to power the fire control scanners."

"That's fine, Netty. Drain the tanks as dry as you dare."

While we waited, we tried quizzing Torina's father to see if he might have any idea who on Helso the Tenants bore their grudge against. But he was as in the dark as we were.

"Van, I have Groshenko," Netty said, replacing Torina's dad's image with his.

"I understand you're at Helso, Van."

"We are. But I doubt that you're surprised by that, or the fact that a squadron of League ships controlled by the Tenants are inbound with vengeance on their minds."

He shook his head. "I'm not, no."

"Who are they after, Petyr?"

"That *is* protected GKU information—"

"It's obviously not protected from the Tenants, so the only ones being kept in the dark are us. Now, we've got about thirty seconds more of twist comms with you, so please don't dither over this. Who are they after?"

Groshenko hesitated a moment, then shrugged. "To hell with it. You have a right to know—Torina in particular."

We exchanged a quick glance, and I again braced myself. Wherever this was going, it didn't feel like it was anywhere good.

"Who, Petyr."

"Her name was Elanora Dunlevy. She was a senior GKU operative, responsible for overseeing the project to relocate the Termigu—and that included authorizing the biological changes necessary to allow them to live on their new homeworlds. She died in battle about sixty years ago, when she was eighty-six."

Torina shook her head. "I don't know any Elanora Dunlevy."

"No, marriage does that—it has a way of obscuring the original family names of your ancestors," Groshenko replied, then took a breath.

"Elanora Dunlevy was your great grandmother, Torina. The Tenants blame her, and therefore her descendants, for what happened to them."

I'm NOT sure how long the silence lasted. Long enough for Netty to shut down twist comms, preserving our remaining antimatter fuel to give us real-time fire-control scanners. It was Perry who finally broke it.

"Dun-dun-DUH!"

Torina and I both turned on him.

"Sorry, but that was one of *those* revelations, really dramatic and unexpected and all," he said.

I just shook my head at him, then turned to Torina. "I... gather you didn't know."

"Hell *no* I didn't—sorry. I mean, this is just," Torina gave a helpless shrug, coupled with an expression so bleak I wanted to hold her. "I didn't know. At all."

Torina sent a deluge of comms to her father, demanding to know what he knew—and when. As the time gap finally diminished to something reasonable, Torina's father assured us he'd known nothing about this, and I sensed he was telling the truth. His face, usually beaming with confidence, was stricken. He was a man confronting his own past, and on terms he hadn't set.

"Your great grandmother, my grandmother, was Elanora Dunlevy, yes. But as far as we knew, she was an explorer who documented her experiences as a freelance writer. And she did die when she was about eighty-six, but we understood it to have been in an accident while spelunking some cave on some asteroid in the Wolf 424 system."

Torina sat back. "So let me get this straight—I'm the bloodline of a woman who corrupted an entire species, turning them into parasites that are dedicated to—I don't know, at least wiping out Helso, but probably taking over known space on top of that."

"Interesting family," Perry said, but I held up a warning finger to him.

"Perry, let's stay on target, okay?" I looked back at Torina. "What your great grandmother, or any of your other ancestors did or didn't do has nothing to do with you, Torina. I mean, my last name's Tudor. We're distant cousins to the former English royal family, which means I've got some real pieces of work in my background—including a guy that had two of his own wives beheaded."

"I'm descended from a mass murderer," Icky put in.

We all looked at her, and she nodded.

"Yeah. My father's—uh, grandfather, I think. He wiped out a rival Wu'tzur faction's colony on some moon, for—I don't know, something about mining rights." She shrugged. "I don't lose any sleep over it."

"That explains a lot," Perry said. Icky replied with what I'd learned was a particularly rude Wu'tzur gesture.

"Anyway, if I were the type to believe in conspiracies—and these days, I definitely am—I might wonder if us first meeting back at Procyon, courtesy The Quiet Room and one of my very first jobs as a Peacemaker, was *actually* just a coincidence," I said.

Torina sighed and lolled her head back against the copilot's seat. "If it wasn't, it still worked out pretty nicely."

"I agree. But that should make you feel better about all this. Regardless of what happened in the past, especially involving our ancestors, doesn't matter. What matters is right now."

Torina sat up, nodding. "Fine. If there's some accountability owing in my family, then we'll deal with it—not them," she said, pointing at the three icons depicting the onrushing League ships.

"Again, I agree," I replied, noting that we'd almost finished matching speed and course with the Helso fleet. "And to that end, let's go to battle stations, folks. We've got a much *less* lopsided fight ahead."

I WINCED as Zeno put a burst of mass-driver slugs into the League frigate, causing bodies to spill into hard vacuum as small, tumbling points of light.

"Firing guns," Netty said, raking the frigate with a hundred massive rounds. "She's ventilated—"

"And there she goes," I concluded as the ship's reactor lost containment in a searing bloom of light.

Torina held one hand over her station, poised to attack the next target even as a battle roared to life around us. Beam weapons lanced out in flickering displays of energy, some hits, some misses, but enough action that I cut the controls hard astern to engage the next target.

"Send six birds in two waves, delay by ten seconds, Netty." My order was crisp, and the *Fafnir* twitched—barely—as our weapons raced away at hideous velocity.

The League ship began sending fire back, but then the Milon family cruiser scored two surgical hits that neatly cracked the enemy craft along her keel.

"Fine shooting, sir," I said over the comms.

"We'll address the next target," came the voice of an unknown Milon crewmember—young, female, and competent. "Your missiles should strike in just over a minute. They're burning all out down the ecliptic to get away, so you've got some downtime."

"This is boring," Icky said.

Perry piped up. "You don't know boredom. I was doing intel for Mark in 1998—"

"Where?" I interrupted.

"Hollywood, Florida. Local cop was selling stolen tech to someone he thought was a sheik from some vague, shadowy place overseas. Anyway, I'm watching this clown so your gramps can swoop in and grab him, with a good case—"

"Thirty seconds until the missiles strike," Netty said.

Perry went on, unfazed. "And this goober went into a place called Blockbuster Video to return some VHS tapes he'd rented. Apparently, this was a ritual for people back then?"

"You haven't *lived* until you've gone to Blockbuster on a Friday night," I enthused.

"I'll have to take your word for it. This… Blockbuster… had a sidewalk sale of some used tapes, and I swooped down and lifted one. You know, just to see what the fuss was about."

"Hooligan," I said.

Perry shrugged. "It was the 90s, Van. So I grabbed a videotape entitled *Scarf Tying Made Easy With Marianne*, which turned out—I could watch the tape by remote scanning—to be ninety-three minutes of a middle-aged lady from Minnesota teaching you, the lucky viewer, how to make knots in a yarn scarf that could be worn almost anywhere."

"Even a funeral?" Icky asked.

"Maybe, if the deceased was a Lutheran. Marianne really knew her stuff, Van, but that video taught me the meaning of boredom, and since enduring that experience, I've never really been bored again."

"Scarf tying?" I asked, still trying to visualize the need for an instruction manual on such a thing, let alone *ninety-three minutes* of said activity.

"Impact. Target gone," Netty said.

"See? Marianne kept us busy while we waited to rain hellfire on those miserable bastards," Torina said, giving Perry a nod of approval.

"I miss her to this day, dontcha know," Perry said, miming wiping a tear.

"Any targets left, or has the Helso crew finished up?" I asked.

"Two live enemies left. Attack?" Netty asked.

"By all means. In the name of Saint Marianne of the Scarf, we attack with the fire of heck and darn-nation," I said.

Zeno's whiskers twitched. "I'll still fight angry, if it's okay with you, Van."

"By all means. Stop the closest League ship from running, and spare no expense. I want them as a cloud of gas or a drifting hulk," I ordered.

Lucky howled over the comms, having taken a direct hit that shut her ship down for a moment. When her lights came back on, she was good and pissed, driving head-on for the same target we were. In a brilliant bracketing maneuver, our missiles punched through the enemy defenses to carve an entire engine away from the ship's frame, and atmosphere began venting in brief, violent plumes from several holes.

"They're done, boss. I'm getting returns that they're about to—" Netty began, but she didn't need to finish her report. The League ship was already cooling gas. "We've got eight ships on one, boss. Any need to mix it up?"

Icky's father showed up at that moment in his massive battleship, the *Nemesis*. Without a word over comms, he unleashed a torrent of fire on the final League ship, tearing it to scrap before I could formulate an order.

"I would say no, Netty. That won't be necessary, courtesy of the *Nemesis*. That's one deadly ship, there."

"Hi, Dad," Icky said.

"Hello, daughter. Anything left to blow up?" Urnak asked, his face beaming as he saw his daughter.

"No, dammit. They all went boom."

Icky and her father wore identical expressions, earning a round of silent laughter from me, Zeno, and Torina.

Perry laughed out loud.

I glanced at the rearward display, confirming there were no contacts.

"Van, that last frigate transmitted a twist comm right before Urnak fired. I was able to catch enough of the spillover to narrow its destination down to a point somewhere on the coreward edge of League space, not far from their border with the Eridani Federation," Netty said.

I nodded. "That must be where they're assembling their fleet, so they can confront the GKU." I glanced at Torina. "We can be thankful for that. If they weren't facing that threat, I suspect they'd have sent a lot more ships here, and this might have turned out very differently."

She nodded.

"That means the big fight is still ahead of us," Icky said.

"It is. But that comm message Netty traced might give the GKU a leg up. Netty, use the last of our antimatter fuel to send whatever data you managed to grab to Gerhardt. Meantime, we're going to have to swing by Helso to gas up."

I frowned at that. A quick mental calculation told me we were going to lose several hours dropping down the gravity well of Van Maanen's Star to Helso in order to refuel and then rejoin the fleet.

By then, it might all be over.

But Icky's father came to our rescue. "Van, I know you're off to some big battle, and no, I don't need to know the details. But I'll save you time and refuel you out here. Also, I have a suggestion."

"What's that?"

"Your ship, the *Iowa*, is as ready as she's ever going to be for battle using automation alone. And that's an awful lot of firepower to leave just parked back at Sol."

I turned to Icky. "Can you handle her?"

"I can keep the automation running, if someone else can do the flying."

"I'll do it," Zeno said. "I've been helping Icky tinker and fiddle with her automation, so I know what she can do—and what she can't—pretty well."

I turned back to Icky's father. "I think we'll take you up on your offer. If you can gas us up, then take Icky and Zeno back to the *Iowa*, we'd definitely owe you one."

I switched the comm to Torina's father. "Starting to feel like bring your daughter to work day," I said, waiting for him to answer.

I felt Torina looking at me. "What?"

"It's—I'll tell you later," I replied as her father came on the comm and I explained what we were doing.

"Which means we've gotta run. Meet for drinks on the veranda after we do a little housekeeping?" I said.

"You're sure we can't help?"

I shook my head. "You need to stay here and protect Helso in case the Tenants decide to try this again. Icky's dad will come back here to help as soon as he can."

He nodded. "Van? Son? Be safe."

I glanced at Torina.

"Always. I mean, we've got a lot to look forward to."

31

By the time we made it back to rejoin the GKU fleet, its numbers had swelled dramatically. It now numbered thirty-two ships, ranging from class 6 craft that were little more than up-gunned workboats, to the ferocious might of the *Righteous Fury*. It looked to me like the very definition of an unstoppable force, but Gerhardt wasn't so sure.

"Our current intelligence puts almost all of the Seven Stars League's fleet under Tenant control. That's nearly sixty ships, ranging from corvettes to a trio of purpose-built battleships," he said over the comm.

I sank back. "Sixty ships? Holy shit." The unstoppable force suddenly didn't seem so unstoppable.

"It's not quite as dire as it seems. The Eridani Federation has moved the bulk of their fleet in the direction of their border with the League, so we're projecting that they'll leave a dozen or so ships back as a reserve."

"Still, that gives them a major edge over us—at least ten or fifteen ships," I said.

Gerhardt nodded. "Which is where the late-breaking intel you provided to us about their likely assembly area comes in. We've sent a scout ship to confirm that they're there. If they are, we're going to immediately attack and try to catch them before they're ready to deploy."

"Ballsy," Perry said. "I like it."

"Is there any chance we can get the Eridani Federation to join us?" Torina asked.

Gerhardt shook his head. "Moving their fleet to make it more threatening is as far as they were willing to go. Now, if they sense an opening, they're opportunistic enough to try and exploit it. But Tau Ceti has made it clear that they're uncomfortable with the idea of the Eridani seizing a bunch of League territory, so they've started mobilizing *their* fleet. That's going to force the Eridani to be cautious."

I sighed. "This is starting to sound like Europe in 1914. Everyone's positioning themselves like dominoes, and if one falls—"

"Indeed. Preserving the stability of known space is our overriding goal. Both the Eridani and Tau Ceti know that, so they're holding back for now. But we're going to have to figure out some way of maintaining the balance of power—ideally by preserving the Seven Stars League as a major power."

"Sounds like you're looking for a regime change," Perry said.

"That's what we're hoping. We have some people inside the League who are helping a loyalist faction quietly position themselves to seize power, but that's only going to happen if we take out their fleet."

"Which means a whole lot of League ships, and their crews, are going to have to die," Torina said.

Gerhardt returned a grave nod. "Sadly, yes. Now, if you can propose an alternative, I'm certainly listening. But in the absence of that, our fleet will be getting underway in one hour. You should receive the final operations orders shortly."

Gerhardt signed off. I glanced around the *Fafnir*'s cockpit. With both Icky and Zeno gone, it suddenly seemed awfully empty.

THE REPORT HAD COME BACK from Gerhardt's scout ship—the League fleet was, indeed, marshaling at the coordinates Netty had traced back from Helso. The countdown had accordingly started on our own fleet preparing to twist. We were still in company with Lucky and K'losk, forming our own little squadron. And since this *ad hoc* fleet hadn't ever worked together before, that was really all it was—a conglomeration of little squadrons of ships that had. It was still an immensely powerful force, undoubtedly one of the single most powerful in known space, but that struck me as a potentially severe weakness. Compartmentalized outfits like the GKU might enjoy better security because of it, but it certainly didn't promote coherence or unity of purpose, did it?

I watched the time. We would twist in groups, with the most powerful, built around the *Righteous Fury*, leading the way. Successive groups would follow on a staggered schedule, to coordinates far enough apart that the risk of twisting things on top of one another was minimized. Our group of three ships would be the sixth one to go.

"No sign of the *Iowa* yet," Torina said. Not that that was surprising, and we'd even planned for it. Once we'd gotten confirmation from the scout ship, we sent word back to Zeno and Icky to twist right to the expected location of the battle if they couldn't join us here by our go time.

Which left us waiting, watching as the menacing bulk of the *Righteous Fury* and her escorts—three heavy cruisers, three destroyers—lit their drives and accelerated away. I drummed my fingers on the armrest.

"I don't like this," I said without really meaning to say anything at all.

"What, the *Iowa* not being here? Or going into a huge fleet battle? It's certainly not what I expected I'd be doing today," Torina replied.

I shook my head. "No. Or—yes, but that's not what I'm talking about. It's—"

I waved my hands around. "It's all of it. This fleet, which exists, but doesn't. And the League, controlled by the Tenants—and neither of them truly bad guys. I mean, sure, the League's amoral and opportunistic, but the line forms to the left on that in known space. And the Tenants are vile parasites, but they didn't start out that way. And now we're going to execute a plan specifically intended to clean up the GKU's mess, which seems to be code for exterminating them."

Torina nodded. "And on top of that, my great grandmother is the one responsible for setting all of this in motion."

"Sure, but even she wasn't being a bad guy. She thought she was helping the Termigu escape the collapse of their planetary environments." I sank back in my seat and closed my eyes. "I wish there was some way we could peel apart the Tenants and the crews of those League ships. I doubt that the League wants this fight, so if we could get through to them, even briefly—"

"Maybe there is."

I snapped my eyes open. It had been Netty who said it.

"Go on, Netty. I'm listening."

"Remember when you were speaking to that League officer, Killian, and he kept having those bouts of discomfort? That struck me as odd. If it's normal behavior by someone joined with a Tenant, then it would tend to stand out, right?"

I sat up. "Go on."

"Well, Perry and I have been chewing on it, and we came up with a possible explanation."

Perry, who'd been silent until now, spoke up. "Actually, credit where due—this is really all Netty's idea."

"Netty's idea, got it." I glanced at the time. The *Righteous Fury's* group, and the two following it, had twisted away. We were just under five minutes from our own twist time. "Let's press on."

"When you were talking to Killian, the twist comm was running to let you do it in real time. But since we were so short of fuel, and the range was so low, I ran the twist comm in its lowest possible power mode to try and conserve as much antimatter as possible," Netty said.

"And that's significant because—?"

"Low-power mode doesn't enable twist comms over more than a few light-minutes, at most. At that range, and in that mode, there's a tendency for harmonic gravitational effects to occur between the transmitter and receiver—essentially, you get a sequence of standing gravitational waves generated across the channel. The effect is slight and really has no meaningful real-world impact. But what if it was interfering with the Tenant's ability to control Killian?"

I sat up even more. "Do you have any evidence that that's what was happening?"

"No, of course not. It's all just conjecture. But for some reason, that Tenant gave up and just—I don't know, kind of shut down Killian, its host, and assumed complete control."

I remembered the way Killian's face had gone slack and lifeless, his voice a flat, uninflected monotone. I'd realized that the Tenant had turned him into a sluggish meat puppet, but I hadn't thought through why.

I glanced at the time. Just over three minutes. "Okay, Netty, let's assume you're right. How can we use this to our advantage?"

"This is where I come in," Perry said. "Netty and I have analyzed the shit out of this, as much as we can with the data we have available, and run some simulations based on it. We've figured out a way to enable our twist comm to produce the same gravitational harmonic effects, but at much higher power settings. If we generate that effect, maybe we can inhibit the Tenant's ability to influence the actions of the League crews."

"Won't the Tenants just take over complete control, the way they did Killian?" Torina asked.

"They might, but then they wouldn't be a symbiotic union of two beings, they'd be one being controlling another directly. And how many of the Tenants do you think are skilled crewmembers of advanced warships, able to operate every system, knowing what button to push when?" Netty said.

"Okay, but can't they end the effect just by turning off their comm?" I asked.

"That's the beauty of it. Even if they close the comm channel, the harmonic resonance effect between our twist comm transmitter and their receiver will still exist, for as long as we keep broadcasting. The only way they could end it would be by shutting down their twist comm system entirely, which at least *still* restricts them to light-speed comms," Perry said.

I thought about the message broadcast by the League Satrap, the devilishly handsome man with the perfect hair. The woman in the background—clearly one of his senior advisors, since she was on stage with him—had fidgeted restlessly throughout his pronouncement of my nefarious deeds. Had she contained a Tenant? And had whatever twist comm system carrying his broadcast been resonating in the same way?

Two minutes.

I nodded. "Okay, let's do it. Configure the twist comm to do whatever you need it to do. Which means now comes the inevitable part where you tell me the downside to this plan."

"What makes you think there's a downside?" Perry asked.

"There's always a downside—*no free lunches* is a universal constant, remember?"

"Unfortunately, you're right. Netty?"

"To maintain this effect, we need a fixed spatial reference point. I can adjust for the movements of the other ships—well, probably up to something like twenty of them, anyway, as long as I've got good scanner data on them. At that point, the math becomes too complex. But I can only do that if the *Fafnir* isn't itself moving. Alternatively, if the bad guys would indulge us by all staying perfectly still, we could move the *Fafnir*, but I kind of doubt they'll be obliging."

"Wait—the downside is that we have to stay perfectly still, in one place, in the middle of a space battle?"

"Like you said, Van, *no free lunches*."

"But we were moving relative to the League ships back at Helso," Torina said.

"We were. But note that the effect was only intermittent, and of varying intensity. We're talking about deliberately generating a continuous effect strong enough to make a difference over something on the order of twenty ships. For me to do that, either we have to be stationary or they do."

The group of ships preceding us abruptly vanished into spatial distortion as they twisted away. That left us with one minute to go.

"Will the Tenants be able to figure out what's happening?" I asked.

"Those aboard the ships that aren't affected will probably be able to work it out pretty quickly, yeah," Perry said.

"Great. So not just sitting in one place, but attracting the full attention of the enemy while we do it." I glanced at Torina. "What do you think?"

"I think it's a horrible idea. But I also think we need to give it a try."

"Yeah, pretty much what I'm thinking, too." I sighed. "It would be so much easier to just shoot stuff, you know."

I shook my head. "Netty, Perry, do whatever you have to do. Meantime, open a comm channel to K'losk and Lucky. They need to know what's going on—and that we are *really* going to need their help."

I turned to Torina. "You and I need to finish suiting up, then depressurize—"

Without warning, Torina abruptly leapt out of her seat, grabbed me, and kissed me. When she pulled back, she smiled.

"That's just in case—" She shrugged.

I nodded. Nothing more needed to be said.

32

SPACE BATTLES—FOR that matter, space*flight*—is all about motion. The weird, almost supernatural physics of twisting aside, ships obey the laws Isaac Newton discerned underlying the movements of things in nature. They have inertia, based on their mass, and they accelerate by the application of forces from things like thrust and gravity, the extent of which over time is determined by that inertia.

All of which was to say that spaceships are *not* supposed to just sit still, particularly in the midst of a space battle.

But, as soon as we'd twisted into the shitstorm of laser, mass-driver, particle-beam, and missile fire that raged between the GKU and League fleets, that was exactly what we did. Netty put the *Fafnir* into station-keeping mode, using miniscule bursts from the thrusters to keep her locked in position relative to a specific set of spatial coordinates. Or, more to the point, she kept the twist comm transmitter locked into that place. We could roll, pitch, and yaw the ship around that point as long as we didn't pull the transmitter more than a few centimeters away from it. She could do it, but between that and doing all of the simultaneous, myriad calculations to account for the observed movements of the League ships now blasting away around us, she was pretty much tapped out capacity wise.

"I've started broadcasting, Van," she said. Lucky and K'losk had taken protective stations on either beam, covering the *Fafnir* with their weapons. Torina was operating ours in manual mode, while I—

While I sat there. I had only one immediate job to do, and that was talking.

When the channel-open indicator flicked on, I did just that.

"To all Seven Stars League ships hearing this broadcast, we are well aware that you are under the control of the Tenants. We urge you to resist it because we don't want this fight, and we don't believe you do either—"

A flash to starboard announced the detonation of a missile that managed to sneak past K'losk. I heard a REAB module fire somewhere aft, but none of the *Fafnir*'s system-status indicators changed. A moment later, Torina fired the glitter caster, enveloping us in a sparkling cloud of laser-attenuating chaff.

"Again, we urge you to resist," I went on. "And when you do, stand down your fleet, and we'll do likewise—"

"Van, there's an incoming message from Gerhardt," Torina said.

I ignored it and just kept talking, delivering the same message over and over, while ships poured destructive energy at one another all around us.

We attracted some more sporadic fire, but the bulk of the League's attention was focused on the bigger GKU ships, the *Right-*

eous Fury, and the various heavy cruisers bulking up the fleet. For them, it was very much a fight. Lasers and particle beams gouged glowing furrows in hulls. Missiles detonated, shredding armor and hull plating with shrapnel. Streams of frozen atmosphere jetted into space through gaps and rents. Debris whirled about. Smaller ships accelerated on bursts of fusion thrust, twisting and turning in response to puffs of thrusters.

And the League fleet just pressed on with its attack.

I felt the cold chill of uncertainty, because it might not work. Maybe Netty and Perry had been wrong. Maybe we were just wasting our time—

Another missile detonated nearby. This time, the *Fafnir* shuddered under the impacts of shrapnel, REAB modules taking some of the hits. Netty kept applying thrust, keeping the ship locked so firmly into place we might have been bolted to this arbitrary point in space. Torina did her best to shoot back, but she was eyeballing her shots, through a cloud of glitter at that. We'd elected to keep the *Fafnir*'s active scanners dark, trying to make ourselves less of a target, but it meant she was literally aiming and firing with virtually no automation to assist her.

And yet, she managed to land hits. I caught a glimpse of a League corvette whipping by, our laser tearing into its hull while Torina tapped furiously at the weapons panel. She refrained from firing the mass driver to avoid its recoil disrupting Netty's careful positioning. K'losk's ship appeared ahead of us, its point-defense batteries spewing streams of tracers at yet more onrushing missiles—

Something slammed into the *Fafnir*—a particle-beam hit. It ripped through the hull, triggering a sudden series of warnings.

Another hit followed, bluish arcs of electrical discharge momentarily flaring around us from the sudden, excess charge. A mist of vaporized alloy fumed the air.

"Van, fusion containment has switched to backup mode. The primary is offline," Netty said.

I swore. Fusion containment—the powerful magnetic bottle that enclosed the howling heart of the reactor and provided thrust for the drive—had two redundant backup systems. With the primary off-line, we were now relying on the first of them to keep us from vanishing in a glorious burst of light. That left a single backup system.

I unstrapped. "Torina, I'm going aft. Try to keep things in one piece up here!"

Her only reply was a raised thumb amid her rapid stabs and taps at the weapons. I hurried aft, clunking my helmet on the hatch coaming at the back of the cockpit.

"Perry, on me!"

"Right behind you, boss."

I stopped briefly in the galley. A circular hole the size of a dinner plate, still glowing around the edges, gaped in the overhead. Another corresponding hole had been drilled through the galley table and out the other side of the ship. A similar through-and-through wound marked the passage of the second particle beam through the *Fafnir*. Smaller holes in the hull showed where we'd been penetrated by shrapnel.

I hurried on. Another missile detonated close by, a piece of shrapnel slamming through the *Fafnir* less than a meter ahead of me. I pushed past the airlock and into the engineering bay. Warnings flashed, yellow and red, on the status panels. A quick scan of them told me that things had gone terribly wrong in the time it took me to even get here from the cockpit. More holes torn in the hull, and a smashed control module told me why.

"Shit—the first backup containment system's offline. We're on the second backup," I growled.

"That's not good," Perry said.

"Perry."

"Yah, I know. Sorry. Nerves."

"You're only human."

"Thanks, boss."

It was *another* thing that didn't need to be said. I eyed the emergency shutdown. I could scram the reactor, but if I did that, the *Fafnir* would effectively go offline. We'd still have some basic function running off the power cells, but that would be it. We wouldn't just be stationary, we'd be dead in space.

I turned to Perry. "Can you do it?"

"Do what?"

"Act as an emergency controller for the containment system."

"Uh—well, I don't have that programming—"

I yanked open a tool case fastened to the nearby bulkhead, dug into it, and yanked out a patch cable. "Well, you're about to get a crash course, courtesy of me hacking you into the system—"

Something else hit us. I felt the thrusters thrum through the deck plates as Netty fought to keep us in place.

"Kinda sensing I don't have a choice."

I plugged the cable into a data port in the engineering console, then gestured for Perry to come closer. "Sure you do… that, or probably blow up."

Perry landed on the console and reared up, opening the data port on his chest. "Well, since you put it that way——"

I jammed the cable into him, and he squawked. "You could at least buy me dinner first——"

"Later, bird," I said, turning back to the console. *Okay, Tudor, you've spent hours and hours learning how to hack these extraterrestrial computer systems. It's time for your final exam.*

I touched the console, hesitated, then tapped at another control. "Anything?"

"Working on it," Perry said. I waited.

"There, I'm connected. Holy—look at all this engineering data."

"Aren't you an expert in it all?"

"Actually, I'm not. My programmed expertise is in general ship flight and operations, not the details of her engineering——"

"Well, let's change that," I said and got to work.

THE NEXT FEW minutes passed in a rapid-fire blur, while also somehow dragging along forever. I racked my brain, trying to figure out how to turn Perry into a fusion containment controller. As I did, I kept casting a worried eye on the last backup. And the whole time, the *Fafnir* shuddered under incoming fire. More systems had gone red, leaving my poor ship in a sorry state—it was easier to see what was still working than what wasn't.

But I grimly pushed on. I finally managed a workaround, treating the fusion reactor's maintenance system as a bridge between Perry and the containment system. The maintenance system was, in terms of its general architecture, similar to others used on the *Fafnir*, and that included one that Perry had learned with intimate familiarity.

"There—you should be connected. Can you access it now?" I asked him.

"Yes."

"It should be similar to the waste reclamation system——"

"It is, thank you very much."

"And you know that system well——"

"Yes, Van, I've got it. Perry ran the ship's toilet, so now he can run the fusion reactor, haha——"

"Can you handle this shituation or not?"

"Solid joke, despite the awkward timing. I'm downloading the firmware from the backup controller now. And—there. Okay, I now officially know how to run the toilet *and* the reactor."

"See? That time you spent running the reclamator wasn't a waste."

"Oh, very funny——"

"Okay, I'm leaving you here to take over containment if that last backup fails, going back to the cockpit."

I hesitated. Perry suddenly looked—I don't know, vulnerable, cabled into the *Fafnir*'s engineering panel, stuck and unable to move. I had a sudden flash of Rolis, keeping the automated terror we'd called a junkyard dog under control while he bought me time to escape. He'd been stuck in exactly the same way.

"Van, go. Finish winning the war. I'll be fine," Perry said.

I nodded, then hurried back forward. Along the way, it struck me that he'd known what I was thinking.

Which was very human of him.

I PICKED my way through the *Fafnir's* battered midships. The galley had more holes than intact structural members and hull plating. Through the slowly expanding cloud of glitter, I actually saw a ship through one of the rents explode in the distance, though whether one of ours or one of theirs I wasn't sure.

When I made it back to the cockpit, I went to sit back in the pilot's seat—to find half of it gone. A big-assed chunk of shrapnel had punched through the overhead, straight down through the seat and out the *Fafnir's* underside.

"Oh. That would have left a mark," I said.

Torina shot me a glance. "I don't want to talk about it, thanks."

"Netty, is there *any* indication this is actually working?" I said, settling myself into Zeno's place behind the pilot's seat.

"Several League ships have broken off. And six more have started firing on their comrades. So, yes, I'd say it's working."

Something suddenly loomed ahead of us—a League heavy cruiser. I swore and looked at the tactical overlay repeated on Zeno's console. K'losk's ship was drifting, powerless. Lucky had taken as many hits as the *Fafnir* but still valiantly tried to cover us with what remained of her weapons. The *Righteous Fury* had started a slow roll, trailing atmosphere from dozens of holes punched into her hull.

It had worked. But it still hadn't been enough to carry the day. And now, the League heavy cruiser sliding menacingly toward the *Fafnir* had us in the sights of banks of laser batteries and particle cannons. Hell, she could just shred us with her point-defense batteries, and there was nothing we could do to stop it.

I stood to reach for Torina, but a voice over the comm cut me off.

"Peacemaker ship *Fafnir*, this is the League cruiser *Dawning Star*. I am here to assist you."

I sat back down. "What?"

Netty spoke up, sounding smug. "I suggested that the League crews turn their ships over to the control of their AIs with orders to stand down, then lock themselves out of further control. The crew of the *Dawning Star* did that, and her AI and I have been talking—he's actually pretty cool."

"Cool? Really?"

"Yes. Cool. Anyway, long story short, the *Dawning Star* is here to protect us from further attack."

I let out a shuddering sigh. Okay, that meant we were out of immediate danger, but the overlay still showed the grim truth—even with a portion of the League fleet either standing down or turning on its fellows, we were looking at a bloody stalemate, at best. The GKU had no more reserves, nothing else to influence the battle. Worse, it might still end in a League victory—a Pyrrhic one, sure, but that was the worst possible outcome, wasn't it? A horrific death toll on both sides, with nothing resolved, the Tenants still in control of the League, and nothing but the Eridani Federation and Tau Ceti to stop them.

In other words, all out interstellar war. The death toll from that might be in the millions, even the billions.

I slumped. I was out of ideas. Whatever was going to happen was—

"Van, *what the hell did you do to my ship?*"

It was Icky.

A new icon had snapped onto the overlay. It was the *Iowa*.

My eyes opened wide as I hit the comms. "Icky, the *Dawning Star* is a friendly."

"Got it. She's broadcasting a guild code. Now get the hell out of my way!"

Her enormous bulk swept past us, charging the League's remaining battleline. Her missile launchers coughed out ordnance, and her lasers and mass drivers poured out punishing fire. I knew her reliance on automation dramatically limited what she could do —basically, fly in a straight line and let the version of Netty that was her AI engage targets of opportunity. But she was a battleship, making her the biggest ship in the fight, and her arrival tipped the balance.

"Not to be petty, but it's about time you guys showed up," I said, grinning at Torina as I needled Icky. I saw Torina slump back as well, relief marking her features.

"Well, excuse us. You try to get a big-assed ship that should have a crew of at least thirty underway when there's only two of you," Icky said.

"Excuse me," Netty added with an electronic cough.

"Oh. Right. Yeah, Netty as well."

"Van, what's your status?" Zeno asked.

I looked out at the *Dawning Star*. Her point defenses almost casually swatted away a missile that had been streaking toward us. I took a slow, deep breath.

"In one piece, more or less. You guys go help finish winning the fight. We'll be good until you get back, I think."

Torina clambered out of her seat and moved to Icky's, so she was again sitting beside me. "K'losk just called. He's wounded, but okay. And Lucky's taking off after the *Iowa*. Apparently, she's still got some fight in her."

I gave her a tired smile through my visor. "I don't."

"No, me neither. I just need to… sit. Just sit for a while." Her eyes were on the ruined pilot's seat.

So were mine. But not for long. Instead, I looked at something much more pleasant. Torina must have felt my eyes on her, because she abruptly turned, then smiled.

So did I.

A voice suddenly cut into the moment. It was Perry.

"Uh, hello? Somebody want to fill the bird in about what's going on?"

EPILOGUE

I'D NEVER BEEN to the capital of the Seven Stars League, partly because my Peacemaking work had never brought me, and partly because I'd been a wanted man here for what felt like forever.

It was actually quite nice. The sky was a darker shade of blue than I was used to on Earth, and the vegetation was more rusty red-brown than green, but the day was nice, not that much different than a warm summer day in Pony Hollow, Iowa.

The man, the head of a local school, walked up to the booth enclosing the ballot machine and paused to give the media time to get some images of him, poised on the verge of voting. With the Tenant control of the League overthrown, the provisional government that had stepped into their place had moved swiftly to hold a genuine, open election. And they'd invited the leading families of Helso to act as observers, a small act of contrition for what could have been a catastrophe if their attack on Torina's homeworld hadn't been stopped.

We watched as the educator entered the booth, then emerged a moment later to a round of thunderous applause from the gathered crowd.

"So there it is, the very first vote of the election, ushering in a new day of true democracy for the Seven Stars League," a voice boomed.

I turned to Torina's father. "You going to go and check it? You know, make sure it was on the up-and-up?"

He gave me a wry look. "We're expecting about fourteen billion votes to be cast, Van. I don't think we'll be able to review them all. That's what audits are for."

I laughed and looked at the crowd around me. Torina, Zeno, Icky, and Perry were all here, as was K'losk, whose arm was held in a sling, and Lucky, who'd taken a hit to her leg that left her with a cast. They'd been the fortunate ones. The total dead for both sides of the battle had topped two thousand, with nearly as many injured. The reality of what it had taken to get here, to this moment, made the whole day a little more somber, the sky seem a little darker.

Gerhardt pushed through the crowd and gestured me aside.

"First of all, Tudor, that was damned good work. So good, in fact, that I'll overlook the fact that you ignored my calls to you."

He said it with that thin smile of his, but I caught a trace of genuine humor. I shrugged and smiled back.

"You sure? You're not going to give me a reprimand or something?"

"As long as you make it a point to only violate protocols and procedures to save the world, I think I can live with it."

The crowd around us started to disperse, people heading for the voting booths that had been set up around the park. I watched them for a moment, then turned back to Gerhardt.

"Actually, most of the credit has to go to Netty, and to Perry. They're the ones that came up with the idea of using the twist comm system to screw up the Tenants' control over their League hosts." I narrowed my eyes. "It's why I consider them such valuable members of my crew, as much as Torina or any of the others—and why I'm not going to let Master Kharsweil or anyone else treat them like property."

Gerhardt said nothing for a moment, then nodded. "I understand," he said, and that was it.

He didn't want to talk about Kharsweil, which was fine, so I changed the subject. "Any word about the Satrap? Or his fidgety aide?"

"All that the provisional government knows is that they've disappeared. They probably had a contingency escape plan all ready to go, for that very reason."

"Great. Someone else who's still out there, along with the Sorcerers, the Stillness, what's left of the Fade, and the Salt Thieves—"

"Indeed. And to that end, you need to return to the *Fafnir*. I've provided Netty with a set of nav data."

"To go where?"

"To see something you should definitely see."

"'Ahh, the old *you need to come and take a look at this* cliché," I said, grinning.

"What?"

"Just—something I heard once. A dozen times if you count 80s cop movies. Doesn't matter. I'll just round up my crew and head for the *Iowa*. My poor *Fafnir* needs a complete rebuild in the shop."

Gerhardt nodded. "Her, and many other ships. There is a bright side to it, though. It's about time for you to upgrade the *Fafnir* to something closer to her full potential."

"Sounds expensive."

Gerhardt smiled. "I think you've earned some financial assistance." But his smile faded.

"Besides, I suspect you're going to need the extra capabilities and firepower. Things are only going to get more difficult from here, Tudor. Whether you realize it or not, you're now on the scanners of a great many more people. Some of them are enemies. Some are friends. But some are both."

"You suck at giving pep talks, you know?"

I stood on the bridge of the *Iowa* with Torina, Zeno, Icky, and Perry. We'd just twisted to the set of nav coordinates Gerhardt had given Netty, a point on the edge of known space, remarkable only for the presence of a rogue planet-wannabe-star, a dim, brown dwarf cutting a lonely trajectory through the Milky Way.

Except it wasn't lonely anymore. There were ships here. A lot of them.

"Who are they all?" Torina asked.

Zeno stepped closer to the big display, pointing.

"That's a… a Frostborn. And that one, I'm pretty sure that's a Serpenta." Her finger moved again, touching the image of a massive ship, something in the class 15 or even 16 range. "And, if I'm not going crazy, that one's a—"

"It's a Dark Star!" Icky bellowed. "I had a schematic for a Dark Star in my room back on the *Nemesis*." She shook her head. "But I thought they all came apart in the Shade War."

"They did, which means these are all off the books," Perry said. "Who's piloting these things, anyway?"

Netty cut in. "Van, there's an incoming message for you. It's Valint."

I nodded. "Why am I not surprised? Put her on, Netty."

A window popped open, revealing Valint sitting in the cockpit of her ship, which was somewhere among those gathered. She seemed strangely uncertain, as though she had something to say but wasn't sure how.

"Hello, Van."

"What the hell is going on here?" I asked her. "What are all these ships? *Who* are all these ships?"

"They're all GKU. They're responding to the Heracles call that was put out."

"Uh, little late."

"Yeah, we could have used all this firepower," Torina said. And she was right—there was enough combat power here that we could have easily overrun the League fleet. Of course, the death toll would probably have been far worse, and in the wake of something like that, the transition through a provisional government to democratically elected one might not be so smooth.

Valint smiled, as bleak as January. "The GKU didn't just break, Van. It shattered. And some of the splinters never came back into the fold. Not all the way, anyway. But they're here now."

"To do what?"

"Whatever needs to be done. But I think you need to talk to someone first. To the extent there even is a commander of these many GKU factions, she's the one you need to get on board."

I stared back at Valint for a moment. "Netty, a general broadcast channel, please."

"Done."

"This is Peacemaker—actually this is GKU Van Tudor of the *Iowa* and the *Fafnir*. I'm addressing all of you, but particularly whoever considers themselves to be in charge. A wise man recently said to me that things were going to start getting dangerous in known space. Between the Tenants, and the Sorcerers, and all the rest of the bad guys out there, I happen to believe him. So, we've got a job for you, if you're interested."

"Ballsy."

The voice was female, low, resonant, and devoid of warmth or cheer.

"But then you always were," it went on. It carried a tone of menace, one that said the speaker was feral, dangerous—a killer.

A new image abruptly appeared on the screen, originating from the ship Icky had identified as a Dark Star. It was a slender, human woman with angular features, like they'd been chiseled in ice. Probably in her fifties, she had iron-gray hair and was clad in a dark uniform. I'd never met, or even seen this woman before, although I had heard her voice once over the comm.

Except I *had* met her at least once before, even if I didn't remember it. Because even not knowing her name, I knew exactly who she was.

I stepped up to the screen.

"It's been a long time, mom."

Amazon won't always tell you about the next release. To stay updated on this series, be sure to sign up for our spam-free email list at jnchaney.com.

Van will return in FIELDS OF FIRE available on Amazon.

GLOSSARY

Anvil Dark: The beating heart of the Peacemaker organization, Anvil Dark is a large orbital platform located in the Gamma Crucis system, some ninety lightyears from Earth. Anvil Dark, some nine hundred seventy years old, remains in a Lagrange point around Mesaribe, remaining in permanent darkness. Anvil Dark has legal, military, medical, and supply resources for Peacemakers, their assistants, and guests.

Cloaks: Local organized criminal element, the Cloaks hold sway in only one place: Spindrift. A loose guild of thugs, extortionists, and muscle, the Cloaks fill a need for some legal control on Spindrift, though they do so only because Peacemakers and other authorities see them as a necessary evil. When confronted away from Spindrift, Cloaks are given no rights, quarter, or considerations for their position. (See: Spindrift)

Dragonet: A Base Four Combat ship, the Dragonet is a modified platform intended for the prosecution of Peacemaker policy. This includes but is not limited to ship-to-ship combat, surveillance, and planetary operations as well. The Dragonet is fast, lightly armored, and carries both point defense and ranged weapons, and features a frame that can be upgraded to the status of a small corvette (Class Nine).

Moonsword: Although the weapon is in the shape of a medium sword, the material is anything but simple metal. The Moonsword is a generational armament, capable of upgrades that augment its ability to interrupt communications, scan for data, and act as a blunt-force weapon that can split all but the toughest of ship's hulls. See: Starsmith

Peacemaker: Also known as a Galactic Knight, Peacemakers are an elite force of law enforcement who have existed for more than three centuries. Both hereditary and open to recruitment, the guild is a meritocracy, but subject to political machinations and corruption, albeit not on the scale of other galactic military forces. Peacemakers have a legal code, proscribed methods, a reward and bounty scale, and a well-earned reputation as fierce, competent fighters. Any race may be a Peacemaker, but the candidates must pass rigorous testing and training.

Perry: An artificial intelligence, bound to Van (after service to his grandfather), Perry is a fully-sapient combat operative in the shape of a large, black avian. With the ability to hack computer systems and engage in physical combat, Perry is also a living repository of galactic knowledge in topics from law to battle strategies. He is also a wiseass.

Salt Thieves: Originally actual thieves who stole salt, this is a three-hundred-year-old guild of assassins known for their ruthless behavior, piracy, and tendency to kill. Members are identified by a complex, distinct system of braids in their hair. These braids are often cut and taken as prizes, especially by Peacemakers.

Spindrift: At nine hundred thirty years old, Spindrift is one of the most venerable space stations in the galactic arm. It is also the least reputable, having served as a place of criminal enterprise for nearly all of its existence due to a troublesome location. Orbiting Sirius, Spindrift was nearly depopulated by stellar radiation in the third year as a spaceborne habitat. When order collapsed, criminals moved in, cycling in and out every twelve point four years as coronal ejections rom Sirius made the station uninhabitable. Spindrift is known for medical treatments and technology that are quasi-legal at best, as well as weapons, stolen goods, and a strange array of archaeological items, all illegally looted. Spindrift has a population of thirty thousand beings at any time.

Starsmith: A place, a guild, and a single being, the Starsmith is primarily a weapons expert of unsurpassed skill. The current Starsmith is a Conoku (named Linulla), a crablike race known for their dexterity, skill in metallurgy and combat enhancements, and sense of humor.

CONNECT WITH J.N. CHANEY

Don't miss out on these exclusive perks:

- Instant access to free short stories from series like *The Messenger*, *Starcaster*, and more.
- Receive email updates for new releases and other news.
- Get notified when we run special deals on books and audiobooks.

So, what are you waiting for? Enter your email address at the link below to stay in the loop.

https://www.jnchaney.com/backyard-starship-subscribe

CONNECT WITH TERRY MAGGERT

Check out his website

http://terrymaggert.com/

Connect on Facebook

https://www.facebook.com/terrymaggertbooks/

Follow him on Amazon

https://www.amazon.com/Terry-Maggert/e/B00EKN8RHG/

ABOUT THE AUTHORS

J. N. Chaney is a USA Today Bestselling author and has a Master's of Fine Arts in Creative Writing. He fancies himself quite the Super Mario Bros. fan. When he isn't writing or gaming, you can find him online at **www.jnchaney.com**.

He migrates often, but was last seen in Las Vegas, NV. Any sightings should be reported, as they are rare.

Terry Maggert is left-handed, likes dragons, coffee, waffles, running, and giraffes; order unimportant. He's also half of author Daniel Pierce, and half of the humor team at Cledus du Drizzle.

With thirty-one titles, he has something to thrill, entertain, or make you cringe in horror. Guaranteed.

Note: He doesn't sleep. But you sort of guessed that already.

Made in United States
Orlando, FL
11 July 2022

19647950R00271